Fat Chance

www.oldcastlebooks.com

Other books by this author

The Rainbow Weaver

Fat Chance

Lyndsay Russell

Illustrations also by Lyndsay Russell

OLDCASTLE BOOKS

First published in 2008 by Oldcastle Books,
P.O.Box 394, Harpenden, Herts, AL5 1XJ
www.oldcastlebooks.co.uk

A CIP catalogue record for this book is available from
the British Library.

This is a work of fiction. Names, characters, places, and incidents either
are the product of the author's imagination or are used fictitiously, and
any resemblance to actual persons, living or dead, businesses, companies,
events, or locales is entirely coincidental.

978-1-84243-299-0 (Hardback)

978-1-84243-300-3 (Trade Paperback)

2 4 6 8 10 9 7 5 3 1

Typeset by Matrix Media Services, Chichester, West Sussex
Printed and bound by J.H. Haynes Ltd, Sparkford, Yeovil, Somerset

For my gorgeous husband Mike, the best
chance I ever took!

Acknowledgements

As an author, you're asked to write this page before the book has even been printed. It feels a little weird and premature to say all those pompous 'I'd like to thank my editor' bits, because, even though I want to, who knows if the book will actually be a success? Indeed, with so many books out there, one could probably say… 'Fat Chance'. So instead, I thought that maybe I could share something personal with you that happened to me last night.

I had a dream…

I'm on a stage (but, for once, not naked).

Firstly, I'd like to thank… Annette Crossland. My eccentric, but utterly brilliant, publisher. Taking chances on new writers is always a gamble. A huge thanks for publishing my first book, and now for having the belief in this one... the second.

Ms. Crossland is a remarkable woman whose intelligence, unstinting enthusiasm and love of her job make her a joy to work for – I suspect that any company she chooses to go into partnership with is very, very lucky.

Publisher smiles warmly, and waves contract for third book.

I'd also like to thank my team buddy and husband Mike, whose fantastic support, talented mind, critical eye, and editorial suggestions were invaluable. I'd also like to hug our adorable daughter Tippi for her understanding when I was 'too busy'. By the way, sorry kiddo – I'm not changing my mind. The 'naughty bits' will be blacked out in your edition.

And highlighted in my husband's.

Wild applause and laughter. I pause - smile sweetly, and look earnestly into camera.

I'd also like to thank my mother, Reeva. Hi, Mum, I know you're watching... Thanks, you've been a terrific help with the book. I'll never forget the 'night of the cocktails' at The Petersham, bouncing ideas off you in the rain. Or the day in the pool in Antigua, bouncing ideas off you in the sun. I love you. *Blow kisses.*

The same goes for my sister-in-law, Anita – who was there for me when my father was ill and my inspiration flagged. Great suggestions. You are so much more creative than your family

give you credit for. I won't name names, but he's my brother…
he's a sod. What can I tell you?

My voice breaks, voice gently wavering with emotion.

At this stage I'd also like to send a big thank you to Diana at
Guards Polo Club for the low-down on Cartier International,
(any tickets?), Julie D. on PR, and Patty on Fashion, Hannah
my editor, and Ion – publishing head honcho and signatory of
important monetary contracts. Kiss, kiss.

I wipe a tear as I clutch statuette of the Booker Prize to my breast…

Finally, it's truly vital I thank you, the press, for supporting a
book that tries to correct the sad, twisted notion that ultra skinny
is desirable, and that we're all butt-ugly if we're above a size 10.
Together, we can address this mess…

*Paparazzi photographers and journalists rise to their feet, and
applaud.*
   I sob unashamedly and place a steadying hand on the lectern.

But most important of all… Sorry, please – I just need to take a
moment. *Dramatic pause as I swallow deeply.*

… Most important of all, I don't want to forget YOU, the public –
for buying a novel that hits back at the celebrity fashionistas. A novel
that struggles to correct the model images that have so distorted our
minds. A book that fights to give us back… our dignity.

Thank you, thank you. This statue means so much to me, I will treasure this moment forever... *Uniformed Body Police march on stage. They try to drag me off. I resist, bearing a martyred facial expression. I raise a fist, I cry out...*

Comrades! Sisters ! Join forces ! Do whatever you can... Just remember these words... It's better to light the candle on the triple-layered birthday cake, than to curse hungrily in the dark.

Chapter One

Poor, sad, lonely Sharon Plunkett. She had tried every fad, every diet, every exercise and every cream. But like a stain of grease on a pure silk blouse, her rolls of fat refused to budge. Life had never been a bed of roses… Instead, just a solitary thorn of despair that constantly pricked at her fleshy existence.

Blinking away bulbous tears, she savoured the square of milky chocolate, marvelling at the way it melted on her tongue. It veritably oozed. As always, the guilty pleasure hit her taste buds with masochistic force.

Clutching the giant chocolate bar to her bosom, the ridiculously expensive, low-calorie salad waiting in front of her seemed deeply unappealing.

The mushy grated carrot and sesame-seed coleslaw looked like something prised from the cheeks of a hamster, whilst the black-eyed prawns stared at her reproachfully. Avoiding their accusing gaze, she disdainfully tipped the plastic package into the office bin. There… I've just saved myself a few calories! she reasoned, trying hard not to think of the squandered pounds. Then shifted uncomfortably in an effort to release the digging pressure on her waistband.

So what if the other girls hadn't invited her to the wine bar for lunch? She knew the reason they left her out. A tight little coterie of skinny girls obsessed with fashion, they saw themselves as 'cool', and she cramped their style just because she was a bit plump.

Who was she kidding? screamed her inner voice. Size 18-20 is not plump. It's fat, Sharon. FAT, FAT, FAT. The only thing she hated more than her life were the bathroom scales. Had it always been so? Throughout her 21 years she couldn't really remember a time when she hadn't felt 'lumpy'.

As a child she had usually been first in the school-meal queue, often up for 'seconds', and always last in the Sports Day run. Nope, there wasn't an age she could remember when what she ate hadn't ruled her day.

Now halfway through the chocolate bar, she had to make the rest last as long as she could. She sipped her tea, dunking a precious square… and sucked noisily on the sticky chocolate like a baby finding comfort at a nipple. As it dissolved, so did her resolve. She sighed, and reluctantly let the sad memories of the weekend re-enter her head. The night had started off as usual…

Her 'bestest' friend Debbee had insisted they go to a kitsch Country & Western theme night at Kingston's hottest club *Kool Kat's*. So Sharon had dressed with care. Well, sort of. She'd applied a splash of blue eye shadow, donned a black A-line tent dress, and half-heartedly curled her long, shiny hair in a Tammy Wynette, sixties style. But it had started to drizzle. Fearing her damp waves would turn into a frizzy tsunami, Sharon grabbed a spotted headscarf she'd picked up in Top Shop, and in an attempt at 'trendy' tied it under her nape.

Alas, instead of 'American Cowgirl Chic', the effect, she feared, was more 'Mexican Peasant Crap', and she desperately wanted to change. But as she surveyed the dismal choice in her wardrobe Debbee was honking the car horn, and Sharon knew she hated to be kept waiting.

As expected, her friend sat impatiently clicking her acrylic French manicured nails on the steering wheel – a habit that made Sharon grit her teeth.

'What took you so long?' Debbee sighed. 'Strap in, kiddo! Yeehaw! Hey girl, it's time to round 'em up!'

For a split second, Sharon didn't know if she meant the male population of Kingston, or her large, spilling breasts. As she struggled to pull the seat belt over her stomach, Sharon jealously glanced over at Debbee's lithe form. It was Saturday night, and as usual Debbee had morphed from trainee suburban beautician, into a sexy, sophisticated, wannabe WAG – her perfect, pert breasts displayed in a tight leather waistcoat, coupled dangerously with white, kitten-heeled cowboy boots and a short, suede Versace skirt from eBay.

As Debbee's long, St. Tropez fake-tanned legs pressed the accelerator, Sharon couldn't help admiring how the outside of her smooth thighs hollowed. Like an athlete. She felt her own thighs spreading over the plastic front seat, like melting margarine.

'You look fantastic,' said Sharon, hating herself for crawling. But somehow she fell so easily into playing her expected role: making-Debbee-feel-great. In response, Debbee preened her blonde Farrah Fawcett mane in the car mirror.

'Do you think so?' she asked, knowing the answer.

'Sure, every man'll drool over you. They always do.'

Debbee smiled at Sharon warmly. 'Actually, that outfit's pretty trendy you're wearing,' she said, awarding Sharon a rare compliment. Sharon smiled back. A tiny glow-worm of confidence lit up inside her.

'Not sure the "look" is you though.'

The worm curled up and died.

Applying a slash of crimson *Urban Cool* lipstick at the next traffic light, Debbee teased, 'I heard Simon's coming tonight, Sharon.'

Sharon's heart did a dozy doe as she heard his name. Simon Mercier. Sleek, handsome Simon. Like a shaggy-haired lurcher. A vision in denim. Secret crush of her life for two, yearning, burning years of unrequited lust.

Something about the way he always looked deep into her eyes made her feel he could see the real her buried under the mounds of massive flesh. His smile made her feel special… Normal.

Last time they'd been to *Kat's*, he'd even bought her a drink. But not long after they actually sat down to talk, Debbee had staggered over and said she wanted to leave because she was feeling sick on Sea Breezes. The two girls had made a hasty exit, and Sharon hadn't seen him since then, which she knew was exactly four weeks six days and twenty-two hours ago.

'I said – I hear Simon is definitely going tonight… really sorry about spoiling it last time. If you see him, use your brains – offer him a drink or something and go for it!' Debbee patronised, applying mascara in the car mirror as she accelerated through the changing lights.

'And you could use your brains to take a PhD in "Transit Make-up Appliance," quipped Sharon in an attempt to deflect the comment.

'Don't ignore me… I know you think he's gorge. Tonight could be your *big* chance!' Debbee giggled. Big was the operative word, sighed Sharon. Big, indeed.

'Simon? Nah, do I look bothered…?' she said, with nonchalance so naked her real feelings were completely exposed.

'Yeah, right. Whatever,' laughed Debbee, who had heard every detail of that famous 'drink' more times than she could bear to swallow.

As Debbee concentrated on crashing the gears of her Clio convertible and cursing the lack of parking, Sharon made occasional clucks of sympathy, secretly letting her mind wander back to when she first met Simon.

He'd walked into her life the moment he stepped through the door of her office to chase up a missing invoice. For the first time since joining top advertising agency Sharpe, Bates and Colt, Sharon was thrilled her job was only Junior Accounts Filing. Because it was HER he had to talk to.

'Hi, I work for your company as a freelance photographer, and there seems to be a problem with my invoice… the account exec's told me it's been lost,' he'd said, shooting her a sparkling, I-floss-twice-a-day smile. As Sharon's heart did a springboard high-jump-double-twist in response, she knew there was no mix up at all. The agency had a mean-spirited, secret policy to ensure three-month delayed payment to lesser mortals by any means, fair or foul. The 'sorry we lost your invoice' schtick was a rite of passage reserved for the absolute newcomer who they could always replace.

Yes sirree, SBC wasn't a successful conglomerate by advertising talent alone. But Sharon couldn't resist his lazy charm. She'd dug out his invoice and promised to put it through ASAP. But as she glanced at the address, she caught her breath for the second time that meeting. HE LIVED IN KINGSTON! Same suburb as her.

'Ohmigod! We're neighbours…' she blurted.

'Really? You live in Kingston? Whereabouts?' Sharon began to describe the University area and the flat she owned around the corner. They fell into an easy, laughing conversation about the joys of drinking down by the river and picnicking in Richmond Park.

It turned out Simon had studied photography at the College, and decided to stay because he loved the buzzy little market town and its holiday atmosphere.

'Condé Naste say there's now an open-air coffee bar for every three residents,' joked Sharon.

'Then we must go for a coffee sometime,' he said, leaning on the desk towards her.

'A coffee? Sure, whatever, I'll see you around,' Sharon answered curtly, looking down at the paperwork to hide her reddening face. He leaned back, a bit surprised.

'Oh, okay then. Another time,' he said, slowly, studying her.

And Sharon realised she had done what she always did when anyone *showed the slightest bit of interest. She'd come across as cold, uninterested and dismissive. A protective habit she'd adopted from an early age, even if people were just being friendly. Poor man. Perhaps she'd trapped him into suggesting coffee because she'd waffled on so much about the coffee bars? She just wanted to let him off the hook – having to arrange something he couldn't possibly want to do. Silence hung in the air like a frosty mist. She tried to think of a witty icebreaker… but her mind was an empty deep freeze. She looked up to see him heading towards the door. Politely, he turned and thanked her again for sorting the invoice.*

'I'll no doubt bump into you around town,' he added.

For many days after, Sharon would analyse whether he had been making a reference to her mammoth size. If he had, she felt she deserved it.

But the strange thing was, they had bumped into each other. Quite a few times. Nearly always at Kat's.

And whenever they saw each other, he always stopped and chatted…

'How's Sharke, Bait and Caught?' he'd tease her about the agency – now wise to the fact the Sharpe, Bates and Colt was run by a board of heartless bastards.

'Still reeling the clients in,' Sharon would laugh, enjoying their mutual bond.

'It's looking goooo…d, girl!' growled Debbee, parking the car and bringing Sharon's attention to the nightclub queue ahead of them. It was long, and as always Sharon quaked with nerves that she would be turned away. But as usual, Debbee had it all under control. Guarding 'the door' like a pompous pit-bull, Debbee's bouncer cousin was playing 'god' with the crowds. Sharon pondered which was thicker – his neck or his head? He was currently arguing with two skinny young teens who, despite the chill night air, insisted on walking around with bare midriffs and indecently fringed micro-minis. 'Are you *sure* you girls are 18?' he asked uncertainly.

'...*Course* we are.'

Of course they *weren't*, thought Sharon, you could practically see their nappies. Debbee unceremoniously elbowed the kiddies out of the way and, after air kissing the bouncer like a famous VIP greeting an equally famous VIP, she swanned through the crowd, Sharon waddling in her wake, the perennial ugly duckling.

The club's 'DENIM AND DIAMONDS' Country Night was in full swing. The wooden floor was a mangled mob of bobbing cowboy hats and clicking, tripping, pointed boots as the drunken British attempted a display of line dancing.

Blocking the bar, a gaggle of three tarty girls looked like backing singers out to upstage Dolly Parton.

Sharon felt like the tour's big, butch roadie as she elbowed through them to reach the counter.

The barman took her order. 'Okay, I'm just going to have a *diet* coke,' she emphasised loudly (and totally unnecessarily, as she was the one getting the drinks).

'Well, make mine a Tequila,' shouted Debbee over a sea full of floating bottle blondes. Turning her back to the bar she stuck her thumbs in her rhinestone belt, flashed her flat midriff, thrust her slim hips forward and struck a raunchy cowgirl pose. Men turned and stared. Women turned and glared.

As Sharon waited for the drinks, she pondered for the triple-trillionth time why someone like Debbee was happy to hang out with her? Fair enough when they were best friends as toddlers – they'd grown up next door to each other, shared nursery toys, and gone to primary school together. At secondary though, the balance changed. Sharing the same class, they'd stayed mates throughout teenage acne, angst and adolescence – but Sharon had grown in weight and size as Debbee had grown in looks and vanity.

Regardless, Debbee still chose to see her when she was at a loose end. And Sharon was grateful – though a deeply insecure part of her suspected her girlfriend liked to have her around purely because, when they stood next to each other, Debbee knew she appeared even more pretty and petite.

Sharon hated the way those two words went together. Pretty and Petite. But there was no getting away from it. And as they sipped and slurped on their purple straws, Sharon was painfully aware they looked like a gazelle and a buffalo sharing the same watering hole.

Together they surveyed the cattle market. Dusty images of Dallas sprang to mind, with the dazzlingly tacky outfits more Rodeo Drive than Rodeo.

Dirk, the club owner, sat in his usual booth alone and aloof, eyeing up the women. With an Indian bootlace tie, white hair and a fake moustache, he looked like General Custer surveying the last one-night stand. His wife Kat was busy chatting to the DJ, her hair so teased it could perform its own strip.

'Howdy gals!' They turned round to see an extremely cute-looking cowboy doffing his hat and directing his white smile totally at Debbee.

'Gee, are you a real cowboy?' she flirted back.

''Course, ladies – I'm Chuck from the States – Tucson, Arizona.'

'Nah, are you really?' simpered Debbee, eyes wide… 'Hey Sharon! He's the real thing! A gen-u-ine cowboy!' she giggled, nudging Sharon so hard her face dipped into her glass and emerged with a frothy coke moustache.

'Sure am. I'm visiting ma' English cousins. We thought this would be a hoot for a night out. Show them ma' roots. Ya don't believe me, do ya?'

'Umm… no,' said Debbee, sucking on her straw and batting her eyelashes like a newborn colt.

'Okay, lady – d'you know how you can tell a real cowboy?'

Debbee shook her mane of hair and practically neighed.

'First, check out the boots. None of that fancy pointed crap. They've gotta be ropers.'

These were round-toed versions, apparently ideal for roping steer.

'Now, check out ma' jeans. Wranglers.' He flashed the label, which sat perkily on an even perkier, perfect male butt. 'Gives you more room when you're in the saddle,' he whispered suggestively, his accent changing mysteriously mid-flow. Yeah, right, sniffed Sharon, narrowing her eyes. She reckoned the nearest he'd ever got to a steer was eating steak.

But too late. With a whooping 'YEEhaw!' from 'Chuck', Debbee was on the dance floor doing a two-step and Sharon was alone at the bar. Feeling hungry, she asked for a packet of crisps… barbecue steak flavour. She shrugged and reasoned she was just getting 'into the evening'.

Although Sharon felt painfully self-conscious standing on her own, watching Debbee struggle to keep in step was highly amusing. It was impossible to say whether the toe crunching was the result of her inept dancing, or his adept drinking.

But then, as the music wailed 'Ma Man Gone An' Did Me Wrong', in walked Sharon's ultimate 'Mr. Right'.

And Sharon panicked. Had she time to race to the loo to re-apply some lippy? Rooted with indecision, she watched Simon fall into relaxed chat with some friends and down a swig of beer from the bottle in a very languid, sexy way. He looked so damned cool, Sharon actually moaned.

Wearing his usual faded denim shirt, he resembled a young, laid-back Clint in a Sergio Leone movie. Suddenly, as if sensing he was being watched, he turned his head and squinted through the dark in her direction. That was it. Too late. She was dead. He caught her eye, smiled – then sauntered towards her…

Stuffing the crisps in her bag, Sharon grinned a warm welcome.

'Hey, how's it going, partner?' he asked, giving her a friendly kiss on the cheek.

'Well, not so great. Debbee's abandoned camp and gone off with an outlaw!' Sharon laughed. Despite the nerves in her stomach, something about Simon made joking so easy. Normally she would mumble like a moron to any male between sixteen and sixty. But not with him. No, there was no doubt he brought out the best in her.

'An outlaw? Who with this time? The Good, the Bad… or the Lousy?' laughed Simon.

'Judging by the way he just stomped on her toe, I'd have to say the Clumsy!'

'Drink?' he offered. *Oh, yes!* screamed Sharon's inner voice.

'Err… okay, why not?' she answered serenely, asking for a spritzer – sophisticated and refreshing, she reckoned, without getting her too light-headed to make conversation. As he turned to order, Sharon spotted Debbee now rowing with the guy on the floor. She pushed him back, and he slapped her bottom, laughing. But Debbee wasn't. And stomping off the floor, she stormed towards them in a furious mood.

'Bastard says I dance like a heifer! He's got a bloody cheek… told me to call him when I'd learnt to walk. I'll show him… how dare he?' Seeing Simon, Debbee grabbed his arm. 'Hey Simon, I need you…'

'*No*,' whispered Sharon pleadingly, 'he's getting me a drink!' Debbee shot her a shucks-too-bad look, and pulled him away from the bar.

'Honey, can you come with me for a while… I jus' wanna have a little ol' dance with you,' she said huskily, in a tone developed to melt the one male brain cell that controlled 'decency'.

'Umm, err… I was just getting dri… well, okay – sure. Sorry Sharon… maybe later?' he muttered, as she trailed him onto the floor like a lassoed stallion.

Crestfallen, Sharon watched the couple move to the music. Chuck the cowboy was wrong – Debbee was a great dancer normally, and she took great pains to show just how good she was. Her sinewy silhouette snaked sexily against Simon and, as he instinctively moved towards her, she threw back her head with a throaty sigh.

The cowboy watched amused from the sidelines, as Sharon stared aghast. The music changed to 'Jolene', and as Dolly Parton trilled, *Your beauty is beyond compare… I cannot compete with you*, Sharon's eyes welled with emotion. She leant forward to pick up her bag, and a tear plinked onto her ample cleavage – lost like a drop of rain in the Grand Canyon.

What the hell was she thinking? As Mr. Blobby's ugly sister what on earth did she expect? Simon probably didn't even recognise her as female, let alone an attractive mate.

Debbee now draped a loose hand over Simon's shoulder and whispered in his ear. He whispered something back… she twiddled her hair extensions coyly.

Sitting there like a plum pudding, Sharon dug her fingers into her pudgy, sweating palm to stop the sobs. Debbee, her closest friend, was moving in on the only man Sharon had ever confessed she wanted. She caught Debbee's eye with a look so plaintive it would shame a puppy.

Deliberately ignoring her, Debbee just pulled Simon closer and rested her head against his shoulder.

It was a calculated move, as if Debbee was flaunting her power over her.

You can have your choice of men… I could never love again, he's the only one for me, Jolene sang dear ol' Dolly, inadvertently edging Sharon's bitterness on. She literally saw red. Painful, red-raw scarlet. Crimson. Blood. She saw his muscular arm brush Debbee's naked shoulder. And with that simple move, he began ripping Sharon's heart out of her body. Moving towards them, unsure what she was going to do, she had to find a way to stop Debbee. Tell her she had a call on her mobile phone… trip her up… blowtorch her smug face off and stamp the scorched flesh into the ground… whatever.

As their lips danced closer and closer with every gyration from Debbee, Sharon felt a loaded gun was pointing at her chest. She had to stop it before it exploded.

Seeing the ladies' room behind them, she decided to head that way and gently remind them she existed. Pushing past a smooching couple and two girls swaying round a handbag, she found herself in earshot of their conversation…

'So my place, about eight o'clock then…' said Simon.

'Sure, I'd love to come… I'll see you then, sounds fun,' said Debbee, breaking free and wiggling her pert ass to the instrumental.

The gun had gone off. Sharon could not deny what she heard. She was dead. Killed by her best… well, actually only friend. Slayed by the betrayal of her erstwhile 'love' – a man like all the others, weak and stupid, who fell for Debbee's quack-doctor charms.

Stumbling past them, she headed into the foyer, and the cool night air. If only she could just ride off into the horizon and never be seen again. If only she could disappear. But this wasn't a movie, and she would never have a happy ending.

She hated herself. Every single hundred, thousand, million inches of her fat, fat self.

~

The phone rang. Sharon sat up at her desk, startled. She had been so immersed in re-living that night, she had almost forgotten where she was.

It was unbearable. She had been a means for Simon to get to Debbee, that's all. A pathetic joke. And as for DEBBEE – she could rip her foxy little face to shreds. The bitch. And an affected one, at that. Fancy changing your name to put two EEs at the end. So pathetic.

Sharon felt so desperate. She couldn't bring herself to be friends with her. But as the loneliness of night after night stretched ahead she was at a complete loss. Sharon stared around the empty office. Time to kill, but she'd already read the morning's paper and had forgotten her book.

Glancing up at the office clock, so cool in design you had to struggle to read the time, she worked out there were still another twenty minutes before the girls would come back from lunch.

The chocolate bar she'd been eking out was now down to a mere three squares, and, as usual, she craved more. To take her mind off it, she looked around for something to read. She noticed Lou Lou, the daffy blonde in the office gang of six, had a stack of rag mags beside her desk. On the top lay a couple of NOW magazines, a glossy dedicated to celebrities and their body image. She flicked through the top one, consuming the endless pages of slim Hollywood stars, studying their slender limbs and lithe bodies in envy. Then she looked down at her own reality.

Compared to the celebs, she could have been an alien reject from the planet Heffalump. Miserably she reached for another square of chocolate to comfort herself. If she could only be slim, her life would be so different…

Sharon picked up the second issue of NOW, read the headlines, and nodded, shocked.

98% of women are unhappy with their bodies!

31% throw up after eating.

62% feel unlovable because of it!

Opening the pages, she read on, eyes widening at the statistics, yet identifying with each one she digested.

69% would rather be an unhealthy size 0 than a size 16.

How ridiculous, she snorted. Though she knew she would eagerly choose size 0 herself. How the hell had it come to this madness, she wondered? Yet every single statement rang deafeningly loud and true. She tossed the publication back on the desk.

On a neighbouring chair, she saw a different kind of magazine poking out of a recyclable hemp shopping bag.

'What's Saffron got in there?' thought Sharon. Saffron, hippy child of the office was the only one who was vaguely pleasant to her… But then, she was nauseatingly pleasant to everyone, from snotty little kids to Teutonic traffic wardens. She was 'at one' with the universe and always muttering on about 'Karma'.

Predict said its title. Well, I predict this is a load of old crap, thought Sharon, feeling like a thief as she leafed through its pages. Guiltily she flicked through – past the '*I talked to Elvis*' article, past the '*My Granny Runs A Coven*' exposé, and past the '*Do You Have Alien Blood?*' quiz.

Instead, her eyes alighted on the small ads at the back of the magazine. Along with '1/2 price Crystal Balls' and 'Navajo Indian Dream Catchers – buy one get one free' nestled three little lines that leapt right out of the page.

MIRACLE WEIGHT PILLS
HATE BEING FAT?
A MAGIC CHANCE TO CHANGE YOUR LIFE

Underneath, it stated:

**A celebrity remedy from Beverly Hills
— end of stock offer
Only £80**

There was no telephone number… just an address.

**For an appointment write to:
DR.MARVEL'S
Miracle Weight Clinic
150 Riversal Road
London W1**

**Director: Dr. Maximus Marvel Bsc DDc. T.G.I.F.,
A.C.D.C. Assoc. Hon. Diploma Neuro-nutrition**

Sharon studied the advertisement, sensing herself hooked by the dream, as always. The doctor had so many degrees, titles and diplomas. She didn't recognise the letters after his name but they looked impressive. The man must know something others didn't. The advert was so tantalisingly simple, and to the point. Could it work? Maybe this was the answer to her problem – the 'big one', she thought ironically.

Nah, this was ridiculous. She worked in an advertising agency, for crying out loud. She knew all about false claims and irresistible promises. Every time she looked at the back of shampoo bottles she'd remember not to be fooled. Not since the day she came across one of the agency's creatives writing copy for a new conditioner.

'**Senses**. *Give your hair the scent of fresh air – a touch of silk with the sheen of ice,*' read the mock label he wanted to test out on her. But when she asked to smell the product scent to see if it lived up to the claim, the writer laughed arrogantly. He had no idea what it smelt like, because the manufacturers hadn't produced a single drop of the product yet. The production depended entirely on whether the agency could create a brand image to fill a perceived market gap.

The experience served as good warning to Sharon never to believe a single word of packaging descriptions – 99.9% of the time.

But when it came to slimming, such was her desperation she'd believe anything. Against all her intelligence, she couldn't help thinking *something new*! Feverishly, Sharon copied down the advert and address. MIRACLE and MAGIC.

The two words missing from her life.

Chapter Two

Lonely, the Saturday-morning blues felt just as bad as the Sunday-morning blues, thought Sharon. And in fact, with nothing planned, twice as bad as the Monday-morning blues.

It had been nearly a week since she had posted off her request for an appointment. A long, miserable week in which Sharon had refused to answer any attempts at contact from Debbee. Well, actually there had only been one attempt, on the answerphone. But to be fair, it was a long, rambling diatribe – and the slagette did say the word 'sorry', twice.

'Still, that's not good enough,' huffed Sharon. 'May her Manolo fakes snap, and her highlights turn green,' she cursed, looking in the mirror at her own puffy eyes.

Her head felt muzzy from last night's three-quarters finished bottle of Merlot. Not a staunch drinker, to down this much on her own made her feel she was spinning out of control and into the depths of alcoholic dependency.

'My name is Sharon, and I'm a chocoholic. Err… sorry, wrong meeting,' she practised in the mirror with a wry smile.

She looked so pathetically sad, she put her hand out to the glass to touch her own reflection in comfort. The ache in her eyes was always there. The look of a kitten that had been abandoned by its mother. Which was, in effect, what had happened all those years ago. And her mother had been truly beautiful. A glamorous, graceful creature.

'Geez, I look nothing like her… Maybe we have the same-shaped little finger,' she sighed. Maybe, if she could just hack off the fat, she would see some similarity. She pulled back her cheeks. She did have very high cheekbones, but they were more curved than razor sharp like her mother's.

Dispassionately, she studied herself. And, as always, decided her hair was her best feature, putting her hand to the small of her back and feeling it brush softly against her fingers. Long, straight and white-blonde, she was aware it had the touch of silk with the sheen of ice… and that had *nothing* to do with conditioner. It was also the one part of her that never changed, whatever she ate.

As for her eyes… no matter that they were large and almond-shaped, they were just too damn tragic. Green. Unusually luminescent in hue, they had a strange tendency to match and reflect whatever shade of green she wore. Her eyes could change from palest duck-egg, to a rich peacock. But right now, they looked a delicate shade of puke. Currently tinged with bloodshot red. A charming look, thought Sharon. Matched her blotchy cheeks perfectly. What was to become of her…?

As always the bathroom scales stood waiting; lurking behind the door like a silent assassin ready to stab her self-esteem.

And every morning, before getting on, she first had a pee on the loo, took off every bit of jewellery (including studs) and every item of clothing.

This morning was no different. Standing sideways so she could see past her tummy, she gingerly placed her feet on the surface.

'It should be good today…' she thought. Mentally she swiftly raced through all she had eaten the day before. She'd been good. VERY good. Only a wholegrain cereal for breakfast. Ummm, she'd had a little bit of double cream with it, but only two spoons of low-cal sugar to make that lovely, yummy creamy crust. For lunch… she'd had a chicken Caesar sandwich, very good for you. And, okay, there were those peanuts, and a bar of chocolate on the way home, but for dinner she'd only had scrambled egg, a couple of low-fat sausages, some fresh bread and butter…

As she stepped on the scale, the figures 210lb flashed alarmingly before her eyes.

'Ohmigod! 15 stone! This is insane!!' she cried. *Another* pound gained. How could that be? Hitting the 15-stone mark for the first time made her heart palpitate in panic. Mentally she calculated, and felt sick. She redid her maths. But no getting away from it, 210 pounds divided by 14 equalled what now felt like 15 giant slabs of concrete blocks.

Impossible. She'd starved herself yesterday. The scales had to be faulty. She lifted them up and checked the pointer was spot on the centre. Her desire was to hurl the hideous mechanical object out of the window, but she contained her pain, and put it on the floor again.

She stepped on once more, as lightly as she could, balancing her body by holding onto the towel rail… then gently released her hand. To find it read exactly the same. Despair weighed her down like a bowl of stodgy dough. As tears welled up in her eyes, she struggled to understand why on earth she had actually gone up?

'After a day of being good, not even the same weight,' she wailed. Again, she counted the calories in her mind… cereal… did she eat two? No…it was three Weetabix… Oh, and there was that banana as well. She'd forgotten that. The first thing she ate, in an attempt to get into eating more fruit.

Then she remembered there was also a mid-morning break. What did she have? The latte… but that was liquid, and didn't really count. She only had two sugars with it, and the spray of cream on top was so light and fluffy, it surely couldn't be many calories. Not even worth counting. Oh, there was a slice of pizza too, but the topping of artichoke and pineapple was healthy.

The flapjack she ate with afternoon tea was full of raisins and oats … good for you, all fibre. In the evening, she remembered she'd also finished off a carton of Stilton soup before it went off. But she had missed pudding with great resolve, and just hit the bottle of wine. Liquid *again*, like the soup. No, she just couldn't understand it.

She pulled a fluffy dressing gown around her for comfort, and stuffed her swollen ankles into a pair of matching slippers. The bulky wrap added stones to her frame and she looked like a pink, pregnant polar bear. But, what the hell, it was cosy.

Sharon knew her dress sense was always struggling to surface but was daily drowned in sail-sized clothes. Still, at least her surroundings had some style, she reasoned.

Her home was her sanctuary and every penny she earned that didn't go on the odd night out or straight in her mouth, went on her studio flat. For the third time that morning, she re-arranged the sweetpeas in the triangular glass vase from Habitat, polished the glass table and plumped up the deckchair-striped cushions on the soft leather sofa.

The colours of the room were peaceful, ice-cream pastels. Pale peppermint, pink and duck-egg blue. It reminded her of happier, younger days by the seaside. Then she heard the iron path gate swing open.

Since answering the *Predict* advert, Sharon had watched the post flop through the communal hallway door every morning. The draught swept around her feet as she went downstairs to wait, turning them a fetching shade of purple. Then finally, at last… a curious pale pink envelope poked its nose through the letterbox. It was addressed to her, marked 'URGENT'.

'A reply!' she squealed, excitedly. Ripping it open, she found a gold-edged appointment card with the address of the clinic, the date, and time of her appointment with Dr. Maximus Marvel.

'Ohmigod!' gasped Sharon. It was *that day*, at noon.

She raced back up the stairs grabbing the banister and heaving herself up two at a time – it was already ten-thirty, and she had to get dressed and find the place. London W1. From Kingston to the West End would take at least an hour and a half.

Then Sharon panicked. Would she have to undress for this appointment? Possible. The thought filled her with dread. It was a clinic after all. They may want to measure her, or weigh her accurately.

Avoiding any activity that involved a communal changing room and a thousand light years away from ever having a lover, her underwear drawer held every conceivable shade of grey. Well, at least they all matched and toned, she groaned. Grabbing the only bra that didn't currently cut under her arms, she teamed it with a high pair of knickers, favoured for not creating an extra ridge around her tummy.

Yanking on a kaftan top and an elasticised skirt she picked up her rucksack and headed towards the train station.

Everyday events made her aware of her size. She always dreaded going through the automatic ticket barrier, squeezing through sideways, terrified she wouldn't clear the swing doors in time. Boarding the tube or train meant either squishing into a seat with arms, or spilling over her 'allotted' space and elbowing the poor sod reading the paper next to her. So she usually stood. Which made her legs ache, and worry that an unexpected lurch would send her flying, flattening some poor toddler or helpless pensioner to the ground.

But more than this, she hated the advertising that surrounded her everywhere.

As she waited for the train, she eyed the giant advert for a new range of lingerie opposite her. The model's body was amazing, with a firm, impossibly long waist, metal-smooth stomach and long, slender limbs. She posed provocatively, one knee perched on a velvet boudoir pouf, flaunting the daintiest, cutest bra and chiffon panties in the world. Edged in running-stitch satin and frothy chiffon frill, the soft, pleated grey set mocked the dingy nylon undies Sharon was wearing. Well, at least the colour of my knickers are 'in' she laughed bitterly, sad that she knew she could never, ever wear such glorious confectionery.

The tube was even worse. The posters led the escalator up an endless line of thin girls wearing bras, thin girls advertising make-up, thin girls advertising cars. And today, at the top, the perfect irony… a thin girl clutching a box of ribboned, designer chocolates and popping one between her moist, damson lips.

Yep, thought Sharon enviously, studying the model's form. No doubt a skinny cow like her would have the willpower to always control herself. The strength of willpower it took to stay slim enough to keep the kind of man who could *afford* to spoil you with such luxury. The model was probably like Audrey Hepburn, who legend had it limited herself to just one chocolate a year, on her birthday… Sharon bristled at the irony of the confectionery campaign, and looked away.

Instead, she decided it was time to play her regular 'Who's fatter than me?' game going up the series of escalators. If it were a good day, there would be four or five commuters, which made her feel better. And worse, because at the same time she would check out the figures of all the other women sailing past in the other direction, or walking up the stairs to her left. Surreptitiously she'd peek in envy at slim, young girls flaunting bare midriffs and skinny jeans. Or gaze despairingly at older women in their forties, fifties and even sixties who had better bodies than hers. No doubt she would grow old and grey, never knowing what it felt like to wear a mini-skirt.

On the other hand – maybe today her life would finally change? She glanced down at the gold-embossed appointment card in her hand. It was suspicious that his name was Dr. Marvel. It made him sound like a real quack. Still, she knew of a dentist called Dr. Savage… and there was an undertaker in Kingston called Fred Paine. Besides, the advertisement had said it was a celebrity remedy from Beverly Hills, and they loved flash names out there. He'd probably changed his surname to fit in, she assumed – chances were it was phoney.

Although an intelligent woman, Sharon refused to consider the next logical step, which was: perhaps the miracle remedy she was chasing would be just as fake? She ignored the possibility because she was so desperate for an instant cure. In her mind, anything was worth a gamble. However stacked the odds.

Checking her watch, she scoured the A-Z with growing anxiety. Riversal Road? The newspaper vendor she asked had never heard of it. But finally she found the name in the book near Oxford Circus. It was a little road behind Harley Street, famous for its leading doctors and medical consultancies. Well, that made him seem a lot more bona fide, she thought, encouraged. And if he wasn't such a mega-success, surely he couldn't afford the rent, she reasoned.

Oh hell, that meant the clinic would be smart, Sharon suddenly thought, apprehensive that the £80 might only cover the initial consultation.

Pushing through the crowds she glanced at her watch again. Only six minutes until she missed her appointment! The hordes thinned as she reached Harley Street and turned into Riversal Road, but spotting a grand house sporting a No. 2 plaque, she realised she was at the wrong end. *No.150 must be miles ahead*, she sighed, quickening her pace along with her quickening heart. She hurtled down the street, counting down house after house. Then she stopped, out of breath and confused. The road had finally turned from elegant period properties into a series of smart boutiques and shops. She felt the time sift away like sand through an hourglass.

Scanning the names above the windows for numbers she realised her side of the street jumped from 148 to 152. On the other side of the road they read 147, 149, 151, 153… She crossed over. She crossed back. Still no sign of 150. A bead of sweat trickled down her neck, her heart pounding with the unexpected stress. She asked a couple walking past, but they were tourists and didn't even speak English. Turning away, her mind rambled in panic. She was late. She was going to miss the appointment. They would be cross. They would refuse to make another one… she would be fat forever.

She steeled herself to look at her watch once more, and let out a breath of relief.

Still one minute to go… Casting around helplessly for a traffic warden or someone else to ask, she saw two workmen carrying a heavy horizontal mirror out of a white van. As they crossed the road in front of her, she called out to see if they knew where No. 150 was.

'What's that luv?' answered the older man, straining with the weight of the long, ornate gold mirror.

'I'm looking for 150, Riversal…' But Sharon stopped short. There, reflected in the antique looking glass was the series of shops behind her, plus a red Regency door, with the title above clearly reading **Dr. Marvel's Miracle Weight Clinic**. Good grief, thought Sharon turning around. And there it was… right behind her all the time. She turned back to look at the shops in the mirror.

Something was odd about the reflection, and she paused, trying to put her finger on it. But as a nearby clock started its midday chimes, there was no time to think. She'd found the place and that was the important thing. And she was on time.

Crossing back over, Sharon looked for the buzzer. But there wasn't one. Only a gleaming brass plaque beside the door inscribed with the Doctor's name and host of initials. On the door itself sat an impressive heavy brass knocker of an open-mouthed Gorgon. Above it, in gold lettering, the number 150.

Relieved, she banged down the Gorgon's head.

On the last stroke of twelve.

Chapter Three

The door swung open of its own accord, and straight ahead of her sat a nurse at a smart chrome and white desk, wearing a brilliant white tunic and matching white smile. All the whiteness was dazzling.

'Miss Plunkett? Hi honey! We've been expecting you,' said the nurse, putting down her nail file and standing up in greeting. Sharon tilted her head up in surprise. The nurse must have been nearly six and a half feet tall. And every inch of her was stunning. Her impossibly long, slim, stiletto-framed legs disappeared into the cute pleats of a tiny white skirt that skimmed her thighs like a tennis outfit. She swiftly sashayed round to the front and whipped Sharon's jacket off her shoulders.

'Coffee? Tea? Elderflower Juice? Magazine?' she pouted through bright, glossy red lips. On her platinum blonde, wave-bobbed head perched a ridiculous nurse's hat. She was every hospitalised man's dying dream – a killer blonde who could raise the blood pressure faster than a coronary.

'Take a seat…' she gestured with a nonchalant flourish towards the right.

Tearing her eyes away from the nurse's cartoonesque beauty, Sharon glanced around and noticed the waiting room was also pure white. So white, in fact, it was hard to see where the floor ended and the walls started.

In the corner was a back-buttoned, white suede chaise-longue. The sound of tinkling water came from a fountain on the left wall – the plump mouth of a snowy cherub spouting forth water endlessly into a Baroque white basin. Above the tinkling, she could hear the strains of new-age music… a hideous mix of noises that sounded like Celtic harp, Andalusian sand pipes, and possibly mating hump-back whales.

If God's waiting room existed, this would be it, thought Sharon uneasily. She carefully lowered her bulk onto the spindly chaise-longue and sat in a prim, knees-together position. The nurse was still waiting for the answer to her offers of refreshment.

'Err, nothing thank you.'

'No problem, honey,' replied the nurse in a transatlantic baby voice reminiscent of a gangster's moll. 'I'll just go and check on Maximus… err, Dr. Marvel. Tell him you're here.'

Pressing a lever, it seemed that she simply disappeared through the wall. As it shut, only the faint outline of a door was visible. No handle.

The surreal atmosphere grew as long moments ticked by. The overwhelming whiteness of the surroundings was disorientating, like being in a thin, floaty cloud. And as her head swam with the dreamy sounds, from the corner of her eye she could have sworn she saw the cherub wink at her. When the door finally flew open again, the tinkling, at-one-with-nature Muzak competed with distant funfair organ music – totally at odds with all the new-age purity.

'This way sweetheart... the Doctor is ready for you,' said the nurse excitedly, beckoning Sharon through. The narrow, winding corridor reminded her of an American fifties fun house. The wood-panelled walls were lined with distortion mirrors that made their shapes change from skinny to short to fat (in Sharon's case, even fatter) to wide to tall (in the nurse's case, even taller). Sharon longed to stop at the mirror that made her skinny, but the nurse grabbed her arm to hurry her along.

'This is all... umm... unusual for a doctor's clinic,' said Sharon nervously.

'What is, honey?' asked the nurse, puzzled.

'Well, the décor... and the music,' she added as the fairground organ got progressively louder.

'That's the "inner child" in Dr. Marvel,' sighed the nurse with fan-like admiration. 'He believes we should never lose it. Wrote a thesis in the *Lancet* about it... won three awards. Here we go...' she said, pushing Sharon through a door before she could ask anything more.

Ahead was a gold-fringed curtain more befitting a Victorian vaudeville theatre.

'In here.' The nurse drew it back with a flourish and shoved Sharon forward.

A handsome man in his late forties, sporting sleeked hair, a black moustache and a charming Hollywood smile, grinned, 'Welcome, welcome, I'm Dr. Maximus Marvel.' He talked and looked like a slick, American game show host… complete with an air of insincerity. Still, catching the merry twinkle in his eye, Sharon relaxed. It was as if he was sending himself up, having a private joke with her.

But then she took in the room. It was so not what she expected. Instead of clinical Beverly Hills it was predominantly pink, and in every shade. Pink and fleshy. Dark pink. Pale pink. Rose pink. Deep fuchsia. And almost red-pink. The only other colour was antique gold – beautifully carved filigree wood, which decorated the desk, mirrors and chairs, in the elaborate manner of a steam carousel.

He directed her towards his large, antique desk. 'Yes, yes,' he sighed walking around her. 'I can see the problem.'

He rubbed his hands, as if loving a challenge, and delved into his doctor's coat for a stethoscope.

'Formalities, my dear. Just formalities. A few tests, that's all…' he muttered. 'Nurse, bring the optimum fat measurer,' he instructed, slapping the nurse's cheeky butt, totally oblivious to Sharon's presence.

'Yes, sir,' she giggled back, opening a glass-fronted mahogany wall cabinet and handing him a pair of measuring pincers that Sharon thought were more suited to an elephant. Her instinct was to make a bolt for it. But then, she was an elephant. It focused her mind. That's exactly why she was there. And anything… and that meant ANYTHING, was worth a go.

Lifting her kaftan, he applied the instrument. Sharon winced at the cold metal. 'Lovely, lovely…' the Doctor muttered to himself, jotting down reams of figures and words in illegible handwriting. The volume of the fairground music seemed to increase as the nurse/receptionist returned with an empty test-tube and a giant 'V' shaped glass that contained smoking green liquid.

'Take this, darlin',' she coaxed, sitting on the edge of the desk and crossing her endlessly long legs. 'It's a neutraliser.'

What!! Sharon backed away, nervously.

'Sure, sweetheart. All those nasty little ol' toxins currently swimming around your body, it wipes them out and prepares you for … you wrote and said you wanted the Celebrity Remedy, didn't you?'

'That's right, that's right,' cajoled Dr. Marvel, now studying her eyes with a spotlight and giant magnifying glass, his own enlarged eye looming through with a slightly mad, distorted gleam.

The nurse handed her the glass of swirling green liquid. With no way to escape, Sharon gulped the scary substance back and waited for an explosion of foul taste. Instead, the very sweetest imaginable hit her tongue. Like a juicy mint leaf dipped in sugar and morning dew.

'Well done, darlin'. Now this way,' said the nurse, wiping Sharon's mouth with a silk handkerchief. But as she tried to stand, things seemed to speed up. Sharon's head felt a little woozy and happy. The carousel music grew even louder.

'I just love this music,' laughed Dr. Marvel. 'Reminds me of travelling funfairs… I used to hang out with them all the time when I was a kid.

'Roll up, roll up…' he barked like the great Barnum himself. 'Come and let me do some measurements.'

Feeling like the Fat Lady With The Beard, Sharon let him pull her towards a stark, full-length mirror on a far wall, surrounded by bright light bulbs – the kind you'd find in a clown's dressing room.

Out came a tape measure and a lot of 'Ah… huh… uh… hu… umm…' noises from the Doctor's mouth as he wrapped it round various parts of her anatomy and jotted down yet more figures.

'You're exactly between the classic, official measurements of size 14 and 16.'

'Really?' said Sharon in delighted surprise.

'That's 14-16 *American* sizing… in England, you're a big size 18.'

Her joy popped like a fairground balloon hit by a dart.

In the unforgiving light, Sharon could barely face herself in the looking glass. The white bulbs gave a ghostly pallor to her skin. To the side of the mirror was a giant jackpot handle, and without warning the Doctor put his clipboard aside, and pulled down on it with two strong hands.

Suddenly the lights began to flash in rotation around the edge of the mirror… and it started to change. Like the mirrors she had passed on the way in, her shape began to distort… but this time, all in ONE mirror. With a life of its own, the glass rippled and bulged in different areas altering her image as it did so. From fat to thin, tall to wide… like a fruit machine window gone wild.

Dizzied by the fast, repetitive movement, Sharon felt her head spin. She held her hand out… she was going to faint. The

Doctor slammed the jackpot handle to a standstill. The mirror came to a halt.

'Okay, I have the perfect solution for you,' he gently announced, supporting her by the elbow.

She opened her eyes, and saw her reflection. It was the same as when she first looked.

'It's the lights, my dear. I do apologise, they have the habit of making one feel a little strange.

'Now, there's just one final test we have to do, to make sure you're really suitable – the change is very drastic, you know. We have to be absolutely sure…'

The nurse steered her to a corner of the room where an old-fashioned giant weighing machine stood waiting. It was red, and had a sign on the top that said, *Speak your weight.*

'Are you serious?' asked Sharon, half laughing, half horrified. This was hardly hi-tech Beverly Hills! The doctor and nurse looked at each other, as if sharing an intimate secret, then smiled. Saying nothing, they ushered her onto the platform.

The machine started to groan and creak. It felt like it was actually coming to life. The hands on the dial began to swing round and round, faster and faster… Sharon's head started to swim again as she watched them spin. Above the groans and the organ fairground music a voice from the bowels of the machine growled out:

'She is much deserving.'

'What did it say? Deserving of what?' asked Sharon, confused.

'No, darlin', the machine said "Too many servings…" Here, sit down… take a rest, it's all a bit much to take in, we know.' The nurse helped her take a seat in front of the Doctor's desk.

'…Please, can somebody explain, what exactly *is* this weight loss course? And how well does it work?' asked Sharon.

'Work? Why, it works MARVEL-LOUSLY!' answered Dr. Marvel, holding a test-tube of fluid to the light.

'But how quickly will I lose the weight? Will it really make me slim?'

'So many queries, my dear,' he said patting her knee and winking at his nurse.

'Take the medicine as directed and you'll have the enviable figure of a celebrity… and face, if I'm right,' he replied, cupping her cheeks in his hand so tightly she felt them puff out like a guinea pig.

'But the thing is, my dear… read the instructions CARE-FULLY. Understand? Very carefully indeed.'

He turned to a side-table and began pouring various luminescent liquids and coloured powders into a funnel that led to a small, silver machine.

'Now, whilst I distil the ingredients for you, nurse will take you outside to wait.'

It was all happening too fast, like being on a rollercoaster with no time to ask questions or get answers.

'But… but… what's actually in it?' The Doctor put his fingers to her lips to quieten her.

'Shush…' Leaning confidentially towards her, he whispered, 'It's called a secret remedy because… it's a SECRET!' And he laughed, throwing her another wink.

'Trust me, everything you need to know will be in the instructions.'

The nurse led Sharon out through the corridor, past the mirrors and back into the pure white waiting room.

'It won't take long, honey,' she soothed.

'Err… okay, let me pay you,' said Sharon nervously. She had drawn out cash in anticipation and handed £80 over to the nurse. She counted it with her glossy long red fingernails, licking between notes to check the amount.

'Marvellous, darlin'. We give it back to charity. Every donation is really welcome.'

'Which charity?' asked Sharon, surprised.

'Y'know, the Needy. Those who can't have what they want to eat.' Again, a distinct lack of specifics. Sharon gave up. Whatever.

She sat back on the sofa and flicked through a magazine from the rack at her side. It was *Saga* – a magazine aimed at the over fifties. She noticed how the models were older, not silly sixteen year olds, but *real* women with a few wrinkles. How odd it seemed compared to normal fashion magazines. She read a few articles, and picked up another *Saga*. Flicking through, she realised how swiftly the older models began to look fine. It didn't take long to get used to the change. Actually, these women were really attractive with their elegant, wiser faces and chiselled Garbo cheeks –

'Ready honey…?' trilled the nurse holding a neat white cardboard box in the palm of her perfectly manicured hand. It was tied with a delicate pink ribbon. Like a gift.

Good grief, thought Sharon – taken aback.

'Err… that's it? That's my medication?'

'Sure it is…' said the nurse, sounding puzzled at her patient's reaction. 'Take it with any liquid you want – even a milkshake if you like,' she winked.

'But whatever you do… follow the instructions inside. Don't break the rules, or there's no guarantee the remedy will continue to work in the long run. It could change everything for you. And you won't want that once you've enjoyed its success.'

The phone rang, interrupting them, and the nurse turned her attention elsewhere.

'Dr. Maximus Marvel's office… how can we help you?' she said.

Sharon thanked her with a wave and left. The door automatically opened, the same way it had when she had arrived, and closed behind her. Looking down at her watch, she was startled to see the time. It was only a minute past twelve o'clock. She shook it, figuring it must be broken.

Then, feeling hungry, she cast around for a café.

Chapter Four

The streets around Oxford Circus were swarming with shoppers. After being disgorged from such an extraordinary experience, it struck Sharon as such an ordinary sight.

Unnerved but excited, Sharon hunted for somewhere to sit and examine the doctor's package. She wanted a coffee bar with a table outside in the sun. A coffee bar with a table in the sun that also served chocolate and cookie cream milkshake. For this, she had decided, should be the chosen drink with which to take her medication. After all, the nurse had practically insisted on it.

She finally spotted a pretty, little peppermint and pink cafe that was busy selling cakes in beribboned, French patisserie boxes – a reverence she appreciated. The name on the striped awning said 'Your Choice'... And Sharon *immediately* decided it was hers.

Whilst waiting in line, she eyed the trays of caramel and chocolate shortbread squares, lemon drizzle slices and crumbly walnut cake with desperate desire. In her rush to get to the appointment, she hadn't even had breakfast... No, she resolved. This was going to be a new start. But the queue was slow...

Finally, it was her turn next:

'A chocolate and cookie milkshake please... with a little bit of cream on top,' she added at the last second. Then she looked at the package in her hand.

'Can you make the main milkshake semi-skimmed? I'll also have a bottle of water,' she added with a feeling of self-righteous control. But then, as if operated like a ventriloquist's doll, she found herself adding, 'Oh, and just this...'

With a life of its own, her hand reached out for a fat fairy cake. Sitting on a solitary plate, the old-fashioned choice looked incongruous compared to the frou-frou pastries surrounding it. But coated in thick chocolate butter icing, and topped with a plump glace cherry, its nostalgic appeal was irresistible. A *Fairy* cake! She handed over the money and shrugged. What the hell? After all, she hadn't actually started the course yet had she?

Settling down outside, she carefully placed the neat white package from Dr. Marvel in front of her and pulled at the pretty ribbon. Like a music box, the lid sprang open to reveal a bevelled mirror. Blinding her eyes for a second, it glinted in the sunshine sending rainbow shafts skittering across the table.

The interior of the box was even more surprising, for nestling cosily in a layer of fleshy pink velvet sat a pure white egg. It snuggled there, precious and perfect, like something a golden goose would lay. Except this egg was encased in a net of criss-crossed twine. This was truly bizarre, she thought.

Her fingers plucked at the twine. Silver in appearance, it stretched like some kind of weird animal gut. How symbolic, mused Sharon as she snapped it apart. She was breaking the umbilical cord to her past life of being fat.

She held the egg up for examination. Made of some kind of bone or ivory, finely carved with indecipherable swirls and inscriptions, it reminded her of those ancient Chinese puzzles. And of her figure. Spherical. Rotund. She studied the egg and saw that a faint line ran through the centre, but it wouldn't open despite the removal of the twine. Press a lever? Pull a stop?

She stopped and took a gulp of milkshake, contemplating the egg. There were no instructions. She held it in her hand, enjoying the coolness and weight of it… and then it slowly opened of its own accord. Like the petals of a flower opening hopefully towards the morning rays of light.

Out dropped a single, solitary pill. A large, white shiny tablet. And with it, a tiny scroll of instructions. Sharon read it again, and again.

But edged in gold, all it said was:

'AFTER CONSUMPTION, DO NOT EAT FOR TWO HOURS.'

That was it. No side-effects leaflet, no ingredients. She eyed the medication warily. It could be made from Balinese bongo dust for all she knew… But she also knew that, regardless, she would take it. A lifetime of fat was a bitter pill to swallow. In comparison this could only taste sweet. Please God, let it work.

But it all looked so exotic. She had expected something medical and clinical. Instead, this looked more like the latest bohemian answer from a spaced-out Californian guru. Still, who knew? Maybe it contained some magic ingredient? Imagining herself to be a Hippy-Chic High Priestess holding court in a Beverly Hills Yoga Centre, she decided the actual swallowing of the pill deserved a certain druid pomp and ceremony; she would have it with the milkshake, but first perhaps she'd go and get a cream bagel to eat as a main course before the chocolate fairy cake.

Then she caught sight of her chubby face in the bevelled lid. No, this was her last hope, and this time she'd do it right. *This time*, she'd do whatever it took. *This time*, she'd have the willpower.

She held up the fairy cake. Reluctant to simply throw it away as she was mindful of waste, she just took a token nibble of the icing. It tasted so good. She took another nip. Then another. The thick chocolate butter topping tasted perfect with the crumbly vanilla filling. Her tongue scooped a tipful… Enough! That was it. A new beginning. She wrapped the remainder of the cake carefully in a couple of paper napkins and popped it into her bag, resolving to feed it to the pigeons on her windowsill when she got back home.

Ceremoniously, she held up the pill in one hand and the instructions in the other. It was all so simple, she couldn't believe it. No exercise, no starving, no dieting, no grief.

'AFTER CONSUMPTION, DO NOT EAT FOR TWO HOURS,' she re-read out loud.

Fair enough. That'll be a piece of cake.

She said a silent prayer. No, a mantra. And as she prayed, she opened her mouth to take it…

Chapter Five

An hour or so later, 'Californian Princess Sharon, Priestess of Hippy-Chic' wandered into an outsize shop still giggling about the yogic mysticism of it all. She was enjoying this so much. Determined the remedy would work, she'd been shopping.

'If I'm going to lose weight, I'm going to need new clothes!' she reasoned. It was time to spoil herself, ready for the new figure she would soon have.

First stop had been Selfridges, and a delicate pair of high-heeled shoes. A soft leather pair in palest beige. They would make her shapely new legs look even longer. Next, she had browsed along the jewellery counters.

Jingling the shiny goodies like a naughty magpie, she found herself drawn towards the rings. This time, she'd bought a dainty triple ring with matching bracelet – slightly tight in size, but when she lost the weight it would look stunning. Dainty jewellery on dainty little bones. A look she had always coveted.

The weirdest thing was, she hadn't thought about food once. Not once. It was as if the pill was already working, her willpower getting stronger by the second. She thought back to the moment the deed had been done, and smiled again. She'd had a bit of a fright, really. Because the huge pill had caught in her throat. Almost choked her. Finally, washed down by chocolate milkshake, it had slid lower, into her cavernous stomach. The irony of 'death by slimming pill' hit her later, and she hadn't stopped chuckling – she was experiencing a feel-good factor that was making her giddy.

Sharon loved the outsize shops because they were the only place she felt normal. She adored the fact that the assistants were large too, not like the usual skinny bitches that manned changing rooms, or the snooty model types at the till.

Sweeping up handfuls of clothes she headed towards the cubicle, stopping only to check out a beautiful fifties-style yellow dress with a tiny blue cornflower print. Made of crisp cotton, it was so sunny and fresh – like the way she was suddenly feeling. As she struggled to hold all the clothes so she could rummage along the rail, she was disappointed she could only find it in a size 16.

What were the chances of it fitting? Nil, she thought, aware its slightly boned waistline made it look an even smaller size than it was. Whatever, she decided, adding the size 16 to the pyramid pile in her arms – she would fit into it soon enough!

The shop was hot, and as she waited in the queue she longed for a cold drink of something. She hesitated, trying to calculate if the wait was really worth the goodies in her hand. It was, she decided, feeling the gorgeous stiff cotton of the yellow dress. For a split second, she wondered what Simon would think of her in it? Then blanked him from her mind. Simon would think what he always must have thought. By being friendly with the 'fat girl', he would get to Debbee.

As a large woman finally padded out, Sharon told the assistant she had eight items and held out her hand for a tag. It never failed to annoy her how the sales girls liked to double-check despite the fact they could clearly see how many she was helpfully holding out. A pathetic power-trip, they may as well call you a thief to your face, she sighed. She was getting irritated. Being overweight, the heat was beginning to get to her, and she felt her good mood start to evaporate.

Her armpits and neck felt sticky and her head hot. Shoving the hangers on the changing-room hooks she knew she'd picked out too many clothes, but couldn't resist trying them on anyway.

It was always a nightmare finding the right size, as she often had to take two or three of the same style in with her to see which worked the best. The gamble of which to try on first would depend on whether she was feeling fatter or thinner that particular day. Well, today was a good one, she told herself, trying to keep her mood buoyant.

Undoing the side button on her skirt, she felt her flesh spill out. Taking off her kaftan she ran her finger under her bra-strap, and took the opportunity to soothe the deep ruts. This is all going to change, she comforted herself. And optimistically, she launched into a size 16 blouse.

Made of a shiny, stretchy, red-and-blue fabric, she was disappointed to see the buttons pulled across her bosoms like two beach balls in a tug of war.

Annoyingly, it did the same in a size 20. The material was too cheap. She progressed to a T-shirt but hated the way it puckered in the same place. Worse, in all three sizes, the material bulged around the back, showing the deep indentation of her bra.

By now her throat felt cracked; then she remembered the bottle of water in her bag. A swig later, and she was ready to try the trousers… They zipped up fine, but the material was too tight in the crotch and looked obscene. The larger size was too baggy round the bum. Despite her original happy mood, the clothes shopping was swiftly evaporating into the usual hell. The heat increased and she felt beads of sweat form on her brow.

But there was still the yellow dress. By habit she always left the best to last. All hopes pinned on this creation. The petticoats rustled as she lifted it over her head and gently shimmied it down. But halfway, it stuck. She checked the zip was undone, and it was. She struggled aimlessly, like a porpoise caught in fishing net. The tight sleeves had her arms in a vice grip; the bodice was trapped halfway over her breasts. She struggled some more, determined to get it lower, to see how it could look if she lost a bit of weight – when she heard the most terrifying 'rip' of cotton thread.

Tears sprouted at the hopelessness of it all. Trying to backtrack the dress off a shoulder she twisted it inside out, and as the whalebone dug into her rib she felt like the very same beached creature – stuck, stranded and unable to move. Somehow, the more she squirmed, the more her semi-naked body became exposed. The heat and humiliation made her head throb. She couldn't possibly ask for help. Swimming in panic and hopeless despair she shut her eyes and felt herself almost black out. The ground gave way, and like a demolished building she sank to her knees in a dishevelled heap. Her bag spilled open on the floor beside her, contents scattering. Sobbing, with her one free hand she reached out for the cold bottle of water and pressed it against her forehead.

Chanting, 'I am not a fat whale, I am not a fat whale,' she took control. Taking a series of slow, deep breaths her panic subsided and her logic returned. Arching, she released pressure on the back of the dress, wrenched it back over her head, and stuffed it on the chair. There was a knock against the cubicle frame.

'Miss, are you all right in there?' said the assistant.

Sharon didn't answer. The heat of embarrassment burned her face, and her nose ran from hot tears.

'Miss, I've something I think you'd like to try on…' coaxed the shop assistant.

With no option, Sharon opened the curtain slightly and peeked out, red-faced, guilty and miserable.

'Don't worry, this is perfect for you,' she said.

The assistant was brandishing the most hideous frock Sharon had ever seen. Yards and yards of garish green fabric overlaid with wavy brown horizontal stripes and dotted with large yellow sunflowers. It looked as if a blind farmer had ploughed a field on LSD.

'I promise it will make you look *really* fat,' smiled the shop assistant sweetly. At first Sharon thought she'd misheard, but the woman blithely continued. 'Horizontal stripes – they always add pounds, you know. I bet you'll look divine in it.'

Sharon was speechless with hurt. How could people be so cruel? Now, even a shop assistant in an outsize shop was making fun of her. Shaking her head in disgust at the dress she snapped the curtain shut and withdrew into her cell. Blinking back more shameful tears, she hurried back into her own clothes ready to run out of the shop.

How dare they be so rude? And in this shop of all places. She would complain to the manager. But maybe the manager would laugh at her as well. No, she would just get out of there... Tucking her bulging flesh back into her skirt, she yanked on the kaftan top. She just wanted to get home, to her pastel-ice-cream sanctuary where no one could cause her pain.

With head held defiantly high, she swept up her handbag and sailed out of the changing room, curtain wafting in her wake. Straight past the assistant, straight out of the shop and straight into the high street. The cooler air hit her ample cheeks and she embraced the freedom from the cell of the changing room, like a prisoner on day release. Taking deep breaths she leant against a wall to get herself together... But when she finally looked up, she took another deep breath – this time, for an entirely different reason. A reason that caused her to stand stock still, her eyes dilated in shock.

All around her were fat women. Not twenty, not forty... but hundreds. Roly-poly shoppers waddled up and down the road like Sumo wrestlers on a coffee break. Puzzled, she walked on. Was there a Fat Persons Convention in from Vegas? Yet it continued endlessly. Fat girl after fat girl passed her. Occasionally somebody really slim, but so occasionally they stood out. The cars were full of chubby women. The buses. The taxis… the female traffic wardens, the policewomen. All plus size 16. Where had they all come from?

Breaking her golden rule, she glanced at the shop windows to look at her reflection – an action that used to make her cringe in horror. But, for the first time in her life, she looked the same as everyone else. And then she noticed something even more amazing.

Unlike the male mannequins, which were normal, the female mannequins were enormous, and sporting hammock-sized dresses. Not just that store, but also the one after. And the store over the road. And the store after that. Two young men in jeans and tattoos walked past her in deep conversation. Then unexpectedly, one turned, looked her up and down and let out a loud wolf-whistle.

Sharon gasped in bewilderment. She sat on a pavement bench to catch her breath. Her heart palpitated. Was she dreaming? She shut her eyes tight, counted to ten… then opened them again.

They focused on a mega-large poster on a billboard opposite. She remembered it being there last week; a model was sexily flaunting her skinny butt in a pair of Calvin Klein jeans whilst wrapped around a male with the torso of a re-touched Adonis. But what the hell had happened?

Instead of the model with third-degree anorexia, there was a young Roseanne Barr look-alike grinning like a Cheshire cat, squeezing her huge bottom into a pair of denims.

Next to her, a semi-naked male model was pressing his toned torso into her back suggestively. The caption read:

**'MAXIMISE YOUR CURVES WITH
THE CALVIN CUT.'**

Shaking her head in confusion she wandered a few paces down the street. A newsvendor called out. Sharon surveyed his stand. The latest edition of *Hello!* magazine stared back at her.

On the cover was a picture of Oprah Winfrey, fist punching the air in victory – huge beaming smile on her face. Looking happy and bloated, the banner headline underneath her screamed:

**'OPRAH OVER THE MOON!
16 stone 6lb again!'**

Next to it sat *Grazia* magazine. On its cover stood a very pretty, very plump girl in a short silver skirt. At her podgy waist she clutched a tiny fluffy dog. The cover line read:

**'MILANA SHERATON INVITES YOU INTO HER
HOLLYWOOD HOME.'**

Further up, on the cover of FHM was a cover line:

'WHO'D LIKE A GO WITH JO?'

And Sharon recognised a famous comedienne known for her keen wit, feminist patter and mega-sized body. But there she posed, grinning shamelessly in a bikini, with the tag line: *'Voted older woman we'd most like to sleep with.'*

On a lower rack, the most curious of all… Sharon picked up a magazine called *FATTIES* and studied its cover 'FATTY OF THE YEAR.'

Enough! Head spinning she hailed a taxi and headed straight to the safety of home.

'Can you see what I see?' she asked the driver.

'What 'yer talking about, Miss?' Sharon gestured out of the window.

'All these people. Fat women… everywhere. What's happened?'

The driver fell silent. He had the resigned look of a cabbie that had picked up yet another weirdo.

She kept her mouth shut as she avidly watched the endless procession of paunchy, bosomy, busty women swarming the streets. Her heart stirred with a strange emotion of fear… and incredible, undeniable hope.

Entering her flat with relief, she swiftly locked the door behind her and sat on the edge of the bed, pulling the pastel quilted eiderdown around her shoulders for security. Then, hand trembling, she dug out the remote control buried under the biscuit tin at the base of her bedside table, and switched on the TV.

Maybe there was an explanation on the news. Glancing at the clock she saw it was coming up to the hour. Perfect timing. She flicked the screen guide on to BBC News and watched as the familiar icon and newsbeat sounded out. And then Sharon jumped. Jumped out of her ample skin. Instead of the usual sleek presenter, the newscaster's bulky bosoms filled the entire screen. She was massive. Her chunky jowls delivered the latest disaster with sincere gravitas.

Switching channels, Sharon caught a recipe programme. A gargantuan female chef was gesturing wildly at her newly baked creation. It was the most decadent chocolate cake Sharon had ever seen. It looked like a cocoa-covered Tower of Pisa.

'Now, don't forget,' twinkled the beautiful dark eyes of the mammoth cook as she licked her fingers. 'Serve the portions to your guests with lashings of cream. And don't cheat, you naughty viewers. By that, I don't mean single cream or, heaven forbid, crème fraiche. Make sure it's DOUBLE. And most important of all, when preparing the icing make sure to be generous with the sugar.' The celebrity chef tossed her luscious brunette locks, ran her fingers round the bowl, and sucked at them seductively.

Sharon felt faint. She started to giggle insanely. There was no doubt about it. She had entered the Twilight Zone. Or should that be the Twiglet Zone? Whatever, it was clear it was a world where it was 'IN' for women to be fat. And 'OUT' to be skinny. A world where heaven is a plus size. How had this happened?

Her mind raced back to the advert in *Predict* magazine… Now she really thought about it, the words never actually stated that Dr. Marvel's Miracle Weight Pill would make you *lose* weight. It just stated it was a '*magical way to change your life*'. And ironically, that had happened when she stepped into the changing room. How the pill had worked, she didn't question. Didn't want to. Why question a miracle? She felt her soul surge with joy – joy as free as a bird. An eagle. A wild, soaring creature whose possibilities knew no bounds.

Whooping round the room she manically switched channels on the TV screen.

A popular blonde presenter in her late forties called Vanessa was hosting a daytime chat show, and listening attentively to a slim woman sobbing into a handkerchief.

'…The truth is, my husband was repulsed by my weight loss. Though personally I blame his unfaithfulness on HER.'

A picture flashed up of a huge female mud wrestler entitled *My Husband's Mistress*.

'… I was so jealous when they were working together, I just couldn't eat,' continued the sobbing guest. 'Before I knew it, I went the other way. But look at me, why would he want me now…' she cried, indicating her slender frame as the very voluptuous Vanessa sympathetically handed her another tissue.

Yes! Yes! Yes! screamed Sharon frantically pressing the channel buttons again and again.

Next, came 'Slob' high-calorie yogurt. An actress in a white track-suit sat on a white, cushioned stool. She looked like a fat snail on a puffball mushroom.

'At 400 calories a pot… can you say 'not'?' she chimed, spooning her face with a toffee-flavoured substance.

'Mmmm… and packed with goodness to match your greatness!'

Sharon collapsed on the bed in hysterical giggles. For the first time ever, she thought it could be incredible fun to be in the world of advertising, instead of despising just about everything it stood for.

Next the screen flashed up a large people-carrier car.

'Enough room for FOUR people,' boasted a sincere voice-over. Oh this got better and better! Sharon felt so light-headed she wanted to throw open the window and yell Hallelujah! She settled for tossing all her pastel-coloured cushions in the air like a juggler in the circus. But it was the final advertisement in the break that really hit home. She turned back to the TV and watched in dumbfounded silence.

A pretty-faced model was smoothing some kind of cream into her wobbly, tree-stump legs. Winking seductively to the camera, she husked, 'Try *Pig Lard*. Just smooth it on your body every morning for three weeks, and you'll see an amazing difference. Apply with our special rubber mitten, and, within days, your skin will develop an attractive, bumpy texture. Yes, GUARANTEED CELLULITE! See how my dimples have doubled…'

Oh thank you! There IS a God. Thank you! Sharon paused to let it all sink in, then yanked up her skirt and looked at her orange-peel thighs. Oh, far more than orange peel. More like grapefruit. But somehow, and she struggled to comprehend this, somehow this was now considered beautiful. Could it be? Could it possibly be?

Calming down, she stretched out on the bed and studied her legs. 'I suppose the bumps do create a sort of interesting pattern…' she pondered after a while, trying to observe herself objectively. The blue veins showed through her soft, translucent skin, twisting like rivers across her mottled, purple blotches. In places her skin looked goose-bumped. In others it strained, taught and firm. The more she stared, the more her flesh took on a surreal appearance. With a flash of understanding, she looked at her body again. Like a blind woman seeing for the first time.

The way the dimples on her buttocks popped in and out had a definite cheeky charm… the variation of texture gave excitement to her skin. No *way* could you call it boring. The soft, sagging skin under her arm crinkled delicately, like finest crepe silk. In fact, when you looked closely her flesh was fascinating. Like an intricately woven fabric of different textured threads… cotton, wool, satin.

Miraculously, the colours didn't look so bad either. For the first time, she noticed how the shades of blues, pinks and purples on her pale skin blended in perfect harmony. Like splashes of a pastel, watercolour painting, she decided. An impressionist painting!

'My God! I'm a picture. As pretty as a picture!'

Sharon threw back her head and let tears of gratitude cascade down her cheeks.

FLESH! It was the most glorious canvas in the world.

And she had reams of it.

Chapter Six

Monday morning, and this time there was NOTHING blue about it. Instead it was a rainbow-coloured world of infinite possibilities.

The weekend over, Sharon woke up at 6.00am and, as she had on Sunday morning, flicked on the TV to double-check she hadn't been dreaming.

A mum proudly spooned breakfast cereal onto her plate.

'How many Weetabix does the trick? For a healthy breakfast always eat SIX,' sang out the advertisement.

No, she laughed, the magic was still working. Dr. Maximus Marvel had done just that. Sold a marvel. A maximum marvel.

She brushed her teeth, and noticed how her eyes were sparkling. This was such a fun world. She shook out her long, white-blonde hair, and ran a comb down its glorious length. It hung in a straight line, soft and shimmery, like a Chinese silk wall hanging. For the first time in so, so long she couldn't wait to get to work.

The journey on the tube proved enlightening. Walking through the throng of commuters she noticed that her figure caused a lot of second glances and envious side-looks from skinny girls. What was it about her shape? Carefully comparing herself to the others around her, she knew she was firm for her size, and her breasts were perfectly rounded, even though they were size 36 F. Very tall, she could carry her size better than many, and her legs were proportionally very long. Her neck was graceful, and she noticed she didn't have the 'squat' look that so many people around her now had.

And, of course, she had waist-length, long, blonde hair, which she normally tied up to keep herself inconspicuous. Today, she let it swing free, and it flew around up and around her face like angel's wings as the tube trundled into the station.

The trip up the escalator was brilliant. Poster after poster of plump, pretty women lined the walls, their faces sparkling with health and joie de vivre. She began to count the 'fatties' as usual, but instead found herself adding up the slims and skinnies. Not more than maybe eight.

Tra-la-la-ing a song, she pushed through the revolving door to Sharpe, Bates and Colt and swept into the lift.

'Morning Sharon,' said a quiet voice. Sharon turned round to see Samantha, the ringleader in her office.

'Oh hi,' said Sharon, clocking her outfit and figure. Now that was odd. Really odd. Samantha looked slightly different. Plumper. Or was it Sharon's imagination? She seemed definitely larger, a spare tyre round her middle. Or had Sharon never noticed that before?

'I love your dress,' Samantha added tentatively. Samantha was the kind of girl who was only friendly when she wanted something. Once she got it, she cut you dead – almost taking a pleasure in fooling you. A girl so self-centred she could only relate to a mirror. What was her game?

'Cheers. I bought it this weekend,' answered Sharon, waiting for a bitchy comeback. But there was none.

'It suits you really well…' came a flat, honest response.

She indicated to Sharon to go first, and they walked towards the office. Sharon took her seat in customary silence, just nodding to the others in the room. But in a cacophony of girly voices, they all simpered,

'Hi Sharon, did you have a nice weekend?'

'Err… I did. Really did,' answered Sharon, aware they were staring at her body and flowing, loose hair.

'Do you want a coffee?' asked Alexi half an hour later. The slimmest of the gang, her slender body suddenly looked like a delicate, diary pencil that could easily snap.

'Sure, two sugars… no, make that three,' smiled Sharon gratefully.

'I wish I had your willpower,' Alexi sighed as she delivered the coffee and slunk back to her desk. Sharon was confused. What did she mean, because she took the extra sugars?

She looked at the stack of invoices on her computer and inwardly groaned. So many to print out. The printer clicked into action. And then out of it. Damn it, she was out of ink.

She pushed herself out of her chair, picked up the fresh coffee and walked into the lift heading up for the supplies office. The elevator was crowded, with just six people crammed in. She didn't recognise anyone else. As nearly all exited, she became aware of a man studying her from behind. Glancing over her shoulder her eyes locked with a familiar face. Oh God, she thought. It was Mr. Bates, the chairman of the company.

Shyly, she smiled, but she was holding coffee in her hand and sudden worry flitted across her face. Not only did it look like she was on a permanent tea break, there was probably something in the blasted health and safety rules that said NO COFFEE IN THE LIFT.

A neatly dressed, courtly businessman, he was so engrossed in studying the changing expressions of her face that his folder accidentally slipped from under his arm. The contents spilled open, and Sharon squished down to her knees to help him sweep up the compendium of papers.

'Thank you, thank you so much, that's very kind. Do you work for us?' he asked, adjusting his tie as he straightened up.

'Sure. For over three years. I'm in Accounts Filing.'

'Good grief, madam, you're not!' he laughed. 'What's your name?'

'Sharon,' she stammered.

The man waited for more, gazing into her woodland-green eyes like a mesmerised fox.

'Err… Sharon Plunkett,' added Sharon nervously. Throwing politeness to the wind, he weighed her up silently, from head to toe.

'That's all I needed to know,' he added. 'Good day.'

He stepped out of the lift with a curt nod.

~

Two days later, Sharon was summoned to Human Resources.

'Dolores Drummond has asked you to go and see her straight away,' sympathised Samantha, suspecting it was bad news.

Sharon felt sick. It was the coffee incident. Or was it the computer disaster? Okay, the computer had crashed, sucking the filing she'd done into the ether and setting her back a whole day's work. But it was hardly her fault. And conscientiously, she'd worked late to make amends.

She had sacrificed her first invite to go to West End nightclub *Chinawhite's* with the girls from the office – Saffron and a few of the others wanted to see if they could get in and asked her to come with them. But in truth, she didn't want to risk being turned away, and anyway, since the 'Denim and Diamonds' nightmare, nightclubs had about as much allure as a cowboy's armpit after a week-long cattle drive.

Sharon knocked on the door and Dolores summoned her in.

A large black woman sat behind a huge desk, paperwork piled around her like termite towers. Taking off her thick pebble glasses to flash a crocodile smile, she beckoned Sharon forward.

'Come in, come in, sweet child,' she grinned, strangely friendly for a woman who usually dismissed her with a disdainful sneer.

'Umm, I'm really sorry about the filing system going down… it honestly wasn't my fault. I tried to retrieve it and Frank said it was the software we'd been given…' mumbled Sharon defensively.

'No, no,' said Dolores, waving away the thought as if she was swatting an irritating wasp.

'That's not why I've called you in. I've had a visit from our illustrious chairman Mr. Bates, who I believe you bumped into in the lift?'

'Yes, I did. He dropped his papers, and I helped him pick them up,' explained Sharon.

Dolores watched her silently, fingers pressed to lips. Sharon felt like the woman was appraising her as if it was the first time she'd ever seen her. Or worse, like a slave trader checking out damaged goods.

The contemplative silence was broken by Sharon.

'Okay, look, maybe I shouldn't have taken the coffee with me… I'll never do it again. But it was my break time, and I was very careful…'

Dolores held her hand up like a lollipop lady, stopping traffic in full flow.

'Mr. Bates has had a talk with me,' she said, neatly making some quick notes on a piece of paper. Head down writing, she asked:

'Do you LIKE your job, Sharon?'

Oh no, she was about to be sacked.

'Umm, yes I do.' Sensing this wasn't confirmation of dedication she lied, adding:

'Very much, it means so much to me. Err… I LOVE it. Filing is such fun… a great job.'

'Then that's a real shame,' said Dolores. 'Because you no longer have it.'

Sharon's guts lurched in shock. Her life flashed before her… well, in truth her lovely little flat and the rent bill unpaid on the counter.

'However…' Dolores paused for maximum effect, like a nasty talent panellist. And shot her an almost evil smile…

'He would like to offer you another.'

'What? Really? Doing what?' Sharon was now befuddled, her palms sticky and her heart pounding.

'Head receptionist. Front desk. The greeting face of Sharpe, Bates and Colt. We think your looks and charm are wasted in accounts.' Sharon was startled to hear this, and her large green eyes widened with delight. So it was true, then. Her face *was* attractive. Sometimes she had thought it was, but it had been hard to see past her pronounced cheeks.

All she ever saw was her body and its bulges. And how she had hated it.

'Your duties simply involve greeting guests with your beautiful smile and handing them a visitor's badge. Here is your own badge.' Dolores handed Sharon a special gold badge, embossed with the words SHARON PLUNKETT.

Sharon held it in awe, like she had been given a brooch from Tiffany. Sitting at the magnificent marble console desk in reception was the most coveted job among many of the young female staff. Sure, she'd read *Cosmopolitan*. She knew she should have been insulted. But no way. She was thrilled. After a lifetime of hiding away, now somebody thought she was worthy of being on display.

An agency was judged by its image. And the girl on the desk was always the model of beauty.

'The money is almost double – it includes an extra allowance for dress and hair,' continued Dolores as if it was a completely done deal.

And of course, it was. Sharon was elated. Ecstatic. Free from the drudge of accounts. Free to smile, laugh, greet, talk on the phone and drink coffee. From now on, the only thing she would be filing were her nails!

By the seventh day in her new job Sharon had spoilt herself in TK Maxx, and decided to buy a tight white suit that showed off more curves than a Mr. Whippy ice cream.

And judging by the tongues hanging out, it certainly seemed to whip up the same amount of desire.

It was so strange. From the moment she nervously started a week ago, every time she stood up from behind her marble front desk, both men and women gave her the 'once over'. From big, butch biker boys to effete corporate clients. Sharon furrowed her brow as she smoothed the pencil skirt over her curvaceous buttocks. It was a style she had never worn before, and, as an experiment, she had chosen to wear white. Unlike black – her usual colour of choice – it made her look even larger than normal. But this appeared to attract men even more, she mused to herself, as a pinstripe-suited businessman approached her with a salacious grin.

'Let me take you for lunch,' said Mr. Pinstripe with all the arrogance of a man expecting an instant 'yes'.

'SO sorry, I'd love to… but we're not allowed to date clients,' Sharon apologised sweetly.

'Not even top ones?' he asked, handing her a flash-looking business card stating 'International Brand Manager'.

'Especially the top ones!' she answered, fingering it with a coquettish smile. As he walked off, she casually opened her drawer, tossing it onto a pile of five others.

The idea of dating still frightened her. She had thought of Simon many times, and wondered when he would turn up in front of her. Part of her couldn't wait. The sight of his face... would he now find her attractive? But another part of her still reeled from the fact he'd betrayed her and gone after Debbee.

Deep down, Sharon knew she was being a bit of a drama queen. Simon hadn't actually betrayed her as such, as he was never hers in the first place. To be fair, the poor devil didn't know he'd been 'living' with her for the last two years. Yet that didn't stop the deep hurt she felt. Irrational, ridiculous. But very real.

Her thoughts were interrupted by the inconvenience of a purring ring tone.

'Sharpe, Bates and Colt,' she trilled, flicking the board with newly manicured acrylic nails. As she switched the person through, she admired her hands. So odd, she pondered, that there was a cachet in the fact they were so obviously fake. No one had tips that white, or lengths that perfect – the whole kudos was in the fact you could afford to have them done.

'It's important you look the part,' echoed Dolores's warning in her head. Fair enough, Sharon conceded. The fabulous entrance to the agency deserved it. The building was 1930s Art Deco. High ceilings with ornate cornicing, giant aluminium doors with a revolving centre.

Mixing old with new, SBC had installed a 20-foot plasma screen to flash up the latest TV ads from the agency. It was complemented by a massive, pure-glass coffee table and matching glass chairs by up-and-coming Italian designer Tino Quaradelgini.

Overall, it created a stunning effect. Waiting clients looked like they were sitting on pure air. (And no doubt full of it too – Sharon often mused, studying their painstakingly cool dress codes, designer bags and goatee beards).

But the best bit was behind her marble and glass console desk. Starting from high above her head, water spilled first over a giant steel ball then disappeared – to re-appear from under a long steel track. From here, it tumbled in a backlit waterfall sheet down the white marble wall, breaking in strategic places like splintering glass. It was a masterstroke of design, a dramatic backdrop that took away the breath of even the most jaded art director.

Sharon smiled as in came another cute biker boy wearing more Lycra than a Romanian circus act. His butt was neat and small, his torso long, lean and firm. She eyed him from head to toe, waiting for a jaunty flirt. But instead, he bowed his head slightly, and avoided her eyes. Almost embarrassed.

'Hi, can I help you?' she fluttered, flicking her flaxen hair back and dipping her long eyelashes over her brilliant green eyes. He turned bright red, stammered and shoved her a package.

'For the production office,' he stuttered, casting her a longing glance over his shoulder as he left.

How odd to have this effect, she thought, still unsure of her newfound attraction.

But here was the strange thing. Over the next few days, some of the biker boys and cool guys started to look a little bit scrawny. A little bit weedy.

She slowly found herself eyeing up the beefier despatch riders and wider clients. There was something so wonderfully big and bear-like about these men. Men that could match her for size. She booked a lunchtime make-over at *Cheeky Chops* – a popular new Covent Garden cosmetics boutique – and headed back to work two hours later with a skipload of goodies and the knowledge she would never make the mistake of blue eye-shadow again.

As the attention at the reception desk increased, her confidence grew and grew; and Sharon Plunkett blossomed out like a gorgeous, puffy pink Chrysanthemum.

It was about this time that Simon wandered in. At first he didn't recognise Sharon at all. She, on the other hand, had spotted him coming at a thousand paces. Time to get used to the pounding in her heart and at least look cool.

'My God, Sharon? Is that you?'

'No, my sister died. I'm her beautiful, identical twin,' she shot back with a confidence that shocked her.

'Haven't seen you around for ages. When did you get this gig?'

'A couple of weeks ago – been fun.'

'You look seriously great…' he whistled. Yeah, maybe I do, thought Sharon for the very first time in her life.

'By the way, that Country night at *Kat's*, where did you go? I looked over, and, dear God, you were doing a getaway faster than Billy the Kid.'

'Nah, I was meeting someone… picked up by a cowboy in a pick-up truck!' said Sharon, blurting out the first thing to enter her head. Anyway, not that you would have given a damn, she thought, with your nose nuzzling in Debbee's neck like a pathetic palomino pony.

'Well, that's a shame, cos' I was asking Debbee to come to my birthday get-together and I was going to ask you too, but you disappeared into the sunset leaving nothing but a dusty trail.'

'Birthday party?? Really?'

'Yeah, I… had a few friends round. Thought you'd find it fun. Never mind, there's always next year,' he added.

'Sure. I can easily wait that long,' replied Sharon, with teasing sarcasm, wondering if she had the courage to look up again and ask him for coffee. But too late. Yet again, her words and actions had come out completely the opposite to how she felt. Like a sarcastic, cool snub. When she did lift her head, it was just in time to see Simon shrug and turn towards the lift.

Holy Moses. He had only been asking Debbee to a birthday party! Not a date. It still didn't quite explain why Debbee had her mouth so close to his ear she could suck his brains out, but on the other hand Debbee *did* have the knack of wrapping herself around a man quicker than a fur coat round a hooker, she thought charitably.

Whatever, for the second time she had just screwed it up with her ridiculous behaviour.

All afternoon Sharon action-replayed the moment in reception like a football fan unwilling to accept the final outcome of the game. She had been too offhand. Her mind kept a tight score of the things she shouldn't have said. What she could have said. What she never said.

Amid the remorse, there was one strange fact that niggled her. Of course she still adored him, but he looked like he'd lost weight. The man definitely looked a bit too slim. A bit less impressive, maybe, than she had remembered. Having spent so long worshipping from afar, it was almost blasphemous to think of Simon as less than a perfect god. But she had to concede, a little more padding around the chest and he'd probably look a wee bit better.

~

'Red Alert! They're on their way!' squeaked the junior executive running past her towards the lifts... 'Sharpe says you've got to be extra charming or you're fired!'

The entourage of Zeigfreid and ZaK, the team behind the global brand Z&ZaK, swept into the vast advertising reception before Sharon even had time to fluff her hair. The assorted coterie of cool fashionistas standing arrogantly in front of her made her feel like she was a shop girl from the returns counter of Primark, but she was being paid well to hide her insecurity.

'Good afternoon, we've been looking forward to your arrival,' said Sharon with her newfound, dazzling smile. 'Please go straight up to the tenth floor. Mr. Sharpe and Mr. Bates are waiting for you…'

Zeigfreid the famous designer stopped dead, giving her a harsh, appraising look. Then, licking his little finger, he smoothed down his hair parting, and clicked his fingers imperiously; 'Zis way, team,' he said in a guttural accent, mincing off towards the lifts. With his Mandarin-style coat and floor-length scarf swirling around his portly body, he evoked the image of a half-dressed geisha.

Trailing like a couple of cute kittens, two identical Japanese women dressed as roly-poly Manga schoolgirls, complete with plaid skirts and bobby sox, lowered their orange-dyed hair and followed.

The butch bodyguard put his hand to his earpiece and checked the corridor ahead and behind, muttering sinisterly into his mouthpiece. Behind him stood the cool, impeccably dressed ZaK.

As the entire world knew, ZaK was Zeigfreid's lover, and also his brilliant manager. The man epitomised success in his silver-grey suit and dove-suede tie – a look of colour and texture he had deliberately made his own. He checked his platinum Patek Philippe watch impatiently and signalled a brief nod to the three briefcase-carrying executives at his side. As they swept by, the last executive paused, and winked at her.

'Still waiting for your call,' he whispered, with a leer, tapping his fingers on her desk.

Sharon looked at him, puzzled. Then realised he had been one of the first to hand her his business card a couple of weeks ago when she had just started the new job.

As they disappeared into the lift, Sharon picked up the pile in the drawer and spread them on the counter like a pack of cards.

The coolest one, on the top, stated:

JACK DE WINTER
Brand Manager
Zeigfreid & ZaK
New York. Paris. London. Milan.

It was a designer work of art in silver, grey and black. The exact shades of ZaK's outfit. Well, thought Sharon – good luck Sharpe, Bates and Colt. Word was out they were about to lose the entire £10 million business. It was always a nightmare in advertising. When a new brand manager took over, they always liked to make their own mark. And that usually meant dropping one agency in favour of another (usually run by a good golfing buddy). The creative teams had been working for two weeks in sweaty desperation to come up with a pitch to save their sorry asses, and the whole agency was holding its breath for today's meeting.

She briefly wondered if it would affect her job. Possibly… but SBC was a giant conglomerate and, though heads would roll for sure, chances were it wouldn't really impact on either her or the jets and yachts of The Board.

Nonetheless, a feeling of guilt and power crept over her. If she called this man and arranged a date, could she help keep the business? Would she do it for SBC? Should she? A fantasy started to play in her head.

The agency in despair. The account dribbling down the plughole. Everyone from the mail boy to the chairman dressed in black, widow's weeds, weeping. Her old colleagues from Accounts Filing standing there, eyes red, heads lowered, bags packed. Sharpe and

Bates on their knees in front of her, hands piteously begging. Then she, like the Mother Teresa of Marketing, would smile magnanimously, making the sign of the cross, bountifully lift the handset, raise a manicured fingernail, poised to dial the number ... and make the bastards beg.

Two hours later, and she realised with deep disappointment her martyrdom would not be called for. The lift doors shushed open, and Sharpe and Bates escorted the same ensemble out with laughs and handshakes, guffaws, jokes and pats on the back. The business was undoubtedly saved.

'It's such a great name,' smiled ZaK, shaking hands farewell. 'The concept is spot on. Well done, gentlemen. But we must launch fast.'

Over his shoulder, Jack stole a look at Sharon. Then stopped, seemingly startled. Sharon saw him whisper something into ZaK's ear. He turned to stare directly at her. Then, one by one, so did everyone. Their conversation falling off, until they were all silently staring in her direction.

Following their stares, she glanced over her shoulder; but there was nothing other than the marble wall and the slick, tumbling waterfall cascading down behind her. Deeply uncomfortable, she placed her hand protectively to her neck, surreptitiously checking her buttons weren't undone at the same time.

'Sorry, gentlemen, may I help you with something?' she muttered, trying to work out what she'd done wrong.

'You just have,' said ZaK quietly.

'My God, she looks like a water goddess...' whispered Zeigfreid theatrically.

Sharon wouldn't realise its importance until much later, but at that precise moment, the sun had come out from behind a cloud and was sending rays of brilliant light through the arched windows of the reception.

The effect was mesmerising. As the hall was unexpectedly illuminated, skittering beams bounced off the cascading waterfall behind her, creating reflections that played and danced around her like silvery sprites. As she stood still as a statue, they lit her platinum hair like a silver halo, and made her green eyes sparkle like the wild Atlantic Ocean.

Drinking in the scene, the men looked at one another. Finally, breaking the spell, ZaK nodded, and the others joined in knowing agreement. Then they slowly turned and went on their way.

~

'Sharon,' said the voice of Dolores Drummond a few days later, 'we'd like to see you in Mr. Sharpe's office right away. Joanne is coming down to take over.' The phone clicked off before Sharon could ask why.

She had never been inside the hallowed walls of Mr. Sharpe's office, or even the floor it resided on.

The tenth level had always been viewed with a mix of fear and awe by all the employees. And now she would see it. Applying a quick dab of cheap Boots lip gloss and adjusting her wrap-over dress to hide her cleavage a little more, she stepped out of the glass lift, and onto the polished oak-wood floor. Her heels clip-clopped self-consciously down the corridor, until she came to an original Art Deco desk, and a striking, but cold-looking, brunette with a 1930s bob, who manned it.

'Through there. They're all waiting,' she said with a tinge of disgust, as if she knew what this meeting was all about. Sharon got the distinct impression she was enviously giving her the once over, and not liking what she saw.

Sharon gave her a sweet smile to try and break the ice, but it was met with an uninterested glance away. The other side of the door was a totally different matter.

'Sharon, welcome – do sit down,' smiled Dolores, arms outstretched as if they were long-lost cousins from Jamaica. 'This is Mr. Paul Sharpe, our Creative Head, and I believe you've already met Mr. Gerard Bates, our Chairman?' she said, indicating the older man on the sofa.

'Drink?' asked Sharpe, whilst pouring himself a Budweiser from a mirrored drinks cabinet straight off a Hollywood set.

'Err, no – just a glass of water.'

'Sparkling or still?'

Sharon had to bite her tongue not to answer, 'Tap please.' Instead she replied, 'Sparkling is fine.'

Sharpe settled himself into a leather armchair, leg slung casually over the edge. The perfect 'Creative Head', he looked like Keith Richards' kid brother – his bad-boy image and rock 'n' roll nonchalance impressed the clients no end and netted the agency millions.

'Sparkling it is, my dear,' interrupted Bates. 'Just like yourself. A sparkling example of charm and beauty.' Sharon thought at first he was being ridiculously sarcastic. But Gerard Bates was of the old school. Cufflinks, three-piece suit, pocket handkerchief jauntily matching his pink silk tie. It was all so odd. Was she in trouble? The looks on the three faces studying her only served to confuse her.

'The thing is, Sharon – it is Sharon, isn't it?' said Bates, looking to Dolores for confirmation. 'You're a valued employee of ours, indeed you have been for… ' Again, he looked to Dolores for help.

'Over three years – since she was eighteen,' filled in Dolores.

'Exactly. We gave you your first job,' he guessed.

Sharon nodded. (At this point, she couldn't really see the merit in mentioning her Saturdays spent sweeping the floors at The Cut Above salon in Croydon).

'Well, we've some incredible news for you. Very exciting. Zeigfreid and ZaK are keeping their account with us… you won't have known any of this, but they were thinking of moving.'

Not know? Sharon smiled. *Per…lease.* How little the management knew about the daily tom-tom drums of gossip that beat around the building. Gossip. The lifeblood of any agency. They could pick their noses in the executive loo, and the post room would have already re-ordered the Kleenex.

'Well, not only have we kept the account – but we're also launching a new perfume for them,' continued Sharpe, straightening his Gucci tie.

'A fantastic product, great name.'

Bates held up his hand to stop Sharpe in mid-flow.

'Please, Sharon. Be aware this is top-secret information. Only a handful of people in the world know about this. The scent is going to be called….*DESCENT*,' he announced proudly, as if naming his firstborn at a *Hello!* christening.

'Decent?' repeated Sharon bemused, not at all sure why they were imparting such high-level info to a receptionist.

'*Descent*,' repeated Sharpe. 'A perfume for the decadent, the cool, the laid-back. For a woman who's 'wild'. A 'fallen angel'. *Descent*… for a temptress, like Eve. A woman not scared to experiment… a woman who…'

Noticing the growing look of bewilderment on Sharon's face, Bates cut Sharpe to the chase.

'A woman, who is …YOU.'

'Me?' squawked Sharon, spilling the water down her front.

'Well, maybe not *you*, exactly. But – well, that's how you look,' explained Sharpe with a 'cheers' raise of his glass.

'A woman keen to experiment?' she repeated, horrified. 'Oh my gosh, you've got it all wrong. The thing is, I don't normally dress like this…' Sharon blushed as she realised her new style of tighter clothes had been taken the wrong way. No doubt the attention had gone to her head and she'd got stupidly carried away. The thought she'd let them down in the reception by looking like a roll-mop trollop made her mortified.

'I'm really sorry, the thing is, the only experimenting I've ever done was fourth year chemistry… and I failed at that. I can easily go back to my old style… but please… I love the job… I'll change my look back tomorrow.'

'You certainly won't!' snapped Bates.

'Listen, Sharon… this is an amazing opportunity,' smoothed Dolores swiftly, like a mother duck nudging her fledgling out of the reeds. 'I'm not sure you understand. We want you to be the face of *Descent*. A top modelling job – a new career. Our discovery.'

Big pause. Big, long pause.

'You're kidding, right?' laughed Sharon, nervously. 'That's funny. That's really funny. This is some kind of reality TV set-up, isn't it?' she said, looking around the room for the inevitable crew to jump out. In fact, she had felt like that for the whole of the last two weeks, ever since she had entered what she now called 'The Twiglet Zone'. Her world had turned upside down… but now it was going totally insane.

'We're not. We're seriously not. The contract we want you to sign will show you just how serious we are,' cajoled Bates.

'The fact is, Sharon,' explained Sharpe, 'Jack De Winter, the new brand manager, spotted you in reception a few days ago. He was right… you have the exact "look" we've been searching for. We've had three emergency casting sessions over at the photographer's. Hundreds of girls from Milan, New York and London – but none have come close to what we want. You're "it". We all thought it when we saw you standing in reception in front of the waterfall – it knocked all of us for six. Zeigfreid and ZaK are wild about you.'

'They want YOU. We want you,' said Bates putting a fatherly arm on her shoulder and puffing out his chest with pride.

'Kiddo, trust me, it'll be fun…' said Sharpe. 'You'll do an exotic shoot and get paid shed loads of money. We're planning posters, double-page spreads…' he continued in a transatlantic drawl picked up from years of client-paid trips.

'But I've never modelled before!' said Sharon, terrified of the attention it would entail.

'But that's exactly what's going to be so great about it,' enthused Sharpe, clearly the creative force of the agency. 'You'll be a completely new face, discovered by accident – innocent, sweet, shy… Succulent and perfect. Like a young Eve… a fresh, ripened apple, ready to fall… into *Descent*! The press and PR will go 'f'…ing wild!'

'How much is the contract for?' asked Sharon, in a daze.

'£500,000,' said Bates.

Sharon was so shocked she just shook her head in utter disbelief.

'Well, of course, if you're not happy with that amount, we can up that a bit…' he added nervously. De Winter had sent a fax that morning. This was the girl they all demanded. And he had to deliver. Retaining the account depended on it.

'That's just for the editorial… we'll add a further £100k for the posters, and of course if they agree to a TV campaign there'll be all the commercial repeats.

'You'll need an agent of course. We'll find you one. Don't you worry your pretty little head about the figures. Just sign the agreement in principle, and go celebrate!' Bates pushed Sharon's chair towards the desk where a contract sat on the table. Then, standing back, he handed her a Mont Blanc pen.

All eyes were on Sharon, wondering what she intended to do.

'Sign here, my dear,' said Bates mopping his brow with his silk handkerchief before giving one of his famous, client-charming smiles.

'The perfume may be called *Descent*… but you, my girl, are definitely… definitely on your way up.'

Chapter Seven

'Muss the hair a bit more… and Gilly, she needs gloss. Add more lippy…'

The photographer was in full swing, directing the minions and multitudes buzzing around Sharon like extras in a Cecil B. DeMille epic.

Sharon looked at the palm trees and exotic flowers on the bank ahead of her. The heat was intoxicating. And the spray of the waterfall tumbling down beside her a blessed relief.

The make-up artist had spent nearly two hours experimenting, plucking, smoothing and polishing her face… when she finally steeled herself to look in the mirror she was shocked. With Velvet Moss Mac eye shadow smudged artfully underneath and lashings of mascara and eyeliner layered on top, her green eyes looked mysterious and mesmerising. Like iridescent pools of petrol on water.

The magic the blusher worked on her cheeks was startling too. They looked elegant and high. And her lips… some product had been smeared on to plump them up, and they pouted of their own accord like two pretty pink pillows blowing bubbles.

Sharon felt this was a dream. A weird, never-ending dream. She tried to remember if she had polished off a whole slab of cheddar earlier in the day and this was the result. To check, she pinched her flesh. Nope, it was still all there. Especially around her tummy. But so were all the people crowding around her, making appreciative noises and fussing with her hair, face and body.

Except for one.

'The thing is, she's too sodding small. Doesn't fit the sample sizes… she's an 18, they're all size 22 – you know what the designers are like… they love BIG,' bitched the fat stylist loudly, holding one gossamer top up against Sharon, followed by another. 'Anyway, I don't know why they picked an amateur, she needs to fill out more. Needs to put on a few pounds.'

Sharpe looked furious, and pulled the woman a couple of feet away from the bewildered Sharon.

'We picked her 'cos she's bloody gorgeous,' snapped Sharpe. 'The wind machine will puff out the kaftan a bit, and one look at her face, and no one will care. Stop moaning and do your job.'

Too small! An unfamiliar emotion swept through her. Confidence. So this was what it felt like. She looked at her curves with new pride. If this was small, what the hell was she worrying about?

Holding a green apple, Sharon was posed leaning back against a rock, hair tumbling down behind her, whilst a live snake twisted round a branch just above her head. The spray had made her cotton kaftan almost see-through, and she was only too aware of her nakedness underneath. The cold water made her nipples stick out as clear as a couple of milk buttons. A horrifying thought furrowed her brow. What would her father say when he saw the posters?

'Okay, Shaz, now listen to me… gently bite into the apple again, then lick your lips… but DON'T smudge the lipstick on the apple.'

By the time she bit into the umpteenth apple, the taste was beginning to give her acid reflux. Still, imagining she was biting into a giant doughnut and thinking of Simon she let herself give a wicked little smile as she held the apple up to her mouth.

'Perfect! Perfect!' cried the mockney photographer. 'What a doll… Magic, darlin'. Jus' as you are… again. Hold it, hold it. Eyes to me. Stick yer' bum out more, arch yer' back to balance… Okay, that's it. Done. Relax. Over.'

The room burst into spontaneous applause and an assistant raced over to wrap her in a warmed towel. Sharpe swaggered over, beer bottle in hand.

'Gorgeous darling. Bloody gorgeous. D'ya wanna go out and celebrate?'

But before he could say any more, Jack De Winter interrupted frostily.

'Sharon, there's someone I want you to meet. Jules D. of *Jules D. Creatives*. Our PR lady. She needs to get some info on you, and she's there to help you if you need her. Hurry up and get changed.'

Glancing over to the catering truck, Sharon saw a smartly dressed woman in her late thirties, with short, brown, spiky hair. The thing that struck Sharon was the neatness of the woman's figure. About size 18, she was perfectly proportioned and toned. Wearing enormous black designer shades she currently had her pretty ear glued to a mobile phone.

Sharon disappeared into the dressing room to peel off the wet kaftan, and re-emerged dressed in a casual sweatshirt and jeans, hair pulled back in a ponytail. No make-up.

'Hello, darling,' said Jules D. kissing her on both cheeks. 'Are you having a good time? Or are they being mean to you?'

The woman's eyes twinkled with fun as she linked arms with Sharon.

'Tell me, I hear you were just a receptionist, and my dear employers Messrs. Zeigfreid and ZaK plucked you from behind the desk of depression and raised you to the heights of glamour… now you can tell me the truth. And you always need to. Is that story really true?'

'Err, well yes. It is actually.'

'MARVELLOUS, darling. Mar-vell-ous. What a story.'

'Except the 'desk' was hardly depressing,' said Sharon.

'Yes it was, darling. Very. The press will love that.'

'But it wasn't. I loved the job.'

'No, you didn't, sweetheart. You *didn't*. You dreamed of escape…'

'But that's not exactly true…'

'Listen to me, Sharon – you can trust me.' Jules D. lowered her voice. 'I'm an EX-journalist!' she chuckled.

Sharon laughed nervously, trying to sound relaxed.

'Look, I'm sure this whole thing is totally overwhelming for you. But don't be afraid, I'm here to help you. In fact, I can really help you far more than you realise right now. I have a feeling about you…' She hugged Sharon's arm tightly, sat her down and ordered a glass of milk for her.

Milk? thought Sharon, really wanting a glass of wine now the shoot was over.

'Milk, darling. So good for you. All that calcium to build lovely, strong, big bones. Okay? Now then, back to your history. It says here that you're originally from Bournemouth, and you're an orphan?' she said, flicking through a file.

'No, not exactly. That's an exaggeration.' Sharon wondered just how much private info on her file Dolores had divulged.

'My mother died when I was ten years old… My father re-married.'

'Well, that sounds good, okay?' said Jules, making furious notes.

'What, my mother dying or my father re-marrying?'

Unabashed, Jules D. laughed. 'Both darling. The former is good for the press, the latter for you, dear heart.'

'Well, no… not exactly,' said Sharon, her emotions surprisingly thawed by the warmth of this woman. 'Not exactly "good",' she clarified.

'Why not? What was she like?' asked Jules D., pausing in her note-writing to study Sharon's face.

Sharon hesitated. Then told the truth.

'He tried to rebuild the family too fast and ended up marrying a woman who had two daughters of her own. She threw me out as soon as she could. When I had just turned sixteen… that's how I ended up in London. Never actually chose to live here…'

'Oh no, how dreadful…' said Jules D., looking genuinely sad.

She saw the pain in Sharon's eyes, and decided to change the subject.

'Now listen to this – we're going to run a full PR campaign alongside the advertising… that means press and radio interviews most likely, okay?'

'Sure,' said Sharon, totally unsure.

'Now, boyfriends… got any? Had many? Who was your first?' asked Jules D. matter of factly.

'Umm…' Blank. Sharon somehow doubted that a quick schoolgirl snog in a game of spin the bottle would count as a relationship. Likewise, the tapas waiter, and their drunken dawn tumble on a beach in Ibiza. But it seemed so lame to say 'no' to both questions.

Could she mention Simon? No, that would be a big, big lie. She finally shook her head, a little ashamed.

'None at all?' asked Jules D. kindly. 'I find that hard to believe…' Sharon looked at her puzzled. This world was really going to take some getting used to. Sensing Sharon's embarrassment, Jules D. changed tack.

'This is good. Mar-vell-ous. We'll paint you as still an angel, about to fall… okay? Maybe that's an even better angle. Leave it to me… I'm going to work on the press release tonight… speak to you very soon. Hugs bye-bye. Miss you already.' And with a kiss on both cheeks, Jules D. waved a farewell and headed off the set. It was nearly deserted. Sharon slowly collected her things, reluctant to leave the magic she'd recently experienced.

But around her, the lights were being disassembled, the fake grass torn up and the plastic flowers dumped in a truck. The water pump was turned off. And the waterfall dry. For one brief moment, Sharon shuddered. The strange new world she had entered seemed as surreal as this set. An illusion that could dissipate at any moment.

'How about that drink now?' said Jack De Winter, offering her a plastic flower. 'I think you owe me one,' he murmured suggestively.

Sharon turned and looked into his eyes. Ultra trendy with a tyre-mark goatee running down his plump chin and slicked back hair, he was so not her type.

'It was me that pointed you out to ZaK, you know. He wouldn't have noticed you otherwise.' He placed a hand on her shoulder, twisting her to face him.

'At the very least, I deserve a kiss…' His lips puckered wetly, and he placed a prerogative hand firmly on her breast. Shocked, Sharon looked around for an escape.

'Tut tut, darling. Not a good idea to do that. I don't think Z&ZaK would be too impressed to think you pushed her forward just because she's your girlfriend,' said Jules D., nonchalantly picking up a folder as she re-entered the studio.

'Sharon, sweetheart, would you like a lift home? I live in Richmond, not far from you… we can share a cab… and I can take a few more notes.'

Sharon bolted for the door, giving Jack a shy, apologetic shrug.

'Night, Jack. We'll see you soon,' said Jules D.

Jack laughed, resigned. 'Jules D. … if you weren't so bloody good at your job… '

'But I am, darling. I *so* am.' She smiled, blowing him a kiss.

~

'Hi, darling, it's your publicist here. We have you sorted.'

Two days later, Sharon stood in the reception of Glacé Inc. The world's leading model agency. Jules D. had made a few calls, and they were keen to meet her.

The walls were plastered with huge models in various poses, but no matter if they were wearing evening gowns or swimming costumes, they all looked incredibly womanly. Very feminine, with strong, beautifully bone-structured faces that stared at the camera with a defiant, Amazonian attitude. Sharon found herself thinking that actually, despite any bulgy bits, they all looked pretty cool.

'Hi, I'm Kristen Saint-Donis,' drawled an elegant woman in her late forties. She had the kind of elegance that would make Jackie O. feel like a spotty adolescent.

Jules D. introduced Sharon to Glacé Inc.'s famous boss.

An ex-model, her hair and face were pure Grace Kelly, and, despite the woman's age, she was still stunningly beautiful. Her full figure was encased in a loose, ecru-coloured robe that ebbed and flowed over her considerable shape like poured cream.

'Jules D. says there's a contract in the post for us… We take 20%… of everything. Are you cool with that?' Matching her exclusive style, the woman's voice was frosty, with a tinge of boredom.

'Okay, sure,' said Sharon, trying to work out how much she was going to be giving away… and why.

As if reading her mind, Kristen answered.

'If you do as we say, and that's a big "if"… I'll quadruple those earnings in a year. If I sound unimpressed, it's because we see a lot of girls in here. Hundreds. All with their dreams of becoming the next supermodel. There's only ever been five. Six if you count the scrawny one with a drug problem.'

She pressed a silver manicured fingernail on the intercom: 'Coffee Zara'. There was no 'please'. No 'thank you'. Then she launched into a long speech, without a pause for reaction.

'Fact is, this is a tough, tough business. Z&ZaK think you've got what it takes to be a "high-end" model. But, if that's true, you're going to need to catch up fast. To be frank – you're already old for a newcomer.' The insults just kept on coming.

'To be a Glacé girl, I think you need to work on your butt. Build it up a bit. Add a few more pounds. As I suspect you already know, Glacé Inc. is world famous for our girls - all sumptous "cherries". The icing on the cake. Indeed, you could say we ruthlessly "cherry-pick" the best. It's true.

'In your case, you've somehow got a big contract – and you've been assigned a top publicist who believes you're really going places. Personally, I have my doubts.'

Zara came into the room and placed a cafetiere of coffee and a slice of cherry cheesecake on the table. Kristen indicated her dismissal, and the girl walked backwards, as if in the presence of the Queen.

As Sharon stood there feeling lost and forlorn, Kristen raised one of her beautifully arched eyebrows… studying her like an artist about to mould clay.

'On the other hand…' she added, sucking thoughtfully on a gold pencil then using it to punch the phone. 'There is something vulnerable here. Something fresh. Something undeniably sexy. Whatever, I can't send you on go-sees looking like that.'

Sharon was hurt. She had worn her best dress from Wallis. A wrap-over in small print, with a pair of beige court shoes.

Kristen pressed her pencil on speed dial and picked up the handset.

'Mario, I have a new girl… do your job.'

~

Sharon was on her way to her eighth 'go-see' that week. On the advice of the agency's freelance stylist, she had pulled her hair high, in a glossy fall that swished behind her like a circus pony, and wore a plain black Mui Mui shirt with a simple white Abberfitch and Crombi T-shirt underneath. Her trousers were low slung and flared. A perfect fit that hugged her thighs and bottom like a second skin. Over her shoulder she had hooked a supple, leather vintage jacket that matched the soft portfolio in her hand perfectly. At her throat, a flat, silver Tiffany heart.

The whole ensemble was Mario's idea. And it was working. Of the eight meetings, two had booked her, and three pencilled her in for a recall.

As she walked down Regent Street she hummed to herself… this world was perfect. She felt perfect. For the first time in her entire life. She sashayed down the street, this time daring to look at her reflection in the windows.

As always, they made her look even larger, the dark shadows highlighting her curves. BUT NOW IT DIDN'T MATTER! There were hundreds around her size. But few her height, and now it seemed she had a pretty face. Which gave her an edge. Her mind wandered to Simon… she'd love to see him again. This time she'd make a move. Ask him for coffee.

Or better yet, coffee and *cake*. How great it would be to bump into him. It would be a dream. She turned the corner. And stopped dead. Her breath caught in her throat. Ahead, she could hardly believe what she saw…

Chapter Eight

People were standing, staring. Pointing, talking. Sharon joined their gaze. High on a billboard overlooking the swarming streets was an image so arresting it was stopping passers-by in their tracks.

Everyone was looking at a giant, 48-sheet poster of a lush tropical waterfall. Lit by strands of sunlight the cascade served as a backdrop to the most gorgeous blonde model imaginable. Her lustrous hair was haloed like an angel's, her face innocent… but the misplaced wet strands that tangled down her breasts gave her a wanton, dishevelled look. Her huge almond eyes were smudged, as if she'd been up all night. But nonetheless, they danced with reflected sunlight, their striking green colour echoing the glinting pool of water. In her hand, a juicy apple, her mouth tantalisingly close, in a wicked, lazy smile. But the most breath-taking thing of all was her body – enclosed in a soaked pink kaftan that opened to her waist yet clung seductively to her ample shape. Nipples clearly outlined.

She looked amazing. Firm, buxom, pale-skinned and all-woman. But more than anything, as wanted by Zeigfreid and ZaK, she looked just like man's original Eve eating the apple. A 'fallen angel'. A naughty cherub who was about to practise fellatio for the first time. The line underneath made her want to die. **Descent. Get wild, go down...**

No question, it had a decadent, inescapable double meaning.

As Sharon stared at herself in shock, waves of disbelief and horror swept over her.

She was proud of her face and body but wanted to run up and cover her erect nipples, and tear the line off the poster… anything to lessen its unbelievable impact. In turmoil she scrambled in her bag for her phone. The only person she knew to call was Jules.

'Jules, it's me! Ohmigod. Have you seen the posters?' asked Sharon, aghast.

'Mar-vell-ous, darling. Fab-ul-ous. Leaves you speechless. The phones haven't stopped ringing.'

'But it's disgusting… I don't even look like that'

'But sweetie, who do you think it is? Stop being so modest. Or, maybe you need to take a long, good look at yourself properly, darling. Maybe you need a spot of self-esteem therapy… I know this marvellous man, runs a mind and body course, I'll email you his details. Hell-oow… Just a moment…'

Sharon could hear Jules D. chatting on another of her phones to a newspaper. 'She's a find, darling. A one-off. Practically an orphan… discovered in a boring receptionist job, wasted. I know… I know… stunning. Her name?' Jules D. paused as inspiration hit. 'Her name is "Shaz". Interview? Of course… sorry, just a minute…'

'Sharon, can I call you back?' Then it went dead. Sharon looked at her useless, silent mobile. Then back up at the billboard. It was so huge. SO in your face. A few young men were staring up at it too. Then one glanced at her. Then at the billboard. Then back at her.

'Hey, its YOU!' they chorused, tongues hanging out like excited puppies. 'You look great!' one shouted appreciatively.

'How about an autograph?' asked another. Sharon shook her head, terrified they thought she was up for a blowjob, and ran towards the tube, and the safety of her little pastel ice cream-decorated flat and a comforting tub of Ben and Jerry's.

But the journey home was anything but comforting. Her poster seemed to be up everywhere in all sorts of different sizes. Down the escalator, on the tube platform, in the magazine of the girl next to her…

There was no escape. No Exit. It was even there on the Way Out.

The next week was a smorgasbord of emotional highs and lows.

By the end of it, Sharon had been interviewed by five radio stations, three national newspapers, and two magazines.

As predicted by Zeigfreid and ZaK, the perfume campaign had created an instant and outrageous publicity storm. People campaigned outside the Advertising Standards Authority demanding that it be removed. Church heads railed, talk shows talked, and tabloid sub-editors had a creative field day: '*DESCENT – advertising standards drop to new low.*'

Of course, sales didn't; they zoomed sky high.

Women everywhere bought it to show they were cool, decadent and 'up for it'. Whilst men everywhere were buying for their women… in the vain hope they might be.

Within days, the glass bottle in the shape of an apple sat on the dressing table of thousands of women. However it got there, all wanted to capture the essence of 'Shaz's' angelic, devilish appeal.

'Shaz, listen to me, darling,' said Jules D., pouring her a glass of champagne. This is a turning point in your life. Grab it with two hands, savour it, and enjoy.'

Easier said than done. They had just watched her featured on the six o'clock news – and protesters had branded her a shocking example to young girls.

'Jules, you don't understand, do you? I'm nothing like this creature.' She was still trying to adjust to her new nickname, no matter the image.

'Oh come on, sweetheart… it is fun, isn't it? Look on the bright side; you may come across as a bit of a "goer", but you've got buckets in the bank, international modelling offers flooding in and me as your friend… okay?'

Sharon laughed. Jules was right. The woman had the precious knack of making everything seem 'okay' no matter how bad.

And actually, she was right. Her life was magical really. She'd had an enormous bouquet of lilies from Zeigfreid and ZaK, a giant, triple-layered gold box of Godiva chocolates from SBC and at least five phone calls from an excitedly rambling Debbee, congratulating 'Shaz' on her startling success.

What's more, on her last visit to the offices of Glacé, Kristen had changed in attitude, treating her with sudden respect. Sharon suspected this generosity of character was solely due to the castings and contracts Zara, her appointed booker, was now juggling on her behalf. But nonetheless, during the mid-morning meeting, Kristen actually ordered a minion to pop out and get Sharon a double chocolate milkshake and blueberry cheesecake.

'Now, as for the love life… let's see what we can conjure up, shall we?' continued Jules D. whilst she waited for someone to pick up the phone at the other end of the mobile held to her ear. 'We need to get you out more. You should be "seen" around. Good for publicity.

'Tonight, take a cab to… Oh hello Don, did you get the papers today?… Great piece on your cosmetic brilliance…' Jules D. chatted brightly to another client, a famous cosmetic surgeon, whilst Sharon sipped from her glass and took time to reflect on the way her life had changed.

Jules was right. What was she worried about? The only person whose approval she regularly sought was Debbee's, and they weren't talking. Besides, judging by the host of phone messages she'd left on Sharon's answer-phone, it clearly showed she thought the whole thing was a hoot.

The girls at the office were long gone. In fact, thinking about it, there were only two people in the world whose reactions she worried about. Simon, who was a photographer, and, let's face it, knew how advertising campaigns worked. And her father. The latter was a totally different matter. But he was getting old now, 77. So short-sighted he probably couldn't see a billboard if it smacked him in the face.

On the other hand, if he could… he'd have a massive stroke.

Maybe she should call him. But, as always, the thought of speaking to her stepmother to get through to him filled her with sickening dread. So rude, Carolyn would always snap 'I'll get your father' before Sharon even had a chance to finish the word 'hello'. Regardless, she'd call him tomorrow, just to warn him about the posters. Sharon suddenly felt really peckish, which was amusing considering the next conversation.

'Right, all sorted,' said Jules D., putting down her mobile phone. '*Grazia* want to run a story on you. Particularly, your diet. They'll be asking you questions like, "How do you stay so fat?", "What are your eating habits?", "… favourite recipes?", "How do you avoid exercise?" You know, the usual.'

Sharon giggled quietly to herself. This upside-down world just blew her away! But every time she tried to ask people questions like, 'How the hell did this reversal happen? When did big women suddenly become so desirable, or why?', they just looked at her blankly, with pity – like she was a little crazy.

And maybe she was, because five weeks on, saturated every day by magazines, commercials and adverts, being a large woman was beginning to seem normal. She had learned now it was better to say nothing to anyone. In fact, she was beginning to think she'd imagined a world where it was once 'in' to be 'thin'. Perhaps *that* was the dream and this was reality?

'So, what was I saying…?' asked Jules D., popping her notebook into her Prada briefcase. 'I know, your love life. Let's hit the town tonight. How about we head to *The Sugar Cube*? One of my clients is the owner – a guarantee of champagne and VIP pampering all night. Plus, the truth is he'd love to have you in his club. Adores having the latest models hang around. Kudos. So it's up to you.'

She liked Jules's honesty. It would never have occurred to Sharon that Jules D. would win points for bringing her to the club. But, nonetheless, Jules had told her.

'Sure. Why not? Especially if it helps you,' smiled Sharon sweetly. A night out. Hadn't done that since the 'Denim and Diamonds Debbee Debacle', as she liked to refer to it.

A few hours later, they re-met at the silver VIP door of *The Sugar Cube*. Sharon had donned a cute, geometric, sixties vintage tunic she'd bought off Mario, whilst Jules looked her usual sophisticated self in sharp, tailored trousers and short Chanel jacket.

Burly bouncers nodded and they swept past the glamorous West End crowd outside. The girl on the desk smiled, air-kissed Jules D. and gestured them in a direction away from the coat-checking crowds.

'Straight up the stairs, champagne's on ice.'

Smiling back, Jules D. took Sharon's arm and steered her up an underlit purple glass staircase and through a heavy mirrored door.

The noise on the other side crashed into them like a wave of water, and as Sharon adjusted her eyes, she saw they had entered a three-walled, mirrored room that overlooked a packed dance floor.

Potted palms, chrome armchairs, purple cocktails. Sharon thought she was in Beverly Hills – it made the *Kool Kat* in Kingston look like a half-drowned, three-legged moggie.

The VIP area wasn't that full. But that was the point of it. No shoving your way to the bar in this joint. The image of Betty Boop, a dark-haired girl dressed in titanium shorts with long, shapely, tree-trunk legs, balanced sexily on strappy white heels whilst she took their order.

The Mojito cocktail Jules suggested she try was amazing. It cooled Sharon's throat with its delicious minty tingle. The crowds below looked up at her enviously. People pointed, some even took pictures with their mobile phones. She smiled for them. Waved. This was such fun.

Jules D. seemed to know everyone. And everyone knew her. Visitor after visitor kissed her cheek, and then shook Sharon's hand. Chat, chat, chat... Sharon mentally drifted off as they talked to her PR lady.

The female guests in the club had uniformity. Streaked blonde hair, long extensions, white, French-manicured, fake nails, Gucci belts, Chanel Bags... fake or not, who could tell in this light? Sharon glanced around for Betty Boop, keen to try another Mojito, when the man at the bar caught her eye.

Strikingly handsome. Dark straight hair, chiselled cheeks, tall. He raised a glass to her and then downed it in one. His tight white T-shirt outlined his powerful shoulders. She clocked his arms, muscular and strong.

For the first time since Simon, Sharon felt a tightening in her stomach. A definite lurch. He smiled. The most gorgeous smile of perfect white teeth. Turning his head, she could see his nose slightly dented. But it was a cute dent. Looked like the results of a bar fight he had won single-handed.

Betty Boop placed a Mojito in front of her. Sharon was surprised: 'I was just about to ask you for another one... you read my mind.'

'Not me… he did,' she winked, indicating the stranger at the bar.

Sharon tossed her waist-length ponytail over her shoulder and looked at him, raising her glass in thanks. He smiled, and walked over.

'Dean,' he said, offering his hand in a warm, firm handshake.

'Sharon… I mean Shaz,' said Sharon, tripping over her new 'cool' identity.

'You're everywhere, babe. We're all crazy 'bout you…' he said in a strong Essex accent. Sharon blushed, realising that the poster line *go down… get wild* and its double meaning was probably on his mind.

But he was so hot he veritably smoked. What the hell, if that's what he was thinking. For the first time in her life, she suddenly *felt* like *getting wild*. As if he knew, he pulled her to her feet and led her over to a corner of the room. The music pounded, but he moved slowly, gently placing his hands on her hips and moving them towards him in a slow, painfully slow dance.

'So what do you do?' asked Sharon, raising her voice above the music to try and form some kind of communication through the sexual steam. It sounded so naff; she hated the sentence as she uttered it. But he didn't seem to notice its ordinariness.

'Footballer. I'm a striker for Scudders… Scuddersfield Rovers. You didn't know?' he asked, surprised. Sharon had never liked the game, considered it a pansy's choice compared to rugby. No, she truthfully hadn't a clue, though she did recognise Scuddersfield as a Premier League club.

'Dean. I'm Dean Brockton.' *Ohmigod*, thought Sharon, the penny dropping. It was Dean, better known as 'Hurricane Dean' for his force on the field – and off.

Recently, she'd seen him spread over the pages of the nationals for three different reasons. His amazing skill at footie. His amazing style in clothes. And his amazing success with women. And now she was in his arms. She turned, panicking, to see Jules D. staring at her, in shock, concern and… yes, amusement. After all, her new friend had only turned her back to chat for a second, and there was her client in the arms of a famous hunk just after swearing, 'I'm not that kind of creature.'

Ah well, people change.

Sharon excused herself from his embrace, and walked over to Jules who was busy pouring herself a glass of delicate pink champagne.

'Okay, Jules D., what are you thinking?'

'I'm thinking… it's okay,' laughed Jules. 'Go for it. Why not? I would. Forget I'm here… go, go enjoy.

'Children,' she said, raising her glass, '…you have my blessing.'

Sharon gave her a grateful smile and walked back. Dean took her in his arms as if they'd been a couple for years. It felt natural. Normal. He brushed a strand of hair from her face, then ran his index finger softly over her lips. The tingle she felt was far greater than anything a barrel load of Mojito could conjure. 'Gorgeous. I just had to touch them…'

His dark brown eyes flirted with Sharon's as he tilted her chin. 'Look at your beautiful, high cheeks… like plump, delicious plums,' he murmured, kissing her face softly. 'I could eat you up…'

By the time his lips brushed hers, she had melted faster than a double nut sundae on an August Bank Holiday, the desire making her body shake with anticipation.

'Hey, Dean! Put her down…!' Five or six mates came over to slap him on the back, and get a closer look at his prey. Sharon smiled at them all, shyly.

'Holy shit! It's her!' said one of his team mates…

'Hello, darlin', you don' wanna waste your time on that loser…'

'Yeah, waste it on THIS loser,' interrupted another, jostling to pole position in front of the gang.

'Can I get you a drink?' he laughed, drunkenly, taking a macho swig from his bottle… 'How about an Appletiser. OR should that be APPLE TEASER!'

They all guffawed at his humour.

'Guys, guys, please. Give us some space. This lady is special. Go play elsewhere…'

'Aw Dean, dear boy… you've gone turtle…' said the closest to her, touching her hair.

'Turtle dove… in love – ahhh…' said a mate behind him.

'We'll just leave you two to get DOWN to it!' joked a third, heading off to the bar with winks and thumbs up to Dean.

'Oh God. I'm so sorry, Shaz. I really am. What a bunch of absolute pricks. A total embarrassment. Trouble is they're my team mates. Have to get on with them for the sake of the club.' He looked so upset for her, Sharon was touched.

Dean took her hand firmly.

'Let's get out of here,' and they headed down the stairs, out the club doors and into the fresh air.

It was then that a thousand light bulbs went off. Shocked and dazzled, Sharon shielded her eyes, confused by the firework of flashguns.

'SHAZ, over here… DEAN give us a smile… ' The bank of paparazzi hadn't been there when they went in, but someone had tipped them off. Compete strangers were calling her name, pleading with her to give them a look. Sharon couldn't believe the attention. It was unexpected, but amazing. Like being an old-fashioned movie star. Dean looked pretty happy to be photographed with her too, and drew her close to his body.

She was overwhelmed by the praise being shouted out from all directions: it was her first big taste of celebrity fame, and it was intoxicating.

'Beautiful, Shaz – look this way!'

'Give us a smile… great, really gorgeous!'

And she replied to their incessant requests with, 'Sure… another smile? Is that enough?' The gentlemen of the press loved her. And she liked their love.

Dean opened the door of a limo and they piled in, giggling…

'Doll, fun isn't it! We should hang around a lot more together…' His voice deepened. 'A lot, lot more…'

He pulled her close to his chest, and ran his fingers down her back. For a second, Sharon stiffened as they reached the bulge at her hips caused by her pant elastic. She straightened to try and lessen the bump, but Dean just groaned, 'My god, your body is to die for… I've never felt anything like it…'

As Sharon gingerly ran her fingers over *his* taut, tanned, athlete's chest, she sighed with bliss, and had to agree.

~

Dean's Chelsea Harbour penthouse was a schoolboy's wet dream. Giant plasma screen, black leather sofa, white rugs, sound system as expensive as a NASA console desk.

The bedroom echoed the monochrome décor with a zebra-skin rug. On the bed, black-and-white suede pillows nestled on crisp, Egyptian cotton sheets monogrammed in grey with D.B.

The headboard on one side had a chrome panel with a series of shiny buttons, which monitored everything from the under-floor heating to the over-head Planter's fan.

On the far wall a grubby blue T-shirt encased in a black frame was inscribed with the signatures of the '66 World Cup winners. By his bed, a giant silver football stood on a plinth. Next to it, incongruously sat a plastic green teas-made.

'From me mum,' grinned Dean, patting its vile formica top, and pressing a couple of buttons above it. The lights went down, and the blinds went up. Sharon gasped at the view. A marina of expensive yachts swaying in the moonlight, edged by a city of twinkling lights.

Dean came up behind her and unzipped her tunic. Slipping the dress down, he lifted her bra strap and kissed her flesh where the material had cut in. Slowly, slowly he removed more clothes, ordering her to stand still. He couldn't take his eyes off her.

It felt like he was worshipping her.

And indeed he was. Finally naked, she stood in the moonlight like a celestial fertility statue. Her shiny hair tumbled down her body in a silver stream of light. To Dean, her rounded belly and full breasts were the symbol of femininity from thousands of years ago.

Sharon smiled to herself. Her life was perfect. This was perfect. She… was perfect.

Chapter Nine

Humming merrily to herself she unlocked her front door, put on the kettle, and then headed to the bedroom to change into fresh underwear. Watching her milky breasts plop firmly into her bra, she ran her palms over her mountainous regions of flesh, and found tender miles of delicately dipping hills and vales.

Such a variety of shape and contour, texture and colour. Then she thought how much had changed. Besides the contract, and a model agency, she now had a lover. She was finally like any other normal girl. Well, not quite. Her life was better.

The next few days she learnt being a WAG was a hoot.

Out of the blue, the crabby old manageress of The Cut Above salon in Croydon was on the phone full of smarmy charm and tales of how much fun it had been when 'her favourite trainee' had worked there. The woman was obviously suffering from False Memory Syndrome, thought Sharon, especially when she cut to the crunch, and the offer of unlimited free nail, eyelash and hair extensions – as an 'extension of our esteem'. How ironic, thought Sharon: the last time she'd heard from them, it was to cancel the extension of her Saturday contract.

This was another turning point. The first freebie arrived almost as soon as the tabloids ran the pictures of them together. A Special Delivery boy handed her a box containing a soft, velvet gym bag embossed with the gold lettering of Gucci. From inside, she withdrew a pale, duck-egg buckle bag in kid leather. It smelt divine, and, being large in size, balanced well with her figure. She was photographed swinging it around town the very next day, along with the tag that it cost £1,000.

'WAGS WATCH OUT!'

screamed the headlines.

Cooler, younger, prettier… overnight, '*Shazza and Dean*' were the new darlings of the tabloids. Jules D. was on the phone every other hour with requests for quotes. *Loaded* magazine had rung fifteen times that morning alone trying to persuade her to pose in her undies. The money was good. She was tempted. But her model agency had bigger ideas and firmly took control.

On the instructions of Kristen, Zara had asked Sharon how she felt about New York Fashion Week. The idea seemed thrilling, but terrifying. Tottering in heels down the catwalk in front of *Vogue*, *Tatler*, et al was a far cry from a stills shoot.

It was about this time that she had another message on her answer-phone from Debbee. Only this time, she was tempted to call back.

'Shaz, Shazza or Sharon? Don't know what I should be calling my ol' mate anymore. Anyway, Sharon – give me a call, can you? I doubt you're interested now, but just to let you know I bumped into Simon a couple of days ago, and he asked me for your number… If you want to hear the gossip, speak soon – yeah? Please call…'

Simon. Sharon hadn't had time to think about him for days. Hey, she was Dean's girlfriend now. A celeb. She didn't need him. Still, she really wondered what he'd said to Debbee. A day later, she decided to drop in and find out.

Getting ready to meet her ex-mate was an interesting exercise.

Which dress to wear? Sharon smoothed the silk of her taffeta blue smock with the big green spots; or what about the white flowing number? The 'white' grinned Sharon. It was *so* fattening.

Debbee cautiously opened the door. She looked both abysmal and equally shocked to find Sharon on her doorstep. Her normally slick blonde bob had matted into dull clumps. Wrapped in a frayed greying dressing gown, her gaunt face stared gratefully at Sharon.

'I'm so glad you came,' she gushed, thrusting her skinny body into Sharon's plump, comforting arms. Sharon winced at the frailty, Debbee's bones grating on her senses. It had been a mistake to come.

Seeing Sharon's reaction, Debbee wasted no time in gratuities and went straight for the full grovel.

'I feel really awful about that night at *Kat's*. Such a heel,' said Debbee, mournfully. 'I just wanted to make that cowboy jealous, and poor Simon happened to be there.'

Sharon pulled away.

Debbee pleaded on. 'I never meant to hurt you,' she wailed, 'you must know that. You know me, a stupid little flirt… anyway, all he did was ask us to his party. Both of us. I turned round to catch your eye and tell you … but all I saw was the back of you bolting towards the exit.

'Please forgive me… I'm so disgusted with myself. I know you were crazy about him. But please, Sharon… I care about you far too much to lose you as a friend. Forgive me?'

Debbee approached her for another hug. Sharon started to feel magnanimous, and after all, the way her life was going she certainly could afford to. But she'd let Debbee grovel just a little, no, a *lot* more.

As Debbee clung, Sharon remained unresponsive, carefully untangling herself from her thin, daddy-long-leg arms.

'The thing is, Debbee, I just don't understand why it was necessary to stick your tongue in his ear.'

For a moment, Debbee was startled at the confrontation. This wasn't the easily pliable Sharon she was used to manipulating.

'Well, the main thing is, it's not *me* he's interested in, anyway… it's you,' she said, attempting a side-step with more skill than she'd ever shown on the dance floor.

'As I've been trying to tell you, last time I saw him, all he did was ask me for *your* number. I bet he's cray-zee about you?' continued Debbee, trying out flattery as a defence. 'He said something about "did I think you'd be interested in posing for a shoot for him?"'

Sharon laughed, and looked up at the gods. This had been her fantasy ever since she'd entered this magical new world. And now it was happening… Dr. Marvel's Miracle just never seemed to stop.

'That could be fun. Maybe,' she answered with a casual shrug.

'Glad you said that, because it's too late anyway. I already gave him your number. Mind you, I don't know what you see in him? You're far too attractive, and famous…' said Debbee ingratiatingly.

Sharon paused to mull that over. Casting her mind back, she pictured Simon objectively. There he stood in reception. Tousle-haired, and wolf-like. Lean, mean and hungry. Actually, did Debbee now have a point? What HAD she seen in him? He could certainly do with a little feeding up.

Nowadays, she found she liked a real man, like Dean. A man who could wrap his arms around her (all the way) and hold her tight. A man whose magnificently large and muscled body could shelter her – make her feel feminine, safe and warm.

'Know what, Debbee? – you're so right. Forget and forgive. How about a cup of coffee?'

Debbee did a little clap of glee.

'Sure! Anything! In fact, I can even make us a hot chocolate. Jam doughnuts? Or orange cheesecake?'

'Glad you're trying to eat sensibly,' admired Sharon. 'You don't want to let yourself go.'

Debbee cast her eyes downward, and puffed out her tatty gown to try and make herself look larger.

'I've put on a few pounds by forcing myself to eat, but I'm not sure it shows? What do you think?'

Sharon was so tempted to be cruel. But that wasn't her nature, so she stopped herself...

'Course it does. You're definitely filling out.' Then she added for good measure, 'Have you seen your bum? It looks much bigger.' Debbee's sad eyes brightened.

'Really? Do you think so?' But as she twisted herself to look in the mirror her brightness faded like a dimmer switch.

'You're just saying that to be kind. Next to you, I look disgusting. But thanks, anyway.'

Defeated, Debbee slunk onto the sofa, sipping her hot chocolate and dunking a doughnut. Her slim legs crossed underneath her. Sharon looked at them with new eyes. They looked plain. Uninteresting. Straight. Breakable. Sharon questioned why the hell she had ever wanted a pair like them. She must have been delusional.

'Oh Sharon, I'm so desperately sorry,' wept Debbee unexpectedly. 'My life is hell. I've been so lonely.'

Sharon plopped a plump, comforting arm around her shoulder.

'You've got so much going for you, how can you say that?' soothed Sharon.

Debbee snivelled a silvery line of snot across her hand and let forth a giant sob.

'LOOK AT ME!! I'm a nothing. A … slim… tiny… nothing! I'm not even petite. Let's face it, Sharon. I'm … I'm skinny! A hideous size 8! Probably even a 6!'

'Let's not exaggerate, Debbee. Anyway, lots of men find your kind of figure sexy.'

'Really? Name ONE,' wailed Debbee, in despair. 'That cowboy couldn't wait to get away from me, and your Simon… he just wanted to get to you, through talking to me.' Oh god, this was so weird, thought Sharon. At what point did Debbee remember the old world?

'But *you* always used to be the gorgeous one…' said Sharon, curious and confused.

Debbee shot her a hurt and angry look, as if she was teasing her, and pulled away.

'Don't be cruel, Sharon. You're mocking me. You never used to be mean…'

Sharon sighed in puzzled defeat.

'Fine. Look, all you've go to do is try harder. Y'know, eat more, exercise less.'

'It's okay for you to say that,' sulked Debbee, curling up like a whiny whippet. 'You're naturally fat.'

'Wrong. I have to work at it,' replied Sharon with generosity, cheesecake crumbs making a white moustache round her mouth.

'Well, I've tried everything, and I just give up. I'll never be like you…' moaned Debbee.

Sharon noticed a copy of *In Vogue Beauty* on the table. She flicked through until she came to the page she'd read that morning.

'Good article in here, have you read it?' asked Sharon, nonchalantly. Debbee sighed.

'I bet I know the one you mean. Is it 'HOW TO HIGHLIGHT YOUR STRETCH MARKS'? Sharon nodded.

'Forget it. I bought the pen yesterday. Cost £60!! And all it does is leave something that resembles a snail's deposit on your skin. A total con.'

Debbee picked up the magazine in dismay.

'"MAKE YOUR CHEEKBONES CHUBBIER",' she read out loud. 'I can guarantee another bloody useless article.'

As if to prove the point, she puffed out her cheeks, eyes cross-eyed, like a demented blowfish and counted to ten on her fingers.

'Pheewww… and they tell us we've got to do this 100 times a day! It's hell. I'd rather have one of those bottom grafts.'

As Debbee reached for her coffee cup, Sharon noticed how the angular shape of her elbow stuck out, inside gristle between the arm muscles showing like two lines of a suspension bridge. She could even see the ugly big bump of her wrist bone.

Poor Debbee, thought Sharon with a wry little smile. There's really no hope for her.

'By the way, Debbee – I hope you won't be offended, but can I suggest something?'

'Sure…' said Debbee, looking very, very unsure.

'Why don't you drop the "EE" on your name and go back to "IE". It's so affected.' Debbee was totally stunned. For a moment or two, it looked like she would hit Sharon.

Then she regained her composure, bit her tongue and lowered her eyes: 'Do you really think so?' she asked meekly.

Sharon nodded imperiously, her final revenge for the Simon matter now taken.

'Well, if you think so, Sharon… maybe you're right,' she agreed.

~

'*Shazza and Dean*' dined and clubbed out most nights, trailed by a posse of hungry photographers. They revelled in the media attention. She stayed overnights at his flat, not sure how an Essex footballer would take to her mini-palace of peppermint cushions and pink throws.

He never really challenged her intellectually, but he was thrilling in bed. His strong, large body and athletic build were delicious, edible and yummy. All was fine in that department. Except one niggly, little thing. He loved her going down on him; a new and unnerving practice for Sharon, who had less experience than a novice nun.

Worse, he wanted her to do so as often as possible, and usually in dangerous situations. In a lift, in a taxi, behind his wheel… no wonder they called him Hurricane Dean, thought Sharon wryly… he really loved blowjobs. It sometimes worried her that he so wanted her to act like the poster girl – or was he attracted to the poster girl in the first place because of his penchant?

Whatever. Fact was, he was really fun to be with, kind to her, and she was falling for his boyish charms. It wasn't long before she started to imagine a mansion in Chingford and a wedding in *Hello!* And Dean, he was proud to be seen with her. He was hot, she was cool. Or was it the other way round? It didn't matter, they looked good together and every tabloid said so. But four weeks into their '*Hurricane Affair*', as the *Sun* repeatedly and proudly referred to it, the summer approached and Dean was called up for pre-season training.

It was on one of his visits back to London, he cooed, 'I'm missing you babe,' seductively putting his finger into her mouth. 'Maybe me an' you should think about getting serious. Y'know, come up and live with me. We could get a flat in Manchester together.'

Sharon looked into his deep, brown, lash-laden eyes and nodded. No one had asked her such a thing before. She always assumed she would end up dead in a stinky flat with five smelly cats. It was major. To LIVE with him! The next step would be marriage. To Sharon, that meant the end of loneliness. No more empty Sundays… Well, empty Saturdays too, for that matter. And, come to think of it, Friday nights.

'We're kicking around at a practice pitch in Nottingham next week to get us into playing "away" – join me Friday night, they're putting me an' the boys up at the Hilton. Think of it, plasma screen, Jacuzzi, you me, champagne on tap… If you're coming, I'll get a suite.'

Sharon sighed.

'I'd love to, but I've got a three-day hair shoot commercial booked in Italy until Sunday. That's a real drag.' Actually, it wasn't a drag at all. It was truly amazing. Sharon was thrilled to be the new *Herbal Freedom* girl and the location was on a glorious beach in Sardinia. However, having met a few top models at the agency, she knew the most successful always acted non-plussed and jaded.

'Never mind, babe. Come up the week after and meet me in Manchester. I've rented a big pad there, nothing special. But you'll like it… see how you feel about the city.'

He slowly kissed her neck, moving down her throat… licking at the tip of her ample cleavage. Lower, lower, lower. 'Mmmm…' thought Sharon, this striker certainly knew how to score.

The following weekend the hair shoot went incredibly well. She gave the director exactly what he wanted. Innocence and wildness. In the strong Italian sun, her polished locks shone more brightly than a newly sprayed Ferrari.

During a long afternoon break, she shopped in the little designer boutiques and got photographed by the Italian paparazzi laden with pretty little parcels and bags, tottering down the cobbled streets in the shortest skirt and highest heels she could manage. A gossip mag's dream cover.

In fact, she was also amazingly good as a model, twisting, turning, posing and pouting like a seasoned pro. By Saturday night, the director had pronounced her 'Mamma mia! Naturally Bellissima,' and the shoot was over early with hugs, air kisses and 'Ciao Bellas' all round. After farewell drinks, Sharon found herself alone, sitting in her sumptuous beachfront bedroom, missing Dean more than she could have imagined.

He would have loved it here, she mulled. Twenty minutes of mulling later, she was heading onto a late-night charter plane to East Midlands Airport. Their last conversation played over and over again in her head. He wanted to live with her. HE wanted to live with HER! She could kiss him all over, every muscled inch of his powerful body.

Childishly, she even played a wedding scene in her head…

She'd ask her father to walk her down the aisle, she'd throw her bouquet to Jules D. and the waiting crowds, wave to the paparazzi and ride off with her footballer in the back of a white vintage Rolls Royce.

As the taxi roared up at the hotel, she raced into reception. It was 2am. She would just sneak into his room and curl up next to his body. The male receptionist recognised her immediately.

'Dean Brockton's room, please,' she asked sweetly. 'Do you have a spare key?'

'Of course ma'am. Delighted to have you stay with us. Room 307,' he said, giving her a shy, appreciative look.

Sharon rewarded him with a dazzling smile, then headed up the stairs, too excited to take the lift, and gently placed the card key into the lock.

It wouldn't work. She tried again, turning it around. After three frustrating goes, the door finally opened, and she headed towards the bed, groping in the dark. As her hand touched the tight, neat cover, she realised it was empty. Still made up. Damn, she thought – he must still be in the bar.

Then a better idea struck her. Rummaging through her bag, she quietly got undressed and put on a classic Janet Reger negligee that showed off her every curve with gossamer glee.

After flossing, plucking and brushing in the bright mirror of the limestone bathroom, she slipped between the cool cotton sheets, fighting exhaustion and excitement in equal measures.

Just as she dozed off, she heard a crash – gales of male laughter from next door, and Dean's voice.

Oh no, he was with his mates, she realised in disappointment. Not wishing to brave the gang, but keen to see her babe, she wrapped herself in his dressing gown and ventured outside. The drunken cacophony increased as she knocked loudly on the neighbouring door.

'You go!' cried someone. 'No, after you!'

Come on boys, she thought, irritated; just one of you open the door. She knocked again. But this time there was silence.

The door finally opened and Sharon marched in, ready to handle them all. There they were, the core gang of idiots. Dean's team mates, grinning, tottering, swigging and spilling beer. And there was Dean. He looked at her in shock and disbelief. A soppy grin split his handsome face.

'Shaz! Babe! What a surprise!'

Sharon was touched to see such obvious joy, and stepped towards him.

He went to move towards her, arms outstretched, but, unfortunately, something was holding him back.

It was his cock. Still rammed into another woman's body.

'Oh my God, babe, this is not what it seems!' he blurted out helplessly.

'Yeah, Dean. The bitch has *you* tied to the bed!' snarled one of his cronies, with a cruel laugh. 'Fancy a roasting, darlin'?' shouted another, beckoning Sharon into the room with a lecherous leer.

'Or how about givin' us all a blowjob. Yeah, Dean says you give them all the time!'

Sharon felt shock, shame, anger and hurt. She parted her famous pouty lips to speak… then turned and ran.

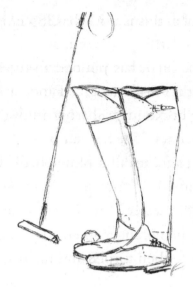

Chapter Ten

'I'm here, darling... open the door!' Sharon wrapped her old furry dressing gown around her tummy, rubbed the mascara grit from her eyes, and slowly opened the door of her flat. Jules D. was shocked by her dishevelled appearance.

'Dear God, Shaz – you look like Chi-Chi the panda on a three-night bender!'

Sharon just let out a giant sob, and collapsed in Jules's expansive arms. They retreated to the squashy sofa, and Sharon blew her nose into a giant hanky.

'How could he do this to me…? I TRUSTED him.'

'Big, big mistake, darling – never trust a man who plays with balls for a living. Here, let me pour you some champagne, and we'll add a little bit of peach juice, okay?' Out of her enormous bag, Jules D. produced a bag of freshly baked chocolate croissants. Her version of chicken soup.

'Now, first thing you need is some media training – you're a celebrity now, and when your world crashes and burns, you must play the fiddle faster than Nero, okay? Happy, happy, happy.'

As she spoke her silver phone began to tinkle the tune of *Mission Impossible*.

'Oh, it's my trouble-shooting phone… Yes, yes… (pause) No. No. He did NOT dump Shaz. She's sitting here with me now, we're having champagne brunch and she's fine. Just got bored with him… I mean, let's be honest, he's just a footballer for God's sake!'

Jules D. scribbled something on a piece of paper and shoved it over to Sharon.

'LAUGH,' it stated in bold capitals. Jules D. indicated it to Sharon again, banging the point of her pen down on the word.

Sharon forced a false laugh out of her throat that sounded more like a croak. She tried again, from further in the background. It worked better.

'Yes, yes… as I said, she's absolutely fine,' said Jules D. in clipped, no-nonsense tones. 'The Hurricane has blown itself out. Totally. You can quote that.' She snapped the phone shut.

'Champagne?' She poured as she continued explaining, 'Damage control, darling… we don't want that prick reaching the press before we do. In fact…' Jules D. dialled again, flicking through her Blackberry with a stern concentration.

'Gerry, yes hi, it's me. Call your man, and tell him that Shaz has called it a day – she's bored, and he's heartbroken. And if one little word against Shaz is leaked by that scuzzbag Dean, the whole story… and I do mean the WHOLE story gets out.

'I hear the girl looked *very* young. You can remind your boy that the only balls he'll be holding are his own, in a cell, trying to protect them from a big, black, horny drug dealer. Okay?' She sharply cut the phone off with a flip of the lid.

'More champagne?'

'I'm not sure. I'll get my people to call your people,' grinned Sharon gratefully.

~

The next few days were a paparazzi blur. Zara had told Sharon that 'paparazzi' apparently meant 'annoying bug' – and for the first time, she felt stung by them.

Jules D. had warned her to show absolutely no emotion, to instead laugh, smile and toss her magnificent blonde mane in the wind.

But it was as if they were holding their breath waiting for her to break down. To show the slightest sign of upset. She would walk along the street, and as she lifted her hand to her face, all the cameras would lift and train in on her, even if it was only to scratch her nose, rather than wipe her eyes.

The good news was her public standing wasn't damaged. She was painted as a femme fatale heartbreaker – a woman even more desirable than before, and the sales of *Descent* perfume went up.

Z&ZaK were rubbing their hands in glee, and Jules D. got a bonus for the handling of the affair.

As for Sharon, she kept replaying their imagined wedding scene in her head…

She'd asked her father to walk her down the aisle, she'd thrown her bouquet to Jules D. and the waiting crowds, waved to the paparazzi and ridden off with her footballer in a white, vintage Rolls-Royce. Then it swept around the corner, and stopped to pick up a female hitchhiker and his ten team mates…

But the odd thing was, a few days later the hurt completely stopped. Was it just the image of being with a top footballer she loved? Sharon tried to recall moments and conversations they'd had, but apart from the first great sex in her life, it had all revolved around ducking cameras, having a laugh, being seen and drinking with his mates.

In a down moment, she'd invited Debbie (formerly Debbee) for coffee and they'd struck up the old rapport. There was a difference, though – and Sharon could definitely feel a shift in weight, so to speak. She was now the top dog, and Debbie, dwarfed by her flamboyant size and fame, happy to trot along at her heels like a little toy poodle.

She'd also had a call from Simon. But it hadn't been quite as she had envisaged. She had wanted to sound his equal and full of confidence, but, instead, he'd got her when she was feeling she was plain old dumpy Sharon again. He sweetly asked and she'd agreed to do a shoot for peanuts – a friend of his was a new designer and had come up with an amazing collection.

All the way through the conversation a little voice buzzed in her head urging her to say 'meet me for a drink, meet me for a drink'. But she felt way too vulnerable for another rejection. Sadly, with a barrage of thoughts whirling round she couldn't concentrate; and when he awkwardly asked if she needed to chat in person about the shoot he was organising, she didn't want to sound like some difficult diva. So, instead, she murmured that whatever he wanted to sort, she'd be happy with – and would see him there, on the day.

Stupid, stupid girl she later kicked herself.

That Sunday, Jules D. asked her to 'come and watch ponies pootling' at Cowdray Park. It was the British Open, and to soothe her broken heart, Pimms, polo and a picnic sounded bliss.

But what to wear? Jeans seemed too casual. A dress looked like she was trying too hard to be an English lady. Digging in the pit of her wardrobe, she finally emerged with a pair of fashion jodhpurs she'd picked up in a charity shop three years ago. They fitted well, her voluptuous shape emphasised by the massive, sensual curve of the thighs. Teamed with a pair of Ravel riding boots, she pulled on a tight, white T-shirt and tied her hair back in a bouncy ponytail with fringe. Without even trying, the look was 'Vogue Stable Girl'.

'Hello darling, you look fab. Absolutely fab,' said Jules D., greeting her with three kisses in the air and a glass of bubbly pink Veuve Cliquot.

'This way, sweetie,' she said, steering her towards the bar. 'You'll get the best view from here…'

Sharon looked puzzled.

'But the pitch is out there…' she said, pointing out of the window towards the galloping ponies.

'True, darling, but it's far more spectacular from where I'm sitting.' Jules smiled, raising her glass to the perfect rear end of a tall Argentinean player clad in white, tight breeches and polished riding boots. They stood in clusters around the bar, soiled, sweaty, but utterly irresistible. Curls of black hair like fetlocks framing handsome, dark-eyed faces. What was the collective term for a group of polo players, pondered Sharon? A Posse of Polo Players? A Herd of Hunks? A Stable of Studs?

Or maybe it was a Thrashing of Thighs? she imagined wickedly.

Before long, the managing director of the drinks company sponsoring the day joined Jules D. Naturally, he was a client. Excusing herself, Sharon wandered out into the dazzling sunshine, and over to the barrier to watch the play.

'Beeutiful, aren't they…?' husked a voice from a husky hunk who swung a boot onto the chair next to her, and casually adjusted the strap.

'Absolutely,' said Sharon, taken in by the most dazzling white teeth she'd ever seen. The South American accent emanating from the most delicious mouth that owned them was so seductive, she shivered.

'Zey are even better to ride… I love thees sport so very much. It ees my life…'

Unsure what to do with this dramatic statement, Sharon replied, 'I know what you mean.'

'Do you? Really?' he asked, eyes catching hers in recognition of a soulmate.

'Err. Yes. I totally understand,' she lied. The last time she'd been on a pony it was at St. Michael's School Fête, and the poor beast had barely made it the once round the playground.

'So whose team are you with?' he asked, curiously.

'Team?' Oh God. She realised her jodhpurs had been a bad, bad mistake.

'Well, I'm not exactly with a team, so to speak...'

'But you ride, do you not?' he asked, puzzled. 'You are wearing the jodhpurs...?'

Sharon hadn't got a clue about the etiquette surrounding polo matches, but she now had a suspicion that the wearing of jodhpurs when you couldn't ride a rocking horse was probably not 'the done thing'.

'Err... yes. I do. Love it,' she lied again.

'I knew you were being modest... your figure is fantastic. The seat of ... 'ow you say? A horsewoman.' Sharon guzzled up every smooth word, noting how Dean's Essex vowels suddenly seemed as coarse as pig pâté.

A furious player beckoned, 'Juan Carlos! What the hell are you doing in the bar! We're playing in a bloody minute, you arrogant sod. Come on, we need you, damn it.'

Damn it, so do I, thought Sharon as he took her hand and slowly kissed it goodbye.

'Will you be here when I finish?' he asked, picking up his mallet and giving it a practice swing.

'If you'd like me to be...' she answered, batting her eyelashes like My Little Pony, and hoping he'd pat her on the head.

'Of course... perhaps you will honour me with a chance to see you away from all this?' He indicated the scene with Latin disdain, as if his soul was born for better things than entertaining the wealthy with his polo prowess.

'No probs,' said Sharon, thrilled. He looked confused.

'I mean, I'd be delighted...'

As the man masterfully strode off to find his mount, Sharon raced inside to tell Jules D.

'Darling, I see you've been hobnobbing with Juan Carlos Garcia…'

'Don't tell me you know him too!' cried Sharon, exasperated and deeply impressed.

'His father owns a magnificent vineyard. Along with half of Argentina. One of the foremost names in the country. Related to the Perons. Good choice, darling.'

Sharon was stunned.

'I just assumed he was a paid rider.'

'Paid, certainly. Probably hundreds of thousands,' answered Jules D., filling a flute for Sharon and handing her a plate of cashew nuts.

'Eat up, darling, nuts are good for you. Nice and fattening too.'

For a split second, Sharon was too excited to eat.

More so when the speakers blasted out his name, describing him as one of the best players in the world. A ten goal. Whatever that meant.

She watched the top sportsman fly over the grass, his pony kicking up the turf as it turned and swung round again and again. Like a winged centaur, they hounded the ball, and shot goal after goal.

In position 2, he was the key player – his pony swerved and turned as he swung and leaned, weaving in and out of their opponents with desultory, effortless ease.

The heat beat down and the game intensified. But regardless, every break between chukkas, he remembered to smile in her direction. She lifted her glass in a return salute.

At the end of the game, he handed his last horse to a young female groom who simpered at him pathetically. He totally ignored her, and headed straight over to Sharon, stripping off his soaked polo shirt, insouciant to his surroundings.

His body was unbelievable. A firm six-pack narrowed at his waist, perfectly balanced by broad, olive-tanned shoulders. He was smooth skinned, apart from a dark, sexy line leading low down to his buckled white jeans. Wiping his forehead with his shirt, he reached down into his saddlebag and pulled out a clean one.

'Congratulations – you won,' said Sharon.

'I always do,' he replied slowly and deliberately, sultry eyes flashing a challenge. He left a deliberate, dangerous pause.

'Do you like England?' squeaked Sharon.

He laughed and shook his head in amusement.

'You Engleesh girls… so sweet.' He leant forward to brush a blonde strand off her cheek, and somewhere in the distance a camera clicked.

'Juan Carlos, come on…' His team were gathered around a manager, and what looked like a cluster of sponsors. A corporate gathering keen to get their money's worth.

'Unfortunately I have a cup to collect. Give me your name and number… we go out, yes?' Sharon nervously scrawled it on a Pimms coaster and, after crossing out and correcting what she wrote twice, handed it to him.

'Until we meet again…' He kissed the back of her hand once more, his lips hovering teasingly before touching the pale, plump skin. Sharon felt scorched. And it had nothing whatsoever to do with the blisteringly hot summer's day.

~

'Shaz, darlin', let me at least see you to explain…' BEEP.

'Babe, it's me again… I know you're pissed off…' BEEP.

'How can I make it up to you…? BEEP.

'You're being a silly bitch, now…' BEEP.

With relish, Sharon deleted message after message from Dean. Though it was six days and still nothing from Juan Carlos, she was still thrilled that the day after the polo, one of the leading tabloids had run a stunning, front-page, sun-dappled photo of her and 'Juan to know you', as she liked to call him. And it was no doubt niggling Dean she was so over him, so fast. And so publicly. Revenge is a dish best served full in the face, she giggled.

But perhaps better than that, there was a message confirmed by Glacé Inc. that Zeigfreid and ZaK wanted her to open their New York show.

Zara at the model agency filled her in on the gossip. Apparently, breaking away from tradition, the show was being held *five weeks* before the start of the official September Fashion Week, and was creating an almighty industry furore.

The world's top designers were livid, as a couture show standing on its own was destined to steal mega-column inches. Worse than that, designers often followed the advice of the 'mood theme experts' at the trade cloth and trimming shows whose jobs were to predict the season's lengths and colours. It was the simple reason why all the designers would suddenly go for orange and silver one year, purple and green the next. The gurus dispensed advice on behalf of the cloth industry to all who asked, and this ended up giving a cohesive look to the season. But if Z&ZaK showed first, to any outsiders, it was going to seem that all the other names were simply following their lead a few weeks later.

Zeigfreid and ZaK were outrageously blasé. They explained, it was because they were 'so tired of being ripped off by other designers' that they wanted to show first. Basically, they were being naughty rebels, and sticking two little pinkies up at the competition.

As for Sharon, she didn't care about the politics – they were flying her out First Class week after next.

'A fashion show… in the Big Doughnut!!' cried Debbie when she rang her. Sharon was knocked out too, and couldn't bother to pretend otherwise.

'Ohmigod! Can I come as your assistant? I'll pay my own way…' begged Debbie.

'Well, in that case, I don't see why not… I know others have their own entourages – maybe I should play the game too?' agreed Sharon.

Debbie squealed at the other end of the phone. 'We'll have such fun! You'll see… like the old days.' Sharon doubted that anything would ever be like the old days. Thank the Lord.

She had to ring Simon to cancel his shoot as it clashed with New York – a phone call she was dreading. Not only did she have to speak to him, but she was also letting him down. Mind you, the fear of the former was a little diluted by the fact Juan Carlos had asked for her number. (She tried to dismiss the fact he hadn't actually called.)

'Simon, hi – it's me, Sharon.' She deliberately used her old name to put them both at ease.

'Sharon, hi – everything okay?' She loved the sound of his voice: deep, warm and beautifully spoken.

'Well, not exactly. I'm so, so sorry but I've just been booked for Z&ZaK's New York fashion show and it clashes with your shoot.'

As Sharon spoke the sentence, the surreal nature of talking to Simon and saying this hit her. Sometimes she got caught out, and the old Sharon crept back in. When it did, it was like a mirror shaking, and she felt momentarily split in half, like being two different people. Before Pill. And After Pill. BP and AP as she secretly referred to it.

'Right … um… what a pain. But that's okay… totally understand. Thousands of dollars walking down a catwalk for the world's top designer, or a couple of hundred quid posing for a loser like me… no brainer.' He laughed.

Sharon fell silent. She felt so bad, if it hadn't been for the fact that she didn't want to risk hacking off Kristen she'd have cancelled New York.

Simon misinterpreted the silence.

'Look, you don't have to do the shoot if you don't want to…'

'Of course I do – we're old mates,' said Sharon, worried he'd cancel.

'Of course we are. "Old mates",' he repeated.

Did Sharon detect a faint trace of disappointment in his words? 'Mates'? Why had she referred to them as just mates? But before she could say anything, she had call waiting buzzing. The incessant beeping made her brain even more addled.

'Oh, there's a call coming in. Can I just take it…?'

'No worries, I'm heading out and it's probably important. Call me when you get back from New York… let me know how it goes, and we'll fix up another shoot.'

The phone went dead before Sharon could say anything to counteract the fact that New York was days away. Mind you, he probably knew that, she thought sadly, and didn't care. She fell back on the fat sofa, and started to munch her way through a deluxe box of champagne and strawberry cream chocolates. On the table sat a stack of celebrity supermarket magazines.

Milana Sheraton was on two covers, clutching different toy dogs and looking more vacant than a parking lot on Christmas Day. But on the inside Sharon was amazed to see herself in three different magazines. Full pages, describing what she was going through, what she was wearing, and how she kept her full, and fabulous rococo figure. Each had made a full-page story over a single, tiny little quote she'd given them. Unbelievable. Actually, even more so when you considered the quotes really came from Jules D.

'I love my life, and don't need a man,' said the headline in *Grazia*, with an image of her, head thrown back, laughing as she downed a glass of pink champagne.

'White is so fattening… it's my favourite colour,' revealed *Closer*.

'The best way to stay fat is to eat late at night,' ran *Hot*.

The phone suddenly rang.

''ello, is thees Shaz…? Thees is Juan Carlos…'

'Hi, Juan – how are you?' husked Sharon back, casually. (She'd been practising saying 'Juan' with a silent, sexy, Spanish J for days.)

'Keen to see you. Do you have Saturday off? I have a surprise for you.'

'I think so, let me check my planner…' Sharon rustled the magazines. From the way he handled his horses, she figured this man liked total control, and Sharon was determined not to be taken for an easy ride.

'Yes, I can clear a couple of things. That would be fine.'

He took her address, they flirted about the surprise, and Juan Carlos said he had to go – he was phoning her from the Hamptons, and the team were about to leave the hotel.

His last words were:

'Oh, just one theeeng… wear what you wore when we met. You were…'ow you say? Really ideal.' Sharon smiled; she had made an impression on one of the most fabulous men on earth.

How was that for a fat girl from filing!

Chapter Eleven

Humming merrily to herself, Sharon heaved her rolling body out of bed. With pride, she watched her creamy smooth breasts flop gently into place. As she shifted weight, she watched her mountainous regions undulate exquisitely, like butterfly wings. The quiver of her stomach, sheer poetry in motion.

It was Saturday morning, so she brushed out her long shower of hair and put on her freshly washed jodhpurs and crisp sleeveless blouse. The curve of her buttocks and huge breasts emphasised her relatively small, curvy waistline. She knew Glacé Inc. wanted her to put on a few pounds before New York.

The models out there were so disciplined; so she added extra double cream to her cereal and three spoonfuls of sugar. It tasted like heaven.

Her mother used to make it for her like this when she was a little kid…

She came down to earth. The one person she still hadn't spoken to for far too long was her father. But she kept on hoping he would call of his own accord. See her in the papers, realise how well she was doing and pick up the phone.

But he didn't. So she steeled herself to ring, dreading the curt tone of her stepmother Carolyn.

'Hi, it's me, is…' said Sharon gingerly

'I'll get your father,' she interrupted, before Sharon had the chance to say another word. The routine was like this every time she phoned. Sometimes the woman's deliberate rudeness made her laugh. Other times it cut her to the quick.

'Hello, my darling, what have you been up to?' said a whiskery old man's voice.

'Loads, Dad. Loads. Can you believe it? I've started modelling. *Me!* Like Mum. I've been doing an advertising campaign for perfume' (although she really hoped he hadn't seen it) 'and a shampoo commercial. Plus I've been dating a footballer.'

'A footballer? Anyone I would know?'

'Have you heard of Hurricane Dean?'

'Harry who, dear?'

'NOT Harry. Hurricane. Hurricane Dean.'

'Harry Candean?'

'Oh, never mind, Dad,' said Sharon sadly. He was really beginning to show his age.

'Sorry, dear, I've not been feeling too well, having some tests …' said her father.

Sharon felt a slight panic, but then her dad was always having tests of some sort.

'Nothing to worry about, darling… got a sore throat, that's all,' he added.

'I was thinking of coming down to Bournemouth to see you,' said Sharon, brightly.

'That would be nice. But you know we don't have anywhere to put you up, and it's so expensive to stay in a hotel.' Sharon grimaced.

Their house had four bedrooms, but Carolyn always made it plain she wasn't welcome to stay.

'Well, I can afford a hotel now – I'm famous!'

'What? Are you? For what!'

'Dad, for being… well, for being beautiful.' She choked on the words.

'What, like your mother?' he asked proudly. 'She was stunning… I remember the time she turned all the heads when she walked into…'

'Joe! Tea's ready…' came Carolyn's shrill, bossy voice in the distance. She'd probably been eavesdropping on the extension as usual. Any mention of his past life set her off in a dreadful strop. Sharon had worked out this was probably why the woman had been so mean when she was just a little kid.

'Got to go, darling, call me again soon,' said her dad sadly, and the line went dead. Carolyn bullied him, but this was a fate *he* had chosen, and Sharon's sympathy was measured. Feeling hungry, she headed to the fridge for a glass of milk, and the packet of Oreo cookies she'd stashed away that morning.

As she dipped the biscuits into the liquid and licked the icing with her tongue, she thought back to when she was just eleven years old.

Her daddy had been attracted to the woman's young but icy beauty, and the fact that she had two daughters. Instant mother and sisters for Sharon, he later told her he had originally thought. She knew he had been missing her mother badly, often hearing him cry in the night.

But why did he have to pick Carolyn? She suspected that his broken heart was one of the reasons the woman snared her father so easily.

She knew he was desperate to replace the loving home he'd lost, and married way too fast in a sorry attempt to make a new family.

Well, they say men hate to be alone. Sharon suspected it was tragically true. Unfortunately, he never got to know his new wife properly, until it was too late – once the woman had a giant diamond ring on her finger.

Sharon recalled how she changed almost overnight, revealing a vile, vitriolic temper that terrified her and, at times, even cowed her father.

Then she shuddered as she remembered her stepmother's face – the first time she showed her true colours it literally darkened and changed, contorting like a woman possessed. Sharon gave a dry laugh: her dear stepmother made Jekyll and Hyde seem like Sooty and Sweep.

She loved her dad dearly, but he was so weak. What had he done at those times? Nothing, thought Sharon, contemplating another cookie. She never knew if he was unable, or just unwilling to protect her from Carolyn's rages. Whatever, she did know he preferred to maintain peace with his young wife at all cost. And that included his daughter's.

Years later, when he was visiting her new flat in Kingston, he confessed that maybe he'd ended up marrying the wrong woman. The bottle of wine loosened his tongue, and he told her rushing the marriage was one of his biggest regrets. But he felt too old and too ashamed to divorce and start again. And Sharon had already left home. It was too late. Certainly way too late for the little eleven-year-old child who had often hidden under the covers of her bed, sobbing, thought Sharon bitterly.

Now, just the sound of Carolyn's voice resonated a dark, sad time in her life – and hearing her curt tone on the phone was enough to make her feel like a frightened little kid.

Then the doorbell of her flat rang. And Sharon the fully grown woman bounced down the stairs, to the open silver Porsche below. She glanced round, hoping the neighbours were taking this all in, and settled into the leather bucket seat.

Juan Carlos drove his car as forcefully as his ponies, the gear stick handled with a firm, Italian leather glove. She fantasised the same gloved hand holding her hair and forcing a kiss on her lips…

As they sped into the countryside, Sharon wondered where the surprise destination was? A cosy pub lunch, maybe? A seaside marina stroll?

Finally the car sharply swung down a magnificent driveway towards a sprawling stately home.

'No, ees not mine!' laughed Juan Carlos, watching her green eyes open wide. 'I use their stables. They like me to exercise their horses…'

'What a fab place… you must love riding around here…'

'That ees why I come…' he smiled, patting her thigh.

The penny suddenly dropped. He had asked her to wear her jodhpurs. Oh no! She felt sick. Panicked. Sweaty. Her mind raced with excuses… Blank. The only one she could think of was 'the wrong time of the month', but that hadn't even got her out of school gymnastics; and it certainly wasn't going to work now.

Maybe she could step out of the Porsche and 'twist her ankle'. But the car was so fashionably low slung, even a vertically challenged pixie would have a hard time pulling that one off.

They walked towards the immaculate stables, he purposefully, whip in hand, Sharon dragging her feet behind him like a terrified toddler.

'Fantastic to see you, Juan Carlos,' said a tall, striking woman with black hair pulled back into a tight Spanish bun. 'Lady Annabel,' bowed Juan Carlos, taking her hand.

'Take your pick...' she offered generously.

The exquisite thoroughbreds snorting and tossing over the stable doors bore as much resemblance to a hacking pony as Pegasus to Dobbin the Donkey. Sharon paled, her firm legs shaking in their boots.

'Is there any chance you'd take Lightning for a ride?' asked a senior stable hand, leaning on his spade. 'He's been giving us so much trouble, needs a firm grip.'

'When did you last have him out?' Juan Carlos replied, soothing the creature on the nose. It bared its teeth angrily in response.

'Been about four days. Even threw Lady Annabel off. Since then, won't let us near him.'

'No problem. Come on, my beauty...' Juan held the struggling head steady as a nervous stable girl harnessed the horse up; Sharon watched from a safe distance.

'Which one would you like to ride?' said Lady Annabel. Her handsome, perfect features gave her an aristocratic air of a bygone age, helped by her smart, black, hacking jacket and side-saddle skirt. A well bred, elegant creature who looked much better standing next to Juan Carlos than Sharon suspected she ever would. The bitch had no doubt been born clutching a silver spoon in one hand, and a pony club rosette in the other, thought Sharon enviously.

'Which horse? Umm… I'm not sure. I'm feeling a bit queasy from a late night, perhaps I shouldn't…' she quietly tried to whisper.

'In that case, you want Fireball,' said Her Ladyship, matter-of-factly.

No, no I don't! I want a Shetland pony called Slugbug, or Snailtrail! screamed a voice in Sharon's head. But it was Fireball they started to harness up. An autumn-coloured horse that loomed much larger as they led it towards her than it had first looked in its shed.

The saddle was high up, and the cotton jodhpurs were a fashion item (as luck would have it, the only fashion item in the Western world *not* made from stretch Lycra).

There was no way she could lift her foot up into the stirrup, let alone swing her body aboard.

'Umm… can I use the Executioner's Block?' she asked, indicating the concrete mounting block by the gate.

'It's been a very long time,' explained Sharon, as two hands attempted to heave her butt up onto the skittering creature for the third time. As she finally settled into the saddle, the pony's back legs buckled a little under her weight. The hard-hat strap dug under her neck, and the fear made her hands sticky as she grasped the reins.

'You hold polo pony reins differently,' called out Juan Carlos kindly, mounting Lightning in one sleek move and cantering over to her side.

He took her hand and put both straps into it.

'The other is free for the mallet... Come, we'll just play around in the field over there...'

Frozen in terror, Sharon just let her pony follow. Why was it even called a pony? she wondered. A misnomer of the sport. It was a bloody great hoofing horse. She caught Lady Annabel looking at her smugly as they trotted past. Fireball? Oh God, the bitch was deliberately setting her up.

The good news was the field was enclosed. The bad news was she hadn't a fucking clue how to ride.

'Always let the beast know you are the boss,' said Juan Carlos, his horse rearing up and kicking out. 'Never show fear.'

Too late, thought Sharon. It knew exactly who was the boss. And she was fully prepared to call it 'Master'.

The pony trotted in a straight line, Sharon's buttocks clashing with the saddle in a slapping motion.

'Rise in the stirrups and indicate right with your rein...' called out Juan Carlos.

Sharon pulled very gently to the right, and the horse responded instantaneously, wheeling around violently, almost tipping her off as it circled.

'They are like Ferraris, are they not!' laughed Juan Carlos cantering closer.

'Gently. You have to use the faintest touch. Zey are like, how you say... Finely tuned. Magnificent.

'Try again, this time just with your knees – push it towards the direction you want it to go.'

Sharon pressed ever so carefully against the pony's silky belly... and it graciously moved in the direction she wanted. The relief was tangible. Only an hour or so to go, she thought bitterly.

'Shaz, now try the other knee.' She did. And once again, the horse responded as she wished.

'Try a fast stop!' shouted Juan Carlos, from the other end of the field.

Sharon pulled very lightly on the rein. And it stopped short, sending her pert nose on a collision course with its head, almost sending her over its head. But as she straightened up, it just waited patiently for the next instruction. It didn't bolt, it didn't buck. It just stood stock still.

Relieved, Sharon's confidence grew. The horse was so perfectly trained, her fear began to slow down to a mere panic. Then, as the pony took her round the field at a gentle trot, she felt the dawning of a little curiosity as to how to control it. Finally, as it responded again and again, she felt a tiny thrill.

The fact they were enclosed removed the terrifying prospect of a bolting mount. A half an hour later, she was cantering behind Juan Carlos round and round the paddock; her own blonde mane streaming behind her, green eyes flashing with excitement and cheeks blushed with exertion.

A couple of times an icy fear would re-grab her, especially when Juan Carlos's black mount continued to rear up again and again, eyes wild like the Horse of the Baskervilles. In response, he lay his whip to its flank, and the creature would snort in fury. But eventually, each time it had a tantrum, Garcia the Beast Master would win.

An hour or so later, she and Fireball were in love. Sharon was ready to bundle her in the car and have her sleep on a blanket in the kitchen. She kissed the creature on the nose as she handed the reins gratefully to Lady Annabel who she suddenly felt like hugging.

By the time Juan and Sharon were nursing brandies in the pretty local pub, the adrenalin withdrawal and relief of finding all limbs unbroken made her feel relaxed and fuzzy. She found herself confessing the truth to Juan Carlos, and he roared.

'Fashion jodhpurs?!' He almost cried at the story. And by the time she added she'd only ever been on a pony for a led ride around a playground, he was not only holding his sides, but suitably impressed.

'Eiy, you are special! Very brave. Fireball responded to your every whim.' His eyes darkened. 'And so do I...my leetle enchalanta!' Sharon was not sure if this meant 'little one who enchants me', or something you ate in a Tacos Bell.

Whatever. The way he spoke it sounded so romantic. She was his little enchalanta...

As he leant across the bar to get a couple of Pimms, Sharon imagined life with this man. Well, actually – nothing that deep. Just the wedding day.

...She'd ask her father to walk her down the aisle; she'd throw her bouquet to Jules D. and the waiting crowds, wave to the paparazzi and ride off into the sunset behind Juan Carlos, masterfully handling a white stallion.

'What are you smiling about, leetle one?' he asked, stroking her thigh lazily.

'Just wondered if you'd tell me a little more about polo, it's so fascinating...' she fibbed perfectly.

'Of course, it ees the game of kings... It was first played in Persia, as long ago as the sixth century BC, with as many as 100 a side...' Sharon bathed in his accent and attention as he told tales of old kingdoms lost in time.

'...And the word chukka comes from ancient Sanskrit, cakra, meaning circle or wheel.' Amazing, she thought. This man could make a game of eight grown blokes chasing a plastic ball around a field sound like a ride on a magic carpet.

The day turned into night, and dinner at *La Corpulent*, an elegant restaurant, so trendy you normally had to put your name down for a table at birth. But a call from Juan to his manager, and they were in.

Sharon loaded her plate with three helpings of starters. Fresh buffalo mozzarella sprinkled with bacon and avocado shavings, delicate pasta shells in oyster sauce and a rich lobster pâté with toasted almond and walnut bread.

'It so good to zee a girl take care of her figure,' smiled Juan Carlos approvingly. She held his dark eyes and saw her desire mirrored back. Leaning forward, he offered her his large asparagus tip. Warm butter dripped off its juicy head.

'You will be at the Cartier International next week?' he asked, dropping her off outside her flat and walking her to the door.

'Sure, of course,' said Sharon, with not a clue how one got tickets.

As his hand wound round her waist, instead of wincing and breathing in, Sharon poked out her already full tummy as far as she could.

It was too much for Juan Carlos.

'Can I come up?' he asked, voice breaking. 'I'd like to stay.'

'Gosh, but we've only just met,' said Sharon, aware she was sounding like a prudish pupil of Miss Jean Brodie.

In response, he kissed her passionately, pushing her hard against the cold wall and thrusting his jodhpur-clad leg between her thighs. His lips were firm, his tongue searching. Then he broke off, and walked away.

Sharon couldn't breath. He was so dashing. This was such fun. And again, a camera flashed somewhere in the dark.

The next few days Sharon bubbled permanently with pleasure, like a fountain of champagne.

'You look better and better, darling,' Jules D. announced one morning, customary croissants in a bag.

Indeed, Sharon did. Her new life had given her confidence, wit and style. Ready for New York, Glacé Inc. had sent her off to get her hair cut at PUDDING BASIN, the most fashionable salon in London.

The result was her waist-length hair was even more platinum than blonde, with a cool spiky fringe. She'd also enjoyed the attention of the make-up artists whenever she did a shoot. As they experimented with different looks, she had picked up every trick. From elongating her almond-shaped eyes, to maxi-plumping her perfect, petal-soft lips.

To add to all this, royalties from her hair commercial were proving astounding. For the two-day stint she did in Ibiza she was receiving thousands of pounds every time it was aired. And it was on daily.

Meanwhile, photos of her and Juan Carlos had boosted her public profile too. Though it had to be said the shot of Juan pressing her against the wall with the tabloid screamer '…**UP THE JUNTA!**' had been more than a tad humiliating.

Nonetheless, the daily diet of glamour was turning into a Bacchanalian feast. And Sharon Plunkett was gobbling up every marvellous millisecond.

Debbie with an IE had latched on as her assistant, and was a good little gofer. Sharon noticed her friend had finally managed to put on a little bit of weight. She might even be a size 10. Whatever. At least it was a start.

It was fun to have her at her beck and call. Easy company when she felt like it after a long day. And after years of having it the other way round, Sharon just *lurved* the way her mate would whine, 'I'm so desperately jealous'. Scraggy little thing, Sharon would think. And with smug superiority she'd force Debbie to eat a full box of chocolates, and make her watch whatever was the latest 'GET FAT FAST' celebrity DVD from the States. Together, the girls would often curl up on the sofa to watch.

'My regime is simple' – said the latest video from Jo-Jo, an American actress and singer famous for skimpy showgirl outfits and sexy toy boys.

'Every morning I get up slowly, and eat three, pure cocoa bean chocolate bars before breakfast. Make sure you stuff them in fast, that way they can't digest quickly…'

That woman looked terrific for her age, thought Sharon. A real icon. Jo-Jo's G-string, sequinned costume revealed a bare navel completely hidden by mounds of excess skin. They viewed the rest of the tape transfixed, Debbie shifting uncomfortably as the celebrity downed plate-load after plate-load faster than a pelican.

'And finally,' gushed the dark-haired beauty, 'the most important thing of all is to have a full dinner as late as possible.'

'Hey, that's my favourite tip too!' grinned Sharon.

Jo-Jo was served a massive portion of cheesecake by a semi-naked youth.

With a salacious lick of her fingers she continued, 'Yes, ideally eat just before going to bed. After all, you don't want to burn off any excess calories girls, do you? Good night. And sweet, sweet, very sweet dreams!'

From the corner of her eye, Sharon watched Debbie turn away from the TV despondently, shoving the tray of chocolates away.

Sharon leaned over to pop another in her mouth, and as the taste hit her eager, trained buds, she couldn't stop the corners of her pretty mouth tilting upwards into a tiny little smile.

It seemed that Jules D. always came up trumps. Like a magician, she always had the right tickets up her sleeve, and producing two for the Cartier International was easier than falling off a polo pony.

'How did you organise that?' asked Sharon as Jules D. flashed a smart envelope under her nose.

Jules D. laughed as if withholding a secret.

'Actually, one came for you, anyway,' she said, tossing a heavy, gold-embossed invitation into Sharon's lap.

'What!? Who from? From Juan Carlos?' asked Sharon breathlessly.

'No, darling, from the Chairman of Cartier. Special invitation to his closest 600 celebrities! We're invited into their marquee for lunch. Best one to be seen in, sweetie, okay?'

Sharon learnt it certainly was.

On the day, Sharon dressed in a cream, floaty chiffon number sent over from New York by Zeigfreid and ZaK which, topped with a wide-brimmed sun hat, looked as deliciously froufrou as a mill fleurs. Jules D. was smart as ever in a tailored navy and white Dior suit that heavily emphasised the size of her hips.

On arrival at the prestigious Guards Polo Ground, the chauffeur heaved Sharon elegantly out of the back seat of the sent limo, and the two girls tottered towards the Smith's Lawn enclosure and its temporary city of white hospitality tents.

The undulating crowd of visitors were all exquisitely dressed. On the lawn, celebrities milled with celebrities, the aristocracy with the aristocracy, and the Royals with nobody.

As they approached the famous flag-flying Cartier marquee, Sharon looked at the topiary arch spelling out CARTIER in awe. She wandered underneath, into the tent, and found the first impression overwhelming.

Every year they picked a top interior designer to decorate, explained Jules D. quietly. And this year whoever it was had no doubt been inspired by peacocks, paradise... and possibly a bong load of seventies pot. Because the tent was stuffed with birds in cages, ostrich feathers in long gold vases, peacock chairs and lava lamps.

'So very retro, darling...' oozed Jules D. to a giant man poncing about in velvet flares and smoking jacket.

'Shaz, dear heart, have you met Nicky Houselman? A roué of extraordinary talent, and designer of this crazy emporium we see before us. A triumph, darling. Love it.'

Sharon held out her hand, and he ignored it, heading for a camp, three-cheek air kiss instead.

The food was also divine. Tucking into a giant starter plate of Norwegian gravadlax edged with fresh king prawns, Sharon counted three celebrities at her table, along with an outcast from Big Brother, who, she noticed from the wrong name on their Cartier name tag, had snuck in on someone else's.

She looked at the name on hers, dangling casually from her cream silk bag and smiled. Sharon Plunkett, you lucky ol' thing. Near her sat three top models, and a Hollywood starlet. Further away, a famous rock star, his wife and model daughter. The place was gleaming with glitz on an unprecedented scale. And she was part of it. People were actually surreptitiously looking at her too. She tried to eat normally, but dropped her bread roll on the floor. Thinking quickly, she gave it a swift kick from the side of her shoe, and disposed of it between the legs of a man at someone else's table. A private polo goal of her own, she giggled.

Three champagne flutes later, and the fact that their spiky heels sunk into the ground were making the journey across the grass to the grandstands deeply treacherous, made Sharon and Jules D. break into a fit of hysterics at their stupid choice of footwear, clinging together like drunken ladettes.

Managing to straighten up just before passing the bank of paparazzi, Sharon proudly flashed her Cartier swing tag at the steward who let them through to the Blue Grandstand for Cartier guests and privileged members. Further away was the Red Grandstand for the day's 'ordinary members'. And over the other side of the ground were the scats for the lesser mortal non-members. 25,000 spectators, all knowing their pecking order. The sport of kings made a game of keeping the peasants in their places.

With this noticed, Sharon proudly took her own place among the 'chosen few' with aplomb, squeezing past the knees of those already sitting – much to the delight of the many males in the row.

But most exciting of all for Sharon was recognising the distant tall figure of Juan Carlos Garcia in the pony line. As the July sun streamed down, the Pony Club Polo Players parade trotted past, followed by packs of hunting hounds and their red-coated Masters.

Then the commentator introduced the players. The distant crowds roared, whilst those around her politely clapped. But ignoring convention, she cheered very loudly when she heard:

'In no. 2 position, the star 10 goal player from Argentina, Juan Carlos Garcia. Highest-ranking rider of the day.'

He tipped his helmet, raised his mallet in salute, and cantered masterfully into place.

The game was a blur of balls, hooves and falls. Fun to watch, vicious and fast. At one point, she recognised Fireball... *her baby*! He performed magnificently, turning complete circles like a whirling dervish, and warding off horses far heavier with his brave little heart.

At half time spectators were invited onto the pitch to tread in the turf. A wonderful tradition where everyone milled around the grass chatting about the weather whilst replacing the cut-up tufts. Unfortunately, with their heels, the girls seemed to be having the totally opposite effect. As they walked, they noticed people behind them were angrily covering their 'plough tracks'. Tipsily racing off the grass in disgrace made them giggle even more.

The second half was even more aggressive. This was supposed to be a friendly game, Argentina invited to play England's finest. But judging by the intensity and fury on the pitch, it could have been the battle of the Falklands with Thatcher cheering on 'our boys'.

The result in the end was a humiliating defeat for the England squad, who, naturally, took it on the chin.

Sharon watched in disbelief as, on behalf of his team, Juan Carlos received the Coronation Cup from the Queen. What was that famous rhyme? *I once danced with a girl who had danced with the Prince of Wales?* Well she had snogged a man who was currently getting a long, friendly handshake from the Queen. Top that!

Finally, the prize giving ended with another surprising high, when Fireball was announced as the best pony of the day. Sharon jumped up and clapped with joy, then watched with ridiculous pride, a tear in her eye, as his owner stepped over to receive the Cadenza trophy.

'What a great day!' sighed Sharon, giving Jules D. a giant bear hug. 'Shall I go over to see him now?'

'Umm, not sure. I'd give him a chance to cool down, pose with the press and talk to the sponsors. Be laid-back. Let's head over to *Chinawhite's* tent for drinks, with a wee stop in the retail village en route.'

The row upon row of tented shopping cubicles held a bazaar of designer goodies. Shopping heaven, there was everything a spoilt, rich debutante could want, from mink-lined dog baskets to thick leather gaucho belts. Sharon held the latter in her hand, feeling the supple hide.

Not interested, she smiled, handing back the latter to the stallholder. When it came to gauchos, she had the Real McCoy to wrap around *her* hips!

Laden with bags, they headed back to the first tent for a much-needed cream tea of scones and chocolate éclairs, then over to the *Chinawhite's* marquee.

The exclusive nightclub regularly took a marquee at the event, and the evening's highlight was offering its London members a chance to boogie away with the players, aristos, celebs, royals and luvvies involved in the polo scene – and as dusk turned into night, what a scene it was. Dishevelled girls, shoulder straps slipping over plump, pretty shoulders to reveal gossamer bras;

men, shirts unbuttoned, ties askew. Champagne flowing faster than the Nile. Amid the mêleé, Sharon spotted her man.

'Juan,' she waved.

He disengaged himself from a buxom brunette and headed over to her.

'Enchalanta,' he whispered, sweeping her into his arms for a deep, delicious kiss.

Sharon's emotions soared. Could a day ever be more perfect?

Crushed on the floor, their bodies moulded together and she could feel his heat. Or was it hers? Every few seconds someone would come over and slap him heartily on the back, or slosh a flute of champagne over them. The music pounded out, and the night threw a dark, quiet cloak over the field. All life pulsated in the tent. All life existed there.

Unfortunately, all manner of top totty existed there too. A blonde called Stephanie, with a voice so plummy you could barely recognise a word, whispered something very rude into his ear about what they did in Houston. Alas, judging by his wicked smile, Juan understood every syllable.

Sharon noted bitterly that the blonde had far chubbier, more succulent legs than hers. Moments later, another aristocratic beauty with enormous hips (again, Sharon noted enviously, a little larger than hers) sidled over and slipped her number into his palm, bemoaning the fact they'd missed each other at the Hamptons. It was a scene Sharon felt totally outside of. They all knew each other intimately. And continued to – it seemed, all over the world.

One glass too many, and Sharon's head began to float somewhere above her shoulders. She tapped Juan Carlos on the shoulder and asked him to take her outside. Excusing himself from the circle around him, he led her through the throng like a docile filly on a leading rein, into the cool night air, towards the dark corner of the grandstand.

Without a word, he spun her around and pinned her back. Finding her body pushed up against a hard wall, she tried to protest as he placed his hands roughly on her breasts. God, it felt good. But also bad. Really, really bad. This was not what she wanted. Way too fast.

They had hardly talked all night. She could have been anybody, and she wanted him to value her. He bit at her neck and she shivered in anticipation, trying hard to remember her resolve. As his hand slid up her chiffon skirt and pulled urgently at her silk panties she placed a hand over his, and struggled to stop him going further. He took little notice. Which made it even more hot and hard to stop him. But she *had* to.

'Oh, Juan, this is… this is … oh God.' By now, he'd unbuckled his breeches with his other hand and had pulled out the most massive, throbbing cock. 'Oh my god…'

Shaking her head, she tried to dispel the lust between them and say 'no' at the same time. It wasn't working, so with one giant effort she pushed him back with both hands.

He looked down at her – shocked and startled. And totally, totally confused.

'I'm so sorry, Juan… I think you're… you're incredibly attractive. This is great, but please, just give me time. Us more time.'

'Time for what?' he asked, genuinely puzzled.

'Time for you to get to know me better. For me to get to know you.' There was an awful silence. Then Juan started to tuck his shirt in, laughing as he did it. Like he was enjoying some hilarious, private joke.

'What's so funny?' said Sharon, nervously, not sure if she should be laughing with him.

'*You* are, my little enchalanta. You are.' Sharon relaxed, she'd made him smile.

But his next words weren't what she expected.

'Why should I wait, hey? You are talking to Juan Carlos Garcia, the best player in the world. I 'ave my choice of zee most beautiful women in every country. Hundreds of them. Sportswomen, models, actresses... Why should I waste my time waiting for *any* woman? Including you?' he finished with a disdainful sneer.

Sharon felt like she'd been slapped across the face. The shock was so numbing, she could only stammer.

'But, but... the day we had… the fun?' her voice trailed off.

He answered with an aloof shrug, and suddenly looked exactly like he really was. An appallingly spoilt, rich, arrogant prick.

As he stalked off, she sank to her knees and cradled her body, the drink making her head swim faster than an Olympic medallist. Through pained eyes, she watched him swagger back over to the party tent, clearly thinking he was the coolest, most desirable man on the planet.

As she slipped away from the scene in a taxi, there was only one silly thing that stopped her bursting into tears. It was the last sight she had of him, gyrating on the dance podium, bathing in the stares of the 'in' crowd below; totally unaware his flies were still undone.

Chapter Twelve

... She'd asked her father to walk her down the aisle; she'd thrown her bouquet to Jules D. and the waiting crowds, waved to the paparazzi and ridden off into the sunset behind her polo player, masterfully handling a white stallion – then the miserable beast reared up and tossed her to the ground.

'Thank God you didn't let him go any further, darling – what a horror. Here, eat a croissant,' offered Jules D., pouring pomegranate juice into the pink champagne.

'I do so like a healthy breakfast,' she said, without any touch of irony.

'He was just so damn beautiful. Every girl's dream,' sighed Sharon, dipping a croissant corner into the jam pot.

'Sorry, bloody nightmare, darling, okay? Can you imagine marrying someone like him?'

Sharon was way too ashamed to say she had.

Jules D. continued without a pause, 'No, this is perfect. We'll just say you're JGF.'

'JGF?' said Sharon.

'Just… good friends,' explained Jules, between bites of her croissant.

'But there was that shot of us snogging against the door!'

'Exactly my point. Keeps the intrigue going. Are they, are they not? Column inches, darling, column inches.' She reached for her mobile phone.

As always, Jules D. was right. A couple of newspapers and two or three weekly gossip magazines ran short photo-caption stories ending with the comment that Sharon had left the Cartier International early and without him, supposedly **'feeling exhausted from too much work. Close sources say "they are just good friends".'**

The first-class flight to New York left Sharon flying high. Having only ever experienced Easy Jet charters to the Costa Del Crappos, the size of the reclining seats was an education. Just two in each row.

She arrived in the 'Big Doughnut' pampered by the hostesses, fattened by the non-stop mid-air banquet and ready and rested for her first ever fashion-show fitting. Debbie, on the other hand, had been squashed in economy, and arrived exhausted, struggling to organise all of Sharon's bags.

But she was happy, because Sharon had actually got her on the official pay-roll as 'assistant' – with Z&ZaK agreeing to cover her accommodation at a Travel Lodge Hotel.

At the other end of the scale, so to speak, sat Boho House. The boutique hotel they had booked Sharon into was an ultra-chic sanctuary for the rich and famous. Quite exquisite. It nestled in the Meat Packing District, the west-side warehouse neighbourhood that had shed its poverty to become a munching Mecca of trendy cafés and restaurants.

Heavenly, thought Sharon, as she sank onto the puffy cotton duvet of her ornate French bed. In the same room, a large oval mirror stood over a thick-rimmed, freestanding, egg-shaped bath that waited for her to dip in her toes. A bath run by her own room butler.

A little later, as she hummed and scrubbed her body, she thought of her little flat in Kingston. Maybe it was time to kiss goodbye to the 'pastel palace' and buy something new? As she shifted her weight, nearly sending a tsunami onto the polished wood floor, the water ran in rivulets down her sides, bubbles pasting themselves to her private bits like a cheeky burlesque dancer.

Singing 'I wanna be loved by you… just you… and nobody else but you,' she jiggled her beautiful, bulbous 36 F breasts to the 'Bo, boo be do' and laughed, looking at herself in the mirror and loving what she saw.

It was a good thing she had this confidence, because it was about to be seriously tested.

International fashion shows were not for the faint-hearted model. Every insecurity was multiplied and magnified by the competition. Zeigfreid & ZaK chose only the best for their line-up.

Visiting their workshops with a host of other models, it was announced that Sharon was to open *and* close the show. The other girls politely clapped. To those in the 'know' (and Sharon had only just qualified when she overheard a loud bitchy voice saying: 'why her?'), 'opening' or 'closing' was the biggest honour a catwalk babe could have.

Hair extensions and fake nails had been pulled out for far less. The fact they had picked this newcomer to do *both* made her the envy of all.

It was also guaranteed to get her coveted consumer and trade press attention.

Sharon was also filled in on the growing practice of the pre-Fashion Week show, where many designers offered their choicest, key items to a quiet, chosen audience a couple of months before the official Fashion Week. Many complained these shows raised the stakes hideously with some designers having to churn out eight collections a year.

But Zeigfreid and ZaK's huge, in-your-face pre-show was going to be far bigger than that. It was the full, all-singing, all-dancing number. The world's press were being alerted. Stars were being invited. The boys were deliberately pushing the boat out… and taking no survivors.

Not only were their rivals now panicked to hysterical hissy-fit screeching-point by the need to do something similar to compete, it also stressed out the fashionista harpies who were terrified they would spend a fortune buying something in the official Fashion Week one month later that was already considered passé by those who had seen it on the catwalks of Z&ZaK. The rivalry was rabid.

Thus, the dogfight to attend and be ahead of the game made this event the hottest ticket in town. Unfortunately for Sharon, it also made her a nervous mound of pink jelly.

'You can do it!' whispered Debbie encouragingly as Sharon faced walking down a mock runway for the first time.

Sharon looked at Debbie's skinny frame, and immediately felt better. *I'm big, I'm bold, I'm beautiful*, thought Sharon, repeating the mantra for the 400th time that morning.

'Walk with more confidence,' barked the artistic director, as she wobbled down the showroom in stilettos. 'You are stunning, show it!' he ordered, tersely.

Luckily, she only had two outfits to wear: a kaftan to open the show, and a bridal dress to close. Sounded simple enough. She hadn't seen either yet, but was told the styles were under wraps. There'd been a shocking number of high-street rip-offs appearing within minutes of the shows recently (not to mention a certain amount of real idea pilfering between designers). For secrecy's sake her 'key' pieces had been fitted on a tailor's dummy matching her measurements perfectly and would be altered on her if necessary.

It suited Sharon fine. She sat munching on a bag of crisps, watching the other models being pinned, pricked and generally ordered around. Many were bigger than her, a few a little smaller. But she felt she measured up fine. There had been a lot of talk in the papers recently about how big was 'too big'. In fact, some cities had taken the step of actually banning any girl over size 24.

'Hey girl, what size are you?' asked a magnificently large black kid of about seventeen.

'Err, size 20,' said Sharon, knowing she was really somewhere between an English 18 and 20.

'Mmm, do you think 24 is a bad thing?' she asked, lowering her stunning brown eyes thoughtfully.

Sharon weighed up her answer carefully. 'Maybe. Though I can easily see how you get to that size.'

The kid seemed momentarily puzzled, and answered Sharon sharply, 'Sister, that may be okay for you, but there are times I *so* crave a fresh salad or crisp apple instead of a cake... I don't know how some of those girls do it.'

Sharon knew that, according to the recent papers, many experts believed size 24 was dangerously big, but it didn't stop young, impressionable models gorging themselves to attain this dress size. Designers were being blamed for encouraging this dilemma. The bigger the girl on the runway, the greater the impact. Oh, how they loved to see yards and yards of their glorious materials floating down the catwalk.

Of course, the more cloth, beads, sequins and work involved, the more they could justify their outrageous price tags. But it wasn't just the designers' fault. The model agencies encouraged their girls to beef up to please them and get the jobs. And some models would eat so much they would be regularly sick. Probably true, thought Sharon. She had noticed there was always a faint smell of vomit in the loos at Glacé Inc.

There was no doubt the pressure was on for models. The sample sizes looked huge on the rails. The idea of filling some of them was daunting. Unlike the consumer sizes in the shops that were made smaller to flatter, these really were size 18 to 24. Anxiously, Sharon asked Debbie to run and buy her another bag of crisps.

She turned back to the kid she'd been talking to and looked over her shoulder at the magazine she was reading. And knew the responsibility fell there too.

Every page was stuffed with stories of how so-and-so celebrity gained their 200lb body to die for. Columns were devoted to 'put on weight' tips, and 'how to look fatter' clothes advice. Massive, proud, buxom, buffed bodies dwarfed sad, grainy shots of skinny-thighed actresses caught out on the beach with their concave tummies and sticking-out hip-bones.

And there was another sick twist to these kinds of magazines, one that screwed up the psyche, for sure. As one story paraded the joys of so-and-so's enviable weight gain, it was counteracted by a snide, cruel tale about another so-and-so's ugly weight loss.

Yo-yo signals with the yo-yo diets, that told women the perfect weight was only safe by a couple of pounds margin either way. The Body Police, beating up the female mind on a daily basis.

But right that moment, Sharon was absolutely thrilled to be one of the fat girls – relieved she never had to worry about being too skinny. The fact was she was naturally fat. Some people found that hard to believe. Girls now envied her for it. There wasn't an interview she'd given where the reporter hadn't asked her for some diet tips on how she maintained her enviable weight.

The other practice she'd noticed was how a few short models – no more than 5' 2" – were getting catwalk jobs. Some avant-garde designers, including Z&ZaK, chose these girls deliberately, because they gave the clothes a more rotund, ball-like quality. Personally, Sharon didn't think people were fooled by this, and was pleased she was nearly six feet tall. Together with her exuberant curves, the impact she caused when she walked into a room was palpable.

Bauble and Bangle, the top salon in the area, arrived to discuss hair. Tingay, their top art director, spread out Sharon's blonde locks like a mermaid's tail, and examined its quality.

'Superb,' she cried… 'We cut this here…'

Sharon gasped in horror.

'No, darling… not her. The others,' interrupted Zeigfreid, bursting through the doors with his usual entourage of Manga twins, bodyguards, et al.

He waved his hand like a queen pardoning a subject from execution.

'Away with the scissors. We love this darling girl exactly as she is… So do the public.'

'Now, my lovely cherub… I need to have a private word with you,' he said courteously, taking her hand in his plump palm and gently stroking it.

'We've got this *marvellous* idea for the opening…'

That evening, when Sharon got back to Boho House, she was stunned to find a massive bouquet of snowy lilies waiting for her, and a tinkling Tiffany bracelet. All from a man she'd never met.

'The model hunters,' Zara had warned. Some disreputable managers and staff at agencies would secretly send out pictures of the new girls arriving in town to the playboys and dirt bags with loads of dosh who helped 'support' the agency bosses. They were a spoilt breed of beauty-obsessed low-life that inhabited the nightlife of the city. They would circle like hungry lions waiting to gobble up a little lamb.

The very young girls, especially the Baltic beauties, often fell prey. Sharon just smiled, tore up the card inviting her downstairs for dinner and ordered room service. Tomorrow was a big day.

The show was due to start at 11.30 am, so at 9 am Sharon stood shivering with fourteen other freezing girls in the unheated back rooms of a meat-packer's warehouse. The tables were laden with piles of doughnuts, cinnamon buns and pretty iced fairy cakes. Copious amounts of hot chocolate were being poured, along with the choice of three vintage champagnes.

Three people were working on Sharon as she tried to calm her nerves. Her hair was being crimped out like an angel's… and a pair of white feather wings were waiting to be fitted onto her back. She tried to remember what the director had told her, and she knew only too well what they expected her to do.

'It's high fashion, darling…. Couture. You'll be fine.' Okay for them, they didn't have to do it. Her stomach churned like ten ferrets bouncing inside a space-hopper. The world would be watching. She couldn't go through with it.

'Here we go…' said her dresser, producing the most fantastic green silk kaftan imaginable. It was sheer, but beaded in all the strategic places – a modesty map, with little islands of mother-of-pearl and shells. To finish off the ensemble, they placed a delicate shell and seaweed circlet on her head, creating an innocent, pre-Raphaelite look to her beauty. She was to walk barefoot.

The crowds filled the seats. Press jostled in the pits, and celebs made their well-timed, last-minute entrances. Finally, the editor of *Vogue* arrived, and, with her, the signal to start.

The music blared loudly in the cavernous warehouse, and Sharon recognised her cue as she heard the cult Reggae song *'Ninety-six degrees in the shade, real hot… real hot in the shade'*. Clammy with fear, she was anything but. There was no turning back. A shove from Debbie, and a deep breath.

She stepped out, spun hair ablaze in the lighting, feathery wings framing behind, conch shell in her hand like a castaway, and faced the sea of darkness ahead.

Light bulbs flashed like a thousand firecrackers, and she heard appreciative clapping as she tossed her incredible blonde mane and sauntered slowly down the runway. Reaching the end safely she turned, lifted up her curtain of hair with her hands, and, crossing one leg sexily behind the other, slowly and deliberately walked back along the runway, swerving at the last moment to the left where a tropical waterfall was pouring. Either side of the stage, they had created a magnificent set of paradise, just like the advertisement for *Descent*.

Shafts of fake sunlight filtered down around Sharon as the rest of the lights lowered throughout the vast loft auditorium. Under the stage lights, the colour of the silk made Sharon's eyes light up like the sheen of a dragonfly.

Turning to the water and looking at the audience over her provocative shoulder, she smiled a wicked smile, then, as directed, stepped into the cascading water. The audience gasped in shock. As did Sharon. It was bloody cold. But as the water drenched her hair, she acted as if she was in the throes of native ecstasy, running her hands through her tresses.

The waterfall undulated down her kaftan, turning it into a clinging, see-through gossamer shift. And there she stood, side on to the crowds, water streaming down her face, hair soaked, wings dripping. Then she turned her back to them. The way she deliberately posed as she held her hands high, as if worshipping the waterfall, water spilling off her upturned palms, made the curve of her long, graceful back carve down like an S to massive, rounded buttocks high and taught as a Venus de Milo. It was one step further than the billboard. A wild, naked angel in front of the entire world's press.

The audience roared. And the lights went out.

For the moment, Sharon's work was done. The show continued with the other models illustrating a Faustian *Descent* into hell via the seven deadly sins...

Sharon was fascinated by the backstage scene breaking around her, and felt just like a romantic heroine trapped in a Georgian brothel. Rouged faces, backcombed, tangled hair... she was surrounded by glorious, painted creatures in various stages of undress as if they'd just stepped straight out of a sumptuous painting.

She heard the audience gasp once more when it got to 'Sloth' and horned satyrs dragged a Titan-sized model standing in a wheeled golden cornucopia down the catwalk. There was a hum of anger too – as she had to be at least size 26 – way too big to *walk* the distance in time to the music. Z&ZaK were deliberately stirring up controversy on a debate that was already boiling hot. And although the garment hung fantastically and she looked like a magnificent, multi-coloured butterfly, many felt this was going one big, fat, waddling step too far.

As the girls filed on and off the stage and panic continually broke out all around her, Sharon had a little more time, as she was being blow-dried and primped again for her dramatic finale.

The 'wedding dress' was finally produced for her to put on. She was astounded. Two assistants carried over an enormous scarlet taffeta and velvet creation. Once on, it swathed firmly around her body, emphasising her opulent proportions, then kicked out with a saucy mermaid's tail. Embroidered with gold leaf, garnets and tigers' eyes along the raised tulle hem, the jewels rose up the calves like licking flames. The robe was designed to sit off the shoulders – the whole effect crowned by a magnificent feathered headdress decorated in rubies. A work of camp genius, the plush red bodice and the red veil were delicately 'singed' as if the wings of a moth had got too close to a flame.

As the dresser sewed her in at the back, three frenetic assistants all working at the same time applied crimson lipstick to her face, red talon fakes to her fingernails, and piled up her hair, letting tendrils snake down. Green shimmery eye make-up and coal-black liner were smudged to give a decadent look… and a live snake placed around her like a living pashmina. The green of its iridescent scales and the reflective colour of Sharon's mesmerising eyes set the vermillion dress off perfectly, and it flared brightly in its own hellish decadence.

'Oh God, does it bite?' she squirmed, as the snake eyed her warily.

'No worries, Sheila,' said the Australian animal trainer. 'I've just fed her. She may like to give you a little squeeze though, but then, who wouldn't?' he laughed.

The music changed to the retro beat of Arthur Brown's '*I AM THE GOD OF HELL FIRE… and I bring you fire*'. Out stepped Sharon again, her heart racing with the thrill, four men dressed as demon ushers leading her to the front of the stage. The audience took an audible intake of breath. Their angel had fallen into hell, and turned into a demon's playmate.

Then out leapt her groom, in a red mushroom cloud of smoke. She was marrying the Devil Incarnate. Or more accurately, a sensational, seven-foot, bare-chested model, dramatically painted red on face and body. Swirling a magnificent peacock-feather cloak, he stalked down the aisle towards her, ruby-studded horns, pitchfork blazing with real fire. Lights dimmed. The paradise set exploded, and flames leapt up along the walkway as the Prince of Darkness passed... The world had blackened into the scene of hell. They stalked hand in hand down the catwalk to the front of the stage. *Fire, I take you to burn...* He reached out to claim his dazzling, virginal, decadent bride, spun her round, kissed her forcefully on the lips... then lifted up a dagger, ripped her bodice open, and plunged it into her heart.

Women screamed.

The lights went out.

The audience went wild.

By the time the lights went on, 2,000 people were giving a standing ovation. As Sharon curtsied, and Zeigfreid & ZaK bounded onto the stage to present her with a bouquet of specially dyed, red lilies, tears filled her eyes. Nothing could have ever prepared her for such an adrenalin high.

Back in the dressing rooms, TV crews, radio reporters and press photographers clamoured around her. She couldn't believe the casual nudity of her fellow models, and the nonchalance with which they stripped off around her, totally ignoring the media scrum, and enviously looking in her direction. But then she thought of what she'd just done. It was worse. But it was wickedly good fun. The microphones thrust towards her.

'How did it feel to open the show?' asked CNN.

'Amazing. Incredible.'

'What do you think of Zeigfreid's clothes?' asked the BBC.

'Incredible, amazing.'

'What was it like to close the show in that way?' asked NBC.

'Amazing, incredible…' Sharon realised she was sounding like an autistic parrot, but she was truly at a loss for words.

'It's been such an honour to work for Z&ZaK, it's the best designer label in the world…' whispered Jules D., giggling from behind her.

'It's been such an honour to work for… etc.' Sharon repeated Jules's speech, laughing at the ludicrous idea of being fed the words – but at the same time deeply grateful for the support from her friend.

At that point, there was a hushed parting of the waves. A very plump woman with sleek, bobbed hair and dark glasses came towards them. Wrapped shamelessly in black-and-white fur, she looked like a very elegant puffin. Then Debbie made a faux pas. Accidentally walking across her path as she hurried to give Sharon a glass of water, she stumbled back out of the way, muttering 'Ohmigod' in recognition – the only one around making a sound.

The 'puffin' didn't introduce herself. No need. Everyone knew she was the editor of New York *Vogue*. Cupping Sharon's chin in her hand, she announced, 'I'd like you to do our next cover.'

That was it. No intro, no exit line. She just walked on past, towards Zeigfreid, who greeted her, arms outstretched, triple air kisses at the ready.

That night, Sharon, Debbie, and Jules D. drank Mojitos and pink champagne in the bar at Boho's. It was an incredible night. They stayed up until dawn, flirting with a host of talent scouts, agency bookers, media luvvies and model hunters. Finally shaking off the hangers-on, they grabbed smoked salmon and cream cheese bagels from Frank's Deli, and headed over to the newspaper stands. Sure enough, Sharon had made the front pages of nearly every single one.

'Dear God! I'm famous!' she squealed, gathering them all up and handing a wad of dollars to the amused vendor. 'Really, really famous.'

'Darling,' laughed Jules D. 'It's just the start.'

Chapter Thirteen

And it was. It seemed that Sharon had that indefinable 'something' that the camera, the media and the public just loved. The Diana factor.

Knocking a top Hollywood actress off the next cover, New York *Vogue* organised an emergency shoot for their forthcoming issue.

The unscheduled session had been a blast. Mauro Testostero, the hottest celebrity photographer in the world, was so endearing and easy-going, she relaxed the moment she met him. Although the studio was vast and teaming with assistants, his crinkly-eyed charm and warm humour brought out the very best in her, and she responded like a child wanting to please a parent. In the end, he shot her naked, arms crossed over her spilling chest. With her hair in pigtails, green eyes twinkling, and head cocked, she looked unbelievably sexy. Like a little girl trying to hold on to a pair of puppies that were struggling to escape.

Where *Vogue* led, others naturally followed. Zara from Glacé was calling Sharon's mobile in New York at least three times a day with castings, spread and cover offers.

Sharon also found it fascinating how the supermarket magazines had increased the status of their pleas. Two weeks ago, they were asking her to pose for a couple of pages. Now they were pleading for a solo cover. Meanwhile, the glossies were offering minimum four-page fashion spreads. In the fame game, she was definitely on the way up.

She was told by her model agency to stop off in Paris, for the cover shoot of *Elle*.

Appointing herself International Travel Co-ordinator, Debbie persuaded Sharon to temporarily employ her, insisting she had done a lot more travelling than her friend, and, unlike Sharon, knew how to handle it all (she argued that as well as their holiday in Ibiza, she'd done a disco cruise on the Channel ferry, been to Amsterdam for a weekend, and once did a student exchange with a girl from Bordeaux).

Whatever. Sharon was happy to go along with it. Suddenly earning skiploads, she was just delighted that Debbie organised the hotel and bags, and took charge of the ticket pick-ups and check-ins.

Both arriving exhausted at the Hôtel de Crillon, Debbie ordered late-night room service in their suite, whilst Sharon popped on the canopied bed like a pooped-out princess.

'This isn't a hotel, it's a palace,' sighed Sharon, fingering the heavily woven drapery. The room was astounding in its graciousness.

Framing the Place de la Concorde with its long line of Grecian pillars, the view from their hotel was possibly the most elegant in the world. The famous Needle pointed up to the cloudless night sky, a few steps away the floodlit promenade of the Champs-Elysées.

'Boy, I can so see why the peasants revolted,' laughed Debbie, sticking an oyster vol-au-vent in her mouth and washing it down with a peach Bellini.

Sharon laughed decadently like Marie Antoinette, kicked off her kitten heels and felt the plush carpet between her toes. In the dark distance, the Eiffel Tower twinkled like a giant magic wand.

It couldn't get any better, thought Sharon, could it?

The session with *Elle* was only one day… but in a subtle manoeuvre to raise Sharon's worth, Glacé Inc. had insisted their rising star have a night of unparalleled luxury so she would look her best for the magazine. *Elle* had balked, bitched, and brindled, before they finally broke. The five-star hotel suite was on them. It set a status precedent that all would have to follow.

For this cover, she was neatly jacketed in vintage Dior. Glossy red, plumped-up lips, and a chic black hat perched on her head, saucily decorated with a luscious pile of ripe cherries. The art director figured the use of strong red would remind the readers of her outrageous Z&ZaK catwalk finale.

Inside, the pages would show her lounging in a bath of profiteroles and cream. It was stylised, rather like a Doris Day movie, with a giant pink powder puff in hand, flowered bath cap on head, fluffy fur mules at the edge of the roll-top bath, and legs kicked in the air.

It was so funny to be lying there in her favourite food, with all the people fussing around her, she laughed the whole day… popping a profiterole in her mouth whenever she felt like it, and driving the poor make-up girl to distraction.

As it turned out, it wasn't for a fashion spread. It was one better. An interview about being one of the world's most in-demand models. After an excited, quickie phone-call to Jules D., she fielded the questions expertly, declaring Dean still a close confidant, (the bastard) and Juan Carlos a treasured friend (the fuck head).

Finally, at eleven o'clock, she arrived home in England, alone, tired and ready for bed. The light flashed on her answer-phone, and she pressed the button sleepily.

Beep. 'Hello, darling, how are you? D'you know, I think I saw you in the papers. Are you modelling or something? Maybe it was just somebody who looked like you. Anyway, it would be lovely to talk to you. Need to tell you something. Give me a call. Thinking of you… lots of love, Dad.' Her father always signed off his answer-phone messages like a letter. Sharon figured it was an old person thing. These days he just seemed to forget everything she told him. It was sad, she so wanted him to be proud of her, to understand how well she was doing.

Hungry, she grabbed a packet of crisps as she listened to the calls.

The next two beeps were from the model agency and her old advertising agency. The girls from filing left a communal message of congratulations, asking when she was coming round to say hello, and have lunch. Yeah, in your dreams, thought Sharon, pressing delete with deep satisfaction.

The last message was from Simon. It felt like a hand had reached inside her ribcage, grabbed her heart and squeezed it.

'Hi Sharon, wow. You are really doing well. I doubt you're going to have time to do our shoot now. Really hope you can, but totally understand if not. But either way, can you just let me know…? The designer is on tenderhooks…'

His voice sounded wonderful. A familiar tone, from the days before the madness. Of course she would do the shoot. No way would she let him down. She started to dial the number… but caught sight of the clock. So late. She'd ring first thing in the morning. That night, Simon filled her thoughts again. She'd missed him, and she enjoyed the luxury of remembering. His smile, his eyes… his laugh.

Next day, the model agency rang first thing. Could she meet an advertising agency team in the West End, to discuss a possible global make-up contract of a hip-happening brand?

They were sending a car for her at 10.00 am.

The fees they were talking were insane. She was never good at maths, but even Sharon could work out she'd be earning something like £20,000 an hour for pouting at a lens four times a year. It was obscene, she grinned, brushing out her hair and pulling on a low-cut Z&ZaK jumper. She couldn't possibly accept it, she smiled, stepping into a flowing skirt. It was too much! She laughed, working out all the wonderful things she'd buy.

Applying her face en route in the limo, she marvelled at how she'd mastered the art of make-up so quickly. Was this really the same girl of a few weeks ago? Cat-like eyes perfectly emphasised with liquid liner, edged with a slash of cobalt green. Mascara'd eyelashes colt-like in their amazing length. Full lips natural, delicately lined and polished with a clear gloss. Skin flawless with the aid of a camouflage stick and a speck of foundation.

Apart from the nights out in Kingston, she had never, ever bothered with make-up before. Her cosmetics bag had consisted of a crumbling *Rimmel* brown eye shadow, dry old *Maybelline* mascara, a bland Nivea chap stick and a mucky tin of Vaseline. If she got this job, the irony of becoming the 'face' of *Urban Cool* was just too much!

Swinging through the Covent Garden doors of De La Guarde Advertising, she was shown straight up to the boardroom. Oddly, she had no nerves. None at all. She tried to work out why, and then realised that so much was going right, if she got the job or not, who cared? Not her. She was already a success. Nothing to prove. It was a confidence that no training could buy, and it explained clearer than any books, or any course, exactly why success …breeds success.

Seven men and women stared at Sharon inscrutably. She just smiled brightly, helping herself to the plate of cookies on the table with relish. They asked questions about her past and current make-up choices, and she told them the blunt truth about the murky secrets of her make-up bag before her recent cannon-shot to fame. Warmed by her honesty, they all laughed. There was something about her so unpretentious – it was achingly cool. She landed the contract before their shoulders had finished shaking.

Leaving by the same limo, on impulse she asked the driver to drop her off near Riversal Road. Part of her still felt she was walking in a fluffy, marshmallow dream… Dr. Marvel's clinic had irrevocably changed her life, and she wanted to thank them with flowers and gifts – and get some answers as to how this miracle had happened.

She passed 'Your Choice', the pretty patisserie where she'd taken the magic pill. The place was still there, exactly as she remembered. On impulse and feeling peckish, she decided to stop for a chocolate malt shake, just to confirm if the cake selection was any different… It was. The choice, including the divine fairy cake, had changed. Still, then again… her entire life had changed. She was having such fun! As the sun shone on her happy face, she flipped out her phone to call back Simon.

'Hi, it's Sharon, I'm back…'

'Hey, great! Are you still up for it?' he asked. Up for it with Simon? She certainly was. Sharon paused, desperately trying to think of a witty answer that wouldn't come out smutty… Too late.

'…Sharon, are you there?'

'Sure. I'm definitely up for it. When do you want to do it with me…'

Oh God, thought Sharon, mortified. It was coming out all wrong. NOT witty Sharon, *so* not witty.

'Well, what are you up to now? The designer will be back by lunchtime – could we set something up right away? Now I've got you… I don't want to lose you!'

Was that a flirt? *Was* that a flirt? Sharon's mind raced.

'You've got me, Simon. You always had. Give me the address, I'm on my way.' Phew. She sounded decisive, flirtatious and professional.

Clipping the phone shut, she looked at the studio address she had just written down. The Coal Face, next to the Steam Museum, Kew. Curious, she sipped her milkshake and finished the crumbs on her plate. Thank heaven she was already looking good from the agency meeting she'd had earlier. She glanced in the direction of Riversal Road. Finding the clinic would have to wait. She was on a confidence roll; this was definitely the right time to face him.

Getting out of the taxi, she looked at the imposing old Victorian redbrick building in front of her. White carved masonry lintels topped the windows, and above the mahogany-panelled door was a large, polished plate of brass proclaiming 'The Coal Face'.

She pressed the buzzer that said 'Mercier Photography' and Simon answered cheerfully.

Third floor up, she pushed open a red fire door, and walked along the corridor. All the way along were various-sized open cubicles buzzing with activity. Artists, iron welders, mosaic makers, fabric weavers…

At the far end, lay Simon's studio. Large open doors into a bright, white room.

He kissed her on both cheeks hello, and then held her by her shoulders at arms length to study her. He whistled.

'My God, you look great! Sit down, sit down. Can I get you a coffee? Or a tea?' Sharon savoured the way Simon looked too. Confident, relaxed and totally at home in his surroundings.

It struck Sharon that it was the first time she'd not been offered champagne at a shoot or show.

'Tea would be marvellous, two… no, three sugars please.'

As Simon headed over to the far side of the room and the makeshift kitchen, Sharon had a chance to take in the large photos running along the whole of one wall. They were stunning: a line of arresting portraits, from a battered, bleeding boxer wiping his forehead with a soiled towel, to a sad old Spanish matador, holding his hat forlornly against his chest.

'My series entry for the Academy of World Arts,' said Simon, noticing Sharon was now walking along the row, studying the pictures one by one.

'God, they're amazing… they all look so, so…'

'*Defeated*. That's the title of the collection.'

'When's the competition?'

'It's just been.'

'Oh, shame. And tell me, were *you* defeated?' she asked, pleased with her Lauren Bacall-style delivery.

'No, not at all actually, I won. The finalists' exhibition is next week. You can come if you like?' he added hesitantly.

Before she could answer, a pretty girl with a purple fringe popped her head in…

'Simon, don't forget to give me your invites; I'm sure I can get a few creatives from Saatchi's to come.'

'Cheers, Darcy… by the way – love the new pottery. Great colours, much better than your usual grey crap! Let me know if you need some press shots.'

The girl laughed, totally unoffended and disappeared.

'Right Sharon, let me show you what we're shooting… it's something special by a terrific new designer called Max Du Pré.' Simon walked over to a clothes rail, flicked through a few items and pulled out a large, chalk-white dress.

'Wow, that's a great tent dress!' said Sharon, amused.

'It is, isn't it!' said Simon, laughing even harder.

And it was. Exactly that. A 'tent' dress. A brilliantly designed A-line frock made from hand-stitched canvas, complete with punkish trimmings of metal tag rings and guy ropes.

Sharon was eager to try it on…

Changing behind a simple black curtain, she stepped out. Simon folded his hands and leant back against the white Victorian radiator.

'It looks so cool… just bloody marvellous.'

On Sharon, it hung perfectly. Scooped around the neckline, it fell in a straight A line, but as she walked it flowed, giving it a sexy, sixties swing. Although it looked like it was made of tent canvas, the material was actually soft, like a silk parachute. The whole design was fun, mad, modern. And a wonderful play on the idea.

'How are you going to shoot this?'

'Et voilà!' Simon produced a huge fifties silver fan, lowered the slated blinds behind her, and handed her a pair of white-patent, seven-inch stiletto heels

'Can you handle those?'

'Sure, I can handle anything you give me,' she winked.

Simon laughed, and brushed her hair off her face with his finger. The gesture felt laced with electricity.

'I think I want your hair wild and free. After all, it's your trademark.'

There was no make-up artist, so Sharon retouched her own face whilst Simon played with the lights.

He switched the fan on, and the dress billowed up. Sharon tried to hold it down with her hands, giggling, her legs splayed like Marilyn Monroe's over the air vent. Her waist-length hair flew up and out, and as she tossed her head against the wind, it fanned out and waved like a stormy sea of platinum satin.

He clicked on a hi-fi, and *Sweet Dreams Are Made of This* blasted out of four speakers.

The Eurythmics' hot electric beat was perfect. Sharon slowly and self-consciously started to move – but as the sounds pulsated through her, she loosened like a wild cat. As Annie Lennox husked '*Some of them want to use you… some of them want to be used by you…*' Sharon imagined Simon doing just that. Flash after flash exploded in time to the music, and as she began sucking her bottom lip, pouting and tossing her hair, the atmosphere in The Coal Face turned steamy, steamy… steamy. And then white hot. A few times their eyes locked above the camera for many seconds longer than necessary.

And as Simon looked through the lens and gave orders, she drowned in the beauty of the moment…

'Beautiful… great.. stunning… this way…look down… to the left…gorgeous…' Sharon was loving it! Simon was fixating on her. Her fantasy come true.

She had his full attention, and he was acting as though she looked amazing.

At times, the dream was briefly interrupted…

'Hey, man,' said a large guy with a goatee and short sideburns.

'…Mike's finishing the CD copy now… are you joining us for the brainstorm later?'

'Yeah, yeah, I'll be there…' answered Simon, not taking his eye off camera… 'Keep that up, Sharon, place your legs wider…'

Minutes later, they were interrupted again.

'Hi, Si! Guys, that looks fab! Great work…' called out another girl as she passed the door – Sharon just had time to note she was a cute size 18, in a swirly seventies top and with pink fuchsia hair.

'What is this place?' asked Sharon, feeling like the outsider of a very, very hip gang.

'It's the nature of The Coal Face. Anyone who takes space here has to be in a creative field. …Look at me, eyes down.

'Y'know… no solicitors or accountants. Makes us a sort of co-operative of talent. A kind of creative hotchpotch. Works really well… Okay, eyes looking past my shoulder, smoulder… that's it!

'Max designs in a studio below, Darcy is two along… we all help each other in any way we can. Don't smile, look mean…horny…

'Mike is a musician, his band's just finishing their first album, and he wants me to shoot the cover. If it's a hit, I get a shit-load of dosh.'

She so wished she was a 'creative'. She envied his lifestyle, and felt, once more, insecure. They stopped as Simon adjusted the lighting.

'What about this job? Are you doing this for free?' asked Sharon.

'Yep. I know this designer is going to be huge. Okay, turn your back to me, look over your shoulder and give me a sexy wink… fabulous…that's it. Hold it…

'But the most Max can afford to pay you right now is the amount I mentioned … £300. Which we're giving all to you. I know your rate's probably a lot higher now, so we really appreciate it.'

'No problem… glad to help out,' she said, knowing he'd be disconcerted if he knew just how much more. But she was equally disconcerted at the use of the word 'we'. How much of a 'we', exactly, were they? Oh no, was Simon bisexual? She'd heard a lot of photographers were…

'Well, I think the designer is a genius! I want to meet him… where is he?' said Sharon with false brightness.

'It's a 'she', actually…' said a smoky voice at the door. 'And I'm right here.'

They both stopped and looked towards a stunning brunette holding a cigarette holder in one hand, trench-coat held over her shoulder by the other. She sported a short, unbelievably sleek, shiny bob, and was wearing a sophisticated black shift dress. Typically French, thought Sharon uneasily.

'Sharon, meet Maxine Du Pré… Max, meet Sharon.'

Sharon winced at the ordinariness of her name next to that of this creature who looked like she should be sitting in a café in a French film noir.

'You can call me Shaz,' she said, embarrassed as she said it. Why the hell was she referring to her press nickname? The woman just made her feel inadequate. She wasn't even as big as Sharon, but it was something about the way she carried herself, that gave the same impact.

'You look exceptional,' Maxine purred. 'Darling Simon, you were right. No other woman would look as good in this.'

Sharon was both mortified and pleased in one sentence. Delighted Simon had said such a thing, but sickened at the way she was so familiar with him. They must be lovers, she reasoned bitterly.

The rest of the shoot didn't go so well. Sharon's sparkle dimmed, and Simon sensed it.

'Let's call it a day, we got some fantastic shots earlier.'

Maxine's hauteur had cooled the room like an iceberg in a hot tub.

As Sharon changed, she heard them talk in hushed voices.

'No, Maxine, don't you dare. Not here. Don't even think about it…' Simon whispered.

A low, throaty laugh emanated from the French beauty. 'Tut, if you insist. You know I always do what you say, darling…'

Sharon felt broken. She was right. It took her a few minutes to compose herself before she brightly pulled back the black curtain.

'Okay guys…I'd better be off. Great dress, Maxine. Love it.'

'Keep it, angel … you deserve it.'

'We're releasing the photos to the press in a couple of days, can you just sign the form?' asked Simon, turning businesslike as he handed Sharon a model release that would allow the shots to be used anywhere, along with an envelope of money.

'So...' said Sharon awkwardly.

'So…' said Simon awkwardly.

'So… are you coming to his show?' said Maxine smoothly.

'Err… yes, if you want me to?'

'Of *course* we do,' said Maxine, using the bloody 'we' word again.

Simon picked up one of the invites on the table. A smart black-and-white card announced that the Academy of World Arts was holding this year's show at the Serpentine.

'One, or two?' he asked pointedly. A leading question she didn't know how to handle.

'Two please,' she replied, mysteriously (but knowing full well one would either be for Jules D. or Debbie). Cheek kissing goodbyes, Sharon said she'd see them there, and left with a deep feeling of anti-climax that stayed with her the whole way home.

Making a concentrated effort to put them out of her mind, the next few days passed in a flurry of 'go-sees' and agency talks. So it was with surprise that she walked into the newsagents for a pint of milk and saw herself on the cover of a major weekly gossip mag wearing the 'Tent Dress'. The shot was fantastic. The silver fan and shadows from the blinds gave it a fifties iconic feel, as her hair and dress billowed about her, and she looked like a younger, sexier Marilyn, all big curves and boobs. But Sharon also had poutier lips, higher cheekbones and gorgeous green eyes.

The same shot was in the *Evening Standard*, and the *Daily Mail*. But, to Sharon, the copy was even more amazing than the photo

– 'LOOKING SHAZULOUS!' said one headline, 'SHAZERIFIC!' said another, and all hailed her as a trendsetter! A fashion leader, able to spot new talent a mile away.

Taken aback, Sharon couldn't believe they were talking about her – a girl who used to think 'cutting edge' meant a pair of scissors.

Shaz shows the way… discovering new designer Maxine Du Pré, she wears one of her witty creations, the 'Tent Dress'.

Within days the dress was a massive hit, and Maxine Du Pré sold hundreds to the department stores in navy, red and white. Its popularity was all encompassing; big girls looked even bigger, skinny girls could hide their lack of curves. The silky canvas made it feminine, yet sporty. Tough, yet girly. Over the weeks to come, it was a style that sold in the thousands – invariably ripped off, variations appeared in every boutique and discount chain across the nation. And Sharon had started it.

Then something else happened to set her above the other models for good, and establish her as *'The Fad Queen to Follow'*. A total accident…

Chapter Fourteen

What to wear? What to wear?

As Simon's exhibition loomed, Sharon learnt that being a fashion icon was fraught with worries. Suddenly, nothing in the wardrobe seemed trendy enough – or worse, too trendy. Sharon had sauntered down Portobello Road the last weekend, and had picked up a few things. High on the possibility list was a vintage gown that skimmed the floor. It was alabaster silk, which scored points because the event was a celebration of black-and-white photography. But was it too dressy? The tiny lines of covered buttons running along the wrists and down the long back were so delicate and feminine, likewise the pinprick ruching under the bust, which gave it an elegant empire line. It was probably perfect.

The problem was, Sharon could only think of Simon's cool crowd. She couldn't imagine any of the women there being seen dead in it. She thought of Darcy, and Maxine and Fi-Fi, or whoever… they'd all be clad in grungy trench-coats and spiky hair, like existentialist extras in a Jean-Paul Sartre documentary.

'Darling, I'm outside, taxi's waiting,' cooed Jules D. on Sharon's mobile.

As they swept down the drive to the elegant, columned Serpentine Gallery, Jules D. smoothed the strands off Sharon's face. For once, she'd tied her hair into a high, loose bun, and it suited her, emphasising her long neck, ample Regency bosom, high cheeks and neat, retrousse nosé.

'Oh my god, what's that?' asked Sharon. This year the gallery had commissioned a Japanese artist by the unpronounceable name of Yoki Yamiharata to build the temporary annual Pavilion, an architectural installation erected on the lawns in front of the traditional building.

Always acclaimed as the very height of innovation and design, the invitation to create the building was an honour internationally craved. This year's results looked like a giant white egg surrounded by spilt yolk. As they got out of the car, they realised the yolk was actually a moat of water reflecting the setting sun, on which swam stately white swans from the Serpentine… with a couple of black swans imported just for the night.

'Black and white? Ahhh, how apt,' said Jules D., noticing the detail. She was referring to the theme of the exhibition – A World Celebration of Black & White Photography.

They crossed the moat and stepped through the 'cracked egg' opening, past a spotlit plaque explaining Yamiharata's architecture:

'This year's Pavilion represents the harmonious re-birth of creativity solidifying the two primal opposing yet complementary principles found in Yin-Yang.'

'Hey, I was just going to say that!' said Sharon to Jules D., both finding the pretentiousness highly amusing.

The scene was exactly what they had expected. The bold, the beautiful, the famous and the über-cool, all floating in a bubble of tinkling glasses and laughter.

Sharon stood and chatted politely to a few people who introduced themselves and asked her about her experiences during Fashion Week, or about the 'Tent Dress' just seen in the *Daily Mail*.

Excusing herself after a while, she caught the eye of a waitress and snaffled a black-and-white sushi off a glass chessboard. Designer delicious, she thought, helping herself to three others, leaving a checkmate scenario on the waitress's board.

No sign of Simon, but she could see his work prominently displayed on the main large wall, spotlights either side. His images were also being projected one by one on a giant plasma screen. She felt really proud, and even Jules D. had to admit his work was really arresting.

Making a beeline in their direction, it wasn't long before a fading actress, hoping *Jules D. Creatives* would relaunch her career, cornered them mercilessly. After the woman's fifteenth sentence beginning with 'I', Sharon excused herself from the humiliating situation and sidled off, leaving Jules D. to let the woman down gently and discreetly.

The other finalists' work adorned the three other walls, and Sharon walked along pretending to study the photos, which protected her from talking to anyone, and gave her an intellectual air at the same time.

The theme was sport – right across the world. Weighed down by their own worthiness, the entries seemed to cover everything from cock fighting in Vietnam to toe fighting in Tibet.

Jockeys in their Jockies read one card, alongside images of skinny white men in their y-fronts. *Stripped bare, the riders show their fragile association with nature and beast… Influenced by the post-Expressionist movement…blah, blah, blah.* Sharon chuckled again at the pretentiousness.

Another series of photos – the third prizewinner – showed an Indian weight lifter, lifting another man.

Günter Andderton's unique series investigates the symbiotic relationship between resistance and force, pushing to the limits the thresholds of pain… a secret and subversive narrative of society's oppression.

Sharon snickered into her cocktail glass, putting her hand around it to hide her mouth.

'I love the way he captures the essence of angst by highlighting the uselessness of man, don't you?' said a deadly serious voice behind her.

She turned, and looked straight into the blue-grey eyes of Simon. They were crinkled with amusement in contrast to his tone. They both started to laugh.

'It's a pretentious load of ol' crap, isn't it? Sorry Sharon, had I known it was like this, I wouldn't have invited you.'

'Don't be ridiculous, this is great,' she said, sweeping her arm in the direction of the whole room. 'Pretentious it may be, but Simon, it's incredibly prestigious. I'm really proud of you.'

'Really?' he said, pleased.

'Yes, really. Your work stands out as… umm, deeply authentic.' She started to laugh at her own words. 'And, err… arrestingly modernist.'

'And, also worthy… don't forget "meaningful and worthy",' he said, ribbing her back.

They then rejoiced in the game of who could find the most conceited description on the walls, finally wandering towards the canapé table to admire the ice sculpture of a swan on a black river of caviar.

As Simon downed a pint of black-and-white Guinness, and Sharon took another mouthful of black caviar, they enjoyed watching people arrive together. One gay couple turned up draped in monochrome kimonos, but they were trumped by a woman in a fifties black-and-white, polka-dot cocktail dress, with two Dalmatians on a chequered lead.

Heading straight towards her, entourage in tow, Sharon recognised Paul Sharpe from her old advertising agency SBC. Black leather jacket, black leather jeans, black shirt, silver earring and black cowboy string tie.

'Shaz, kiddo! The girl's done good,' he schmoozed, swigging a beer in his usual rock 'n' roll fashion, and planting a wet kiss on both her cheeks.

He turned to the people with him:

'I remember the moment we knew we had a star in our presence. There she was, a lowly receptionist, when the sun came out, and made a halo around her… God, it was one of those electric moments you never forget…' As he went on to describe the waterfall and how it had influenced the final poster of *Descent*, Sharon smiled, embarrassed, and edged away to stand with Simon again, who was watching her curiously.

'Simon, I haven't had a chance to tell you how much I love your photo of the Tent Dress. Amazing… been in a lot of papers.'

'I know. That's 'cos you looked so good in it; it was easy to take a great shot. I owe you one. The phone hasn't stopped ringing with job offers.'

'Not at all! You're now in the presence of a "style icon", thanks to you.' Simon looked at her seriously for a moment, locking her eyes with his.

'This is all a far cry from *Kool Kat's*, isn't it? Do you remember that last time we were there…? It was you I really wanted to dance with, not Debbee.'

Tingles shot up her arms. Sharon tried hard to listen, but was uncomfortably aware people glanced at her all the time, and she found it hard to concentrate and relax. Photographers circled, taking photographs of the two of them standing there together, and they carried on talking, pretending they didn't notice.

Simon was the first to break the pretence between them.

'Okay, there's one to your left… run your fingers through your hair, and give me your best model smile,' said Simon through gritted teeth, smiling back.

'Another swooping in at three o'clock… take a sip and look passionate about your work,' countered Sharon. They were having such fun… until Maxine Du Pré tapped Simon on the shoulder. He turned, and automatically gave her a kiss on the cheek…

'Have you missed me, darling?' she asked coquettishly.

At that point, a microphone tapping was heard, and a pompous man in a dinner jacket made a speech.

'Fantastic to have entries from all over the globe…blah blah blah…Nikon… Kodak… sponsors etc. etc. etc.'

Sharon noticed Simon looked a little edgy. Was it because Max had slipped her arms through both of theirs as they listened?

'And our fantastic winner, Simon Mercier…. really captures the essence of man's ability to… blah, blah blah,' said the host.

The room broke out in applause, and Simon walked forward to the podium.

'I am really, really pleased to get this award. It means a lot to me. I've always loved black-and-white photography …' he began. Then hesitated.

Sharon noticed something had caught his eye above the crowds, and she saw a subtle, almost imperceptible, smile play on the edge of his lips. She doubted anyone else had ever studied his mouth like she had, and doubted even more if they could see what she could. So as everyone looked at him in rapture, she, instead, followed his eye line…

Oh no…! She turned back to him with the biggest beam on her face she'd ever had. He saw her turn back to him with a grin. They both knew.

Along the side of his work, a bright banner announcing the awards hung all the way down the wall. The same banner also hung in various places horizontally. But it was the vertical wall banners that made her gasp. She and Simon hadn't noticed it before. It would appear nobody had. Certainly not the graphic designers who had designed the vertical version from the horizontal. But it clearly said:

Academy of
World
Arts this year sponsored by
Nikon &
Kodak

Simon seemed to hesitate, he looked down at his notes, as if he wanted to change his planned speech. He looked once again at Sharon. She knew the acronym was irresistible, and, sure enough, Simon rose to it like a man with Tourette's.

'…Indeed, I'm somewhat overwhelmed at the entries this evening.' He screwed up the paper. 'When mine was submitted to the committee, I never expected to get this (lifting the trophy) W-A-N-K from the Academy.' Speaking swiftly as he said the letters, it was hard to tell if anyone actually realised what it spelt.

Regardless, Simon continued, holding up the silver statuette. 'And I can see tonight that there are many finalists out there who have earned this experience far more than me. What can I say… I'm enjoying this moment right now, I feel ecstatic. And I truly thank you - the organisers - for the pleasure of giving it to me in front… of all of you …' he just managed to finish, disguising his collapse into hysterics with the sudden development of a heavy coughing fit.

The sponsors slapped him on the back and handed him a cheque for £25,000. He struggled with his composure, posed for more photos, then slipped off towards Sharon and Max.

Reaching Sharon first, he finally was able to let out a relieved guffaw, and they both creased up, holding on to each other as they shook. Max looked on, puzzled, in that petulant, sexy way only the French can pull off.

Max finally caught the joke, and smiled. 'Cute, darling, very cute,' she said, squeezing Simon's cheek. At that point, a tray of drinks went floating past, and Sharon twisted round to catch it. She heard an almighty rip. As buttons pinged off the back of her dress, the blood drained from her face. A huge tear now ran from the centre back to under her arm.

The fragile material around the rip disintegrated and frayed… Sharon stepped back in shock, catching her satin Louboutin heel in the long hem as she did so. Tottering dangerously close to the ice swan, she made another twisting manoeuvre to avoid falling face first in the caviar. Another rip was heard, as the bottom half of the skirt split apart.

She looked at Simon, horrified. He looked at her, mock horrified. Jules D. came running over to help.

'Get me out of here! Help…' whispered Sharon, trying to hide behind her. Photographers were circling like sharks about to eat a juicy morsel of photo-gossip.

'Listen to me. Stay calm. Stay absolutely calm. Don't let them see a single sign of worry while I fix this. Give them a little laugh, go on. That's it. Now, lets see… Thank God, your bra's really pretty…'

Then they both started to laugh. Such a stuffy, pretentious crowd, and this was the worst thing that could possibly happen to a celebrity. It was also the funniest. Sharon knew her bra was now showing, but it was new, edged in pretty chiffon, and very clean! As for her skirt…

'Darling, just tie it up or something…' said Jules D., taking control. Sharon did, in a knot at the side, like a sarong. It actually looked pretty good. The frayed rips had a cobweb-like quality, and, without trying, her vintage, full-length gown had transformed into a chic little number. She kicked off her shoes that now looked ridiculously high, and let her hair half down. Barefoot and beach-babe leggy, the effect was very, very bohemian.

Recovering enough to mingle, as their little circle circulated round the room, people stared in admiration and envy at such an 'in' gang.

Max, however, was now acting in a very predatory manner, coming physically between her and Simon at every opportunity.

Jules D. took Sharon aside.

'Sharon darling, I'd give up tonight. She's never going to leave you alone with him. Come on, sweetie, let's head off. Never good to be the dreg at any party. Call him tomorrow, and say you're sorry you had to leave. Gives you a chance to speak to him alone, and maybe he'll suggest meeting up or something.'

'You're right. What's the point?' sighed Sharon. 'She's got her perfect, French-manicured nails into him. I don't want to share. Or fight.'

They walked out into the hot, August night, and, as Jules D. disappeared in search of a taxi, Sharon sat at the edge of the moonlit moat, and dangled her bare feet into the water. It was cool and refreshing. As she watched a serene swan sail silently past on the silvery water, it reminded her of a rubber toy swan she once had. She'd floated it on the Bourne Stream in Bournemouth Pleasure Gardens when she was about five years old. And it had sailed out of reach, under the bridge, past the Pavilion and along, eventually, to the big, bad sea. She'd been devastated. Her mother had tried in vain to comfort her, but all she could think of was her poor little swan, lost and alone in the vast ocean. Right now, just like her.

'There you are! Why are you going? Something I said?' asked Simon, settling down next to her.

'Not at all. I just thought you were busy.' Sharon desperately wanted to say 'with Max' but knew she wouldn't be able to hide the jealousy in her tone of voice, and it would be such a humiliating giveaway.

'Nope, I'm not. I'm all yours…' He looked at her intently. The words hung in the air, suspended by static. They both said nothing, just slowly moved their faces closer and closer. Feeling an uncontrollable force of gravity, Sharon felt the overwhelming pull of her lips towards his. She so, so wanted to feel his touch hers, they actually ached for that moment. Their lips were only a fraction apart. She could smell his cologne… his cool breath…

But the fear of rejection kicked in.

'What about Max? You're with her,' her voice cracked. Simon made a last-minute swerve manoeuvre, brushing his lips against her cheek.

It broke the moment.

'Max? Good God, no! Why the hell would you think *that*?'

Sharon didn't know how much to say. So she started with little things.

'Well, she… she calls you darling.'

'Maxine calls everyone darling, including the tax man!'

'Okay, well, umm… when we were doing the shoot, I heard her come on to you, and you were laughing and said … "Don't you dare! Not here!"'

Simon started to laugh, his shoulders shaking.

'Go on… what else?'

'Well, she doesn't leave us alone – she's been squeezing between you and me all night.'

'Oh Sharon. This is SO funny… you have no idea. Please, go on…'

'Funny? Not to me it isn't,' said Sharon, perplexed.

'Oh, it is, believe me. It *is*. Sharon, I don't know how to tell you this, but... Maxine is GAY. G-A-Y! She's had the hots for you for ages!'

'WHAT!?'

'You were her muse for that dress. She has cuttings of you from Fashion Week up in her room! I knew what she was up to the minute she slinked into my studio. She wanted to make a pass at *you*, and you're right – I said *no way! Don't you dare... not here!*

'Actually, I was really cross with her, because I wanted to go out for a drink with you after, and I think she knew it.'

Suddenly, it all made sense. Max always squeezing in between her and Simon – getting physically closer to Sharon.

And now she thought of it, it was *Maxine* who had insisted she came to the exhibition... How could she have been so blind?

Sharon started to laugh uncontrollably, both flattered and relieved.

'Taxi, Sharon! Come on!' They looked up to see Jules D., door open in a black cab.

'Oh no, now I've got to go...'

'Stay a bit longer...' said Simon, placing his hand over her wrist.

'Ah, there's our boy!' cried a suited organiser, leading a posse of photographers and sponsors behind him.

And the two were reluctantly pulled away in different directions.

'Damn. Sharon, I'm off to Los Angeles for two weeks work. I'm leaving tomorrow... I'll call you when I get back, okay?' called out Simon, retreating towards the Pavilion for more corporate schmoozing.

'Okay, do that!' she shouted back, as she stepped reluctantly into the meter-ticking taxi.

Looking out of the back window, the last thing Sharon saw were two fighting swans, and a soaking gaggle of Academy organisers desperately trying to pull them apart before guests and press realised the anthropological error of mixing the black and white birds together.

Chapter Fifteen

Sunday brunch, Debbie and Sharon sat in Jules D.'s stylish slate-topped kitchen, drinking bucks fizz and guzzling endless croissants.

'Which ones next? Chocolate, almond or plain…?' called out Jules D., pulling out a tray from her designer Smeg oven. The fresh-baked smell of bread wafted through the air, bringing with it dreams of smoky French bistros and Gauloises cigarettes.

'Well, I just can't believe you didn't realise she was after you,' said Debbie, giggling as she topped up her flute.

'No idea. And I'm sure he was going to kiss me! If only I'd kept my mouth shut.'

'…Yes, for once that would have helped,' said Jules, settling at the counter with a stack of Sunday newspapers and a frothy, machine-made cappuccino.

'Now he's off for ages… I can't bear it!'

'LA, did you say? What's he doing there?'

'Absolutely no idea… photographing something or other.'

'Here's a good piece,' interrupted Jules D., as she worked her way through the papers with a yellow highlighter. She held up a spread on the Egg Pavilion, and there, largest picture on the double page, was Sharon, moonlit hair tumbling down, dress suggestively ripped along her shoulder line and hem tied saucily up at the corner. She was sitting by the moat, one foot paddling in the water, other knee up to her chin, showing an indecent amount of ample thigh. She looked like a naughty water-baby about to do a skinny-dip.

The copy trilled, '**Shaz does it again – is she the coolest babe on the planet? On a night out at the Academy for World Arts, her vintage Chanel dress tore, but did she run home crying? No, not this model. A nip and a tuck was all it took to transform her glam gown into a hot little mini.**'

'Coolest babe on the planet? As if… And where did they get the idea it was a vintage Chanel? I just picked it up off a tatty old market stall.'

'Makes good copy, darling – who's going to contradict? Not you. Certainly not Chanel,' explained Jules D.

'Hey, let me see the other photos…' Amid the pictures was a small one of Simon and the organisers. He looked calm, confident and handsome (though perhaps a tad too slim compared to the bear-like men around him), thought Sharon.

'Can I keep this copy?' she said, tracing her finger over his face.

'You'll want this one too, then?' said Debbie handing over a broadsheet showing a picture of the two of them laughing together.

This time the text concentrated on Simon.

'Up-and-coming advertising and fashion photographer Simon Mercier, winner of this year's Academy of World Arts, beat fierce international competition with a striking series of black-and-white images depicting sportsmen at the end of their game. His recent picture of Shaz in the Tent Dress by Maxine Du Pré has started a new fashion craze – the garment sold out in Harvey Nichols last week within an hour of opening, and the names on the waiting list are said to be in the hundreds.

Now Britain's newest supermodel may have started yet another craze when her dress ripped. Tying up the tattered hem, she kicked off her shoes and carried on partying. Chances are this season's new look will be "tatters".

'Wow. Very, very good. Two things in that copy have just earned me a nice fat bonus from Zieg and ZaK.' Jules D. grinned, popping a buttered morsel in her mouth.

'What things?' asked Sharon and Debbie in unison.

'The fact a *broadsheet* is now referring to you as a single name is a mega-sign of your celebrity status. Tabloid or otherwise.'

'Really? I'm just relieved. I've always hated "Plunkett". What's the second thing?'

'Second is the fact they describe you as a supermodel. Horribly clichéd description, I know – but it does put you firmly in the big league. Kristen owes me one huge, fuck-off favour, the stuck-up bitch. Now she can eat her words along with her cheesecake every morning.'

'Everybody owes you a big favour, me included!' said Sharon, getting up to give her a giant hug. 'I was ready to run and hide. It's insane how something like a ripped dress can create such media interest. At the time, I was just mortified I'd stuffed myself so much I split the back – the humiliation was awful.'

Both Jules D. and Debbie looked at her, puzzled.

'You just don't understand, do you? You see, the world used to worship skinny women… that was before I took the magic pill.'

Debbie sighed. 'This again. Sharon, I'm really worried about you. Maybe it's just the pressure you're under? But sometimes you say, err…mad stuff, and I can't help thinking you should see a doctor, or a psychiatrist or something?'

Jules D. nodded. 'I agree, darling. Or if you want to, say it to us. But please, please don't ever repeat this kind of crap to a journalist. Remember how they crucified Cruise?' reminded the PR queen.

Sharon stayed quiet, defeated – and reached for another croissant.

'Good girl. Try the kiwi jam, it's full of nutrients and pure sugar,' urged Jules D., a walking encyclopaedia on healthy living.

~

As the papers launched the 'tatters' look, and Sharon ripped the sleeve off a few old T-shirts to feed the press more fodder, she was surprised to receive a hand-delivered invitation from the States.

Screen-printed on silk and mounted on papyrus it said:

> KOO RANJANI AND ALEX AVALON REQUEST YOUR
> PRESENCE AT THEIR WEDDING IN:
> LAS VEGAS, JAIPUR, LONDON AND REYKJAVIK

With it was a handwritten note from Koo saying:

> *Shaz, I'd love you to join us at any of the venues – and I would be deeply honoured if you would agree to be my bridesmaid. Call me...*

Koo was a massive Bollywood star turned chart-topping singer, and Alex her good-looking US producer/Svengali. Sharon re-read the note. She would have been deeply honoured too. Except for the fact she'd never even met the woman.

'Look at this! Why would they ask me to do such a thing?' said Sharon, showing off the invite next time her little gang of three got together.

Debbie was agog. Jules D. just yawned.

'Well, it's kudos for them, darling. You would be adding a few thousand to their *Hello!* deal, I suspect. Having said that, you should do it, of course. It's a very clear two-way street. Publicity for them. Publicity for you.'

Debbie felt otherwise. 'Well, I think it's appalling. Asking a complete stranger to be a bridesmaid,' sniffed Debbie. 'And look at the itinerary, it's very last minute. The first service is in less than a couple of weeks.'

'Oh, so I gather you won't be going with Sharon, then?' asked Jules D.

'I didn't say that. I just think it's bad taste. But then, I *love* bad taste. Sharon, we should go!'

'But it's crazy… a non-stop marathon. Just look at the venues and dates. London, Las Vegas… India… and …Revjka… isn't that Iceland? Why the hell Iceland, Jules?'

'I suspect it'll be in one of those ice hotels, and then they'll be called the coolest couple on earth. My guess is their PR will already have been seeding that headline with the chosen hacks. Anyway, say "Yes", darling, and I'll give their people a call. Maybe we can get to design some of the bridal party outfits? Zeigfreid would love that… yards and yards of sequins and saris, baubles bangles and beads.'

'How many bridesmaids do you think Koo has actually asked?'

'Ummm, knowing her, however many Liza had, double it. I'll check out who they are first. You don't want to be ending up in a line-up with any of those losers from her days on that X factor show.'

Jules D. was referring to the fact Koo had started out as a hairdresser from Hounslow. She'd made it to the top in a tacky 'Find a Bollywood Star' reality competition and then shot higher, like a comet to the highest reaches of the celebrity cosmos.

'Fifteen,' said Debbie.

'Fifteen what?' asked Jules and Sharon.

'Fifteen bridesmaids. Liza Minnelli had fifteen. And two maids of honour – Elizabeth Taylor and Marisa Berenson.'

Jules D. and Sharon looked at her in pity.

'What?' She shrugged defensively. 'Years of devouring *Hello!* What can I say?'

'Well, that's useful to know, Debbie. Well done,' said Sharon kindly.

Debbie looked pleased she'd contributed something worthwhile, and the three went back to the importance of discussing how good or bad Sharon would look in a sari.

~

As it turned out, with Vegas the numero uno on the whistle-stop wedding tour, she had to look good in Gigi Versale first. Ten days later, the knock on the door of her suite at the six-star Menagerie Hotel told her the bridesmaid's dress had arrived. It came complete with a male dresser from the designer who explained camply that it was 'Kong's Fay Wray meets Vegas Show Girl'.

Made of bright-yellow satin, it clung like a condom-tight sheath, then flared and split at the side like it had been torn.

'That last touch has just been added, and was inspired by you…' said the dresser, placing his hand to his mouth in a feminine flutter. 'We love the "tatters" look, sweetpea, so "in" right now'.'

Sharon hated the hideous frock. Worse still, the spaghetti straps and plunging neckline created a massive headache in bosom leverage. Sharon's 36 F's were pretty good at defying gravity, but this dress had so little support, she could have done with a pair of space helmets. Copious reams of boob tape later, they made two giant steps for mankind. And it looked surprisingly good. Although the crazy choice of colour played havoc with the complexion, it did make her green eyes glint like a dangerous lynx.

There was another knock at the door, and Debbie ran to open it. A distinguished man in green livery with a box of jewels entered.

'Please, take your pick,' said the silver-haired, elderly gentleman, holding open the case with pride. 'They're on loan to Koo and her bridesmaids, compliments of Deia Jewels.'

Sitting down at the marble coffee table to study the contents, Sharon felt in awe as she handled the precious trinkets from the famous jeweller. The multi-coloured stones gleamed in the bright lights of the room like little baby fireworks.

'For the actual wedding service today, may I suggest yellow diamonds…? This set of earrings goes so well with the bracelet and choker,' said the footman politely.

'You may suggest anything you want!' laughed Sharon, holding up a heavy chain dripping with sparklies.

'How exactly "Deia" are they?' gasped Debbie, mouth agog.

'Oh, to the nearest hundred thousand? About two million.'

'Fine. I'll take three – one in each colour!' teased Sharon, '… trust me, I'll keep them Deia to my heart!'

At that point, the footman's mobile began to chime prettily.

'Yes? Yes… oh dear. Okay. Alright, I'm on my way.' He looked crestfallen. 'I'm terribly sorry, ladies, it seems the bride is unhappy with her choice and wants to look at everything we've sent over. I've got to go right now. But I'll be back as soon as I can.'

He swept up the entire pile displayed on the black velvet cushion, and raced out of the room with a harried look on his face.

'Oh well. That was fun while it lasted,' said Sharon flatly, staring at the empty table like a child robbed of its sweeties.

An hour and a half later, as the sun set on the strip, she was in the lobby with 20 other bridesmaids, lining up for the walk into the Wedding Wing of the hotel. The Menagerie was the latest outrageous Vegas construction, a glitzy over-the-top theme palace based on a zoo. Which, quite frankly, was exactly what Sharon found she had got herself into.

From the Concierge desk to the bellhops, staff were dressed as Safari Guides – the boys in tight-butt shorts and butch khaki flap jackets, the girls in mini box-pleated khaki skirts and crisp cotton shirts, rolled-down wool socks and ankle-laced tracker boots. Since 90% of the girls had legs as long as a giraffe's anyway, the effect was surprisingly sexy. The massive real palm trees growing in the centre of the foyer reached up to four floors high. At the top, mechanical monkeys leapt from branch to branch. Below, every ten minutes on the dot a herd of elephants would wiggle their ears, trumpet their trunks, then dip in unison into a pool and spray water into the air like a ten-sprout fountain. The entrance to the Wedding Wing was along a rope bridge, through the splayed legs of a giant giraffe sporting a massive diamond collar.

Watching the unruly commotion outside, Sharon could see the press corps was out in full. As fashionably late guests squeezed through the mêlée, the helicopters came buzzing down like angry wasps desperate to taste the celebrity jam. On the ground, black-suited bodyguards were holding surging crowds in check, all talking importantly into their earpieces, trying to look like stars in a CIA movie.

Sharon glanced along the line at her fellow bridesmaids and gave them friendly nods. Nearly all were recognisable, some far more than others. Behind her was Tricia Trendall, a stunning, forty-five-year-old international soap star so perfectly preserved she shamed the embalmers of Tutankhamun. Whilst sashaying her big, high ass right in front of her was Batista, a street-tough Cuban black singer renowned for her latest mega-hit single, *Beat you up, Bitch…* A slight improvement on her previous release, *I'll Fuckin' Have You!*

Sharon made a mental note not to tread on her hem.

The bridesmaids were all dressed the same, and it was interesting to note how some of the beautiful women in the line-up looked like scrawny little birds in the canary-yellow frocks. You certainly had to be big to carry the look off. But something else united them all. A sickly pallor of green.

Koo must have spent days researching the worst shade of yellow, thought Sharon, irritated. How clever… what better way to make yourself look famously fabulous than to line yourself up against the world competition, and cobble it.

Alas, it also seemed the doddery, silver-haired footman had found the time to visit all the other girls, except her. In true Vegas style, all the bridesmaids dripped in dazzling diamonds. Sharon noted that there was enough bloody 'ice' around to save the polar bear. No worries – she thought bravely. Feeling somewhat intimidated by the amount of fame around her, she was happy being underdressed.

As they waited in the ante-room for the appearance of Koo Ranjani, they were handed pretty bouquets of yellow and white jungle lilies, with trails of creepers twining down.

Finally, the bride arrived; a pure-white, lace-covered bodice encased her ample, curvaceous body, teamed with a Victorian organza skirt, bustled at the back with large yellow orchids. To maximise her girth and impact, she had draped a long chiffon wrap encrusted with pearls and diamonds over her shoulders, and it rested elegantly on her arms. It trailed effectively either side along the floor as she swished towards them, making the idea of a head veil and train seem immediately old-fashioned. In the surrounding jungle décor the overall effect was brilliant. Smouldering sexuality underneath a prim exterior, she looked like a voluptuous Victorian Jane, about to meet Tarzan.

Her entourage of 'closest girlfriends', on the other hand, looked like a bunch of bananas for the apes.

Nonetheless the bridesmaids all warmly air-kissed the bride. As Koo worked her way down the line, Sharon felt nervous. What was she supposed to say? 'Nice to meet you…'

But being a practised ol' pro, when Koo got to Sharon, she simply exclaimed: 'Shaz! How are you?! I'm so, so glad you could make it. I really am,' and gave her an emotional, eyes-closed hug, like twins who had been torn apart at birth… before moving swiftly on.

Jungle drums beat out a rhythm as the bridesmaids led the way in, entering under a jungle ruin into the next hall. A fake stream ran down the main aisle, and the wedding party had to carefully negotiate stepping stones all the way up to the altar. The room had more foliage than the Amazon Basin, with gay birds of paradise tweeting mechanically from the high branches of the plastic mango trees.

Either side, sitting uncomfortably on rocks and trunks and stumps, sat the glitterati. Celebrities, authors, rock stars, artists… all dressed in bright tropical colours. Ahead, looking impossibly LA with a deep tan and sparkling white smile, waited Alex Avalon. His hair was swept back and shaggy, and his white collarless shirt undone to reveal a bronze, hairless (probably waxed), body builder's chest. Sharon was sure he winked salaciously at her, which was a little disconcerting since he was about to be betrothed to his beloved in the eyes of the Lord. Well, sort of.

A large black minister with a necklace of ancient symbols asked everyone to stand, as he 'smudged' the air with incense.

In Sharon's mind there was no doubt the ceremony was pure hokum as the couple recited saccharine vows, exchanged wooden tribal drinking bowls, pinned exotic flowers in each other's hair and ended with an embarrassingly long public snog to make everyone aware of their uncontrollable passion for each other.

The photo line-up afterwards seemed to take hours, as the 'chosen one' did his photos for the magazine that had bid the highest for the exclusive rights to record this holy event for posterity. The security was unbelievable. She had been frisked once and asked twice if she was concealing a camera, though in this outfit she dreaded to think where they thought she'd hidden it.

As the bridal party were asked to pose again and again, she realised this was 'pay back' time for the free flights, hotel and banana dress. Suddenly, a TV reporter who had been staring intently at her walked briskly over, and in a clipped New York accent asked, 'How come you're the only bridesmaid not wearing bling? I hear Deia Jewels has loaned out their top collection.'

Sharon was taken aback. It had been noticed. She felt herself blush as she tried to focus on what Jules D. would say. And then it came to her…

'I never wear anything I can't afford to buy,' she bluffed, with an arrogant shrug. She softened it with a smile, and wrinkled her pretty little nose. Hard to say if she was joking or not.

The newswoman lit up with unexpected joy. 'Great sound-bite, Shaz. Thanks.'

The following wedding breakfast was so gargantuan it could have passed for a two-weeks-all-inclusive.

Laid out on a 150 ft tabletop made to look like a ledge of rock, the buffet of lobster, prawns and crab claws was piled higher than Kilimanjaro. But the centrepiece of the room was a giant open fire, and the kind of sight that would make a vegetarian slit their wrists and drink their own blood: a spit-roast choice of pork, lamb and, in keeping with the theme, antelope.

As for pudding, a chocolate fountain was never going to be enough. Instead, Koo and Alex had a nine-foot-high chocolate waterfall that poured gooey Mocha into a tropical pool, where sweet-toothed guests could scoop up the confection in freshly cut coconut shells.

The roof had been retracted completely to show a vast, darkening Vegas sky. All around the ballroom walls, vines and creepers hung down festooned with flowers and fruit. Real parrots flapped around the edges on gnarled wood perches, and in the far corner a Safari guide handling snakes, tarantulas and two-foot centipedes was entertaining the spoilt brats of the rich and famous.

Koo had now swapped her corseted bustle and bodice for a chiffon Victorian chemise and a tangled hair wreath of ivy and flowers. Very becoming, it looked like she'd been carried off to the treetops and ravaged by her newly married Gorilla.

For a couple who had a daydream life, the Official Wedding List had been a nightmare for someone of Sharon's new celebrity stature. The last time she chose something off a wedding list, it had been a toss up between a sandwich toaster and a bread bin for her cousin Barry.

But not so here. The choice was terrifying. Amid the demands for a Lalique crystal goblet set of fifty and a sack of gold and platinum iron golf clubs rested the sanctimonious suggestion that a donation to their favourite charity would also be acceptable.

The dilemma of being a) an honoured bridesmaid, but b) a complete stranger made the amount she should spend on the happy couple completely unfathomable. Add to this the fact she was now famous and therefore supposedly rich… she was at a loss.

In the end, as she was still waiting for a shed-load of money to come through the agency accounts department, she had plumped for a £500 donation to the couple's pet project – The Poor Children in the Orphanage of Rahdipur.

Now, looking at the opulence of the occasion, she wondered if she had been expected to donate more. On the other hand, it irked her that by cutting out just *one* of the wedding ceremonies, the happy couple could probably rebuild the entire village, complete with plasma screens in every five-bedroom house.

Taking a healthy portion of skewered meat and sweet potato, she sat on one of the tree trunks near the fire, and concentrated on not spilling her plate.

'So what do you think of all this?' said a deep male voice. Sharon looked up, into one of the most famous faces in the music biz. It was Jaz, a laconic, laid-back naughty lad who had made his name by escaping a boy band into mega-stardom. She couldn't believe the huge star was actually talking to her.

'Move that beautiful butt over,' he said, settling himself down next to her on the tree trunk.

'So, how do you know the happy couple?'

Sharon blushed. There she was, a bridesmaid. A woman who had sold her soul for the freebie trip and the publicity circus.

'I don't,' she answered honestly. 'Never met them before in my life.'

'So what did you do? Grab a giant banana, skin it and gate-crash?' asked Jaz, highly amused.

'They asked me, I said yes. Sounded fun,' she explained a little embarrassed.

'And why not, I say. So did I,' smiled the star with a twinkle.

'You don't know them either?'

'Depends on interpretation. I did meet Alex in the toilets once, and he lent me a rolled-up fiver... so in this business, I guess you could say we're bosom buddies.'

Sharon was both shocked at his open reference to cocaine, and amused.

At that point, Koo and Alex could be seen kissing in front of them through a haze of barbecue smoke.

'They look so right together, I wish them days of happiness...' quipped Jaz. Then they looked up, shocked to see a microphone dangling over their heads. And both laughed. No doubt the video of the event would now have a curious mute moment.

God, he was cute, thought Sharon, peeking at his childlike blue eyes, edged in dark, spiky lashes. She noted how strong his arms looked in his white vest, very manly and covered with tattoos. Oh he was so rock 'n' roll. If only Debbie and Jules D. could see her now.

Sharon talked easily with Jaz as they ate, and her excitement doubled when he told her to stay there whilst he got them some rum punches. Three rounds later, the lights went dark and they found themselves surrounded by forty Amazonian fire-dancers, flames blowing at them from all directions.

This was followed by bridesmaid Batista performing especially for her 'good friends', the loving couple (for an undisclosed fee). The woman was a sensational performer. By the third number her sizzling mix of salsa/caribbean beat had the revellers screaming 'Bo-Bo shake your booty', a chant the enchantress was well known for, and more than happy to oblige to.

As she shimmied her massive ass off the stage, African native drummers belted out a hypnotic rhythm from the tops of four jungle tree houses nestled in each corner of the room.

And then an air of decadence broke out. The heat, the bright clothing and the abundance of drink and food made a heady mix. The jungle atmosphere came alive with the lighting of a hundred flaming torches. With the added arrival of maidens scantily clad in zebra skins bearing platters of cocktails, Sharon was reminded of an old Hollywood movie, was it *The Fall of Babel? Sodom and Gomorrah?*

As for the great gathering of the rich and famous, fully aware the press were being held at bay, they gleefully loosened their proverbial ties and ripped off their inhibitions.

Despite being who he was, Jaz didn't seem to want to leave her side. They gyrated to the beat, lost in the heat of the night, pushed close by the pressing crowds. In the firelight, her eyes glowed even more like a lynx, her sleek blonde hair wild and tangled as the sounds swept over her.

This was surely a dream… Sharon closed her eyes to the beat, and then opened them. No, the rock idol was still there, staring at her with a cheeky smile that said: 'Let's get naked.'

Pulling her behind a palm tree, he gave her a spliff, and Sharon took her first ever puff of weed. It made her cough. So did the second puff. But by the third, she had the first floating feeling. A mellow happiness that drifted through her, lifted by the incessant, throbbing beat.

At around midnight, there was a terrifying crash of thunder – then a blue flash of lightning. The sky ripped apart and rain sheeted down, drenching the dancing guests in a torrential shower. Regardless, the frantic pounding of the African drums increased, and hedonistic pagan madness heightened by the natural force of nature swept through the throng. As the storm increased, everyone around her danced with wild abandon, Born Free. Soaked to the skin, clothes clinging to their bodies, Jaz pulled her to him and crushed his mouth on hers, his hands and lips devouring her like a lion that hadn't eaten for months.

As the water poured down her face and between their lips, her head swam, her ears burst. She was in heaven. She was in hell. She was in *descent*. She no longer looked like the girl in the poster... she *was* the girl in the poster.

And she was loving every *fucking* second of it.

Chapter Sixteen

She was drowning, she tried helplessly to float, but wave after wave after wave kept hitting her, rocking her from side to side… she was sinking… she was going under. She was… woken up!

Sharon found herself lolling in a giant, oval-shaped waterbed, and shifting next to her, the toned, rock-hard, rock-solid, rock-on body of a rock star. She almost squealed in delight. Then shuddered. What had she done with him? Her mind was a blank. Well, sort of.

The passion had been crazy, insane. But she thought she'd passed out before they reached 'last base', as it were. She sincerely hoped so, because she had a gut feeling the only way she'd hold onto this boy was to play a little hard to get. A kid at heart, she reckoned he played games.

Jaz sleepily opened his famous blue eyes, sat up on one elbow precariously, and ruffled his hair, giving a rakish look that emphasised his high cheekbones and enormous eyes.

'THAT was a hell of a night… Great. Now be a good girl and go get me a coffee,' he croaked.

Indignant that he thought she was some kind of waitress, Sharon lifted her considerable hips, and dropped them back down onto the waterbed. They sent a mini tidal wave his way, dislodging his elbows and causing him to collapse and convulse with laughter.

'Whatta girl!' He leaned over to kiss her, and the heat re-ignited. But Sharon swiftly turned it down.

'Hey, let's get up and do Vegas!' she suggested, flinging back the hotel's black-out curtains, and staring at the only city in the world that twinkled in daylight.

Four days later, they were still doing it. Vegas, that is.

Like two kids in an all-night candy bar, they gorged on every thing the Sin City had to offer. Bouncing like shiny bright pinballs from street to street, they experienced every theme going, from Pyramids in the Hotel Luxor, to the Gondoliers in Venice. Every over-the-top bar, every eccentric eatery, every feather-fanned show, every far-out attraction… it was fabulous fun, from the Mardi Gras in the Masquerade Village, to M&M's World of Chocolate.

As they spent every single hour together, their friendship grew into something real. Sharon found him really funny and affectionate, but most importantly, despite his fame, the man had a warm heart. She watched him smile and joke with his fans and sign autograph after autograph. It wasn't an act. He genuinely loved people, and made time to chat with them all. He was also generous. Everyone got a great fat tip, from the room maid to the doorman.

'What the hell, I was once broke,' he said to her, after handing a polite taxi cab driver a $100 bill for a ten-minute ride.

Hell, thought Sharon, the paragon even helped old ladies cross the street. Well, not exactly. In fact, he did one better.

Enjoying the people-watching possibilities of this City of Sin, one night they were fascinated by the pensioners pouring dollars into the hungry one-arm bandits – mechanical, heartless outlaws who were holding them prisoner with false hope, and robbing them blind.

One old bird kept pouring money into the Giant Jackpot for thirty minutes straight, until she was finally down to her last nickel. Like every pull before, it lost. Looking forlorn, she started to cry. Jaz just walked up to her, and poured all his dollar winnings into the cup at the bottom of her machine. About $500, just like that. And walked away without a word. The woman looked as if she'd just seen Jesus Christ.

With so much to see and do together, they found themselves on a spinning fairground ride that never stopped. And Jaz was always up for the next thrill. Delaying their flights home three times in a row, by the fourth night Sharon was shattered.

Jaz, on the other hand, had enough energy for the two of them. It dawned on her that it was probably much to do with the white powder he sometimes sniffed. He was generous, always offering it to share. But Sharon remained wary. Apart from scaring her because it was classed as dangerous and illegal, she didn't like him taking it as she wanted him to be just 'high' on her. On the other hand, she was aware from the gossip mags that it was all part of the rock 'n' roll scene. Who was she to stop him?

Regardless, she wasn't keen to get sucked in, and always declined due to an ingrown distrust of the drug ever since she read a horror story about it being mixed with Vim.

As for the sex, she tried her damnedest to keep him at bay. Indeed, she often thought of Simon and whether she was breaking any kind of unspoken bond, or was that just wishful thinking on her part?

But the truth was, Simon hadn't even kissed her. And the other truth was, she was with a ROCK STAR!! Yes, she was being more shallow than a rock pool, but the looks the other girls gave her were priceless. And the looks from Jaz, well, they curled her stomach with strange firework sparkles.

When Sharon finally caved in on day four, it was hot, horny and dangerous in a back alleyway. Leather jacket, leather jeans, he knew exactly how to turn her on, and she adored the way he felt against her. She also loved his boundless energy and enthusiasm. Caressing her body fondly in the limo back to the hotel, he was like a puppy with a new toy.

'Why did you make me wait so long, babe?'

'Because you would have just been bored. Never got to know me.'

'Not true. I knew you the moment I laid eyes on you. Come here, you luscious lump of lurve.' Sharon sighed with contentment. Although she chided herself she'd only lasted out four days, she also reasoned they'd been together non-stop, the equivalent hours of twenty dates. Anyway, in rock star groupie terms, four days was probably equivalent to the chastity of a Born Again Christian.

By the time she jetted back to England, with promises to come to his next music festival, she had no idea the British papers had been covering her non-stop from the day of the wedding.

Jules D. and Debbie met her for lunch, armed with stacks of magazines and papers. Sharon was astounded.

The headlines had her wrongly quoted as saying:

'I WON'T WEAR FREEBIES!'

Whilst the copy stated:

'Shaz sets a new standard in über-cool as she refuses the freebie jewels offered by Deia Jewels. Whilst other bridesmaids decked themselves out in borrowed bling, one supermodel stuck to her principles.

"I never wear anything I can't afford to buy," says Shaz. No question, her understated look set her apart from the rest of the spoiled beauties in the bridesmaid line-up. A refreshing change to the usual greedy grabbing, other celebrities would be wise to follow…'

The photos accompanying showed Sharon looking serene, laid-back and natural, as opposed to her usual green-eyed wild-child look.

'Oh, my god,' said Debbie, excited. 'Now you're leading the celebrities!'

Sharon couldn't believe it. 'I hate the expression "über". It's trying so hard to be cool. This is an über load of cobblers.'

'Darling, well done! I can't believe you turned down all those freebie goodies,' hugged Jules D.

'It didn't exactly happen like that, did it, Debs?' Debbie had been a little miffed with Sharon for running off with a Rock

Star, and had caught the plane home from Vegas the next day. On the other hand, she'd also met the rock star's band manager at the airport, who was in her view 'a real hunk'. With so much in common to bitch about, the two employees had bonded in the VIP lounge. As a result, she was also invited to go to Jaz's next concert. At that moment, she was on a big high, and her best pal Sharon could do no wrong.

'Yes, it did. Well, sort of. Whatever, you had the brains to spin the situation,' Debbie said admiringly.

But when Jules D. heard the whole truth from Sharon, she let out peals of loud laughter.

'Good girl! I'm so proud of you. On the other hand, don't expect an invitation to the rest of the wedding ceremonies… The clip of you smiling like Mona Lisa saying, "I never wear anything I can't afford to buy," was on TV stations all over the world. It's on YouTube as one of the biggest hits. I just *love* what you said, and the way you said it. Leaves one wondering if it's a wind up or not… a real classic on the lines of that ol' chestnut "I don't get out of bed for less than $10,000".

'But the thing is, darling, as big as Koo is, she won't like being overshadowed. I expect a cancellation call to the other ceremonies any moment now.'

She showed Sharon the *HI YA!* magazine marriage spreads, and given equal billing next to Koo were pictures of 'Shaz' simply dressed (if you could call the Banana that). Worse, in a couple of the down-market weeklies, her picture featured at twice the size of the bride and groom's. But who cared? Sharon's star was still on a dizzying ascent.

Amid the recent newspaper cuttings and photos, the glossier magazines that took longer to print were concurrently running shots of her in the Tent Dress, or the Tattered Dress, and finally – in undoubted confirmation of her trend-setting ability – spreads of other models sporting the Tattered Look.

But it was that morning's Sunday papers that made her smile and panic at the same time.

A front-page screamer cried '*SHAZ AND JAZ!*' and there they were, sharing a giant candyfloss, holding hands. The days with Jaz had felt like a holiday romance – that surreal limbo land where whatever you do so far away from home doesn't count. She never expected her exploits to be blazoned across her home papers for friends, family, and – yes – Simon to see. Naïve, really. Someone was bound to recognise them out there, despite dark glasses, fake beards and hats. (Well, the fake beards were just for an hour - Jaz had made her wear hers, and walk into a beauty salon for a bet.)

On the other hand, she was glad it was 'out there', even though she didn't know if Jaz saw the relationship as 'going anywhere'. They did look really good together… and she was learning fast it could only help the career.

'It's great. Footballer, Polo Player, Rock Star… Good girl. So "on the way up".' said Jules D. dreaming of her next bonus from Z&ZaK.

'But what if it doesn't work out? What will people think? Where do I go from here? And Simon… what about him?' Neither of her friends could answer that, and instead brought over a plate of cookies and ice cream to change the subject.

After the news of the Jaz relationship broke, paparazzi seemed camped outside the door permanently. Even trips to the shops became a hazard, and in truth a bit of a pain. She had to slap on make-up just to nip out for a pint of milk, and it became abundantly clear she would have to move from her flat for security reasons.

Three estate agents came round, and she took the middle quote, looking for a fast sale. In return, glossy brochures featuring bijou mews houses and riverside penthouses were sent to her home, and in between modelling 'go-sees' and assignments, she began the trawl of looking for a new place to live. As she struggled daily past the intrusive pap lenses from her car to her door, gated entrances and protective porters suddenly seemed deeply appealing.

Meanwhile, although Simon flitted in and out of her mind, there was no denying the fact that dating one of Brit Rock's hottest icons was an incredible high. She reasoned there was no guarantee Simon would call, or, indeed, was actually that interested. Better a bird in the hand… especially when it was a fab-looking, famous songbird who guaranteed unlimited press coverage.

Confirming her status as his 'babe', she'd been receiving intimate texts from Jaz saying exactly what he'd like to do with her; and she couldn't wait for the weekend. He was tied up recording for the next few days, but the Big Alternative Festival was looming fast.

The Rock Chick look was a tough one for Sharon. Her 'man' was headlining Saturday night (which Jules D. told her was a very, very good thing). The old Sharon had only ever been into folk music and Abba, and had dressed in whatever she had found to fit. For her, the new abundance of clothes for women her size was overwhelming. Designers all pandered to the bigger shape and the choice in the stores had quadrupled.

As for 'celebrity dating', her Vegas walk on the wild side with Jaz had been an enormous step. But this was another, even more public leap. And now aware the press were featuring her every move, from toenail colour to choice of lip-gloss, the dilemma wasn't lessened by the fact they were going for the whole weekend, it was bound to rain, and they were staying in a tepee.

On the other hand, with the growing influx of press stories the designer freebies were arriving daily – fuelled more than ever by the kudos of having one of their products photographed on an icon that chose to 'buy her own'.

Soon, her little flat began to resemble a car-boot sale of stolen goods, with piles of designer handbags, shoes, sunglasses, skirts and tops building up in every corner of every room. But it wasn't accessories that were a problem. It was the whole look.

Finally, a quick call to Mario from Glacé and she was sorted.

It was a strange experience to go into a famous designer shop and be told to take whatever she wanted. All she had to do was let them have the stuff back when she'd finished. And not even take it back. Just ring a number, and they'd send a car. Oh indeedy, life as a celebrity was a blast!

Using a large, soft-suede weekend bag, she packed amongst other items such as her vintage leather jacket, her new floppy sun hat and pink wool beanie and scarf from Gucci, a baby-pink cashmere jumper and grey angora hoodie cardigan from Chanel, flower-patterned Wellies from Kath Kidson, two pairs of wonderfully faded, fattening jeans from Diesel, and a black chiffon kimono from Agent Provocateur. Just for good measure, she also stuffed in her old, fluffy, pink dressing gown. She reluctantly refrained from taking her bunny hot-water bottle, as it was so not 'rock 'n' roll'. Then she thought, why not? Who says what's cool? It seemed that she did. And so she chucked it in.

Running short on space, she only took one bag from the designer pile with her, a supple leather tote with Indian fringing. Very Glastonbury, she reckoned.

Jaz said he didn't want her there for the build up as he needed to concentrate on his act, therefore the Big Alternative Fest was in full swing by the time the manager's white limo dropped her and Debbie off. Sharon noted her assistant was looking better these days, filling out to a more acceptable size 12. However, she'd chosen to wear white cowboy boots and a very short, white-leather skirt, topped with tight, white T-shirt and cropped leather bomber.

Hair messily backcombed, lips stained with red, and make-up deliberately smudged, the look was porn-star-groupie-meets-group-for-group-gang-bang. Still, it was rock 'n' roll so maybe Debbie had got it 'bang-on', so to speak?

The grounds were bursting with people, colour, tents, stalls and noise. And loud, very, very loud noise. A massive stage with banks and banks of speakers either side dominated the skyline. Handed 'Access All Area' tags by an assistant as they arrived, they were whisked through a backdoor maze of corridors and curtained areas.

'Debs, there you are babes!' said the manager, sweeping Debbie away from Sharon and crushing her to him in a giant bear hug.

He wasn't what Sharon had expected at all… wearing a suit, he could have been a city boy. But his face was fun, round and jolly… and Debbie looked smitten as he chucked her under the chin.

'Shaz, your man's in there…' he said to Sharon with a friendly smile. 'But I have to warn you he gets really uptight before a show. So, go easy on him, okay? Keep him cool.'

Feeling nervous, as she hadn't seen Jaz since Vegas, she popped her head around the door. The room was a mess of guitars, ashtrays, and beer bottles. In the corner, yelling at a girl holding a black sparkly jacket, was Jaz, his face tense and angry.

'Why do you think I'd wear that? For fuck's sake – what kind of prick do you think I am?'

'I thought you said this was the one you wanted to wear today… don't you remember? I spoke to you about it yesterday morning.'

'Well, that was yesterday… you should have checked with me today, stupid cow. What else have you brought with you?'

The girl tremulously opened a suitcase and pulled out a striking blue silk shirt.

'It's so great… I thought you'd love it. It will match your eyes, and catch the wind when you dance around.' She swirled it to demonstrate.

Jaz's eyes softened a moment as he took in the beautiful item. And he sighed, resigned.

'I wanted the white silk, but since you've fucked up… this'll have to do.'

Sharon coughed, shocked at what she saw but determined not to show it. Maybe this was what rock 'n' roll stars did. Act like monsters to their staff. Maybe it was acceptable? Normal, even.

'Shaz! At last! Welcome to the house of hell! Come here, great to see you… ' From a spoilt bully he suddenly changed into an adorable little boy. All big eyes and winning smiles. Looking every inch the mega-star, he swept her up into a delicious snog, but as he held her close, she felt his hands on her back shaking.

'Are you okay?' she asked him gently. He imperceptibly shook his head. Then turned to the poor girl backing into the corner, unsure what to do or where to look.

'It's okay, Dee, sorry about… you can go. Shirt's fine.' He waited until the girl left the room, cleared the mess of magazines and cans off the sofa, and sat down, pulling Sharon close to him.

'No, Shaz, I'm not okay. I hate this bit. The nerves. I can't stand it. I just don't know why I'm in this business. Hate it. I'm such a fuckin' loser. People just don't see it.' He ran his fingers helplessly though his hair, and sat dejected, elbows on knees.

Sharon forgave the monster she'd just seen, and melted protectively over him, pulling him into the safety of her luscious curves.

He let out an enormous slow breath, and she rocked him back and forth, like a baby. He murmured, lost in the delicious smelling, enveloping comfort of her body. 'Geez, I wish I could stay here like this forever… you're just so soft, warm, soft… soft…' he swallowed back a sob.

'Jaz, you're great. The best. Everyone loves you. You'll go on stage, and be fantastic. Magic. And I'll be right in the wings, watching,' soothed Sharon, her heart breaking for him.

'Will you? I'm really glad you're here. I think you're the greatest.' He squeezed her hand, then walked over to the dressing table. A little cellophane packet was tucked next to a tissue box. 'Back in a sec… ' he winked, and disappeared into the WC.

Sharon sighed. She figured he was getting some chemical help. But then, who was she to criticise? After all, she wasn't going outside to face 200,000 screaming people.

There was a tentative knock on the door. 'How's my boy doing?' asked the manager. 'Are you ready for it?'

Jaz emerged from the WC at the same time, bouncing out with a big grin and high fives to everyone. He ripped off his T-shirt and pulled on the silk blouse, staring at himself in a large, bare-light-bulb stage mirror as he buttoned it up.

'Shaz, come here, what d'you think?' Sharon walked over, and stood just behind him, looking at the two of them in the glass. Her heart lurched as she suddenly remembered the mirror in Dr. Marvel's clinic.

Now here she was, the girlfriend of one of the biggest stars in the country, and he was asking for her opinion on his stage outfit. Would he have given a damn what she thought in the old world? No way. She wouldn't have even got an autograph from his roadie. Pushing away the negative vibes she answered him.

'I love it. Fab colour on you'.

Jaz turned, pecked her on the cheek, and simply said, 'See you later… It's Showtime!' and slapped his manager on the back. The two turned and left the room. Unsure what to do or where they were supposed to stand, both Sharon and Debbie trailed behind, flashing their Access All Areas at all and sundry. They parked themselves in the wings, beside a mammoth speaker.

The lion roar of the audience was so strong it was physical. Jaz was blown a few steps back… then he came forward, and bowed.

The band opened with the deafening decibels of 'I'm Just a Jester', his first solo number one, and Jaz illuminated the world around him. Electrifying charisma shot off him like a superhero. He only had to look in a direction for the crowds to scream in response. A cheeky wink here, a saucy bum pose there… he was conquering the universe.

Shaz was entranced. Blown away. Was the little-boy-lost in the dressing room really the confident entertainer straddling the stage like a Colossus?

As his silk shirt floated in the breeze, and the lights bathed him in a golden glow, she watched the fans surge forward, time and time again, desperate for a touch of his hand. She smiled secretly, knowing exactly where that hand had been, and where it was probably going to be that night. It was an unbelievable thrill to know he was hers. As he turned and blew a kiss to her just before his fourth single, a hit ballad entitled 'Cup Cakes', Sharon exploded with euphoria. He glanced to the side of the stage at least four times during the song, and she knew he was letting her know he was singing it to her.

Unfortunately, she was so excited as he trilled *'You're the one for me, we have to be, I need you to see…'* Sharon simply needed to pee.

'Debs, I'm desperate. Where can I go for a wee?'

Debbie leaned against the manager and whispered in his ear. Not taking his eyes off the stage, he indicated to go down some stairs and turn right. Sharon raced off, determined to miss nothing.

On her return to the wings, she heard the packed fields clamouring for an encore. Two songs later he had revved them up so much, fans were burning and crashing, being carried over the heads of security to the safety of the perimeter.

'Goodnight, God bless, and be GREAT!' yelled Jaz, ripping off his blue shirt and waving it above his head in a farewell salute. His incredibly fit, tattooed torso gleamed with sweat as he flung it into the grasping crowds. Screams went up as it was torn from hand to hand, the lights went out, and Jaz raced off backstage, a hundred backstage hands clapping him on the shoulders, shaking his hands, all wanting to touch the glistening, golden god.

'Let's go!' is all he said to Sharon, and she dutifully followed the entourage back to his dressing room.

'Man, you were smokin', man.' 'Wow, awesome.' 'Coolest ever.' 'Vibes amazing, man.' The accolades poured in faster than the booze poured out as band members, camera crews, record bosses and other stars surrounded him in a galaxy of star worship. Sharon hung back, waiting for him to signal whatever he wanted to do next.

Joints came out, and were passed around, little packets exchanged hands, and bottles of Jack Daniels were heavily swigged. Debbie looked right at home in the corner of the room, fag in one hand, beer bottle in another. Sharon felt awkward, and wished they were alone.

Finally, pulling on a clean T, Jaz walked over. Once again, he simply said:

'We're outta here.' He picked up a duffle bag, picked up a bottle of whisky, and picked up Sharon's hand.

'Thank you and goodnight…. Jaz has fucked off and left the building!' Everyone laughed and clapped, and he saluted farewell.

They pushed their way backstage, past major stars who were either leaving or getting ready to go on stage… en route, the same exchanges passed from artist to artist to artist.

'Hey man, you missed the after show.'

'Yeah, I bailed, man.'

'You missed it man, it was all happening.'

'Have a good one, man.'

'Cheers dude.'

'Fuck off, cunt.'

The rock 'n' roll banter that clearly said: 'We're all in the same Fame Club.'

As they hit the cooling night air, he led Sharon to a private performers' area. Fires were lit, and yurts and tepees glowed in the dark like coals. Coming to a white cone with Indian drawings on the roof, he flipped the entrance flap open, leading her inside. It was beautiful.

Moroccan, coloured-glass lamps edged the walls, and in the centre a real fire gently burned. Thick Persian rugs covered the ground, scattered with sheepskins, and, in the far corner, a raised pallet strewn with fur throws and silk beaded cushions was lit by a high stem of gothic candles. Tribal hangings decorated the walls, and on a rock by the fire stood a pot of melted chocolate and a bowl of pink and white marshmallows. It was Nirvana.

Sharon dropped her bag to the side, and sank onto the rug by the fire.

'You were fantastic,' she smiled, holding out her hand to him. 'Amazing.'

'Really?' he said coldly. 'If I was that amazing, why did you leave half way through?' Sharon was completely taken aback.

'Crikey, I'm stunned you even noticed. God…'

'Of course I noticed. But you haven't answered me. If I was that amazing, why did you fuck off?'

'I didn't "fuck off" – I went off to find a loo. I was desperate.'

'I think you were bored.' He looked at her icily.

'WHAT? I was bursting, if you must know. So excited, I had to go. What's got into you?'

'I'm pissed because you missed the best bit. The first encore.'

'For me, the best bit was when you sang to me…' she placated.

'Fucking don't know why I bothered!' he said petulantly. Sharon was lost for an answer.

He silently rolled a big, fat joint, and took a big, fat drag. As he blew the smoke up towards the fire hole in the roof, he pursed his lips, making a blowing noise. She watched, hurt and unsure what to say as his eyes closed in meditation.

After a while, he seemed to calm down visibly, as he handed her the joint. Sharon was actually far more interested in the chocolate and marshmallows, but took a small puff of the weed to show solidarity. She tried to forgive him; after all it had been a tough night.

When he opened his eyes, they looked sad, and infinitely softer.

Two joints later, and he had totally transformed.

'Sorry babe, it was great to have you there. Come here...' They curled up at the edge of the fire, and fed each other chocolate-dipped mallows toasted in the flames. As Sharon and Jaz talked through the night, she learned more about this man and what made him the way he was. They had so much in common. As she heard about his weak mother and drunken, abusive dad, she easily related to the loneliness he must have felt. The more she related, the more he opened up. And the more she learnt, the more she forgave him everything.

At times she held him in her arms, at times he cradled her. Two lost souls trying to find their way home.

Taking turns to share their pain, the night wrapped the tepee in a protective blanket. Safe inside, they swapped tales of wicked stepmothers and cold fathers until the grey morning mist broke over the sea of tents, swirling in the fresh breath of a new day.

Chapter Seventeen

The festival atmosphere was infectious, and Sharon loved it. Venturing from the tepee for fresh coffee and muffins, they wandered through the throng towards the hippy hip-hop stalls. Likewise, hundreds emerged blinking sleepily into the daylight, many dressed in bright, crazy colours and second-hand clothes. In this supercalafragelistic world, anything went with everything. Feather boas with leather bondage bodices, fairy dresses with biker boots. She even passed a man naked, except for a tutu and flip-flops.

Apart from the snap of an occasional press photographer or the click of a mobile phone held by a friendly fan, they were surprisingly left much alone to wander and enjoy themselves. Luckily, there were many other stars to watch on stage, and, besides, the laid-back atmosphere was very much the nature of the festival.

Set in the hills not far from the stone circle of Avebury, the event was divided into sections. Among others there were the Performance Zone, the Healing Zone, the Meditation Zone, the Experimental Zone, and Sharon's spiritual favourite, the Shopping Zone. Well, it wasn't actually called that, but there was no doubt in the hearts of the hordes that swarmed over the stalls that it was a dream 'retail park' for hippies.

Browsing lazily along the exotic stands, she picked up shiny bangles made of sweetie wrappers, a shaggy Indonesian bag made of wool and rags, two silk shawls beaded with mother of pearl, and a present from Jaz… a silver cirque that swept down onto the forehead in a point. At the point sat a small turquoise, like an Indian bindi. He placed it on her flaxen head, and stood back to admire. She looked like a warrior princess from the myths of time.

Meandering into the Healing Zone, there was something very appealing about the fact Jaz was up for a session of personal growth, and she stood by amused, watching him torn between two tents: an hour of Reiki by the descendant of Red Bull, or a Shiatsu massage by an aborigine with hot stones. Finally, he chose a third tent offering High Touch Jin Shin Acupressure which, according to the chalkboard outside, was known as 'the Art of the Compassionate Being'.

'Hey, Shaz – it says this is a 7,000-year-old treatment from Japan… Cool,' enthused Jaz.

As he allowed himself to be led by a kimono-clad healer through the tealight-lit petal garden into the bunting-covered yurt, Sharon sat down at the tent next door, and let an Indian woman work intricate henna flowers all the way up her curvy, plump arm. An hour later they emerged from the Zone into the throng; Jaz with his soul re-aligned, and Sharon with a pattern she'd smudged into a psychiatrist's inkblot – and one that would take weeks to wash off.

'That was an awesome experience,' said Jaz like a wondering child. 'The theoretical framework is the Chinese 5 Element System. That means Earth, Metal, Wood, Water and Fire. Which correlates to the physical, mental, emotional and spiritual levels. God, I'm starving…. Fancy a kebab?'

They laughed their way around the festival and back to the cosy, rug-strewn intimacy of the fire-lit tepee and their own little world. It was paradise.

'How about coming with me to Bali?' asked Jaz later that night, passing her a big spliff. 'We could get our union blessed by a Hindu priest. Be fun…' He was serious about her, and he was trying to show it. Sharon looked into his big, baby blue eyes, soft sensuous lips, hard rock 'n' roll body, and drifted into a wedding finale daydream.

… *She'd ask her father to walk her down the aisle, she'd throw her bouquet to Jules D. and the waiting crowds, wave to the paparazzi and ride off with her rock star on the back of a big, black Harley.*

'Sure, why not. I haven't got that much lined up… I could go in a couple of weeks. Just got to do a commercial for *Urban Cool* and a couple of shoots for Zeigfreid.'

But actually, by the time she got back from La-La Land and returned her booker's calls, the line-up was all the way round the corner and along three blocks. Now firmly linked with Jaz, she was dominating the gossip columns and showbiz rags daily.

The press attention was so intense, from snaps of the laughing pair in Vegas, to shots eating burgers in the Vegan Zone, she was the Golden Goose who kept on laying double-page spreads.

'Darling, there's nothing to fear, okay?' soothed Jules D.

'You just go on the show and chat. It's a *chat* show, okay? The man is paid a fucking fortune to make you feel relaxed, okay? That's his job.' But it was live. No matter how Jules D. dressed it up, Sharon knew going on his show she'd feel stark naked.

This particular host was witty and cutting. She'd always loved watching him tease the hell out of his guests. But to be on the other side? Insecurity and terror gripped her in equal measure.

With Glacé Inc. ringing non-stop, offers from all directions were now coming in fast and furious.

Even emptying the rubbish a week or so later became a 'Shaz Sets Style Sensation'. All she did was drag out a smelly black bin-liner of rubbish at 8am dressed in a tight black T-shirt, ankle-length, old black skirt, bare feet and a black headscarf to hide her unwashed hair. She'd donned a big pair of black sunglasses to hide the fact she wore no make-up. Overnight, the 'Greek Widow Look' was gracing the front pages of a dozen publications, with Sharon compared to the elegance of a grieving Jackie O.

Later that week, on seeing the press coverage it had provoked, Debbie, Jules D. and Sharon howled until their giggly, girly tears diluted the contents of their pink bubbly flutes to white.

The funniest comments of all were from female journalists moaning that this head-to-toe 'Widow In Black' new look slimmed down figures too much, and only big women like Shaz could really get away with wearing it. Accused of causing misery to any poor girl smaller than size 12, Sharon was even castigated by one columnist who felt she should have some responsibility as a supermodel, and stop flaunting her fabulous fuller figure.

Whatever. The press fever meant the level of attention rose higher and higher, a fact reflected by the increasing worth of the freebie handbags and shoes arriving throughout the day. The latest monstrosity from Puccinetti was a giant doctor's bag made of silver snakeskin and gold studs. The PR blurb attached pointed out it was a mere £7,000 retail.

That any woman could be foolish enough or brainwashed enough by the magazines and labels to spend more than a couple of hundred boggled Sharon's mind. But she was also aware now that, as a celeb, she was expected to 'look the part'. In return she was expected to 'play her part' in fuelling public envy and aspiration – resulting in designer-label sales. It was a symbiotic relationship that Sharon struggled to resist.

As for her relationship with Jaz, it went from strength to strength. The papers seemed to adore the rhyme *Shaz and Jaz*, repeating it ad nauseum.

Deeply attracted to him, she adored the fact he needed her. That he was mad about her was obvious from the frequent texts and emails that would punctuate her days. His dependency grew. But he had a mysterious trick of disappearing faster than Houdini, only to reappear as if nothing had happened three days later. It wasn't just her that got this kind of treatment. Debbie's man, the band manager, would ring her regularly to see if she knew where the hell Jaz was. It seemed he was always late for a photo shoot or missing a radio interview. If ever she managed to pass the message on to Jaz, he'd act paranoid.

'The bastard won't leave me alone. I swear to God, he's having me followed. I saw this guy in black the other day. Trailed behind me like a spy,' he complained.

'Could have been a fan,' reasoned Sharon.

'Nah, it's someone the fucker's hired. He thinks I'm going to sign a fucking deal behind his back, asshole.'

As for the times Jaz stood her up, poor Sharon didn't know how to handle it. Afraid to make a scene in case he thought her 'too heavy', she'd say nothing. Only to send Jaz into a furious rage that she hadn't even noticed he'd gone. Either way, she began to fret she was on to a lose/lose situation.

But then he'd do something to surprise her. Take the night she finally had to face the Nathan Boss chat show. Jaz turned up, drove her there, and sat in the green room holding her hand like it was an injured little bird he would cherish and nurture. He told her time and time again how amazing/witty/clever she was, and how she'd be the perfect guest. It was the confidence and support she needed.

As it so happened, he was right. As she stepped out to the studio applause and the band of singers welcoming her to the show, she smiled. It was fun! The nerves disappeared as Nathan kissed her warmly on both cheeks and led her to the sofa.

'Would you like something to eat…? An apple, maybe?' he opened with, cheekily offering her the fruit bowl on the table.

The audience roared at the reference to *Descent*.

Sharon shook her blonde locks, saying: 'No thanks, I ate earlier…' and glanced up at Jaz who could be seen on a screen that showed the goings-on in the green room.

The audience roared even more at the unintentional double entendre. Sharon picked up the cue, licked her finger and winked. That was it. From then on, Nathan and the Nation were putty in her paws.

By the time the floppy-haired charmer had smooched her off the stage, he was already begging her to come back in a few weeks. She stepped back into the green room flushed and excited. It had been an amazing high.

'Let's celebrate,' suggested Jaz, sweeping her off in the car and into the West End. 'I know just the place… Do you realise, we've been together exactly a month? It's perfect.'

They ended up at Waikiki's… a tackily decorated Hawaiian nightclub more renowned for young royals, Sloanes and aristos than rock stars. But that made it fun for Jaz. He was approached time and time again, with 'Jolly loved your last CD, ol' man', and the two of them practically drowned in the crazy array of coconut cocktails thrust at them from all and sundry.

As they slow-danced on the floor, and Sharon caught the eye of a young prince staring longingly at her, she shook her long hair and gave a deep, throaty laugh. How had all of this happened? The Easter Head spewing steam in the tropical pool beside them had no answer. As '*Shaz and Jaz*' shared straws in a £175 jungle-green concoction, and pinned flowers behind each other's ears, they recalled the night they met, in equally ridiculous tropical surroundings.

'Oh how I miss that Banana dress,' moaned Jaz, teasingly.

'I know… you're dreaming of peeling it off me!' Sharon flirted back.

Later that night he teased her in a far more merciless way, and after, like a pair of spent puppies, they fell asleep content and warm in each other's arms.

…Until the cool air hit Sharon's bare flank.

Chapter Eighteen

Feeling chilled, she sleepily stretched out to find the duvet and Jaz's warm body. But it wasn't there. She opened one eye to see the light under the bathroom door spreading out like rays from a spaceship. She lay there a while, looking at the bachelor pad of a rock star. It was messy. Black walls, cans of beer, discarded T-shirts. Very reminiscent of the backstage dressing rooms he frequented.

In the kitchen she knew washing up was piled on the draining board, and cigarette butts and tea bags left brown stains on the aluminium sink. On the wall hung a giant Andy Warhol painting of Keith Richards, his ultimate hero. The bookshelves brimmed with rock 'n' roll memorabilia, and the hard floor was strewn with Tibetan rugs and leather poufs.

A mess, but nothing she couldn't sort out in an afternoon, she smiled. Jaz was taking quite a while, and Sharon suddenly had the urge to pee. Well, just in case he came back and wanted to have her again.

Throwing on his white, collarless shirt, as she knew it gave her a sexy 'girlfriend of boyfriend' look, she padded over to the bathroom, and put her hand down on the door handle.

'No! Not now. Just… go away,' followed by a moan.

'Jaz?' she asked, 'what's wrong? It's me…' Alarmed, she pushed the door open a little, worried he'd hurt himself, but it wouldn't budge, held in place by something spongy. Peering through the crack, she could see it was his foot.

'What's going on… are you hurt?'

'I said, FUCK OFF! I mean it… don't come in.'

'Don't be daft, let me in!' said Sharon, all the fears of something 'not being right' flooding her mind. She still reeled from the last time she'd stood at a door, and found her man in the middle of a gang-bang. With that image in mind, she gave the door an extra hard shove and Jaz let out an angry yowl.

Sharon stood in the doorway, looking at him sprawled on the floor. Between his legs lay a couple of red, plastic-topped vials, and on the tile next to them, little cubes of beige soap. Or was it sugar? Sharon bent down to see what he was doing. That was when she noticed he was awkwardly holding his hand behind his back.

'What are you hiding?' she asked. He looked like a guilty toddler caught with a packet of sweeties. Then, suddenly, he didn't. And his face changed, contorting into an ugly sneer.

'Aw, what the fuck. You were bound to find out soon enough. Fair cop.' He held up a glass instrument. Sharon then noticed the strange long lighter in his other hand. A sick feeling churned her stomach. It was drugs. *Serious* drugs.

Jaz kept flicking the little lumps across the floor like a game of tiddlywinks. 'Rocks… sugar… ice… twinkie… It's called getting your rocks off. After all, baby, it's ROCK 'N' ROLL!' He laughed, hollowly.

Sharon slumped down, her heart raced. 'It's cocaine, isn't it?'

'Crack. Crack cocaine, darlin'. The best.'

Crack? Surely that was the drug of gangsters and yardies? Quietly, in shock, she asked with dread, 'How long have you been taking it?'

'Umm… let me see. Well, I guess it's got to be pretty much full on from my first smoke …err, three or four months, I guess. Who knows?'

'We've got to get you help! You can't keep taking it. It'll kill you.'

He looked at her bemused. Ignoring her, he lit the burner in his hand and took a hit. She felt totally out of her depth. The closest experience Sharon had had with drug dependency was a packet of Panadol for period pain.

She sat on the cold floor watching him, lost for words. It all slowly made sense. At the beginning, feeling herself daring, she'd joined him in a spliff or two, and accepted he snorted the odd line, which she had been hoping to tackle him about once they were even closer and more 'established'. But *this*? It explained so much. His mood swings, his aggression… and even the weird little burn marks on his fingers that he had joked were down to him being a lousy cook.

It scared her so much. This abuse was way out of control. As the drug hit his brain, Jaz laid his head against the toilet and closed his eyes in pleasure. He had gone somewhere else.

A minute of silence later, Sharon decided she had to do the same. And left.

This time it hurt. It really hurt. Sharon went into her own depression. Not even the feeding drip of chocolate doughnuts and crispy croissants from Jules D. could lift the dank feeling of despair. It was tinged with the awful urge to 'do' something about it. To help him in any way she could, even though she had read enough articles to know 'addicts have to help themselves'. Debbie was deeply worried for Sharon, and rang her from Jaz's manager's pad three or four times a day.

Jules D. was already working on a damage limitation 'break-up' story, even though Sharon told her she was going to stand by him.

As for Jaz, he was silent for two whole mysterious days. Then he started emailing, texting and ringing every hour, on the hour. Sharon took his first call, and asked him if he would get help. He agreed. The next he said he'd changed his mind, and told her to 'fuck off'. The third, he cried for forgiveness. The fourth, he begged her to come over. The fifth, he swore because she hadn't come, and called her a whore. The sixth… she hung up the second she heard his voice.

'He's so, so lost. Like a little boy. I can't abandon him, can I?' sobbed Sharon to Jules D. and Debbie. They just looked at each other helplessly, pity in their eyes, and no words in their mouths.

The dilemma Sharon found herself in was utter hell. Loving, talented and fun, the man was like a drug himself. They were both famous, both successful. But mutual experiences and low self-esteem bound them to each other tighter than an addict's tourniquet.

Oh God, he was *her* heroin, cried Sharon, hugging herself to sleep in a foetal position of anguish. And indeed he was. Her moods would alter like a condor in a canyon – up and down, up and down, riding the very air he breathed. He could change the current in a flash of crack – one moment she was soaring high only to be sucked back into the deep abyss of despair. Sharon tried to focus on work, but found she was sleepwalking through important castings and forgetting to return calls.

Her head told her to get out now. Before she got too involved. But instead, she spent hours and hours scouring the Internet trying to find out the success rate of coming off crack. It didn't look good. 'Harder to crack than heroin.' Maybe that's why they called it crack, she sighed, miserably. Then he went silent again, for another two days.

When the phone rang at 1.00 am and she heard Jaz crying and pleading with her to pick up the phone, she had no choice. He sounded so desperate. Completely out of it.

'Babe… oh God, I need you. Please, please come and get me. I… I love you. God, love you so much. I can't do without you. Please, I'll give it all up, I promise. Just come and get me…' She knew she had to go. She tried to work out the rambling address he'd given her on the street map as Debbie drove her car down Hackney High Road. His manager wanted to get him, but Jaz had *insisted* he stayed away.

It was down to Sharon to go – with Debbie for moral support.

'I'm going to stick by him,' announced Sharon as her friend screeched round the corners like a demented bat. 'No one else ever has, and I'm going to show him I will.'

Her resolve to help him was strengthened by the fact he had actually used the 'love' word for the first time. Admittedly, it wasn't in quite the Mills and Boon setting she had hoped for, but he obviously cared. The hard fact was, she'd missed him badly – and, needing her own fix, couldn't wait to see him again. But now the two girls were terrified. Following the garbled instructions, they found that the streets got more and more deserted, the area swiftly turning shabby and destitute.

'Oh God, it's here.' They looked at each other, wide-eyed and fearful. The wet street shone in the nicotine-yellow lamplight, iron stairwells and soggy cardboard boxes slumped against brick walls covered with graffiti. A drunken tramp eyed them suspiciously as they got out of the car – Debbie, ridiculous in a pair of red stiletto Manolos, Sharon ready to run in a pair of old trainers.

She pressed the dirty buzzer. No one answered. But the latch on the door was broken, so they pushed it open and walked up the harsh, concrete stairs. It was disgusting. The smell of urine and vomit assaulted the nostrils. A pile of soiled nappies permeated the landing, the surrounding steps littered with used condoms and a scattering of syringes. Picking their way up to the second floor flat, 2b, they walked in.

There must have been about seven people lying around the squalid room. A couple were burning a light under a spoon as they sat on a springless sofa so badly stained it was more brown than its original orange. It was so dark, it was hard to tell if the shapes in the room were all people; two or three were so skeletal they looked like a pile of discarded clothes.

'Babe, you made it…' croaked a voice in the corner. And there he was, dazed and smiling like Dopey in *Snow White*. The kitchen door opened and a violent-looking Korean in combat gear and tattoos emerged with a thick-set black guy in tow.

'Hey, bitch, who the hell let you in here?' said the Korean, pulling out a knife.

'Cool it, man. She's my girl,' said Jaz proudly, as if introducing Sharon to the in-laws. He staggered to his feet like Bambi on ice. Indeed, as he stood up, Sharon could see he clearly was 'on ice'. And something else, even worse. A syringe slipped off his lap and clattered to the filthy floor. Disney? This was pure Tarantino.

'My God! Jaz… what have you been doing to yourself?'

'He's been havin' a fun time with the Cotton Brothers…' laughed the black guy. 'Dynamite, man… like you, Shaz.' Sharon felt sick just hearing him say her name, the real price of household fame.

'Have you got any cash…?' asked Jaz lamely. 'My friends want me to give them some.'

Stricken, the girls looked at each other. The Korean walked over and put his grubby-finger nailed hand under Sharon's chin. He tilted it up to his pockmarked face and smiled. A whoosh of foul breath escaped his blackened, rotting teeth. 'Your boy's been criss-crossing the line, ladies, and owes us a ton,' he hissed like a snake.

'Criss-crossing?' repeated Sharon, confused.

'He's a regular speedball artist… hey, Jaz – you been keeping secrets from your lady? How'd you 'spect to form a relationship?' He snorted with laughter, thinking the whole situation highly amusing, and ran his eye over Sharon's body. '…Hey, you're that fuckin' fancy model, aren't you? Jackson, where are your manners, man!?' The least we can do is explain to the lovely lady…' He turned and slapped the black guy on the back, who joined in the fun. Like a teacher explaining the facts to a dyslexic child, he spelt out the truth.

'Okay, baby, lesson one. You've just busted into a one and one. That means a house that serves its honoured "guests" heroin and crack.

'Lesson two. Your boy here likes both. It's called speedballing.'

'He's injecting *heroin*?' Sharon gasped, stating the obvious but desperate to be told she was making a big mistake.

'That's right, sweet cheeks, the candy brings you up, and the smack mellows you out. Up and down… quite a ride. Ever tried?'

'Inject, smoke, smoke, inject, what the hell…' groaned Jaz groggily. 'Shaz, please just give the man the fuckin' dosh.'

Sharon looked at the squalid mess her boyfriend sat in the middle of. His lank, greasy hair, sick-soiled clothes, the cesspit surroundings – and the paraphernalia of death. She helped him to his feet and simply handed her bag to the Korean.

'Hey, what the fuck's this shit? I want money. Two hundred quid. NOW.'

'It's worth £7,000,' she replied coldly. 'I'm sure you'll get 10 times what he owes you on the black market.' The men grinned in delight.

'Nice doin' business with you, honey. Fancy a takeaway?' asked the Korean, offering her a grimy cellophane packet. 'It's on the house…' They cackled like a pair of happy hyenas as they held up her bag to the single, bare light bulb, to check out its designer label.

Dragging Jaz between them, the girls hobbled past and out, down the fetid stairwell, into the cool night air. The putrid smell continued to fill their nostrils as Sharon shoved Jaz into the back seat. The stench of his vomit and shit killed any hope of a future relationship. Hooked on crack was a living nightmare. Hooked on heroin was the road to hell. But hooked on *both*? Rehab was a daydream. The man was too far gone to ever make it home.

He knew it. And she knew it.

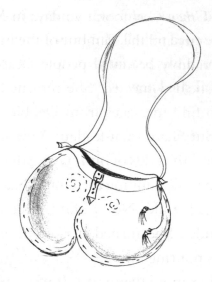

Chapter Nineteen

...She'd asked her father to walk her down the aisle; she'd thrown her bouquet to Jules D. and the waiting crowds, waved to the paparazzi and ridden off with her rock star on the back of a big, black Harley. Then there was the scream of police sirens. They were pulled over by the cops, and strip-searched.

It was a strange phenomenon. With every downturn of her love life, the higher her work life soared. As the tabloids began to splutter with speculation about the demise of '*Shaz and Jaz*', the invitations and offers kept tumbling in.

The shoot for *Urban Cool* took two days in Manchester, and the buzz of a new city and the glamour of the impossibly trendy shoot full of incredibly beautiful people cleared her mind of the fetid scenes she'd witnessed. She returned to her London flat exhausted, to find messages from Debbie. Jaz had booked into the Priory. But Sharon felt leaden. With such a cocktail of addiction, she knew the odds of him staying the course were less than a one-legged mule winning the Grand National. Make that a blind, one-legged mule. No, a blind, pregnant, one-legged mule with 'attitude'. She turned her attention to the pile of letters and emails pouring in.

One amused her more than most. It was a plea from a pupil from Saint Martin's College who had sent Sharon illustrations and photos of her end-of-year collection – a cute range of clothes with an iconic cowboy theme. The student begged Sharon to design her own bag to accessorise the show.

She was flattered. What the hell did she know about design? But then, glancing at some of the freebie monstrosities piled in the corner of the living room, she smiled mischievously. A couple of bags had even come with matching purses full of money – not-so-subtle bribes for her to use them. No question, the whole 'celebrity bag' thing was created to fool the public into drooling over celebrity photos, or, even more incredibly, parting with huge amounts of money. And to think she had once been on the other side, envying the women who could afford these luxuries. Luxuries that probably only cost a 100th of their publicised price to make. Suddenly, she felt like mooning the designers. The 'buttock' bag, she giggled. That's what I want to make. She studied her behind in the mirror. Two very large, creamy globes, with deep dimples at the small of her back.

She scrawled her design on a piece of paper, and posted it back to the student.

Five days later, together with a letter asking for her approval, Sharon opened a parcel and pulled out a large, soft, supple, leather bag in the rounded W shape of a curvaceous bottom. It was a peachy tan suede with two stitched circles at the top where she'd made the dimple marks. The long, adjustable riding strap meant you could wear it across your body, or on your arm. It reminded her of a well-worn saddlebag and smelt deliciously of saddle soap. She loved it. A hand-made one-off, it looked amazing, and she wore it out that night with a pair of riding boots and an Australian bush hat. By morning, it was in every paper.

'SHAZ GIVES JAZ THE BUM'S RUSH!'
'BOTTOMS UP SHAZ!'
'BUTTOCK BAG GIVES STUDENT LEG-UP.'

and so on…

With the Tent Dress, the Tatters Look and the Greek Widow fad still all the rage, the addition of the Buttock Bag prompted a surprise request through Glacé Inc. for lunch with Michael Grey – the entrepreneur behind *Bessie B's*, a chain of boutiques found in every British high street.

'The thing is Shaz,' he said, pouring her a third glass of Chateau Latour, 'you've got that undeniable "it" thing going. Kids love you. They want to be you… I'd like to bottle it.'

Sharon wasn't sure where he was going with this, but, as he waffled on, she tucked heartily into her Scottish fillet on nutmeg mash and caramelised shallots. With all the stress over Jaz, she hadn't eaten for a few hours, and now she was making up for it with gusto. By the time she'd finished her maple leaf treacle and clotted cream tart and polished off coffee and petite eight, the smooth talker had produced a contract for her to 'think about'.

She eyed it curiously. It was the offer of a range of clothes bearing *her* name. It seemed so simple. All she had to do was give the designs the 'once over' and agree to model the collections four times a year. The amount for this 'exclusive designing' was awesome. The repetitive zeros on the last line looked like his PA had got her fingernail stuck in the keyboard.

'But I've got to be honest, Mr. Grey. I'm just a model. I know nothing about design.'

'What about your Buttock Bag?'

'That was a joke! The student wanted something to give publicity to her show. A one-off. I had no idea it would look so good.'

'A joke, eh? You *cheeky*, *cheeky* girl!' He snorted, even more pleased with his own. 'I think you underestimate yourself, young lady. Anyway, design, schmezine! Who cares?! It's how you wear the clothes that counts, Shaz. It's what you stand for. Just a model? So sweet.'

'Don't you worry your pretty little head; we'll do all the hard work.'

Then he winked conspiratorially. 'All I want you to do is just tell us your favourite looks *before* you get photographed in them, that sort of thing. Keep us ahead of the game, y'know.'

Actually, Sharon didn't know. Not a clue. How the hell could she have guessed the ripped dress would have caused such a storm? Or the back-of-the-wardrobe pile of black crap she'd thrown on to empty the rubbish? But she nodded back with a confidential wink of her stunning, long-lashed green eye, and the steel heart of Mr. Grey turned molten. The deal was done.

Later, as she was sitting at an outside table in Soho's Bar Italia relating the meeting to Debbie and Jules D., she realised what good friends they'd all become. The laughter tinkled in the air, as Jules joshed Debbie for having a fruit salad instead of a Danish pastry. 'Darling girl, you've been doing so well, don't weaken. You're going to fade back into a size 8 or something. Sharon, the girl has *no* willpower to eat. And I envy her!'

'I am what I am. I've always been slim,' smiled Debbie, 'and luckily my man likes it that way.'

Jules eyed her fruit salad enviously, 'Mmm, that pineapple looks good. I really fancy the fresh taste… can I just have a spoonful? Just a teensy one…?'

'Anyway, Debs, how's it going with… err…?' asked Sharon, realising in deep embarrassment that she didn't even know the name of Debbie's manager boyfriend. She had only known him as 'that bastard' or 'the fucker', thanks to Jaz's paranoia.

'Jack. His name is Jack Delany,' said Debbie, hurt. Sharon apologised with a quip about early Alzheimer's, but she caught a look from Jules D. that warned her she was falling into the celebrity trap of self-absorption. It was an easy thing to do. As a 'celeb' everybody asked about *you* all the time. How do you feel? What do you think? What are you doing next? And the awful truth was, when your life was more colourful than an opium butterfly, everyone else's news sounds pretty mundane in comparison. Generally speaking, the barbecue at the brother-in-law's or the boss's bad habits didn't make for natural conversation after questions about dating movie stars or filming in Hollywood. So it was easier for the famous to stop asking. And once they stopped taking an interest in others, the more self-centred they became - the more the world revolved around their brilliant, shining sun. But Sharon knew it was wrong.

Besides, she did care about Debbie, and she was keen to hear (now she had time) what was going on.

'Well, biggest news is, he's asked me to meet his parents!' The girls squealed in delight for her. It seemed so un-rock 'n' roll, it was hysterical, and they fell about imagining his folks were either going to be like Sharon and Ozzy Osbourne, or the Waltons.

Then Debbie went quiet… 'The other news is… is not good. And I don't know how to tell you this, Sharon?'

Sharon indicated her to go on, regardless.

'I'm so sorry, but Jack told me just before us meeting up that Jaz has done a bunk. Disappeared from the Priory. Probably be in the papers by tomorrow, if they can't find him soon.'

Sharon's shoulders slumped. She had known this would happen, but nonetheless, when he entered the rehab clinic he'd lit a tiny matchstick of hope for her; a small glimmering flame that, against all the odds, just maybe he'd stick it out. Clean up his act. With this latest news, the flame blew out – the dark trail left behind symbolic of their relationship finally going up in smoke.

'There is ab-sol-ute-ly nothing you can do for him, okay? It's his journey. Rock 'n' roll is all very well, darling, but let's be frank - you don't want to be seen hanging around a junkie,' said Jules with stark honesty.

Sharon winced at the word 'junkie', but knew its truth.

Jules took a sip of strong coffee, and continued, 'You could lose contracts worth millions, he could just drag you down. I'm not sure I could even stop Z&ZaK from cancelling. I mean, it's not like you're in too deep. Get out now. Onward and upward, okay?' Finishing her speech, she patted Sharon's hand in comfort.

'Anyway, changing the subject before you can cry, this'll bring a smile to your gorgeous face…' She handed Sharon an envelope. As she pulled out a thick invitation, tiny crystals spilled over the table like baby tears.

Seeing Sharon's sadness well up, Jules snatched it back off her – 'Right, listen to this… you are invited to the Crystal Ball Gala! Hollywood's biggest "charity do". Glamour! Film Stars! Directors! Producers! Everybody will be there… and get this. You're not just going as a guest, you're going as a prize in the charity auction!'

'I'm going as a *what*?' said Sharon, choking on her coffee éclair.

'The prize, darling.'

'The prize is a kiss from *you*!' Debbie interrupted. 'Jules said you had the option of a kiss or a date, and I figured "kiss" was safer. God knows who you could end up with otherwise, boring you all night. I thought you'd prefer just giving a kiss.'

'Oh my God, guys, how do you know I'd prefer doing anything? You should have asked me first.'

Jules D. looked affronted. 'But I know your diary, you're free, and it's going to be such FUN. Besides, it's for a good cause.'

'Yes, think of the charity. *Hands Across America*, or something…' interrupted Debbie again.

'No, it's *Reaching Home*,' corrected Jules D. 'Helping runaway kids call home. The Ball is always amazing, darling – biggest event of the year. It's such a fab event, to be honest, even I can't wait!'

'Well, I'm glad you two are so excited, whilst I get auctioned off like some kind of fat cow.' They both looked at her, startled.

'What's the matter? What's wrong?'

'I just don't want to do it, okay. You should have asked me first.' The three fell silent. Jules D. signalled to the waiter to bring another round of drinks.

'Darling, what's wrong? Explain the problem…'

Sharon looked pained as she tried.

'Have either of you considered the hideously embarrassing thought that nobody will actually bid for me?' They both looked at her as if she was totally insane.

'You are kidding us, aren't you?' said Jules D., puzzled.

Sharon wasn't. Beneath the veneer and success, her childlike insecurity meant a part of her still believed she was plain old Sharon Plunkett, from Accounts Filing.

'For a top model, you sometimes say the stupidest things,' said Debbie, as if stating the obvious.

'Now, your dress…' continued Jules D. dismissing Sharon's fears as clearly the ramblings of a mad woman. 'Zeigfreid has told me he's going to create something utterly sensational just for you – he wants you to be the Belle of the Ball. Which isn't easy considering we're talking Hollywood, and mega-competition'.

'Let me guess, this is all happening because another one of your clients is organising the event?' said Sharon, relaxing a little, their enthusiasm thawing her doubts.

'Naturally,' said Jules D. shamelessly, as if insulted it should be any other way.

'Your network web would shame a Black Widow!' laughed Sharon, her mood lifting. 'Okay, when do we leave?'

The days leading up to the ball were pretty busy. Sharon signed the exchange contract on a chi-chi little mews house in Chelsea, and, to the delight of Glacé Inc., concentrated on her castings and bookings. For a girl who once thought the height of travel was a ride on a Ferris wheel, she was rarely off a plane now. Debbie, working full time as her PA, made the trips far more fun than travelling on her own, and the whirl around her continued to swirl.

The papers broke the story of Jaz, found comatose in a gutter by a prostitute. Everyone had sympathy for Shaz, and totally understood why she had walked. Now it was clear the relationship was over and she was exonerated, she even had the courage to call Simon, though painfully aware she was publicly in 'break-up' mode again. He never said a word about it. Instead, he just invited her for a drink at *The Pissed Piggy*, a cosy pub that served good food and real beer, and had a roaring fire lit nearly all year round. Sharon turned up dressed in black, straight jeans, crisp shirt and waistcoat. Dressing carefully, she deliberately put on pointed boots as she knew they added a few pounds to her thighs.

Simon looked as cool as usual. Straight, sandy-brown hair flopping over his eyes, black leather jacket, soft, faded, blue jeans.

As always, she felt immediately comfortable with him. The humour always there between them. Luck was with them, the seats by the fire were empty, and they sat chatting about the ridiculous Vegas wedding, his trip to LA, her commercials and adverts. But any discussion that could lead to their love lives was pointedly avoided.

'Well, well, well… is that the famous Buttock Bag?' he laughed, noticing it hanging on the back of her chair after they'd downed a couple more drinks. 'Can I caress it?'

Sharon offered it to him, smiling in the flickering light, her hair a pinky red in the glow – which was a good thing, as she knew she was blushing scarlet.

As he ran his hands over the suede, he looked at her – his eyes narrowing. And they both fell silent – shocked as each suddenly imagined him doing it to the real thing. Sharon felt her stomach contract, and her throat go dry. She stared at the perfect shape of his lips, and couldn't speak.

'Why did you go off with him?' asked Simon huskily. Sharon didn't know what to say, gulping back her spritzer to buy time.

'Oh, Simon. I was flattered. He was… was so keen.' She carefully avoided adding the words 'and gorgeous'.

'And world famous,' sighed Simon, pulling back.

'Well, there is that.' Sharon broke into a grin. They both started to laugh, and then pushed and poked each other, teasing.

'Fame hag!' insulted Simon.

'Better than being a "worthy" drag!' threw back Sharon.

The evening was fantastic. A night full of banter and fun. But Sharon noticed he was starting to act like a big brother or a great mate. Slinging his arm around her shoulder, he insisted on buying her dinner, but was not intimate again – the intense moment with the Buttock Bag was a one-off.

It also worried Sharon that when they talked about her success, he did so as if she was somehow out of his league. How could she broach this? What could she say to counteract it, without sounding conceited? The words never came the whole evening, and when he dropped her off and kissed her pointedly on her cheek, she felt at a loss.

Apart from Simon, the other important phone call she made was to her father. He had left a message way back saying he wanted her to ring, but every time she called, she either got the answer-phone or Carolyn saying he was asleep.

She decided to drive down to Bournemouth and tried one more call to say she was coming down.

'Hello, can I speak to...' but as always Carolyn cut her off before she even had the chance to finish.

'I'll get your father,' she said, colder than the Ice Queen.

'Hello, darling,' said her dad in his whispery, old man's voice.

'I hear you're doing well? As your agent, where's my cut? I only want 80%, I'm not greedy,' he jested, voice fading with the effort.

Pretending to be her agent had always been their long-standing joke, ever since she started her £10-a-day Saturday job in the hair salon.

'Cheque's in the post, Dad,' she laughed back, knowing he was probably unaware she had a real agent who was now getting thousands.

'Darling, I hate to mention this, but I didn't get the keys to the new Ferrari – post has been really bad, dear. Best to bring the cheque down with you!' He seemed on form, smiled Sharon, also pleased he mentioned her coming down.

'That's what I was ringing about. Thought I'd pop down this weekend.'

'Okay. (Big pause.) Just a minute. I'd better check with Carolyn.' She heard a muffle as he put his hand over the receiver.

'Carolyn, can Sharon come down this weekend?' Sharon hated the way her father always had to ask her stepmother for the normal right to visit her dad.

'No Joe. We've got my family coming, remember?'

'No, when did you organise that?'

'Well, I was going to do it this afternoon.'

Sharon bristled, knowing her dad didn't realise she could hear.

'Hello darling, it's a little difficult this weekend. Though I'd love to see you.'

'Right then, I'm coming *now*,' said Sharon. 'I'll see you in a couple of hours.'

'Oh, lovely…' said her father, a little confused, but obviously delighted he would be getting to see his daughter so soon.

Alas, the traffic down to Bournemouth was appalling. The weather had turned nasty and rain made the visibility almost nil. Exacerbated by road works, jams from the Southampton Junction onwards made progress excruciatingly slow. As hailstones bounced off her new silver BMW (on loan via a client of Jules D.), she wondered what her father would make of her success. Her mother had always made him proud. Now, maybe she would.

Five hours later, she was in tears. The road had seized up tighter than a rusty lid of homemade pickles, and her car was sandwiched between lanes with no way off. She rang her dad to apologise…

'Don't worry, dear… I can't wait to see you. I'll wait up.'

But by the time she walked up to the door of her father's crumbling Victorian house she was drained, hungry and tired, and it was nearly nine o'clock at night. Carolyn's sour face as she opened the door made Sharon's heart plummet.

'Hi Dad,' she called out brightly, seeing a shape coming up behind her. Her father hobbled towards the door, leaning heavily on his brass, dog-head walking stick.

She was taken aback at how frail and skinny he looked since she last saw him, and was careful to hide her reaction.

'Darling, I've been so worried about you, I thought you were coming straight down?' he said, concerned.

'Oh God, dad. You would't believe the traffic. Horrendous. Tried to get here as fast as I could.'

'Well, that's strange,' said her father. 'Carolyn told me her friend came down this afternoon and the traffic was straight through. No problems.'

What!? Sharon felt her temper flare and fought to control her tongue. Oh, there were problems all right. And it was Carolyn up to her usual manipulative mind games. More lies to make her out to be the 'bad daughter'.

'No, Dad, believe me – I've just spent hours in a bloody awful traffic jam down the A3. Got even worse after Ringwood. Tried every single side road down here… all blocked.'

'But that's so odd. Carolyn…?' he turned to ask. But she had disappeared.

'So, Dad, what's been happening?' asked Sharon. They sat at the kitchen table and chatted as Carolyn returned and placed some cold meat cuts in front of them. It wasn't long before her father confessed he'd been booked in for some serious tests. He was losing weight. He didn't know why. Worried, Sharon gave him a warm hug, and was shocked by the skin and bone that once used to pick her up and toss her into the air.

She hoped they would retire to the antique-stuffed living room for a cosy bed-time drink, but instead her father apologised.

'Darling, I'm so tired, do you mind if I go to bed?' he asked, giving her a gentle kiss on the forehead. 'I believe Carolyn's got the room made up for you.' Sharon turned to see a wicked glint in his wife's eye.

'Joe, I really don't want to touch the guest bedroom as I'll have to do it all over again when the family arrive. So I've put a camp bed up in the office.'

Sharon knew it was a deliberate snub that her father was either too gutless to stop, or too insensitive to see. Either way, he said nothing and tottered off towards his own bedroom.

Smug with her little victory, Carolyn silently led Sharon past the pretty pink guest room towards the cold office at the end of the house. In it, next to the filing cabinet, was a single camp bed on iron, pull-out legs. Her father had retired to bed without a word about the sleeping arrangements, pretending not to notice the cruel snub. The man was so weak it broke Sharon's heart time and time again. She lay in bed, trying to convince herself that he was simply just too naïve to see through his wife's clever little games.

She remembered the first time he'd brought Carolyn and her children home. *Haughty, high-cheek-boned and heavily made-up, the woman looked like the Wicked Stepmother from a Disney movie. Nonetheless, it all started so well. Originally her new 'mother-to-be' had been a paragon of kindness to her, fussing over her like her own two daughters, doing motherly things like taking them all shopping together. An elegant, beautifully dressed woman, Sharon remembered that time she offered to style her hair. Though it had to be said the flick fringe did nothing for her, she agreed happily, finding herself behaving like a desperate puppy seeking praise and affection. With her mother gone, she felt so alone and abandoned and had badly wanted Carolyn to love her like own daughters.*

She knew her father was so keen to make a new family home for everyone, especially his precious child, he told her. So what did he do? Get engaged within six months, and married within a year. But the day he put the ring on Carolyn's finger, he put a rope around Sharon's neck. Secure in the marriage, Carolyn swiftly revealed her true colours. And they were all darker than black.

Sharon shuddered with the memory. She called that period 'the Change.' The atmosphere in the house altered dramatically. Her stepmother's sudden coldness towards her coupled with a truly vicious temper was a shock. Feeling there must be something deeply unlovable about herself, Sharon had tried everything to try and win her over. She'd even agonised for days about how to give her stepmother a Mother's Day card that meant something, but wouldn't betray the memory of Sharon's own mother.

Settling on writing the endearment 'Dear Ma', she thought it would show Carolyn that she cared and wanted to be loved as a daughter. She had fervently hoped the woman would melt a little, and show some warmth towards her like she did towards her own children.

Excited, Sharon remembered how she had come into their bedroom on the morning and tentatively placed the card on the silk eiderdown. Carolyn picked it up with her daughters' cards. But Sharon had made a terrible mistake. For when the woman finally read Sharon's, instead of the hug she had hoped for, Carolyn's face frowned, she tore the card up and shouted at her for calling her 'Ma' - it was 'common', she spat. Her name was 'Carolyn'. And that was what she wanted to be called.

As Sharon lay sobbing, clutching her pillow like a lifebelt, her father had stroked her hair, and confided something that only made the matter worse. His new wife had confessed that, after their first date, her dream life had been to be with him and her own daughters on a desert island. Insensitively, he thought this information would help, telling his little girl it wasn't her fault; she had never been included in Carolyn's picture, and therefore she shouldn't take the rejection personally. But she was only eleven years old. Too young to understand. How could she? She felt more unwanted than ever. The feeling had stayed with her ever since…

It was turning into a bad night. Sharon tossed and turned, plumping up the thin pillow as best she could. But the memories were hard to blot out…

When she was fourteen, Uncle Albert, a lovely man who'd been her dad's friend for centuries, had taken her aside one day, taking pity on her because of the way she was being treated. It seemed the real trouble was clear to all of her father's old friends who watched sadly from the wings.

'Listen, little one... you have to be a grown-up and try to understand. Your father's wife is more insecure than a tin-pot dictator.'

Sharon had asked him to explain more.

'Thing is, your dad adored your mum. Let's face it, she was a very special lady, hard act for anyone to follow. Carolyn is only too aware.'

Sharon recalled how Albert looked around him nervously, knowing he was speaking out of turn.

'Please, go on...' Sharon had begged, keen to understand what she was doing wrong.

'Your only "fault" is you look like your mother. She's jealous, Sharon. Jealous of Joe's love for your mother. I know your dad well, and I don't think your father has ever got over her. Carolyn knows this, of course. She knows she can never compete. The whole of Bournemouth knows it. Unfortunately for you, little one – you look the spitting image of your mother. I think it's driving the woman mad.'

Albert was right. Carolyn took it out on her with a scolding mood that would flare at the slightest cause. Leave a jumper on the chintz sofa... drop a spoon on the wooden floor... Sharon learnt to walk on eggshells, but often missed her step simply through nerves. Every time, the results would be a shattering telling-off.

The bedsprings dug into her shoulder blades like blunt knives. But they were not as sharp as the pain she felt as she allowed herself to remember the whole past.

Ahh, the grand finale, thought Sharon bitterly. The day Carolyn gave away Beau, her little dog. Sharon was on a school trip, and returned to find him gone. No warning, no words.

The woman had given him to her parents, people Sharon barely knew and rarely saw. Beau had been her companion since she was seven. And the only tie left to her past family life. How she had cuddled him when her mother died. How he had licked and snuggled her through all the tears. She still missed him now.

With the only thing left to love gone, and her older stepsisters determined to make her feel like the outsider, life for Sharon became a lonely, living hell. It was compounded two years later when Carolyn triumphantly announced she was pregnant, and, like a fat cuckoo, threw Sharon out as soon as she turned sixteen.

The memories of those days caused a night of pain far deeper than the cold metal of the hard camp bed.

The next morning Sharon rose stiffly at 8am, and left for London.

Chapter Twenty

A week later, Sharon, Jules D. and Debbie stretched out on the green-and-white-striped lounge chairs and felt the Californian sun warming their skin.

'Be careful, darlings – I think we might end up getting a tan. So unflattering.'

Jules D. clicked her fingers to summon a pool boy, and in seconds a white canopy was erected to protect them from the rays.

Sharon sat up. 'Oh come on, Jules, that's hardly necessary, it's September!'

The weather was sunny, but the air whispered with a cool breeze. Nonetheless, the three of them couldn't resist lounging around Hollywood's most famous pool posing like movie stars. With its azure-blue pool, sculpted bushes, and towering palm trees set majestically against the walls of the hotel locally known as the *Pink Palace*, the art deco beauty of the Beverly Hills was breathtaking. Even its evocative location on Sunset Boulevard was a thrill. Since the 1930s it had been the scene of a thousand stills, films and commercials; set amid twelve acres of lush, tropical gardens, it was in this setting that Gregory Peck wooed Lauren Bacall, the Rat Pack played cards, and Gloria Swanson … simply swanned around.

Now Sharon and her team were there; dolled up in dark glasses, scarves and floppy hats, sipping cocktails and eating canapés in the same holy spot, like pilgrims paying homage to a bygone age of glamour.

Debbie sounded like a stuck thirties vinyl.

'I can't believe we're here. I can't believe we're here. Really, I can't believe we're here.' The mantra was finally broken with 'Loooook!' squeezed out in a hushed tone.

Taking seats over the other side of the pool were a famous power couple often hailed as Hollywood royalty. The man stopped to invite some obviously big 'players' to join them, whilst his much younger wife dropped her peach chiffon beach robe.

'Mmmm, since the last baby looks like she's managed to keep the extra pounds,' muttered Jules D. jealously.

The dark-haired beauty flaunted the tiniest bikini, her body no doubt stretched, plumped and honed by personal trainers 24/7.

As one, all three girls glanced down self-consciously at their own bodies to see how she measured up next to the female star.

Debbie had chosen a green, fat-striped tankini in a desperate attempt to look bigger. Alarmingly, it seemed to match the lounge chair. Did she look like the staff? Or worse, like a long, skinny, peppermint stick? She panicked and hid her body with a thick towelling robe

Jules D., on the other hand, looked full and fab for her age. She knew it, and had the confidence to stop comparing.

As for Sharon, she was wearing a white, cut-out swimsuit that had a pearlescent sheen to its soft fabric. She noticed when she stood up that the producer's eyes strayed in her direction. Amused, Sharon deliberately stretched her hands above her head in a sensual yawn, shook her long, platinum hair loose from her headscarf, and combed her fingers through it.

Every man around the pool swivelled to look in her direction. Her rounded belly curved outwards like a beautiful full moon, her magnificent breasts two perfect orbs that rested in its orbit. Jules D. just sat back, smiling at the effect she knew her protégé was having on the producers and directors dotted around the sundeck.

Tonight, she suspected the effect would be even better.

~

'"All expenses paid." How I love that expression!' laughed Sharon dancing round the luxurious living room of her suite.

She'd just returned from the hotel spa after a pedicure, manicure and full body massage with enough free products to launch her own salon. Jules D. was sipping champagne by the fireplace, and Debbie was tinkering out 'Chopsticks' on the white baby grand piano. The textures and furnishings of the surroundings were in distinct Beverly Hills accents of greens, pinks, apricots and yellows; all elegantly subdued into a palette that splashed the word 'success' across every wall. A pink Grecian marble and Italian granite bathroom completed the picture of her deluxe suite.

'What time did you say the hair *artiste* is due to arrive?' giggled Sharon, emphasising the pretentiousness of his LA title with glee.

'Just after the make-up *artiste* – and before the nail *artiste!*' laughed Jules, replacing the bottle in the ice bucket.

'Is that before, or after the "doing up the zip" *artiste*?' shrieked Debbie, mincing around the room like a camp stylist. She was planning to wear a white, loose, empire-lined gown that did much to hide her lack of curves, whilst Jules D. had opted for a classic Dior satin crossover in ice blue. This time, the bling was on full beam. They draped and dripped themselves in as much crystal and diamond glitter as a woman could take. Which, actually, was quite a lot.

'Diamonds are a girl's best friend,' trilled Sharon, admiring a delicate diamond ring sent over by Tiffany's. As for her rule about not wearing anything she couldn't afford… well, now she could. And she slipped it on her finger.

'Did you know that in Japan, models are sacked by agencies if the rings on their fingers slip off?' she asked her friends.

'What the hell are you talking about?' asked Debbie.

'Honestly,' said Sharon. 'I met this model at Fashion Week who'd just got back from a stint out there. She told me they're all given rings by the agency when they arrive. And if they make the sinful mistake of losing weight it shows by the looseness of the ring. And the girl is dropped.'

'That's tough on the young kids,' commented Jules.

'That's the most depressing thing I've heard,' sighed Debbie. 'If it were me, I'd go straight out and find a friendly jeweller for regular resizing.'

Waiting for her dress to arrive from Z&ZaK, Sharon was padding endlessly around the room in a thick, terry-towelling robe and slippers, holding a martini like a fifties starlet. Nervous of the evening ahead, she jumped subjects like a cat on a hot tin roof.

'Oh wow! It says Monroe stayed here many times too!' she said, flicking through the Room Information folder.

'Which room? One like this? Or even this one maybe? Is it this one!? Tell us!' asked Debbie, star-struck as ever.

'Apparently, one of the bungalows,' replied Sharon, nose buried in the *History of the Hotel* leaflet. 'Oh, and get this! Marlene Dietrich too… she walked into the Polo Lounge in slacks and got them to change the rules about women having to wear skirts. What a woman.'

Engrossed in the conversation, all three of them jumped when there was a knock at the door. In walked a bellboy pulling an elegant thirties trolley from which hung a covered ball gown.

'Delivery from Z&ZaK for Miss S. Plunkett,' he announced theatrically.

Crowding around, the girls saw there were two dresses. The first was white velvet and chiffon, with a slim, white velvet throw. It was exquisitely elegant. Straight, low cut and Grecian in style. The second was protected by paper cellophane. They carefully peeled it off, and gasped.

~

271

Snow fell gently from the sky and settled like a soft icing on the white magnolia trees and marble statues of the Crystal Garden. Only in Hollywood could it snow this time of year. Nothing, of course, to do with freak weather, just the special effects machine making real snowflakes from its hidden spot on the top of the hotel roof.

No question, the illustrious Crystal Ballroom in the Beverly Hills Hotel was the perfect place to hold the Crystal Ball. For this auspicious, $8,000-a-seat occasion the hotel had even agreed to paint the apricot ballroom a cool winter white. White church candles glowed from silver candlesticks on every table and in every corner. The famous massive chandeliers overhead added a frosted glow, as did the magnificent white velvet drapes and glass icicles dripping from the pelmets. Outside, a thousand tea-light lanterns lit up the bushes and flowers in the scented gardens, sending silvery rays through the fallen snow.

On every table, giant arrays of white crystallised branches were set in sculpted ice blocks and hung heavy with sugared almonds. Dainty Gypsophila garlanded the tablecloths, the centre further adorned with bouquets of lilies – their stamens carefully removed and supplanted with swaying crystals – elegant in tall, slim vases at least four feet high. The table settings gleamed with the finest silver cutlery perfectly embellished by Venetian crystal napkin rings threaded with glazed snowdrops.

As a final touch, all the tabletops were scattered with Swarovski crystals, which caught and reflected the light like tiny, twinkling stars. It was as if the Snow Queen had waved her frosty wand and turned the land to Narnia. A scene so full of fairy magic, you'd only ever find it in a little child's dreams.

Or, of course, in a Disney movie.

The place was packed. Everyone who was anyone, and anyone who thought they were someone, was there.

Looking divine in her white Grecian gown, Sharon sashayed through the throng like an Athenian statue that had climbed down from the Acropolis to walk amid the mortals. As she mingled with the guests, famous movie actresses glided all around her, like swans on a lake – large, languid and serene. Most gowns were body-con; suggestively revealing, designed to show every capacious curve and catch the eye of a top producer.

Sharon noticed the male actors seemed bigger than expected too. Taller and more well-built than she imagined. No doubt necessary to match the glorious race of Amazons on celluloid.

Quelling any feeling of intimidation with a creamy Snowball cocktail, Sharon took her place at a table for ten near Jules D., whilst Debbie was assigned organisational duties off stage.

A highly fashionable charity since a powerful director's child had run away from home, there were more famous faces than not, and Sharon kept sending secret nods and winks over to Jules every time she spotted another star. At her own table, she watched Maria hold court. The undoubted queen of pop, Sharon remembered her from a different time. But this woman now looked amazing for her age. All trace of her past hardness had gone. As she expressively moved her arms, her beautiful bingo wings flapped like delicate butterflies, the soft fullness of her face giving her a kind, gentle countenance. Very like a virgin, in fact. Next to Maria sat hospital-soap star turned matinee idol George Spencer, more handsome in real life, more suave and sophisticated than his images ever portrayed.

Every time she caught his eye, Sharon would lose courage and swiftly look away, unable to play 'the flirt' at such a high-stakes level. But she was kept busy, anyway, because immediately to her left was a hot young producer from a famous dynasty – Quinton Selsick – who chatted animatedly about up-and-coming casting for *The Banquet*, a sci-fi movie set in a world where food was at a shortage, and the rich were growing crops of brainless people to eat.

Sharon paled as he ploughed insensitively on with the gruesome plot, but, it had to be said, not enough to put her off the feast set before her by white-liveried footmen wearing snow-white gloves. Served on crystal platters, the food was themed white. To start, there was baked lobster, and crab pâté, of which Sharon savoured every morsel she devoured. The second course was described as: *Pousses en Claire OYSTER SURPRISE* – a title engraved on the mother-of-pearl menu adorning each table.

She was about to wave hers away, convinced there was no way she could actually swallow the oyster, when she realised from Jules's expression what the *Surprise* bit was. A little unladylike, Sharon grabbed the waiter by the sleeve and pulled him back. For there, on the open shell of the Mediterranean crustacean, sat a glistening, real pearl! Delighted, she fingered its smoothness, and for a second she was reminded of the single magical pill she had taken so many weeks ago. How long was it? She worked it out in her head and realised, with the time difference, it was exactly 150 days ago that very moment. How weird, she thought; then turned her attention to the Russian Vodka sorbet just placed in front of her. The main course of wild chicken in a white truffle sauce was only just surpassed by the dessert of white Belgian chocolate profiteroles with Chantilly cream.

Just as Quinton was asking if she was interested in doing a screen test for *The Banquet*, Debbie came up and whispered, 'It's time.' Sharon's stomach flipped with nerves (and, it had to be said, the second portion of profiteroles) as she rose to follow her out of the room.

All the men stood up politely with her, and she was startled at the unexpected attention.

'Good luck,' mouthed Jules D., tilting her champagne flute upwards in a private toast.

Heart pounding like fists against a door, Sharon stood backstage whilst hair and make-up fussed around her. By the time she was attired in the second ball gown, the auction was in full swing. It had started with a set of four Venetian brandy glasses that fetched $10,000.

The highest since then had been a ski weekend in Vermont that nearly went for $100,000. Nearly, because just as the auctioneer was about to slam down his hammer, he mischievously announced that he had forgotten to mention it was Spielberg's chalet, and that he would do the cooking and cleaning for the couple. The audience roared, and the bidding shot up to $500,000.

At this point, the celebrity host reiterated the reasons for the auction. The image of two forefingers touching in the manner of E.T. was beamed up on the screen behind him. 'Phone home' said an alien voice over the PA system. There was something about the auctioneer that reminded her of someone. His smooth patter, false game-show smile… Then the man hit his stride:

'*Reaching Out* sends teams of people into the heart of the ghettos, the cold streets, the brothels and the bars to look for our lost ones. Posters, advertisements, leaflets… all asking for the children – our children – to 'Phone home'. Please, I ask you… as one American citizen to another, I beg you… to dig deep into your pockets… into your hearts.'

Sharon now felt sick. And it wasn't just the sloppy, sentimental speech he was churning out… it was nerves. What if no one bid for her?

'I ask you to turn to the person next to you and touch fingers…' urged the auctioneer. Damn, thought Sharon, trying to take her mind off the moment ahead. If only she was back at the table and next to George Spencer.

It was nearly her time. She took the fifth and last peppermint off Debbie, who almost had to shove the shaking Sharon into position. Finally, she was ready to go out there; her new dress arranged carefully around her, headdress adjusted into final position.

'Next, because this is Hollywood and our lives are all about magic and fairytales… we're offering a pair of glass slippers by Louboutin!!'

A silver-liveried footman brought out a cushion bearing a sparkling pair of transparent stilettos.

'You can actually wear them, though they look just as stunning in a glass case… who will give me $1,000?'

Shoes, women, wine and showing off resulted in a staggering final bid of $50,000.

'That's it,' panicked Sharon. 'Debbie, get me outta here! No one's got any money left! I'll be going for a fiver, if I'm lucky…'

'Now, honoured Hollywood royalty… You can't have a glass slipper without Cinderella…' As the lights dimmed, the host turned to the wings, hand outstretched, welcoming Sharon with a big smile. He winked…

'Oh my God, it's Dr. Marvel. He reminds me of Dr. Marvel!' uttered Sharon as she jerked towards the stage.

The audible 'wow' as the audience saw her entrance gave her an unexpected surge of confidence.

There she sat, in a giant glass pumpkin pulled by two tiny, white-plumed ponies. When a footman opened the door, she emerged from the carriage in a fabulous ball gown made entirely of edible sugar crystals. The tiny icicles formed a giant bell skirt, with sugar-glazed roses garlanding her shoulder to hip. On her head she wore a glass tiara tinkling with crystals. With her Nordic hair crimped and fanned out like a fairy queen and ice-cool emerald eyes, she looked as close to a fairy princess as was possible to imagine.

'Of course, we now need to find a Prince Charming to kiss the fair maiden.' The auctioneer took her hand and paraded her across the stage. She walked with her practised model sway, and smiled prettily at the blur of faces scrutinising her face and figure. Inside, she was dying of embarrassment and fear.

'A kiss from the striking… the stunning… the intriguing… international supermodel SHAZ! Ladies and gentlemen, who will start the bidding?'

There was complete silence. She was right. No one wanted to pay for such a ridiculous thing.

But actually, it seemed no one had a clue where to start. Even the host, thrown by how stunning Sharon actually looked, felt the original reserve was too low, and perhaps insulting. He thought it best to leave it up to the audience. But maybe not… The silence was finally broken. '$20,000,' cried Quinton Selsick, the producer she'd been sitting next to.

Sharon was so grateful she would have slept with him for less. Relieved the ordeal was over she smiled at him welcomingly and took a step in his direction.

'\$30,000,' said another voice. Startled, Sharon looked across the other side of the room. There was a portly gentleman in white tie and tails waving a catalogue at the host.

'\$45,000,' cried another, 'for my wife!' His wife happened to be one of the most beautiful women in Hollywood, and the fantasies of every man in the room were fuelled by the Sapphic thought.

The bidding grew faster. Sharon couldn't believe what was happening. It suddenly became a laugh, and she was enjoying it.

'Walk around again, sweetheart,' urged the auctioneer, loving every minute of it. 'Blow them a kiss…'

Like a naughty Queen Titania, she pouted her shell-pink lips as she blew – adding a slow, seductive wink for good fun. The men groaned in pleasure. And she threw back her flaxen head, giggling, exposing her perfect, alabaster neck.

'\$100,000,' said a deep voice from the back. Sharon recognised it almost at once, and put a shocked hand to her mouth.

All heads swivelled to see Brett Stone, lounging back on his chair, casually tilting a catalogue a couple of centimetres.

Sharon couldn't believe it. The A-list actor voted the 'sexiest man on the planet' had bid to kiss *her*! More than that, he was actually willing to *pay a fortune* to kiss her. Not in her wildest, craziest fantasies could she have dreamed up this insane moment. Brett had been the subject of avid fanzine stories recently. Since his split from one of Hollywood's most stunning actresses they had tried to link him with various hot babes. But it seemed he preferred to hang out with his gang of A-list single mates. He was free, single… and raising his finger to bid again!

The portly gentleman bid against him. 'One hundred and twenty five to Mr. Krogenheimer' said the host. Sharon recognised that name too. A top producer known for his hard-hitting violent movies.

'One fifty,' countered Stone, coolly. It was becoming a macho battle, and the room fell silent in lurid fascination.

'One seventy…' shouted Krogenheimer. Sharon wondered if she could offer a free consolation prize to Stone if he lost?

'$200,000,' said Stone unemotionally.

Krogenheimer hesitated, and looked like he would pull out.

Sensing an end the auctioneer suddenly had a brainwave on how to get a little bit more out of the situation.

'Gentlemen, it's for a good cause. Shaz, how would you feel about kissing both of your bidders for $125,000 each?'

'Err… sure. Umm… of course. *Reaching Out* is a very good cause,' she murmured, unable to think of anything other than reaching out for Brett Stone.

'Gentlemen?' he asked, inviting them to reply to the idea.

'Sounds good to me!' snorted Krogenheimer, wiping his mouth with a napkin and rising from his seat. Everyone applauded enthusiastically.

But Stone raised his hand, silencing the crowd.

'$255,000. And I don't share.' The audience roared its approval. Flash bulbs popped and hands clapped even louder. Krogenheimer sat down again, shaking his head and shrugging his hands in smiling, magnanimous defeat.

'Well, Brett – we all know you're good for the money, you had better come up here and claim your prize!' The orchestra struck up the hot, soulful song of 'Sealed with a Kiss', and Brett picked up his glass of wine, finished it…then walked towards the stage, all eyes darting between the two of them.

Sharon stood frozen as her idol got nearer and nearer. His perfect features were just as handsome as on the screen, wicked blue eyes, sensual mouth and blond hair swept back – a lock fallen nonchalantly over one eye. Even taller and more muscular in real life, shirt collar and black tie loosened. He stepped on to the stage and the room held its breath. Like a scene from a movie, he walked over, put his hand under her chin and tilted up her perfect mouth. They locked eyes. Then he turned his back to the audience, swinging her round to shield her, and let his lips touch hers. A warmth spread through every nerve in her body as her head swooned with the knowledge that his lips were actually on hers. Then firmly on hers. She felt her mouth soften and open, and let his tongue enter her. Her body went limp, and his arm tightened to support her. Feeling her relax, he gave her a long, hard, slow, deeply passionate kiss. He deliberately breathed in, taking her breath with his in an unbelievably sexy, intimate moment.

Then somewhere in the far distance, she heard the voice of the host.

'Enough, kids … break it up. We're going to have to charge another $100,000 at this rate! And that's just for watching!' he said, sweeping his hand over the guests, so that everyone roared. They roared and clapped again as Brett bowed slightly to her, kissed her hand and left the stage. Curtseying coyly in return, Sharon was led off in the other direction by the footman. Debbie was in the wings jumping and squealing with excitement like a four-year-old on a sugar-rush.

'Ohmigod! Ohmigod! He's a God! What was it like? What was it like!!'

'Heaven!' sighed Sharon dreamily. 'Like tasting… ambrosia.'

Chapter Twenty-one

Climbing out of the sugar creation, which was actually shedding its icicles faster than an igloo in August, Sharon relaxed back into the Grecian Goddess number, and tried to take in the experience again.

Debbie was busy fluffing out her hair and pinning some strands back up in the mode of Juno. 'I can't believe what I saw! Shaz, he PAID for it! $255,000!'

Jules D. came rushing in from the audience.

'Darling, what a coup! You'll be on every cover, every front page! You mark my words! The press will go cra-zy!' said

Jules D., snapping off a sugar icicle and giving it a curious lick. Actually, the press coverage was the last thing on Sharon's mind. All she could think of was The Kiss.

'What the hell do I say to him if I bump into him? How do you do? My name's Sharon, nice to snog you?'

She was handed a mirror as the make-up artist re-applied her lipstick. Once finished, she looked at her lips carefully. Did they look the same? How had they seemed to him? They were perfectly curved, equally full on top and bottom with a neat bow shape. Okay, kissable. Definitely kissable.

By the time Jules D. and Sharon returned to the ballroom people had started to gather outside the white-pillared gazebo for a nightcap. As they walked through to join them, guests raised their glasses and smiled at her, jokes about her doing so much for charity abounded with good humour. Sharon bubbled with the attention of it. Above in the night sky, Cirque de la Craze trapeze artists were performing a heart-stopping act. Dressed in ivory corsets with white ostrich plumes, they sailed against the starry backdrop like Arctic birds of paradise.

A big band played inside, and through the French glass doors she could see the revellers dance and jive. Keen to get her bearings and decide how to greet Mr. Stone should she get the chance, she headed in the opposite direction, to the outskirts of the group. She couldn't see him anywhere. Debbie was still sorting out dress and travel, and Jules was busy chatting to a potential client.

Sharon wandered past a white dovecot and deeper into the garden foliage. There, amid the swinging lanterns and tea lights that peeked through snowy branches, sat a little white-and-silver tent, the entrance lit by two flickering candelabra. It was small, round and medieval in style. Curious, she strolled over, and, peeking inside, found a gypsy woman with a crystal ball sitting at a little table. Gloriously attired in veils and silks, she sat amid the lush draperies with a gold-toothed smile. How apt for a Crystal Ball! smiled Sharon.

'Come in, come in… be my first lady of the night,' said the gypsy.

Sharon took her place on a silk cushioned stool, placed her hands on the table, and stared into the shiny globe. She fought a childish urge to shake it in the hope of seeing snowflakes.

The gypsy lit another candle, then followed her gaze, looking first into the ball, and then at Sharon's expectant face.

'You have had a very unhappy past. But recently, you have had an unbelievable amount of magic and mystery in your life… it has changed your world beyond all recognition.'

'True. Go on…' urged Sharon, astounded.

The woman caressed the ball with her long, spidery fingers.

'Success gave you its calling card – and you picked it up. But now…

'You are looking for love. You will find it. I see a man involved in "pictures". A tall man – talented, witty, handsome… he's very keen to know you much better…'

'And he's standing right behind you!' said Brett Stone, handing the gypsy a large bill and taking Sharon's hand to lead her out.

'Oh my God!' she laughed. 'Hi, again!'

'I've been looking for you. Everywhere.'

'Really, why?' asked Sharon, unsure what to say to this amazing news, and finally, finally, really feeling confident of her beauty.

'That was some kiss… thank you,' he said gallantly.

'Well, that's a relief. I thought you were going to ask for your money back!'

He paused, taken aback at finding a gorgeous woman with humour.

'Cute,' he replied, breaking into a broad grin. 'Beautiful… *and* funny. I like that. Where do you live?'

'Kingston.' It seemed a ludicrous place to name here, in Hollywood.

'Jamaica?'

'Err, not exactly.' A vision of the grey streets, shopping mall and local pubs flashed into, and just as quickly out of, her mind.

'What about you? LA?' she asked, sensing from her own appalling behaviour with Debbie that this level of celebrity would love nothing more than to talk about themselves.

'Right now? Tonight, right here. Beverly Hills Hotel. The Presidential Suite.'

'You're kidding! Is that where Kennedy stayed?'

'The very same room.'

'Oh my God, what's it like?'

'Want to see?'

'Yeah! Absolutely… I mean, no. Err, not yet. Err, no… not at all.' As she realised she'd just agreed to go to his room she was mortified, and had tried to back-pedal. It was all coming out wrong, like she intended to eventually. 'Not at all,' she repeated, primly. 'But I'm sure it must be fascinating.'

'Absolutely,' he mimicked. 'Not every day you get to sleep in the bed where he screwed Marilyn Monroe.' It was the way he slowly said the words and looked into her eyes that made Sharon aware he was deliberately playing with her. As he probably did with every single woman he met.

Fine, she thought. I can play too.

'It's suddenly turned chilly here, I'm heading back for a drink…' She walked off, interested to see if he would follow. He did. Inwardly, she was screaming: Yes! Yes! Yes!

The man voted the world's most desirable movie star had just paid $255,000 dollars to kiss her. He had then hunted her down, told her, face to face, he'd been looking everywhere for her… and was now following wherever she went like a tamed wolf! Things just couldn't get any better, could they?

She stopped at an ice cream parlour stand set up in another corner of the garden, and as he came up behind her she felt his breath on her neck. He asked if he could share a spoon of her four-scoop coconut sundae.

They sat on a white stone bench feeding each other mouthfuls until the heavenly concoction was demolished. Then, together, they rejoined the main party – chatting, drinking and dancing. Marking his new territory, he never left her side. The studio fat cats were particularly impressed by his obvious attention to Shaz, trying to assess if she had the staying power to become a GOS – the Girlfriend Of Star. If she did, they all knew the ensuing publicity could make her a potential Hollywood player. History had shown it happening so many times before.

The question was, was it likely? Was it worth the effort of going over to say 'hello'?

Either way, press cameras flashed, and smiles were thrown at them from all directions as Hollywood's latest 'beautiful couple' stared deep into each other's eyes. Amid this dream bubble, Sharon also felt the sharp prick of a couple of drop-dead glances from three or four starlets. Judging by their killer stares, she got the impression Brett had probably pissed them off in the past.

Maybe with a one-night-stand.

Looking at his wicked, playful smile and feeling his strong arms around her, she could easily guess how that would make them feel – and sent a silent prayer to the goddess Aphrodite that this gorgeous 'god' wouldn't do the same to her.

As they slow-danced seductively, they were both well aware of the sensation they were creating around them.

Quietly talking as they swayed to the rhythm of the beat, she relaxed and forgot the circus around them. Despite her first impression of a Hollywood movie star, he was actually more normal than she thought. It turned out he loved the same music – who'd have believed he liked traditional Irish folk? But then, coming from an American immigrant family, he had strong ties with Ireland, and was proud of them.

Fascinated about Hollywood, Sharon encouraged him to tell her about his life. He told her about his new film, *The Descendant* – a serious script the studios had finally allowed him to make. He was starring, and for the first time, also directing. It was his shot to do something 'real'. Passionate about the story – a quiet, unassuming man believes he is a direct descendant of Mohammad, and is mercilessly persecuted by the CIA for his beliefs – Brett wanted to 'make a difference'.

As they danced closer, Sharon became very aware they were being scrutinised by press, producers, directors, waiters, starlets, actors and writers. It was fame at its very highest, giddying level.

'Let's head out of here... have a quiet drink back at the Presidential Suite. It's pretty impressive. Has its own pool.'

Hot Night... Movie Star... Private Pool... no brainer. It seemed a wonderful idea for two reasons:

a) She was curious to see exactly *what* could impress a world-famous movie star.

b) To see the look on the faces of Jules D. and Debbie as they left.

She was also aware he could take her acquiescing to go to his room totally the wrong way. But she said yes anyway.

'Okay, I'll come. But only because I'm interested in American political history.'

As Brett unlocked the door to luxurious Bungalow Five, Sharon had misgivings. She was feeling uncomfortably like a 'push-over'. But twenty minutes later, as their bodies embraced in the spotlit art deco lap pool, she was ready to 'roll over and die'. It was surreal – like being in an old movie – and, for Sharon, a case of, 'Frankly, my dear, I don't give a damn.'

Against the silhouette of palm trees, inky sky and mottled white moon, Brett's face wavered in front of hers. Surely she was swimming in an oasis, and he was just a mirage. But when she touched his flesh, it was warm.

She just couldn't believe that the perfect features she'd idolised on a twenty-foot screen were hers to touch, caress and kiss. The thrill was indescribable.

Sharon got the impression that Brett was just as smitten. He confessed he'd seen her face on the billboards, and wondered many times what her succulent lips would feel like to kiss. How they would feel on his body. As her eyes echoed the pool's deep aquamarine, each was enamoured with the image of the other. It was a hot combination, which reached boiling point when he touched between her thighs. She felt her legs part as he pressed her against the poolside wall, and the image of what he would feel like burned inside her. She lifted her hands to his neck, and then ran them down his broad, muscular back to encircle his slim waist. His chest was unbelievably smooth and hard, like a flint stone – leading down to the taut stomach and a finely tuned six-pack she'd seen in countless films, now hers to stroke.

In turn, he ran his hands over her shoulders, down to her waist, tracing every curve, mound and dimple with his long, manicured fingers.

'You're unbelievable. Beautiful… bewitching. I bet you're a real handful? Maybe two handfuls,' he added softly, cupping his hand on each breast. 'I've got to have you,' he whispered in her ear, the tickly, tingling sensation spreading all the way down to her tippy-toes.

With an admirable amount of mega-willpower, Sharon ducked under his arm, and emerged from the water a few feet away.

'I think we need to cool off,' she laughed, pushing the water off her face. 'So, can you imagine? Marilyn Monroe and Jack Kennedy, where do you think they did it?'

'And you're trying to cool me off!?' grinned Brett. He duck-dived, and pulled her down under, to join him in an underwater snog.

Actually, Sharon had still to get her Primary Width Swimming Certificate, and this wasn't a good move on the part of Brett. She surfaced spluttering and struggling like a victim in *Jaws 3*.

'Shit, sorry,' said Brett, genuinely surprised, seeing her pretty nose wrinkled and eyes squeezed tightly shut. The pool culture was so ingrained in LA, he just assumed everyone in Hollywood was a good swimmer. She coughed and coughed, blindly reaching for the stairs out.

Tenderly wrapping her up like a baby in giant towels and a robe, he led her to a pool chair. As her fit subsided, he sheepishly confessed that, actually, he knew the pool was built in the early nineties, and that Jack and Marilyn probably only got together in her bungalow, somewhere else in the grounds. He apologised for getting her to his room under false pretences, and she relaxed at his honesty. Sipping freshly squeezed mango juice, they curled up on the lounger together, looked at the stars peeking through the palm trees, and talked until dawn chased them away with a turquoise hue.

She learned a lot that night, mentally ticking a list as he talked. Brett hated drugs. Major relief after Jaz. Born into the Beverly Hills scene, both his parents had been abusers, and he'd seen more than enough directors, actors and producers unable to walk on set unless they'd had enough 'ice' to create a private rink.

He also believed in fidelity. Well, at least he seemed to dislike the regular LA orgy scene, which was good enough. Another box ticked.

As for waiting for the right girl, he was cool with that too. Hollywood had spoilt him, and he'd 'stuffed himself at the candy box for far too long'. Plus he mentioned something about a religious group he was interested in. They had some neat ideas about monogamy, which resonated with his feeling of isolation at the top of the movie tree.

All of this vital data, she recounted at a scrumptious brunch with Debbie and Jules D., who hung on her every word like baby bats at a feeding fest.

'So how are you going to play it?' asked Jules D.

'I don't know… day by day. Every girl wants him. I think I need to be different.'

'Be cool! Be really cool!' suggested Debbie.

'Be yourself,' insisted Jules D. confidently.

'How do you know that's the right thing?'

'Experience, darling.' Sharon and Debbie were intrigued. Jules never talked about her love life, preferring instead to advise on theirs.

'I just wondered, have you ever been in love? Really in love?' asked Sharon cautiously, dying to know more.

'Have you ever been married?' blurted Debbie, far less cautious.

'Of course, darling. It was… err, fun. Interesting.'

'Would you do it again? Have you ever been tempted?' asked Sharon.

'No, darling. I've been there, done that. Read the book and got the T-shirt.' She said it in a tone that suggested the book was now firmly shut, and the T-shirt returned for a refund.

The girls were itching to know more, but they didn't get the chance.

The subject was neatly avoided by Jules when her mobile phone rang for the tenth time that morning.

It was, naturally, the Press - and, as always, Sharon's PR friend was right. That day, front pages all over the globe carried photos of 'The Kiss'. This time, the headlines didn't shout. They screamed. 'Verkdentdkit!!' and 'サスツオカホ' and 'ΕÆμnnvlμκtμ', which roughly translated meant:

'SHAZ MELTS HEART OF STONE!'

'STONE THROWS $255,OOO FOR A KISS.'

'STONE KNOCKED OVER!'

'$255,OOO A SNOG? STONE THE CROWS!'

And back in old Blighty, *The Sun*'s Booker Prize-winning effort:

'SHAZ'S SEXY SMACKEROONY!'

With a few days free before returning home, Shaz was delighted to take up Brett's offer of lunch on Rodeo Drive, and asked the girls what they thought she should wear. LA was so casual, it had a uniform all of its own. Khakis, chinos, tassel flats...

Finally she decided on a pair of classic linen trousers from Prada, but as she pulled them up she was surprised to feel that the waistband was slightly loose. Surprised, because she had worn them for a recent shoot and they had been tailored for her measurements exactly.

Humming to herself, she stepped on the glass scales parked neatly at the side of the sumptuous, sage granite bathtub, and looked down. She tried to work out the kilogrammes in her head, and it looked like she'd lost about three pounds. Odd. She'd been eating as much as normal, if not a whole lot more. Well, that was cool, she'd just enjoy a really large meal with Brett. Such joy!

The three blocks of Rodeo Drive was an experience. Just like the scenes in *Pretty Woman*, she flounced in and out of the luxury stores, attended to like royalty, whilst Brett looked on, amused. As a gift, he insisted on buying her *First* in Van Cleef and Arpels – a sophisticated perfume that made her feel his number one.

Unsure what to expect when they had started the expedition, Sharon was amused that the most ostentatious part of the most famous shopping district in the world looked like Disney Main Street: fake boulevard with fountains, wrought-iron balconies and cobbled streets. But it was enchanting in a movie-set kind of way, and, amid the Coco Chanel, Christian Dior, Valentino and Tiffany, there wasn't a Primark or New Look to be seen. Sharon dipped in and out of the stores soaking it all up, like a biscotto in a frothy coffee.

In these designer boutiques, they were used to serving only the kind of woman who truly pampered and looked after herself – and that tended to be the rich, famous and elite. There was one very easy way you could tell. The items were straight from the international catwalks. That meant the size 18 really was a size 18 – not like high-street stores that would copy the lines and often call a size 14 or 16 size 18 to flatter the customer.

As Brett waited patiently, Sharon marvelled at the choice and quality in such quantity, but what amused her most were the displays. On every rail and on every stand, the large, flamboyant sizes were up front, the clothes diminishing until at the very back, the odd, embarrassed American size 2 or size 0 dress resided, for the customer who had more money than chic. So hard for skinnies to find designer stuff, she grinned.

Not her problem. Two cashmere sweaters, a Valentino skirt and a pair of Cartier earrings later, Brett steered her towards the Mediterranean-style entrance of *Bijan* – a men's boutique so exclusive customers had to make an appointment in advance. Naturally, Brett hadn't – but one charming, famous smile through the window later, and they secretly let him in, anyway. He loved the look on Sharon's face when he bought a couple of pairs of silk socks for $100 each – and she was even more horrified when he explained the average customer tended to drop in the neighbourhood of $100,000.

After, it was lunch on the terrace at Spago, Beverly Hills. Boyish and spiky-haired, a gentleman introduced as Wolfgang Puck came out to say hello personally, kissing Brett and Sharon like long-lost cousins. This name meant nothing to Sharon, but Brett explained he was a Master Chef extraordinaire, and owner of Spago. He'd been meeting, greeting and feeding the good, the great and the dissolute of Hollywood since the early eighties – the likes of Jack Nicholson, Sean Connery, Clint Eastwood, et al. had all regularly rolled up at his ramshackle restaurant on Sunset Boulevard. This new eatery in the exclusive postcode of Beverly Hills had now replaced the original, and was even more elite (away from les touristitos). Bookings had to be made a month in advance, and if you weren't famous, you needn't even bother trying for a 7–9pm table.

'Spago?' Sharon vaguely recognised the name from Oscar Night – the place the parties were always held. As they sat on the pretty patio, the tall pepper trees kept the hot Californian sun from off their faces. A fountain tinkled merrily (making her occasionally nip to the loo) but, apart from that, she knew she was sitting in one of the most romantic settings in the world, opposite one of the most romantic faces. She glanced around, and again she noted the famous all around her. Meryl, Leonardo, Whoopi, Oprah… They were sending over friendly, acknowledging nods in response to Sharon's smiles.

'You should come over for a while, they love English girls here,' said Brett, pouring a cool, crisp glass of Californian wine. 'And you'd love Hollywood, it's a great neighbourhood,' he added, as if talking about the joys of living in Surbiton.

Over a lunch of Austrian white asparagus with brown butter sauce, followed by roasted filet mignon and Maine lobster with celery root purée, he told her his dreams of running his own studio.

'I know I can do it…' 'I've got these ideas…' 'I had a meeting with…' 'I so want to make this work'. It was fascinating watching his beautiful lips move, and his eyes light up, but by the time they reached the Mocha-Macadamia Nut-Chocolate Cookie Ice Cream Sandwiches, she realised he hadn't asked her one, single question about herself.

But she was nit-picking, wasn't she? In fact, it was refreshing. As a 'celeb' in her own right and used to being asked about herself all the time, it was quite a change. It wasn't her ego that was worried, it was something else. She put her finger on it by the time she was halfway through the main course. It was the fear that she could really be any girl right now, listening to him chatter on. Unless he had a chance to discover her likes and dislikes, hopes and dreams, how the hell would he ever get to know her? She feared he just wanted a pretty ornament, and she wanted to be a lot more than that. As he went on to describe why he had dropped his last agent, she suddenly thought of Simon, and how they bantered together… taking turns to listen, laughing at each other's foibles.

She cleared her mind to concentrate again on Brett. Hardly a hardship, she grinned privately, drinking in his sculpted cheeks and dimpled smile.

It was early days, and it really was a minor worry because the rest of the week was spent in a haze of film-star glamour. When Sharon looked back on her time with the footballer at *The Sugar Cube*, she thought how naïve she'd been to think it even resembled the glorious reality of Hollywood. Forget palm trees in plastic tubs, now she was relishing the real world – tea at The Beverly Wilshire Hotel à la *Pretty Woman*, swimming in the *Pink Palace* pool, and cocktails at the Polo Lounge.

All the time, Brett was shaking hands with friends, producers and agents. Always introducing Sharon proudly, like they were together. On the last night, as they walked through the gardens of the hotel, he mentioned his film *The Descendant* again. Would she like to be his date for the premiere? Sharon was astounded, and deeply flattered. That was like announcing to the world they were a 'couple'. By the time they'd reached his bungalow, she fell into his arms, and tumbled into bed.

Roughly pulling each other's clothes off, the sexual attraction was sizzling. He was divine in every department, and she discovered first hand that he was a 'long-standing member of the Academy'. No question, he certainly knew how to give an Oscar-worthy performance, because he left Sharon feeling she'd just been handed the Lifetime Achievement Award.

Later, as she spooned her body around his magnificent form, and tenderly held his 'Supporting Roll', she knew if any woman were sleazy enough to do a 'kiss and tell', it would only serve to help his career.

Chapter Twenty-two

...She'd ask her father to walk her down the aisle, she'd throw her bouquet to Jules D. and the waiting crowds, wave to the paparazzi and sail off with her actor in a golden, hot-air balloon.

The farewells next morning were worthy of Romeo and Juliet, with the star-crossed lovers torn apart by their rival entourages.

'We're going to miss the plane!' huffed Debbie, guiding Sharon towards the white limo.

Sharon blew a final kiss to Brett, who was checking out and heading off for a few days to his home in Arizona to chill out before mounting the publicity treadmill leading up to his film premiere.

'I always find that spending time at the ranch helps me cope with all the horseshit around here,' he joked. 'Come with me, you'll love it,' he added, with a dazzling white smile. Tanned and muscular, casually dressed in a checked flannel shirt, tight, pale, faded jeans and worn cowboy boots, he looked like a hot, horny ranch-hand. For a second he reminded her of Simon. No doubt, she had a thing about cowboys; but it was High Noon and time to leave town – she was a cowgirl too, and needed to return for a shoot with Luxury Leather Wear, and a showdown with Kristen over foreign commission.

However, she was in for a tougher ride than she bargained for.

Arriving back home, the photographic crush at the airport took her off guard: the news of her relationship with Brett meant all hell had broken out. Worse waited at the flat. She could barely see the door for the number of 'paps' lining the street. The group had grown in size, and the mood had darkened in intensity. As the price on her head had tripled, so had the determination to bag an 'exclusive'.

They now looked so intimidating, hooded and rough, that when she got out of the taxi she kept her head down and headed straight for the door. When she didn't look in the direction of a couple of new faces, she was shocked at their attitude and language.

'Look this way, slag!'

'Oi, you fuckin' bitch!'

Horrified, she turned to look at them… and they got the shot they wanted.

As she finally shut the door on the mêleé, and went through her phone messages, she was thrilled to see she'd exchanged on the Chelsea mews house. One month and she'd be out of here. There was also a message from her dad. For some reason, his whispery voice sounded like it was fading on the wind. She had to call him back.

But first, desperate for a shower and soak, she ran the bath and went through her mail. Bills had mounted up, and a quick glance at her credit card statement made her realise she was spending quite a bit. No problem, as she had over a million in the bank, and plenty more to come, but still, it was surprising where it all went. Taxis, limos, champagne, and, of course, clothes. One could not live by freebies alone. The trouble was, she reasoned, once you were at a certain celebrity level, you couldn't do ordinary things without looking 'cheap'. Travelling by tube was out of the question now, as was shopping in Asda. She'd replaced both with taxis and limos, visits to Harrods Food Hall and a delivery account with her local delicatessen.

And it seemed buying clothes from a chain store was at your peril. She swiftly glanced through the stack of cuttings the agency had sent over to her. The last one, dated yesterday, showed her wearing a smock top she'd recently bought from H&H. One of the tabloids (one she'd refused an interview with) had taken a photo and called her: **'SHAZ – QUEEN OF SCHMUTTER'.**

It was her first negative piece, and, unused to it, Sharon felt deeply upset. She rang Jules D. who told her that all publicity was good publicity. 'Par for the course, darling. Rise above it – and get a good night's sleep, okay?'

A week later, Sharon was generally feeling more relaxed and refreshed. The meeting with Glacé Inc. had gone very well, and she'd negotiated a good rate for future work. Michael Grey wanted her to look at some designs next Thursday, and there'd even been a surprise phone call from a company in France keen to discuss the launch of her own fragrance. She suspected her contract with *Descent* would put a stop to it, but no harm in talking.

For once she only had a relatively short list of things to do – firstly, try her dad again; he hadn't returned her calls. Other than that, she just needed to find a removal firm to do the move, and source something fab to wear for Brett's premiere.

Munching on a fresh apple she'd picked up at the deli, she pulled out her drawers, mulling what to wear. Suddenly feeling creative, she wanted to mix and match what she had; see if Michael Grey was right... could she really conjure up a combination that would generate column inches whenever she felt like it?

Fixing her bra on, she noticed the cups looked a little loose. Strange, she thought. It wasn't a cheap bra, so surely the elastic hadn't gone already? Opening up her wardrobe she picked out a bronze blouse.

Mmmm... would a metallic look work? She fingered the silver pleated Valentino skirt she'd bought that wonderful day on Rodeo Drive – a crazy spend, but hey – she was dating Hollywood royalty. She could team it with bronze and silver bangles. Why not? she decided.

Adding a slip over her silk cami-knickers for extra bulk, she smoothed the silver skirt down over her head. That's odd, she thought. The waistband felt a touch loose. Checking the button wasn't coming off, Sharon felt a teensy wave of panic. She was surely imagining it. She puffed out her belly. No... she wasn't. The skirt was definitely a little bit loose. Just around the top. She made a mental note to eat even more than usual, every day for a week.

'Well I suppose I could make it,' sighed Sharon like a trapped hare caught unawares when Debbie phoned later that day. Debbie, unexpectedly free because her boyfriend had to rush out of town to sign a hot new group, kindly offered to cook Sharon a special gourmet supper. But there was a little problem with the cooking. Debbie couldn't do it. No wonder *she* was thin, thought Sharon uncharitably, a seasoned sufferer of Debbie's Dinner Specials.

'So, tell me, how's the love life?' asked Debbie that evening, after she'd told Sharon how Jack's parents turned out to be just like Richard and Judy (not the Osbournes *nor* the Waltons).

'Love life's brill!' said Sharon between mouthfuls of yellow rubber on charcoal, which had started out hopefully in life as scrambled eggs on toast. Sharon had just had a phone call saying Brett was flying to Europe via Heathrow, just so he could stop over and see her.

'We're going out for dinner tomorrow at *Trotters*.' It was another of those fingers-down-throat, so trendy, 'eat all you can' restaurants whose tables required either a month's booking in advance, celebrity connections or Russian mafia money.

'Good idea. Looks like you're losing a little bit of weight,' said Debbie innocently.

Sharon blanched.

'What?' she demanded, rubberised egg splattering Debbie, and bouncing off her face.

Debbie looked deeply uncomfortable. 'Err, sorry – I didn't mean to upset you. Forget I said it.'

Sharon fluffed up her pink angora jumper and stuck out her chest.

'Where?! Where have I lost weight? TELL ME?' Her voice rose in a long squeak like the lips of a pulled balloon.

Debbie hesitated, like a lemming about to fling itself off a cliff.

'Well… umm… maybe… I think, perhaps all over.'

Sharon leapt up defensively.

'You're just being bitchy. You haven't changed, Debbie. You love making me feel bad.'

Debbie responded angrily, 'How can you say that to me? I'd give anything to have your figure.'

Sharon pointed haughtily at the bathroom. 'Bring me your scales. We'll soon see if you're right.'

Like a dog in an obedience class, Debbie fetched her blue bathroom scales and reverently set them down at Sharon's feet.

Surreptitiously, Sharon picked up her wool cardigan and tied it round her waist.

'I saw that! That's cheating,' whined Debbie. 'Anyway,' she added quietly, 'you're only fooling yourself.'

Ignoring her, Sharon placed her legs firmly onto the machine. The needle landed squarely on 193lb – she had lost well over a stone since the ball.

'These scales can't be right!' said Sharon. 'They *can't* be. Since I went on those scales in the Beverly Hills, I've been eating more than ever!'

'Well, you must be doing something wrong,' commiserated Debbie, trying hard to hide the hint of triumph in her eyes. 'Maybe you're exercising more than you used to?'

Sharon looked away – maybe sex burnt off more than she realised. A headline she'd recently read in Debbie's pile of supermarket mags said '**68% of women would rather eat chocolate than have sex.**' Would she?

Sorry – when the sex in question was with Brett Stone, the answer was no – she'd rather have the sex.

The following night, the date with him was preceded by a nerve-wracking mirror session before she left the flat for his hotel. What outfit made her look the biggest? She rushed out of her room leaving the bed strewn with a heap of rejections. She began to hate every single item in her wardrobe. What on earth was she going to take with her for the premiere trip next week?

'Darling, you ought to try and exercise a little less control,' said Brett as they lay entwined in each other's arms much later that night. 'I'm not sure, but I think I can feel a rib bone.'

Ashamed, Sharon flopped onto her belly.

'Don't be hurt, babe – I'm worried about you.'

Sharon felt sick. She'd just eaten a gargantuan meal, and yet her stomach seemed deflated.

'I bet you wouldn't love me if I was slim,' she found herself saying before she could stop the words spilling out.

'I never said I did love you,' he replied, coolly. But seeing her huge, viridescent eyes, Brett softened, and gave her a kiss on the forehead. 'Who knows, maybe I will someday soon.

'But let's face it sweetheart, I live in Hollywood, and nobody loves a thin girl.'

Sharon smiled weakly, and laughed. But her emotions tumbled like Size 0 dresses in a dryer. He's going to leave me. I know he's going to leave me, screamed a voice inside her skull.

She lay against him all night, unable to sleep – determined to gain weight and keep this perfect creature she was curled up to all hers.

The following morning there was a knock on the door, and in came a French waiter bearing breakfast. Silver domes wafted wonderful smells. Sizzling crispy bacon, fluffy scrambled eggs embellished with dainty slivers of smoked salmon, plates of cured meats, five flavours of home-made jam. As the linen tabletop filled up, a pile of freshly baked baguettes fought for room against iced cinnamon buns doused with dripping clover honey.

Sharon sat up, her large breasts tumbling over the duvet. But suddenly conscious of her body's new imperfection, she leaned over to the chair and swiftly hooked up her silk blouse. Slipping it on, she glanced at the pyramid of food. For an instant, she felt nauseous. It's just emotional nerves, she reasoned.

Her hand shaking, she dipped the silver knife into the curled creamy butter and wiped it on a baguette.

A tiny dollop plopped onto her shirt. Sharon gave a sad sigh.

A stain of grease on a pure silk blouse. Almost impossible to budge.

Chapter Twenty-three

Following her night with Brett, as soon as Sharon got home she dragged out her old scales from the broom cupboard, dusted them off...and eyed them warily. For over three months she hadn't stepped on them once. Like a prisoner who had shaken off their jailor she was reluctant to go anywhere near them. But she was losing weight in a world where it was 'in' to be a plus size; and like the old days before she'd taken the Pill, the daily treadmill began once again.

It became a ritual. Every day her weight changed, often dramatically. Occasionally up a pound – she was happy. Down three pounds – she was depressed. Slowly, slowly, like a helpless junkie, her life began to revolve once more around 'the needle'. Any special occasion or casting involved ripping her wardrobe apart like a frenzied burglar.

Another week later, a niggling feeling pervaded her as she looked at the unexpected apple in her hand. Had something happened the night of the Crystal Ball to change the magic?

Stepping on the scales, and despite a night of binging, she reluctantly looked down. The needle wavered, and then fixed on 177lb. Sharon looked at it incomprehensibly. Two pounds less after a full night of binge eating, making that another 16lb in total! She had slipped down to less than 12 ½ stone.

Impossible! There *must* be something wrong with her scales? her mind wailed. Sharon kicked them back into the corner. Panicking, she pulled on the tightest jeans she could find in her wardrobe. They hung baggy around her bottom, like a loose nappy. Weird, confused emotions coursed through her shaking body. Years of conditioning meant she'd felt an initial elation at finding the clothes loose, but it was misplaced, and seconds later she was hit by a wave of fear. As a bountiful star in this world of the Botticelli beauty, she didn't want to be slim. It was insipid. Not only that, she was well aware that if she should lose much more, the agency would kick her out… and Z&ZaK would be furious. How could she have let it get so out of control, for God's sake? Looking good was her job. Her business. Her life.

She speed-dialled Debbie, who listened in horror, and came racing over to Sharon's flat. On first inspection, Debbie thought Sharon was looking far lighter, but this time couched it carefully, so as not to offend her friend, and celebrity boss.

'Well, I can notice a little difference – but you can easily hide it with your height,' said Debbie with unaccustomed diplomacy.

She had arrived with a dozen Krispy Kreme doughnuts, but for some reason, probably anxiety, Sharon couldn't face the sticky, sugary softness she normally craved.

Together they examined her wardrobe, and after she'd tried on a couple more outfits, they scooted past the paparazzi, and snuck into the lingerie department of M&S cloaked in dark glasses and hats.

The 'push-out' pants and 'tummy release' vest their expert suggested seemed a comforting answer. Padded and moulded to emphasise a woman's bumps, Sharon relaxed a little. But she knew the truth, and so did Debbie. Shaz the Supermodel had gone down to size 14.

She called an emergency meeting with Jules D. who kindly put her weight loss down to all the emotional turmoil she'd been going through with her love life. But Sharon knew it wasn't that. In truth, overall she'd been having marvellous fun, each time meeting a more fabulous man to swiftly take her mind off the last.

Changing the subject she asked Jules D. about her immediate dilemma: what to wear for the forthcoming premiere. Could her brilliant PR conjure up a fabulous dress?

Not sure what the reaction from Z&ZaK would be to creating a high media profile dress for a celebrity with a weight problem, and, more importantly, not wanting to alert them to the change, Jules D. diplomatically thought she would try elsewhere, whipping out her Blackberry before you could say 'Google'; but the problem was unexpectedly solved by a timely call from Maxine Du Pré, who had learned from Simon how Sharon had misread her advances at his exhibition. Ever the egoist, and convinced all women had a secret desire for Sapphic assignations, she decided to ring Sharon and make her feelings very, very clear. After Sharon had declined coffee, lunch, dinner and breakfast in bed, Maxine exasperatedly husked was there was *anything* she could do for her?

Sharon asked her what she had in the way of red-carpet frocks, and Maxine veritably purred with pleasure.

'Darling, if I can't take your dress off you… let me drape one on you! I have the perfect creation.'

That afternoon she turned up with a black crepe dress that crossed in the front with large satin panels. Its most distinguishing feature, though, was a giant bow perched on the shoulder.

'It's divine on you, darling,' muttered Max, between a mouthful of pins. Sharon wasn't convinced, but the fact she'd already had a 'successful dress' with Max, and that the designer was prepared to take this one in to fit her perfectly, made it a more attractive option. To be frank, she didn't fancy contacting any of the PRs and asking them to send two sizes smaller than 'sample' – you just couldn't trust anyone not to leak the story.

'I think I'll just add some tulle around the hem to fill out the effect, and, of course, you also have the stole…' purred Maxine, sucking on her ciggie holder dramatically.

Even with the special underwear, Sharon noticed she looked somewhat slimmer. Was it really wise to wear black, she worried? It was so slimming. Still, the stole was great for hiding all sins… and she still had a whole week to go on a crash binge.

As for her relationship with Brett, it was going brilliantly – in the virtual reality world – with emails, texts and phone calls every day. She guessed this must be how it was for film stars. She used to read how actors always complained break-ups occurred because of work. Perhaps it was true? Meanwhile, there was the move to organise, and as the freebie pile of goodies grew, Sharon was faced with clearing out skip loads of her old crap.

As she started the painful process, she unearthed an old album from underneath layers of school reports and certificates. Inside, there were pictures of her mother, father and herself. Sharon realised that actually she looked quite a normal, rounded child. Although she had always felt fat since she could remember, maybe she'd got it wrong. Maybe the weight hadn't started piling on until after her mother died?

She decided to try her dad again, and once more, steeling herself to speak to her stepmother, she waited patiently whilst he came to the phone. It was then he gave her the news of his tests.

'Darling, you know I've not been able to eat much recently? Well, it's a problem with the oesophagus. Don't be upset, but I'm afraid it's cancer.' The word hung in the air like poison. A powerful word that clutched at her heart with giant, crabby pincer-like claws.

'How bad?' she croaked out, not wanting to hear the answer.

'Pretty bad, darling. In fact, very. No hope, I'm afraid. They've said it's terminal.' The floor dipped under her, and her legs gave way. She stumbled backwards and dropped onto the sofa. This couldn't be happening. Not to him. Not to her.

'I'll come right away,' she said, tears pricking her eyes as she thought of her dad, needing a hug to get over the shock – to make it not real. To make it all right again.

'Err… I'd better check with Carolyn, just a minute. Carol, can Sharon come down?' Sharon felt the flicker of anger that he had to ask at this time in his life. It burst into a searing flame when she heard the woman's heartless response.

'Well, we've people coming over to see you later, and I don't want her to come if she has a cold, or anything.'

'Darling…' said her father weakly,

'I don't have a cold,' snapped Sharon. 'Do you want me to come?'

'Of *course* I do…'

'Then I'll be there.'

'Better make it the weekend, darling, could you come then?' Sharon agreed, not wanting to upset him, but boiling with rage at being sidelined at a time like this. As she hung up, Sharon reached for a box of chocolates, and sobbed into her glass of milk.

That Saturday, the drive through Bournemouth to his home was agony. A trip that took her down memory lane at every path she took.

Sharon looked to the left, peering down a cul-de-sac. There was the old school where her daddy used to drop her off. To her right was the restaurant he took her to on her tenth birthday. And as she rounded the corner, she braced herself to see the skating rink where he taught her to skate. She remembered the first time. Oh, how nervous she was… yet her daddy held her hand and she never fell over, not once. As the ghosts of childhood cried out from every street corner, her eyes filled with tears of good times long gone. Times that could never come again. Those days were lost forever. The skating rink was now a duplex cinema.

She drove through the town centre engulfed in loneliness, knowing the memories would be even more poignant and hard to deal with in just a few months time. Or would it be weeks? Maybe days?

Finally, she nervously knocked on the door to his house. Their house. No longer her home. As usual, her heart pounded at the thought of having to face Carolyn, made a thousand times worse by her father's illness, and the reality of dealing with eternal goodbyes.

Even though he was expecting her, when she entered the cluttered living room it was full of Carolyn's relatives, including Sharon's step sister, Esme, who sat there with her fiancé, and Sharon's half-brother Damien. Everyone was engrossed in watching tennis on TV. Sharon took in the array of antiques and photos crowding the parlour: pictures of Carolyn's children receiving diplomas, getting engaged, laughing, having fun. There wasn't a single photo of Sharon to be seen.

On the sofa opposite, looking somewhat lost, sat her father, visibly shrunken in size and stature, his jowls a ghostly grey colour. Sharon smiled at Damien, assuming he *was* her half-brother? He wasn't even born that night Sharon was dismissed from the family home. Despite asking her dad many times about him, and wondering if he ever asked about his big half-sister, her father admitted that Carolyn was determined to keep him away from Sharon. He sadly said he didn't really know why.

Her father was blind. Sharon suspected the reason was very simple. His wife never wanted her son to know the cruelty she was capable of to another man's child.

Maybe one day when the boy was grown up, she would get the chance to tell him the truth. But that was a long way off.

She stared at the green-eyed, dark-haired youth. Same eyes. This was her flesh-and-blood brother. She didn't even know the first thing about him, but now was too tragic a time to start.

Carolyn, true to form, was busy putting on a 'show' of the good wife, making a real fuss of her father. It seemed to Sharon she was trying to claim her role as his loving, caring partner. It all looked a bit staged. 'Joe, would you like some more tea? Soup? You must eat that up, it's so good for you.'

Her father told her the latest medical situation. It was awful. The tumour now blocked his passage, and all he could eat was liquefied food. Although he wasn't hungry, he was basically starving to death. He had to eat something to stay alive, but all he could swallow looked like baby goo. As Carolyn tucked a napkin on him, Sharon sadly thought how weird old age was… a complete circle from helplessness, to grown adult, to helplessness again.

Conversation was stilted due to the fact her estranged family sat there the whole time listening to every word they exchanged. Sharon couldn't believe their insensitivity. She'd driven hours to sit with her father – who had just told his daughter he was going to die. His *real* daughter. His only daughter. And there she was, trying to make final memories with her Dad whilst her step sister and strangers lounged around chatting and watching the telly.

Worse, despite driving well over two hours to get there, she knew she'd only have a little time with him, no more than twenty minutes due to his tiredness. Yet Esme and the others sat there, refusing to move.

Sharon fought the urge to scream at them to leave. But years of abuse and fear of Carolyn's temper cowed her instinct to ask them to go. Was it deliberate? Her step sister Esme lived around the corner, and had all the time in the world to spend with her father; why on earth were she and her fiancé insisting on being there now?

When Sharon nipped off to the loo, that thought was confirmed.

'Don't worry, mum, I'm making her feel uncomfortable,' Sharon overheard Esme saying to her mother as she brought more tea in from the kitchen.

So, that was it. A ploy to wind her up. She tried desperately not to let it get to her. She knew Esme had now been totally brainwashed by Carolyn, and tried hard to forgive her.

Then her mind drifted back to the time she was thrown out.

On the 'night of a thousand daggers' as Sharon called it. She was sixteen. Esme had been fourteen. Mona, seventeen. That night, Carolyn had come home from dinner with her father in a foul mood, no doubt aggravated by her pregnancy. She had stalked into the living room, and Sharon had looked up, nervously knocking over a glass of water on the table as she did so. The woman went mad. Her face darkened and she screamed at Sharon's clumsiness. It was the final straw. Sharon was getting older, and she was finally building up the courage to answer back for the first time. As Carolyn culminated in a screech that Sharon was the spawn of her mother, she had retaliated with, 'I hate you!' And run, hysterically upset, to the safety of her room.

She heard Carolyn order Esme and Mona into her bedroom. Sharon could only guess what lies they were being told about her.

When they all emerged, they had entered Sharon's bedroom, her private sanctuary. Esme stood hugging her mother's side as she ordered Sharon to leave the home, whilst Mona screamed at her to 'Fuck off'. They snarled like a pack of she-wolves. Cornered in the far end of her room, Sharon looked to her father to stop them. But his anguished face just peered round the door, his shoulders shrugging helplessly. As the screaming increased Sharon simply felt her body leave the scene below, and float above… removed. Left by her mother. Betrayed by her father. Hated by her step-family. The hurt was too much to bear, and her mind had taken its own steps to save her. As the screaming around her continued, her father sadly took her by the hand and drove her to the station. He put her on a train to London with an address to stay with one of her mother's old friends. It was 10pm, it was raining. But the drops pounding on the window pane of the train were nothing compared to the tears tumbling down her cheeks.

Forcing the images of that night to recede, she tried to concentrate on talking to her dad, phasing out the others in the room. Giving her a big, bespectacled smile, he put his skinny arm around her, and she lay her head upon his chest. They chatted quietly about the old days whilst the step-throng around them watched sport on TV. The situation was totally surreal, but Sharon was torn. Did she stay, drinking in every feature, every gesture her father made, committing it to memory? Fearing this would be the last time she'd ever see him alive? Or should she leave? Escape the awful atmosphere and gain back her sanity?

Carolyn brought in mushed peas and some gruel substance and Sharon watched in pain as her father tried to swallow. The irony stuck in the throat even harder. For there she was, obsessed with her physical appearance, trying to gain weight, and here was her father unwillingly starving to death, dying from the loss of pounds. Gain weight/lose weight/right weight/wrong weight. In the end, surely none of it really mattered, not when it could come right down to this?

'Darling, I'm not afraid of death, you know… never have been.' It was one of the many things she loved about her father. Not worried about age or dying.

'How long do you think it… how much time did they…?'

'Oh, well played!' said Esme's fiancé loudly, as they watched the game of tennis on TV.

'Don't know, darling. I think it could be six months…' Looking at his shrunken form, she somewhat doubted he was telling her the truth, but it was a comfort.

Finally, biting back the tears, she hugged her dad and said goodbye, and that she would see him very soon. As he hobbled to the door like Yoda, a sliver of his normal size, she stared at his face and tried to freeze-frame it. A sweet man she loved who had failed to protect her. Who now, never would.

She turned to Esme and, seeking an act of kindness to try and rewrite the terrible history of their youth, asked her if she would let her know how her dad was doing. To which she replied non-committally, 'Someone will.'

She spoke in the exact tones of Carolyn.

Sharon sighed. As she walked out towards her car she knew the wicked stepmother had won. And, unlike in fairytales, there would never be a happy ending.

Driving along the motorway it hit her that, even though he was still alive, her father's life had now reached its conclusion. Told its tale. So that was how his story ended. As she sobbed all the way home, she had never felt so alone.

Back at the flat, she realised the opposite. With a growing pack of paparazzi at the door, the chances were she really wasn't ever going to be alone again. As the premiere neared, so did the interest in her.

The attention was fuelled by the announcement of her fashion deal, and screen test for *The Banquet*. Actually, the latter she'd found out in the press, along with everyone else. She laughed, thinking it was a joke. But it was a clever, publicity-generating move by Selsick, who deliberately leaked the story before he asked her agent. That way, even if she said no, the story had made column inches.

Worn down by 'Is it true?' questions from the 'paps', the official offer was confirmed two days later by Zara; by then Sharon had decided, 'What the hell, why not?'

In truth the idea of acting had terrified her ever since she had screwed up her role of a bush in the school nativity play. (Her branch poked Mary in the eye so that she then cried louder than Baby Jesus.) Still, she was heading out to LA for the film opening, so she might as well give it a shot. In for a penny, in for the big green bucks! she figured.

This time, when she arrived at the Beverly Hills Hotel, she was shown straight to the Presidential Suite, where she ran in and fell into the arms of Brett. He seemed delighted to see her, and after a screen-worthy passionate kiss, he hugged her close to his chest.

She told him how she'd missed him, and how much she wished he'd been there when she'd found out about her dad. He fell silent, stroking her hair. Then he stroked her back, encircling her waist. Sharon felt comforted. The silence continued. Until she felt uncomfortable. 'What's up?' she said. 'Are you okay?'

'Actually, I was wondering if you were. You've lost so much weight, it's… it's quite a lot.' Sharon stood back, not sure if he was genuinely concerned, or worried about her being his arm candy.

'I'm going through a lot right now…' she countered defensively.

'I know that, and I'm here for you. But still, at our level, we have to have some control.' Sharon felt speechless, and burst into tears.

'Look, forgive me. I'm a prick. An absolute prick. I'm sure it's just what you're going through, with your dad and all that. Come on, babe, make yourself beautiful and let's go see a movie!'

Sharon disappeared into the pink granite bathroom to shower and repair the damage. Three hours later, following a visit from the hair artiste, make-up artiste and nail artiste, she was ready for her first public premiere. But as she slipped on the black creation from Maxine, she was horrified to see it was loose.

Well, more than loose. It gaped under her arms, and bagged around her buttocks. She gingerly stepped on the hotel scales, keeping on rings, shoes and diamond necklace. Regardless, she'd dropped another eight pounds. Fear gripped her. Was she sick like her dad? Was something seriously wrong? In panic, she even considered stuffing her bra and pants with toilet paper for extra padding, but the horrifying image of her trailing white loo roll down the red carpet put a stop to the idea.

Pale, she walked into the living room of the suite, wrapping the stole around her body to hide her disappearing voluptuousness.

'Are you okay?' asked Brett, concerned. He looked impeccable in an Armani black suit and tie, like a classic Hollywood leading man. He led his lady out to the limo, and she chattered nervously, trying to hide her sudden body insecurity, which made her quake with the public scrutiny she knew lay ahead.

Timed to perfection for maximum impact, their car swung down Sunset Boulevard towards Grauman's Chinese Theatre – the crowds roared as it pulled up, and Sharon squeezed Brett's hand for good luck. He smiled. 'Nothing to worry about… it's Showtime.'

With that, he stepped out of the car, and waved like an old pro, his switched-on, mega-watt smile more eye-dazzling than the searchlights that swivelled over the crowds.

Sharon got out her side, and walked around to join him on the red carpet walk. Security men in black were all around her, urging her to join Brett. She held one end of her long stole, but suddenly she couldn't find the other end! Groping behind her like a blind woman as she smiled and worked the crowds, the cameras flashed, thousands stared. She was faced with a choice.

To make an inelegant turn and stoop, which would show off the looseness of the dress, or to trail the stole dramatically behind her like a catwalk model. She chose the latter.

The crowds roared again as she took her place next to him, he smiled at her, and arm in arm they walked towards the magnificent piece of kitsch – a green Chinese pagoda – that marked the entrance to the historic cinema. The flash bulbs were so intense, spots danced before her eyes. As Brett stopped to sign books, and shake hands, Sharon posed on the carpet, a giant circular bank of photographers crying out her name from all directions. It was wild!

As he took her hand, they posed together,

'Kiss! Kiss!' chanted the crowds. He looked into her green eyes, and smiled enigmatically. They didn't kiss. Instead they waved and walked into the buzzing foyer to be greeted by the microphones and booms of various TV crews, keen to hear Brett's thoughts on foreign policy and America's stance.

He rose to the seriousness with passion and belief. Sharon was impressed – this was his big break from being a pretty boy, and she knew how much it meant to him.

As for her, she was asked more important, life-affecting questions, such as: 'What designer are you wearing?' 'Whose shoes are those?' and 'Which is your favourite lip gloss?' The attention was overwhelming, and she was having a blast. They took their seats in the auditorium, and as the lights dimmed, she detected a nervous twitch on Brett's fine-boned cheek. The first betrayal of anxiety from him she'd ever seen.

The film began with explosions, death and destruction. Brett was playing a cool CIA agent who finally let his principles rule his head. A lot of Muslims died. Also a lot of Americans. Depressing, heavy and meaningful, Sharon was unsure if it was bloody brilliant, or bloody awful. The only thing that really moved her throughout was the really odd sensation that the giant face on the screen was also sitting right next to her – the same hand brandishing a Kalashnikov, the same hand caressing her thigh.

Afterwards, applause filled the cinema, and they swept out with the producers and headed off to Spago for a celebratory dinner.

Deeply conscious of her figure, anxiety dulled her appetite, and as they sat at their table, she felt her dress ride up under her armpits, no flesh to keep it in its rightful place. Yanking it down, she quietly asked a waiter to get her some safety pins.

Everyone was congratulating Brett, shaking hands, back slapping, laughing and joking. Two producers asked him to come to their offices next week to discuss a couple of projects they thought he may like to direct. It was looking good.

Sharon, meanwhile, was looking in the sparkling goody bag hooked on the back of her chair. It was astounding. Inside was a crystal Swarovski bikini, a diamond-studded eye mask, a new perfume called 'Flesh' encased in a glass-sculpted bottle of a large woman reclining, a four-foot adjustable tummy chain from Gucci, and some Godiva chocolates. For a film that was so meaningful, the goodies were outrageously meaningless. That was Hollywood, she guessed, irked by the tummy chain, realising she could probably fold it in half and still wear it.

That night, they returned to the suite and had a wicked time. But Brett made a couple of comments that really jarred. 'Eat some more cheese,' he'd insisted as they enjoyed their alcoholic nightcap. 'It's wonderfully fattening – you don't want to let yourself go now, do you?'

And worse, as they curled up together, he placed his hand on her hip. Then withdrew it a few seconds later.

'Something wrong?' asked Sharon, nervously.

'Your hip just felt a bit… bony, that's all. No worries, Shaz – go to sleep.' And he kissed her shoulder softly. But she couldn't. She tossed and turned, knowing this man was used to absolute perfection, and she was no longer the ultimate.

The next morning the papers were hand delivered early by his producer. And Sharon's life fell apart.

Chapter Twenty-four

'FILM FLOPS MORE THAN DATE'S DRESS!' announced one paper.

'Brett Stone's directorial debut, a mish-mash of meaningless drivel designed to whip up anti-American sentiment was bad enough, but his girlfriend Shaz, a multi-million pound international model known for her taste, wore a dress by up-and-coming British designer Maxine Du Pré, that looked two sizes too big…'

Underneath was a shot of Sharon leaning forward… the dress so loose her left breast was falling out of the cup. Worse, you could even see the clear shape of a collarbone.

'THE DESCENDANT? Stone's film – or Shaz's dress?' captioned another paper, picturing her hiking up the bodice. **'After last night's premiere, both were on their way down…'** it continued, mercilessly.

'Oh God, I'm so sorry,' said Sharon, burying her face in her hands. The embarrassment of him being shamed even more than necessary by her attendance as his date was unbearable. Brett sighed long and hard – like a condemned man.

'It's okay. It seems the film would have been slammed either way. You've just given them fodder for a funny headline. They'd have found others, I'm sure.'

'It's not all bad,' said his producer, handing him the *Washington Post*.

'Brett's attempt to wake up America put most of us to sleep. However, there were moments of sheer genius…'

'"Sheer GENIUS." Brett, that's good enough to get you another film, my son!' said his producer, desperate to find something to redeem the situation.

Brett snatched the paper eagerly, then re-read it out loud, trailing off at the end: 'However, there were moments of sheer genius. Just not nearly enough,' it continued. He tossed it on the sofa in disgust.

'They just don't "get" my work,' he snarled sullenly.

Sharon looked at the photo accompanying the story. Her dress bagged and drooped around her body like a black bin liner. How apt; she certainly looked a pile of rubbish, she thought.

At the bottom of the piece there was more:

'Supermodel Shaz, famous for the Descent perfume campaign, draped her stole in imitation of a vintage movie star outside

Grauman's famous Chinese Theater – but without the voluptuous curves to back it up, the flaunting "descended" into a joke.'

What! It was so unjust, she wanted to scream; to explain to each and every one of the readers that the stole was ridiculously long, she'd simply dropped the end and was too nervous to pick it up. But there was nothing she could do.

Brett's producer left them alone with a servile bow, and they sat in silence, picking at the stack of waffles, French toast and bacon.

Half an hour later, the phone rang for Sharon. It was Quinton Selsick's assistant, confirming the time of the screen test.

Knowing she was a total novice, Brett was being kind, telling her the whole thing was going to be a cinch. But her confidence was badly shaken. She dressed carefully in a white voluminous blouse, with pleated tennis skirt for added fullness. She judged her legs in the mirror – the calves and thighs were still nicely plumped, but was that a concave curve appearing at the top? No, it only seemed to show when she flexed her ankle and lifted her leg.

On her flaxen head, she popped an Alice band, leaving her hair to cascade loose. It was very California 'preppy', in the style of the 'victim' part she was up for.

Brett kissed her good luck on her perfect little nose, and, settling down at the bureau in the living room of the suite, said he had loads to sort, but would be there waiting for her to come back, to find out how it went. The studios were only round the corner from the hotel, and they arrived at the giant hangar far sooner than she would have liked.

As she tried to go over the script, she was clucked and fluffed over by a batch of 'mother hens' making concentration impossible. With make-up and hair finally perfected, an assistant led her out to the floor. Quinton came over and gave her a hug like a long-lost brother – then steered her over to another actor holding a script.

'This is Luke, he's going to read the part of the killer… your boyfriend. You've just found the boiled head of your sister in the kitchen pot. Now I know this is in at the deep end for you, but I need to know you can handle the script. Come the real thing, we'll have plenty more time to develop the scene, so for now – just give it what you can, okay?'

Sharon nodded, fearfully. So many people standing around, all scrutinising her from head to toe. The script had been sent on to her in England, but, try as she might to remember the lines she'd learnt on the flight over, her mind was a complete blank; she couldn't even remember her surname.

The back lot darkened, and three spotlights were trained on the set of a Martha Stewart country kitchen.

'So, you think you know me, do you?' said the actor, narrowing his eyes wickedly.

The words and direction clicked into place.

'Not really, there are times when I haven't got a clue who I'm with.' She edged towards the knife in the drawer.

'Does that worry you?' asked the boyfriend killer, menacingly.

'No… *(wavering tremulously)* I… I like a bit of mystery. Really. I do…'

'Did you see me in the woods with Nikki yesterday? I sensed you were following me…'

'No. No… Of course not. I was in town all day… shopping. I saw a dress I really liked…' *(wide-eyed innocence as she gropes behind her back for the protection of a knife).*

'Liar. You've been watching me. Like I've been watching you. Every moment.' *(Walking slowly towards her.)*

'I didn't see anything. Please, Luke… please. You're scaring me; please, back off…' *(biting her lips in fear, sweat bead trickling down forehead)*. 'I want to go home, it's getting late.'

'I love the smell of fear… makes me hungry, Lucy. You're so tasty … *(sniffs her neck like a dog)* I could eat you up.'

(He goes to kiss her, then yanks her by a handful of her hair, and grabs her hand and twists it.)

'Ahhhhggg….' *(Screaming ear-piercingly loud, and dropping the knife to the floor.)*

'What's this, my little love? A knife? And just what were you going to do with that?' Long pause. Very long pause.

Shaz's mind blanked again. No idea of the next words.

'…Err, peel the potatoes?' she offered, desperately.

'CUT!'

After screwing up the last line, Sharon expected to be thrown off the set, but, instead, Quinton came striding towards her, grinning like a cat who'd just downed a gallon of cream.

'I love you, you're brilliant!' The people on the set burst into applause. Sharon was stunned at his response, although, to be fair, she had really 'felt' the part as she acted it.

'You were so good, you passed the ol' Jonesy test. He beckoned to a set painter smoking a fag in the corner of the room. 'He had hairs standing up on the backs of his arms when you screamed, isn't that so, Jonesy?' The old man nodded, proudly showing off his arms.

'We'll be in touch, Shaz. There's a couple of … minor things that are worrying me, but, other than that, the part is yours.'

'Oh, what kind of things?' said Sharon, deflated.

'Oh, you know what Hollywood can be like. A bitch dominatrix that rules us all! But nothing that can't be sorted, I'm sure. I'll talk to your agent, we'll sort it out. How about a spot of lunch?' Sharon declined, innocently thinking it was more important to get back to see Brett than to lunch with the producer.

By the time she drew up at the *Pink Palace*, she was feeling high and low about the audition. Keen to ask Brett for his advice, she bounced into their suite, but he wasn't there. Instead, there was a note propped on the antique mahogany table.

'Sorry, Shaz – had to go to an emergency meeting, not sure what time I'll be back. May not be able to take you to the airport, but my driver is at your beck and call – ring front desk.
Love, Brett.'

She sank onto the sofa in despair. She knew he was losing interest, and why. Glancing in the mirror, even the new outfit she'd worn for the audition looked a little loose. Sharon reached for a chocolate from the elaborate box of truffles on the table. But somehow, the stress of it all had taken away her appetite.

Back home, over the next few days the papers were even more cruel. The British press had a reputation for building up and pulling down, and Sharon's star was certainly 'On The Descendant'. At least that was the lousy pun three papers used – complete with visual of Brett's film logo.

Worse still, the waiter she'd asked for a couple of safety pins had sold his story to the scummiest Sunday tabloid entitled,

'SHAZ'S SAFETY PIN SHAME.'

The bastards ran a front-page story on how he'd **'found her crying in the toilets and she'd begged for my help'**.

A few days later she got 'papped' and more was to come: a picture of Shaz getting out of a car and accidentally flashing her slimmer thighs. Placed next to an image of her original poster for *Descent* perfume, the headline ran '*GOING DOWN!*' with a big circle ringing her smooth, cellulite-free legs. The same shameful story ran in three supermarket rags.

Her heart was plummeting with her weight, and the latter truly did seem to be falling. Two days after binging on Chinese takeaways and thick-crust deep-filled pizza she braved her scales again. This time, the needle flicked over 160lb – 11 stone 4 pounds. At this rate, she was hurtling towards being an English size 12! As for her body mass index, she suspected it was around 23 – though maths had never, ever been her strong point.

This was bad, really bad. She couldn't even face the castings lined up on her answer-phone. She'd also started sleeping badly, weight paranoia gripping her at three in the morning, and holding her in its tight grasp until daybreak.

Debbie headed over armed with the latest books, complete with a diet disc to help her put on weight.

'This is the biz!' announced Debbie, heading towards the hi-fi.

She read the back cover: *INNERSPEAK – using subconscious techniques of self-hypnosis and affirmations, we guarantee the pounds will pile on in days. Just believe in what your mind can achieve, and your body will follow.*

'Okay, you ready?' asked Debbie, having made Sharon comfortable on the sofa, feet up. Sharon studied Debbie's figure as she fussed around her.

'Actually, Debbie, you look like you've put on a few.'

'I have! This tape is fantastic. Trust me, it'll work. You just have to play it every day in the background and repeat the affirmations.'

The disc began with the sound of waves breaking on the shore, followed by whispering.

'I can't hear a thing! How the hell is this going to work?' asked Sharon.

'It's sinking in subconsciously – now say these words…' Debbie handed her the cover of the CD. Inside was a long list of affirmations.

'My body is feeling warm and rested.'
'I feel fat cells growing on my thighs.'
'I feel large, lumpy and tired.'
'I am always hungry. I need food to survive.'
'My body wants regular meals.'
'I care about myself, and reward myself often.'
'My body needs snacks.'
'Sugar is good for me.'
'I need to rest lots, and often.'
'I nourish my body with the treats it deserves.'
'Every day and in every way I'm a winner.'

'Oh, for fuck's sake,' said Sharon. 'Next it's going to say "*My body is a temple*".'

'It does, further down. And it is,' said Debbie, hurt.

'Well, its worshippers are deserting in droves,' sighed Sharon sanguinely. Regardless, desperation meant she persevered, listening to the 30-minute tape three times in a row.

'Right, now promise me you'll play it every day, any time you can, okay?' said Debbie, beginning to sound like Jules D.

'I promise. What else have you got?'

'Books. Lots of books. Best sellers,' said Debbie brightly, holding *Eat Yourself Fat* in one hand, and *Fat is a Fabulous Issue* in the other.

Sharon flipped through the pile, picking out the ones that appealed, and settled on *The Re-tox Plan* and *Think Big For A Better You*.

'Jules is also on her way over,' said Debbie, looking at Sharon, deeply concerned.

A flash of irritation crossed Sharon's mind, was it because they were true friends that they cared, or because she was now the cash cow?

'Darling, I came as quick as I could. Is it true?' said Jules D. in hushed tones, as if visiting a sick patient.

'It is,' confirmed Debbie, ushering her through the door.

'Well, I've never heard of anyone dropping two dress sizes in two weeks. Let me have a look at you, darling.' Sharon stood up, turned around, and held out her loose waistband.

Jules D. took a sharp intake of breath.

'Okay, it's not great. But I know it can be sorted. I've got these wonderful vitamins and fattening pills. It's going to be fine, okay?' she said, delving into a large, very expensive-looking crocodile bag. As often as not, Jules D. ended her sentence with 'okay?' It always gave the comforting impression that things would be fine. It was one of the idiosyncrasies she loved about her friend. The other was her endless supply of croissants and champagne. Always adorably generous, she never came empty-handed; this morning she had surpassed herself with a supply that would have sated the five thousand.

'Almond, chocolate, pistachio, marzipan... oh, and I've also got healthy peach... that's the flavour of the champagne.'

Raising a toast to the girls, she added, 'It's just a blip, darling, okay?' smiling warmly at Sharon.

Sharon asked Jules meekly what she intended to say to Z&ZaK.

'It is a little tricky, sweetheart; you know there is a weight clause in your contract. I think I'll have to be unobtainable for a few days. As for Glacé Inc., why don't you avoid going in for a while, and tell that bitch Kristen you're off to a health hydro? If you can drop two sizes in two weeks, I'm sure we can help you gain the same. Now, tuck in.'

As Sharon nibbled slowly, her eyes glazed over with a faraway look. Jules D. lowered her voice, and took a deep breath as she touched on a subject she knew Sharon seemed loath to talk about.

'Obviously, there's also the trauma of your dad's illness: that must be affecting you far more than you think. I can easily put out a press release about it. It will explain a lot, and take the heat off you. People will sympathise, be much more forgiving.'

Sharon didn't doubt they would. But the truth was, she was eating more than ever. It wasn't a question of lost appetite. Her father's diagnosis had only a little to do with the dramatic loss. The pounds had been falling off since the Ball. Tempting as it was, using the 'dying father' card as an excuse was tasteless and immoral, and she shook her head adamantly.

'Sharon, maybe it's not related, but why won't you at least talk to us about your dad?' said Jules D., softly.

'If I don't talk about it, it isn't real,' said Sharon. She took a giant bite of doughnut, and closed the subject.

Luckily, the INNERSPEAK affirmations and the increased intake seemed to work. Sharon's weight went up three pounds in three days, and she felt a little happier.

During this time, Sharon was surprised to find that Simon called often to see how she was. Despite the hoo-hah in the press, and the fact she was now dating a film star, he was incredibly kind and understanding about her dad's illness, not shying away from the fact he was actually dying, and asking her in detail exactly how she felt.

Usually ringing her at night, she opened up to him about her past in a way she had told nobody ever before. They spent hours talking, Sharon curled up on her pink pastel duvet, responding to his velvet voice like a lover of classical music.

Simon had the perfect nickname for Carolyn: 'the Wicked Witch of the West'. It made them both laugh at a time when Sharon just felt like crying.

But whenever it actually came down to arrangements to meet him face to face, she would make excuses, deeply insecure about the way her life was plummeting in more ways than one. Finally she agreed to brunch round the corner, and wore the loosest 'A' top she could find, adding a padded money belt around her middle for extra bulkiness.

'Who cares about weight?' he comforted her when she told him how the press were making her feel suicidal. 'Look at me, probably one of the leanest men you'll ever meet! Most women love a big guy.' He was definitely lean, but now Sharon was shrinking he didn't seem half as slim as last time they met. She guessed it was all relevant.

'Listen, Sharon, there was an experiment done once, a long time ago, called Brown Eyes/Blue Eyes – you can look it up on the Net. A brilliant teacher tried to show her kids the dangers of racism. She told the class that there had been some amazing scientific research that pronounced all the children with blue eyes intellectually and physically superior to those with brown eyes. Thing was, within a day, the blue eyes were lauding it over the brown-eyed kids, and the brown-eyed kids let them, feeling ashamed of their eyes.

'The next day, the teacher came in and reversed the situation, telling her class she'd got it totally wrong, and actually it was the *brown-eyed* kids that were superior. Vindicated, they turned even more viciously on their friends with blue eyes, who suddenly felt totally inferior in turn.

'Thing is, neither attitude made the slightest bit of sense.'

'So what you're saying is that it's the same with body image?' asked Sharon, trying hard to concentrate on Simon's theory, and not his own, beautifully intelligent eyes.

'Absolutely. As a photographer, believe me – I know fashion changes all the time. One minute, velvet knickerbockers look cute as hell, the next they look more silly than a Novice Nun Barbie.

'Same with shape. As long as you're healthy, there is no better or worse size, it's only what the media convinces us looks good. Or bad. Attractive, or ugly.'

Sharon loved conversing with Simon. He was bright, funny and effortless company.

'Tell me, what did Maxine say about the dress? I feel awful. It was a great number, you know – just not great on me. My fault.'

'Ah, don't worry about Madame Du Pré. You got her name known all over the world. She said to say, "All publicity c'est fantastique publicité, daaarling!"' he said, imitating her French accent perfectly.

'So, anyway – how's the film star you accessorised it with it?' Finally he had asked the question she dreaded.

'Brill.' She hadn't heard from him in three days.

Simon started to laugh, 'You know, I just don't get what you see in him.'

Sharon giggled at his joke, remembering the conversation she'd had with Simon over Jaz.

'Well, he was so… so keen. And I was flattered!' she repeated.

Once again avoiding the word 'gorgeous'.

'And universally famous?' joked Simon.

'Well, there *is* that!' They both fell about.

Mascara stinging her watering eyes, Sharon headed to the ladies for a make-up check, but when she came back, she saw Simon had picked up her mobile, and taken a call from Kristen. He held out the phone to Sharon, who grimaced.

'Shaz, I've had Quinton Selsick on the phone, who thinks your acting is excellent.' By the disbelieving tone of her voice you could tell she thought Sharon must have slept with the man to get such a good review.

'However, I'm not going to mince my words. He says you're too skinny.' There was a silence as it sunk in.

'So that's it?' asked Sharon.

'No, not exactly. He says he hears it's to do with family stress, and if you can show you're sorting yourself out in the next couple of weeks, the part is yours. But you need to gain at least two stone before the studio will actually sign you.'

'Oh, well, no problem then.'

'You tell *me*, Shaz. You've been avoiding all our calls, and we haven't seen you since you came back from your last LA trip.' She sounded more cold and uptight than a penguin's ass.

'I suggest you book into a Thin Farm a.s.a.p. If you get this role, it's worth £500,000 – that's half a mill for four weeks work. Not to mention the launch of a whole new career. Is that incentive enough for you?' The disdain in her voice was tangible.

'Sure,' said Sharon meekly. 'I'm sorry.'

'Meanwhile,' she added, 'for the sake of your reputation, I'm holding all bookings and "go-sees" until you've sorted yourself out. So concentrate on it.' The phone clicked.

'Another drink?' asked Simon, seeing her crestfallen face.

'Pint of Guinness, packet of peanuts and two bags of crisps,' answered Sharon, with determination.

~

Lose a pound. Stabilise a couple of days. Gain one or two, lose four. By the end of the following week, despite gargantuan efforts, she had dropped a further five pounds. Sharon had gone to her GP for help. He immediately sent her to a hospital consultant specialising in size dysfunction. After more tests than a laboratory mouse, everything came up negative. In poor comfort, the only thing her doctor could finally offer was a dizzy concoction of tranquilisers and sleeping pills.

That's when she knew she *had* to visit Dr. Marvel again. She'd been trying to make an appointment for days, but, worryingly, the telephone number on the advert was 'temporarily out of order', so she was faced with no choice but to turn up on his doorstep. Taking a taxi to Riversal Road, en route she looked at the throng in the West End streets. In the windows were Tent Dresses, Tatters Dresses and Greek Widow Dresses. But, sadly, not Droopy Premiere Dresses, she mused.

'What number, love?'

'150,' said Sharon. He pulled over at148.

'That's odd, can't find it,' he muttered, scratching his head. 'Are you sure you've got the right address?'

'I do. It's 150 Riversal Road.' She handed him the paper.

'Well, that's what it says,' he answered, puzzled. 'Sorry I can't help you. Dunno where the "150" is. Bloody weird. However, I can tell you it's not called that.'

'What do you mean?' asked Sharon, handing him a fat tip.

'Well, y'know. It's like the way Cadogan Square looks like Cad-o-gan. It's actually pronounced Ca-dug-an. Same with Riversal Road. It's not River-sale. It's called Rev-ersal – as in "reverse".'

Sharon stood there. Digested the fact. And froze.

'Ta-ta luv. Can't wait to tell the missus I had you in the car, so to speak. Cheers!' The taxi drove off.

Reversal Road. The Crystal Ball had marked 150 days since she'd visited 150, Reversal Road. ...And it was the day her fortune changed! Dr. Marvel's Miracle? Her throat constricted in fear. What had they done to her? Why had the magic reversed? She ran up and down the road, eyes filling with panic tears, desperate to find the clinic. People either looked the other way, or at her sympathetically, her distress obvious to all.

Then she remembered how she'd spotted the clinic the first time she came. Through an old mirror two workmen were carrying across the road. And it all fell into place. There had been something odd about the first sighting, and now she knew exactly what it was. It was the name of the clinic – all the other shop names had been *reversed*. Dr. Marvel's Miracle Weight Clinic had read normally. It should have read backwards, like the others. The hairs on her arms stood up on end. Cold fear clutched at her throat like the clammy hands of a witch.

She grabbed the arms of passers-by, interrogated shop owners and begged traffic wardens, but an hour later she had to concede.

The clinic was not there. It was gone. It may never have been there. It would probably never come again. She was alone in this world. Alone with her dilemma. She was fighting unknown magic – magic probably more powerful than anything her willpower could ever control.

Chapter Twenty-five

'Sure I'll come with you,' smiled Debbie. 'I still want to put on some weight myself.' Sharon studied the 'Thin Farm' brochure Kristen had ordered Zara to bike over.

'**CHOMPERS – THE RIGHT WAY TO GAIN**' claimed the front page, showing an elegant fortress set in magnificent grounds.

'Okay, well the deal is you make sure I do whatever they demand, okay? Mind you, it's damned expensive –about 100 pounds for every pound I want to gain,' sniffed Sharon.

'Ah, but think what else you'll gain. Five hundred thousand! A Hollywood contract. You've *got* to do it.'

Of course Sharon would do it, and pay for her assistant too. She only hoped the £4,500-a-week price tag meant that the spa worked.

'The thing is, Debbie, to tell the truth, I'm scared they can't help. The doctors say they can do nothing, and I'm eating more than I ever used to.'

'But what are you actually eating? It's vital. Think about it...' urged Debbie, handing her a Diet Plan notepad and a pen.

She looked at the catchy slogan on the cover: 'What You Eat Should Be A Big Deal.'

'Okay, let me think...' She'd had her usual two bowls of cereal and cream for breakfast, and always made sure she had her two chocolate bars with her morning coffee ever since Jules D. had given her an article in the *Lancet* that showed how milk chocolate prevented osteoporosis.

Lunch? No problem. Always started with two bread rolls and butter wherever she dined, and tended to stick with courses that involved thick, cheesy sauces. When cooking for herself, she was careful to order thick-crust pizzas, or Chinese – and always with either fudge cake or banana toffee fritters. Nope, she really didn't think she was slipping up at all.

But then she reluctantly allowed herself to remember the fruit-stall holder on the way home. Such a friendly chap. They'd started chatting, and it only seemed polite to buy his fruit. Such a delicious display of shiny red apples and plump green grapes. How could she resist?

Guiltily, she recalled buying a half-pound of each. So what? So, she'd eaten an apple. Well, two if she was really honest with herself. No real harm in that. But there was. She had to admit it had filled her up more than she expected, and she missed her usual afternoon tea and cake.

Also true that the grapes had spoiled her appetite just before dinner – and that banana. She'd eaten the lot.

'Any fruit or veg?' asked Debbie with the uncanny perception of a mind reader.

'Just a couple of apples,' Sharon answered, innocently.

Her friend took a judgemental intake of breath.

'Go on, I bet that filled you up?'

'Well, I guess so. But I still managed two puddings after dinner,' she added proudly. Didn't want Debbie to think she was a sad, skinny bird.

'Sharon, this is the kind of stuff you've got to watch out for,' warned Debbie, stretching her sinewy body. 'Trust me, you don't want to end up looking like me.'

A week later, the two of them stared up at the high, ivy-clad, stone walls of CHOMPERS Health Club.

'Looks just like a mental prison,' shivered Debbie, nervous at the prospect of being force-fed. Sharon felt a little more confident just being there. After all, she was practically normal. At least, nowhere near as skinny as Debbie.

The towering medieval doors groaned with exclusivity and torture. 'After you, my lady,' curtsied Debbie. Was that a baby bud of sarcasm? Sharon suspected that Debbie's 'attitude' was increasing in ratio to her boss's decreasing girth. Or was she just being paranoid?

Whatever. Sharon's fragile new confidence felt a little tremble as she entered the high hallway. What if she failed here? Either way, she would be stuffed at the Last Chance Saloon.

Their footsteps echoed on the cold flagstones. Sharon's stilettos, reinforced for her struts on the catwalk, clipped so loudly, she tried to tiptoe up to the reception desk. Behind it, an auburn-haired, rosy-cheeked doctor in a white coat signed them in.

'Woah,' whispered Debbie to Sharon. 'If I come out with a figure anything like hers, it'll be worth the agony... and your money.'

Sharon clocked the woman's figure. The white cloak clung to her perfectly proportioned, fulsome shape, and although she was clearly middle-aged, she had the irresistible appearance of a mouth-watering, treacle dumpling.

'Hello, Sharon, Debbie. My name is Dr. Honey Battenburg. I'll be assigned to you for the entire week. Any problems come to me. In moments of weakness, girls, remember – I'm only a buzzer away.'

She smiled kindly. 'Remember, it's a battle to achieve perfection, and I'm on your side. This way...'

She gave a smile that advertised expensive cosmetic surgery and led them to a sterile white room. Sharon sniffed enviously. Even the woman's name oozed extra inches.

Handed thick towelling robes, and told to strip to their undies, she left them alone. By the time she returned, the two girls were huddled together like Romanian refugees.

'Who's first on?' invited Dr. Battenburg. Seeing Sharon wasn't going to budge, Debbie reluctantly volunteered, and stepped cautiously onto the scales.

'Drop your gown dear,' she instructed gently.

Standing there almost naked, Sharon had to admit Debbie's figure had been steadily improving since she first visited her after their row. She could see the way her bottom had started to spread and dimple prettily. Sweet crinkly wrinkles poked from underneath the rotund cheeks. Her thighs had also filled out. Curvaceously convex at the side, instead of muscular and concave.

'Umm… not too bad.' Dr. Battenburg slid the weights along the top of the professional scales, chewed the end of her pen and did some quick calculations. Okay, we need to get your body mass index up quite a lot, and ideally you need to put on in total about 25-35lb – a nice size 18.

'And now you, Sharon. Please, let me take your dressing gown for you.' Aware she was dealing with a celebrity, Dr. Battenburg's tone was far more obsequious.

'Let's see, here we go… 145lb. About size 10. Umm, I think we can do a lot better than that, can't we, dear?'

'WHAT! No! No… that's impossible!' She grabbed the woman's arm. 'Do it again! These scales are wrong! DO IT AGAIN!' she screamed.

Dr. Battenburg backed away, her hand searching nervously for the emergency button that would bring the men in white coats running.

'I'm terribly sorry, my dear. These are state-of-the-art accurate to the nearest milligram. Calm down, Miss Plunkett, please. I know it's sometimes a bit of a shock to be faced with the truth, but we have to know these things, don't we?'

Glancing round in wild panic, Sharon noted the sympathy in Debbie's eyes, and hated her for it.

'Listen, my little love. You've nothing to worry about,' soothed Dr. Battenburg as if talking to a frightened toddler. It had the right effect, and Sharon sobbed quietly as the doctor patted her hand. 'Here's your activity and health programmes for the next forty-eight hours. You'll be monitored carefully. Be strict with yourselves and you'll definitely see results in the end.'

With a reassuring, motherly smile that made Sharon want to throw herself into the woman's dumpling squashy bosoms, they were led to their sleeping quarters.

It was luxurious beyond belief. Fur bedspread, deep pile carpets. Log fire, and, on the mahogany table, a bunch of pink chrysanthemums with a card saying: 'To one of the world's most beautiful flowers! Good luck, Jules D.' It was so, so typical of Jules, and so sweet. But Sharon was also momentarily deflated. She thought maybe Brett had sent them.

'I love it here! I thought we were heading into a monastery cell, but this is truly the Kingdom of God! Look, television, DVD, bar, and fully stocked fridge,' said Debbie, clapping her hands in glee and opening the door.

'Oh look at that,' she quivered. Alongside milkshakes of every flavour, racks and racks of designer chocolate bars and cashew nut packets, fudge, crisps, and pretzels stared back – each separated and labelled Monday, Tuesday, etc. A red sign stated, 'minimum required daily intake'.

A sight that would have once made Sharon think she had died and gone to heaven now made her nauseous as hell. All she wanted was an iced glass of water. Sharon had kept it secret, but she had begun to hate the taste of junk food. It was weird, but anything too sweet, creamy, sugary or savoury sometimes made her feel sick. On the other hand, she often craved fruit and vegetables like a ravenous rabbit. But, of course, it didn't help her bulk up.

'There's no way I can go through with this,' she quailed, looking at the fire escape already.

'Don't be so pathetic,' chided Debbie, irritated. 'Look, silly, it's simple.' She opened a peanut crunch bar, and ate it in three bites.

Sharon calmed down, and lay on the bed sucking a finger of fudge like a good little girl. On Debbie's advice, she stayed still and saved calories as she watched her friend unpack both their bags.

Later that afternoon, whilst Debbie headed off for an unenergetic game of tiddlywinks in the sports arena, Sharon stretched out for a relaxing massage. As the Swedish therapist kneaded her flesh, she imagined it was being stretched and expanded.

Stretched, expanded… and filled.

'And this final oil contains Factor 22,' grinned the handsome blond Viking. 'After all, you don't want to get a suntan, do you? It always amazes me how it makes women look so much slimmer and smooth-skinned. A disaster.'

Sharon peeked down at the way his hands rippled over her thigh tops. Over the last few weeks, the grapefruit peel had vanished. Now it looked more like orange peel. Nope. Sharon had to face it. More like a slightly bumpy apricot. Talking of which, for some unknown reason she really fancied one right now. Oh, how she craved that tart, fresh taste. Tangy… fruity and light.

By dusk, both the girls had retired for a cosy night with the stack of DVDs. Sharon had become nervous of being seen by the other guests, recognising a famous footballer's wife with a well-known eating disorder in the room next to her.

'I don't understand why you want to hide away here,' said Debbie, desperately keen to star spot. 'There's no shame in being here, it's almost a status symbol.'

'No, it's not, Debbie. You're confusing it with rehab. The press are never so kind about this sort of thing.' Sharon, of course, was right.

And her face was well known to all. Anyone could spot her, anyone could tell the papers. Even the staff. Could she trust

Viking Boy? Could she even trust Dr. Battenburg not to talk in return for a down payment on her retirement?

For the tenth time that night she checked her text messages. Finally there was one from Brett. She replied by pressing the call button

'Hi, babe, how's it going?' said the famous voice at the other end.

'Not so great. I feel so miserable. Not heard from my father, have a feeling the messages aren't being passed on. And I hate it here. I just want to go home,' she bleated.

'Now, come on Shaz, what's happened to that voluptuous big woman I kissed at the ball?'

'She's just thrown up three packets of crisps and a Twix bar,' wailed Sharon.

'Stick at it, sweetheart. I know you can do it.' And the phone went dead.

~

'Well, that's incredible,' trilled Debbie. 'I can't believe the difference.' She had just undergone two hours in an herbal water-retention tank to plump up her fat cells.

Looking at Debbie's pink, glowing, fertile-fleshy body, Sharon nodded morosely in agreement. Unlike Debbie, who had gained 3/4 stone, she had lost a further 14lb. A steady two pounds a day. At this rate, she only had 63 days to live before she simply vanished. At 6ft and only 9 stone 2lb, she was now nearing size 8.

'There is, of course, surgery,' advised Dr. Battenburg, deeply perplexed and worried that a client as high profile as Shaz would leave the premises with *less* weight than when she entered. Considerably less. No question, the sacred reputation of CHOMPERS was dangerously at stake.

'What does that involve?'

'Well, lipo-addition. It's painful, I won't deny. And a fairly new procedure. We use a harmless silicone fat substance that is then siphoned into your buttocks and stomach. I'm not sure with such continuing and dramatic loss that it is the right course for you, though. We need to stabilise you first.'

'So what do we do until then?' asked Sharon helplessly.

'Therapy. That's what we need to try next, my dear,' she said, checking a clipboard of her notes as she talked.

'We've run every test imaginable. Your problem is clearly not medical, and, according to our monitoring, you're not breaking the rules. Sometimes the mind is stronger than any of us give it credit for. It's time to meet Dr. Grotemaster.

'He has his own, shall we say, slightly eccentric methods, but he gets marvellous results. Come with me,' said Dr. Battenburg, leading Sharon down some stairs way down into the bowels of the gargantuan building.

'Dr. Grotemaster, meet Miss Sharon Plunkett, you have her notes.' Sharon looked at the other people sitting in the semi-circle around the room. Most hung their heads pathetically. All were slim. Hideously slim. English size 8 to size 2.

'Looking shocked, Sharon? Ve 'ave here American size 0 and in some cases, stand up Stacy,' ordered Dr. Grotemaster 'size 00.' Stacy, all hair extensions and spoilt pout, was dressed in designer tracksuit and trainers, but you could still see her bones. 'Tell our new friend Sharon how we are all united on one thing. We are, aren't we, class? Tell us what it is.' He thwacked a ruler against his thigh like a Nazi SS officer flicking a whip.

'GAINING WEIGHT, Dr. Grotemaster,' they all chimed, as one.

'Sit down, Sharon. Over there,' he ordered in a thick guttural accent. His balding head and half-moon glasses, mean lips and sharp nose made him cold and intimidating.

Sharon turned with pleading eyes to Dr. Battenburg, but she simply pointed at the chair too. 'Go on, dear. Do as the good doctor says.'

Dr. Grotemaster continued, 'Now, I vant you all to think "fat". Do you understand?' He put on music – an old vinyl record on a vintage gramophone. It scratched out the Pastoral Symphony.

'Ludwig van Beethoven… a master. Like YOU are all masters. Masters of your own minds. Now,' he smacked the ruler down hard on a tabletop. 'I vant you to imagine "fat". Do you understand? Close your eyes and imagine your body growing. SEE it growing. How do you look? Turn around in the mirror of your mind. Now, FEEL it growing. SENSE it growing. YOU can make it happen. It WILL happen. Repeat: "I CAN MAKE IT HAPPEN… I CAN MAKE IT HAPPEN!"'

Three days later, it hadn't happened. Three pounds lighter, she lay on the floor head to toe with the other losers. Soft, tinkling music played in the background, as Dr. Grotemaster tried variations on a theme.

'FEEL those dimples on your thighs. Imagine your skin bubbling,' he urged.

Sharon imagined her thighs. But it was useless. She knew the truth: that her unique, lumpy, soft watercolour skin was turning into a blank, boring canvas. Her hand snuck down to feel it. Smooth, unblemished in texture. Taut and sleek as the flank of a thoroughbred. How her heart cried.

Later that night, it was to cry some more. After days of silence and unreturned calls, she had a text from Brett. Excitedly she pressed the open button. But it simply read:

'Sorry Shaz – not going to work out. Brett.'

That was it. Seven words. Seven short, shitty little words? Sharon threw the phone in anger.

'That bastard! I'm not going to let him finish with me like that!' she railed. 'I can't believe it – by text?'

'Oh, no, that's so *mean*,' said Debbie sympathetically (though she'd done the same thing many times).

'Look at that! The prick couldn't even be fagged to type in the word "it's" as in "it's" not going to fucking work out!' cried Sharon in a fury.

'Bastard! I'm going to tell him exactly what I think!!'

'Please, Sharon, don't do it. He's so not worth it. Let it go…' Debbie tried to stop her dialling with a rugby lunge, but she still had enough strength to shove her friend off.

Trouble was, Sharon had experienced too much pain recently to just 'let things go'.

'Hi, it's me. Thanks Brett. I just got your sweet text. Tell me something, how does a man who pays $255,000 for a kiss just walk away like this? What happened?'

There was a silence.

'Shaz, it was easy. Now leave me alone.'

'No, just answer the question.'

'Okay, if you insist, I will. Firstly, look in the mirror. Word has it you're losing even more weight, and you're as skinny as a sparrow. I don't like slim women, okay? It turns me off. And secondly, if you must ask, that quarter of a million was well-spent PR. Amazing coverage. I got it all back on tax, okay? I have to add, though, that was a great kiss. Unexpected bonus. Take care now, bye.'

Sharon looked at the silent phone, and felt the same dark helplessness she'd felt as a little girl. Unable to answer back. Unable to defend herself.

She howled and rocked like a baby as Debbie tried to hold her in her arms. As she tried to sleep, the despair as her future evaporated kept her tossing and turning for the tenth night in a row – once again, the dark bowl of night made her a murky soup of fear.

... She'd asked her father to walk her down the aisle, she'd thrown her bouquet to Jules D. and the waiting crowds, waved to the paparazzi and sailed off with her actor in a golden, hot-air balloon.

'You're too light!' he yelled at her as the balloon rose higher and higher... Then a scrawny bird flew by, and burst it with its beak.

She tumbled down, down, down. Down, to her death.

The next day, Dr. Grotemaster had a breakthrough as he tried to break her down. But it wasn't what he expected.

His methods had changed. Now, he was getting his class to group cradle each other, and talk about their generally troubled childhoods, though some had obviously suffered worse than others.

'Very good, Stacy. So, your brother flirted with your best friend, and they ignored you. Very good. Now, Sharon, let's hear from you.'

Sharon made no move to lie in the centre of the group. They all held their hands out for her, faces warm and shiny. Sharon felt ridiculously touched. But resisted the naff horror of the idea.

'Trust me, it will work. We've had many famous clients here – people you'd never have guessed needed our help. You do as I say. You need to open up. Discretion is my middle name.'

What's your first and last? thought Sharon bitterly, Hitler and Goebbels?

Half an hour later, Sharon was still talking, face soaked with tears as she described her mother.

'Vas she slim, your mother? Or fat?' asked Dr. Grotemaster.

'Oh, model slim,' said Sharon proudly. The class and the doctor looked puzzled, but Sharon was now drifting into her own past world.

'And what happened vhen your father remarried? How did your new family make you feel?'

'Lonely, an outsider. Outcast. Unwanted, worthless.'

'And why do you think that was?' The people in her group held her close, stroking her hair as she choked out the answer.

'My stepmother was full of hatred for my mother. My father never got over her death… never loved his new wife as much, and I think she knew it. I was so like my mother, everyone used to say so… and when they did, I would catch Carolyn looking at me with such bitterness. I think she… she wanted me to disappear.'

'So, how did you cope, vat did you do?' he said, polishing his round-rimmed glasses fervently.

'I don't know…'

'Yes you do. Picture your life back then, Sharon. There you were, all alone…'

Sharon shifted uncomfortably, hating the feelings that rose up from her gut like the arms of a strangling octopus. She remembered the constant rows. Her stepmother screaming at her because she'd left a drawer door open. Her stepmother storming into the sanctuary of her bedroom brandishing a plate she'd forgotten to wash up. Her father doing nothing to protect her. Her stepsisters quietly smug, watching her get into trouble again, and again. Esme and Mona… Esmerelda and Desdemona. Good grief, she'd never noticed that before… their names sounded like the Ugly Sisters…

'Concentrate, Sharon — follow through the visualisation. What did you do after a row?'

Sharon allowed herself to fully picture one. The row in the kitchen when she'd spilt the gravy dish. Sharon remembered crawling back to her room with a packet of biscuits. The time she left the door unlocked? She'd taken the telling off and then hid in the garden. She sobbed for hours, but at least she had that yummy coffee cake to comfort her.

A pattern was emerging…

'Go on, Sharon, ve are getting somewhere, go on… you ate. Good. Now how did you see yourself ven you looked in the mirror?'

Dr. Grotemaster's excitement was palpable, his magnified eyes peering at her as if she was a slithery specimen on a Petri dish.

Sharon pictured herself in her little bedroom. The full-length mirror hanging on the inside of her cupboard door. She remembered the hours and hours she would stand there, staring at her face, tears streaming down her slim cheeks, hands tearing at her young, slender body.

'I… I looked just like my mother. But *she* hated my mother. I didn't want to look like Mummy… It hurt too much. It really hurt.

'Oh God, I wanted to be loved again. That's all I wanted. I thought if I didn't remind her of Mummy, she would care.' Sharon let out an almighty, shuddering sob and continued, talking to herself almost in a trance.

'Stupid, stupid. If I don't look like Mummy, you'll like me better. She'd like me better. I'd like me better. So… so I ate. I ate and ate. I ate… until I got huge. Until I looked nothing like my mummy, nothing like my old self. I felt better… I felt worse.'

The room fell silent in sympathy, as Sharon digested the revelation.

She looked up at Dr. Grotemaster, and round at her companions, wide-eyed and stunned.

'Oh, my God… I ATE. Non-stop. *That's* why! …So I wouldn't look like my mother!'

It was as if a light bulb had been switched on. No, that was a cliché, and the moment deserved so much more than that. It was a sudden realisation that burned brighter than the Blackpool Illuminations, the Northern Lights, and the Millennium Fireworks against one very dark, night sky.

Sharon cried out in anguish, memory… and relief as she excused herself all the years of loathing her body and lack of willpower.

'Right, so ve have to stay vith zis feeling of wanting to eat, live zis moment again,' snapped Dr. Grotemaster. But it was too much for Sharon; she apologised, quickly hugged the group back in return, and disappeared to her room to make an urgent call.

Chapter Twenty-six

Dialling Bournemouth for the third time, she left a message asking someone, anyone, to call. Her dad had only spoken to her once since her last visit, and it had been heated. Hating going into the house and all the old wounds it opened up, she had asked if she could take him out for tea at a little hotel only fifty yards away from where he lived.

'Yes, dear, that would be lovely, really lovely,' he agreed happily. Sharon was thrilled; the idea of sitting in the pretty courtyard and having some private time with him was vital. At this stage, every final moment with him was precious.

Ten minutes later, he rang back.

'Why are you asking me to do this? I'm a sick man,' he stated accusingly, as if Sharon had invited him to dance naked on hot coals.

Sharon was dumbstruck.

It had seemed perfectly reasonable to her. Even though he was ill, she knew he often went out with his wife to catch the fresh sea air. Indeed, he had told her she couldn't see him the day before, because he was going to Esme's house for lunch.

What had happened in the ten minutes since being so excited about going out with her? Sharon knew exactly what had happened. She could just imagine Carolyn's shrill, nagging voice when her father said he was going out for tea.

'Joe, you're a sick man. You know that. How can you think of going out for tea? I have all your medicines. What if something goes wrong? I'm not taking the responsibility, Joseph – after all, I'm the one looking after you…' etc. etc. The manipulation by his wife was so obvious to her, why not to him? It was as transparent as an oxygen mask what she was up to. The woman was determined to make Sharon's last few times with her father as uncomfortable and as unpleasant as possible. If nothing else, Carolyn was constant.

Compromising, Sharon told him she would come all the way down to see him, if he could make sure that she could see him alone – no TV on, no step relatives in the room. He'd said he'd organise it, and call her back. Two weeks had passed, and she was still waiting.

Debbie joined her in the room a couple of hours later, surprised to find Sharon standing stock still, staring at her slim form in the mirror, eyes distant.

'You know what?' said Debbie, oblivious to the drama going on in Sharon's head. 'Perhaps the answer is not to move so much.' She was towelling her hair from the Jacuzzi she'd been soaking in, and insisted they both try the Stomach Exercise Room.

'Come on,' Debbie cajoled, 'you never know, you might enjoy it?'

Very slowly, as if holding the arm of a sick patient, she led her friend through the meandering corridors until they reached a glass door. Sharon looked inside the large, wood-floored hall. It was too much and she turned to go. Debbie pushed her through. Dressed in fluffy white robes, about twenty guests lay on white leather chaise-longue like a school of stranded walruses. A corpulent customer shifted his weight and clicked his fingers at the staff. Worried at his exertion, one of the attendants immediately ran over and handed him the remote control panel for his personal TV system. They lifted the headphones onto his head, and he grunted a perfunctory 'thank you'.

The table beside each lounger lay laden with goodies. Popcorn, flapjacks, marshmallows, boiled sweets. Without taking his eyes off the screen, the man opened his jaw, allowing the attendant to pop three pink mallows dipped in chocolate into his mouth.

'Take a lounger,' insisted a young, plump female trainer, wearing a white tracksuit embroidered with the emblem of CHOMPERS in gold.

She stretched out, the leather cushioned base hard under her bony frame. It reminded her suddenly of the chaise-longue in Dr. Marvel's waiting room.

'What would you like to watch? Modern, musical or old classics?'

'I don't know, I don't even care. Maybe an old classic?'

She plumped a cushion behind her back, put a disc in the side of the TV and pulled it across her on a swing arm.

'How about this, *The Mirror Crack'd* with Rock Hudson and Elizabeth Taylor?' Sharon was annoyed at her choice. Was she being subversively rude? Then she sat up with interest. 'Stick it on,' she demanded.

She waited for the appearance of Liz – an old film. Would it show her as slim or fat? She sometimes thought she'd dreamed a world where women were idolised for being skin and bone.

But when Taylor made her appearance, it told her absolutely nothing. She was simply plump and middle-aged. A woman renowned for size fluctuations, Sharon could only guess she was somewhere in mid-cycle. Despondent, Sharon flopped back down weakly, and, believing she had acquiesced, an assistant immediately stepped forward to spoon-feed her some cake. She took the first mouthful, and it tasted unbearably sweet. She craved some fresh juice or fruit.

'Come on, just one more,' coaxed the trainer, firmly.

'Please, not another mouthful,' she begged, crumbs of chocolate cake making a dark moustache around her mouth.

Looking around the room at the mouths chomping away, Sharon's stomach turned over. She was going to be sick.

Crying and puking in the toilet, the door suddenly swung open.

'You naughty, naughty girl!' scolded Dr. Grotemaster. 'You're doing that on purpose.'

~

'Ve *vill* get to the bottom of zis… I believe the vay forward is hypnosis. It vill unleash the corners of your mind.'

He was beginning to take her failure very personally, and he scared her. Certainly, a private session with the Nazi was so not what Sharon wanted, but she'd just received a phone call from Kristen: 'Michael Grey wanted to meet with you as soon as you're released – I mean… come home. So be quick, and be fit – if you know what I mean. Size 18, nothing less.'

Sharon was so far from that target, she didn't even have the energy to reply. The moment he saw her, she figured that contract would disappear faster than her skinny butt. But it did spur her on to sort out the rest of her life before it was too late.

'Now go back, Sharon – go back to when you first felt unhappy about your weight.' Grotemaster had her stretched on a soft couch in his office. Books were neatly stacked two feet high on his desk. Walls were covered in packed shelves, apart from one – which proudly displayed obscure certificates from universities and conferences from all over the globe.

The lights were lowered, the blinds drawn. Suddenly, she felt very, very sleepy. His voice drifted in and out, in and out… all she wanted to do was go to sleep, and for his voice to go away. But every now and then she heard a question, and she found herself answering heavily, exhaustedly, in the hope he'd be satisfied, and drift away. Far, far away.

'…And so, you say you took this… this magic pill. What happened next?'

Sleepily Sharon described the hope she felt on that day she went shopping for something new – a wardrobe of clothes to suit the way she was going to look.

'It said I couldn't eat anything for two hours… so I just shopped and shopped, bliss.'

His voice seemed even more distant… she could barely hear. But he prodded her to speak some more. She floated in and out of consciousness.

'I saw this beautiful yellow dress, tiny blue flowers...' Off she drifted again, like a boat softly bobbing on a long mooring rope.

He hauled her back a little.

'You say you were in a cubicle, and the dress was too small? How did zat make you feel, Sharon?'

'Bad, really really bad. I couldn't get the dress off. I remember...'

There was a long, long pause.

'Remember what? Tell me?'

'I remember falling to the floor, sobbing. I was hot, suffocating in there... miserable. Hated myself. So sad... So lonely. So ugly. And then, I... I saw my bag.'

She stopped.

'What was inside, Sharon, go on.'

'Inside was a piece of cake... a Fairy cake I had left over from earlier. I reached for it and...

'OH GOD!' Like a drowning bug fighting a whirlpool, she forced herself fully awake and sat suddenly upright, head dizzy.

'OH MY GOD! OH MY GOD!' She grabbed his collar with both hands.

'Oh God, Dr. Grotemaster, YOU'VE GOT TO HELP ME! I *ate* it. I ATE! I didn't wait the TWO HOURS on the instructions! I ruined the spell. I ruined it!! Do you understand now?'

Peeling her desperate hands off his white coat and trying hard to hide his disgust at their boniness, Dr. Grotemaster looked at her resignedly. He didn't understand, not at all. And with all his professional experience, he didn't think there was any hope that he ever would.

Chapter Twenty-seven

Sharon stood in the shop doorway as the day suddenly darkened. Above, a monstrously bulbous cloud filled the skies, stretched its pregnant belly and released a heavy gush as its waters finally broke. Her phone finally rang. It was Jules D. calling her back.

'I got expelled,' said Sharon ashamedly to Jules D. 'They "asked me to leave".'

'Oh, my poor love, I know. I read all about it.'

'What's been happening in the outside world? Go on, tell me your worst,' said Sharon, wiping the raindrops blown onto her face.

Jules took a deep breath, ready to use years of honed diplomatic skills. 'Okay. Well, Z&ZaK have cancelled the contract for the time being. Thing is, Shaz, it's a really sophisticated brand. They were a tiny bit disheartened when you got mobile phone "papped" at *CHOMPERS*.' That was a Jules D. understatement of the highest order.

The front pages had run a sneaked-out shot of Sharon in a screaming match with a bald-headed doctor, shoving a giant cake in his bespectacled face. And ZaK's actual words were 'Fire the skinny bitch!!'

'*Urban Cool* has, err… cooled off a little too. Slight problem there, from what I hear.'

'But they never put a weight clause in because they were mainly shooting my face. Even though they've dropped me, surely they can't ask for any money back?'

'Umm, well you may have noticed half the name of the product is, unfortunately, "Cool" – and there is a clause about behaviour. Alas, food fights at a Thin Farm aren't quite street cred at the moment. … Although maybe I could put a spin on that?' she added hopefully.

'Don't bother. What else?'

'Remember that cover shoot you did for *Rich Recipes* magazine just before you flew out for the premiere?'

'Yes, in my bikini eating a Pavlova.'

'Well, some bastard from the photography studio sold a story to the tabloids that he spent six hours retouching your image to make it look fatter. Big storm. Readers screaming they're being fooled, and all that.'

'I had nothing to do with it! That's not fair! Christ, how much did he retouch?'

'Oh, I don't know. The usual they always do, probably. You know, teeth…hair. But I think he also shortened the shot to make you look more rotund… and maybe added an unnecessary bump or two. They do it to cover shots all the time. It's just that people don't realise it. Bad luck, sweetie, that's all.'

'Anything else I should know about?'

'Damn, other phone's going. Sorry, darling, I've got to go. Call you later, okay?'

Sharon put the phone down, feeling more alone than ever. She felt Jules D. had lost interest both professionally and as a friend. She was more washed up than the wrappers in the fast-filling gutters that gurgled at her feet.

Sharon walked along the windswept streets, a shadow flitting between the big, the bold and the beautiful. With so many pounds lost, her walk felt airy and light, almost like she was floating. It increased her feeling of invisibility. She spotted a *Minus Miss* shop, selling size 12 and smaller for skinnics. Wandering in, she looked at the other women, heads down, eyes to themselves sorting through the drab, uninspiring clothes to find something, anything, that would flatter them and make them look a size larger. The shop girls employed were minus-sizes, to make the customers feel more normal. Sharon eyed the minuscule American 00 assistant behind the counter, and knew she wasn't that far off. Whatever, at 6ft tall, everything hung on her willowy frame like damp rags on a scarecrow.

She aimlessly wandered out, not caring to buy anything, not caring whether she ate or drank, not caring whether she lived or died.

At first, there had been a plethora of break-up articles in the press – bitchy features with titles like:

'SKINNY SHAZ STONE-WALLED BY BRETT'.

But now they concentrated purely on her weight, with features like 'SKELETAL SHAZ SHEDS STONES!' accompanied by pictures of her tiny frame, hand held in front of her face, hiding from the camera lens. It was utterly insane. How could the number of pounds a girl weighed rate such coverage? How did it ever come to this? But there she was, on front pages alongside global warming, war and world peace.

Luckily enough, Sharon's trademark eyes and hair could be easily disguised with a hat and dark glasses. In the streets, it seemed no one had a clue who she was. Or maybe they just didn't expect to see a face so well known walking around like any other shopper.

As she braced against the wind to head home, there was a tiny 'ting' noise. She thought she might have imagined it. But on checking she saw she had a message from her father's home number.

She clicked, and read with horror: *'Your father's condition has dramatically worsened. Call if you want to see him.'*

Shaking, she dialled immediately, and Esme answered the phone.

'Yes, well, he had a bad night. Don't think he's going to hang on for long. Come now if you want to see him.'

Sharon couldn't drive. She didn't know what the hell to do. Distraught, she rang Debbie, but then remembered she was still at *CHOMPERS* finishing the third week. She rang Simon's studio, but was told by one of his gang that they thought he was out of town on a shoot.

Somehow, three hours later, blinded by tears and the harsh hammering rain, she found herself outside her father's house.

Hands trembling from the hellish drive and fear of how ill he would be, she tried to knock, but failed. She stood there for ten minutes, trying to compose her feelings: anger, betrayal, hatred and love.

Finally she plucked up the courage, and lightly knocked.

Esme opened the door and showed her into her father's bedroom. Like a wizened old warlock who had snuck into a giant's bed, he lay asleep, propped up with a couple of pillows.

No, not asleep, in a far, far away place. He was in a deep coma. Sharon was devastated. The illness had left him almost unrecognisable. She was too late! She thought of all the things she had wanted to say to him, the words she'd been formulating on the way down. But it was all too late.

'When did he get to this state?' she asked Esme, who suddenly looked uncomfortable.

'Well, he's been getting worse day by day. But finally in a coma, well, it happened early this morning.'

Sharon realised they had deliberately left it to text her until he was unconscious, robbing her of any chance to actually talk to him. She fought back the bitter words she longed to say, and turned her attention to the frail shell that barely breathed in front of her.

'I'll leave you alone. Take your time,' said Esme softly, with a concession towards kindness. Sharon stared at her father, and touched his hand. It was warm, alive. He looked so still, she had almost expected it to be cold. His breathing was laboured, and irregular.

'Dad, Dad. Can you hear me?' Nothing. 'Dad, it's me, Sharon. I'm here.' No response. Sharon noticed his walking stick propped up against the flowered wallpaper, and tears fell as she realised he'd never use it again. She tried to wrap his limp arm around her, feeling like a lost little girl and knowing it would be the last time she'd ever have a hug from her daddy. But there was little room to curl up next to him. And she laid it back down, lovingly.

Composing herself, and whispering 'Dad' over and over again, Sharon thought back to the old days when he would occasionally visit her in Kingston. He'd always try and excuse Carolyn's behaviour. Time and time again he'd say to her, 'Sweetheart, I know you two don't get on, but she looks after me.' It had been his mantra for years. Funnily enough, he had never said 'I love her' about his second wife, which in truth would have been easier to take. Just, 'The thing is, darling – she looks after me.' That had always hurt, especially when Sharon was a little girl. After all, *he* was the parent. It was selfish, because what he was really saying was: 'Sorry, darling, she's good to me, even though I know she's horrible to you. If you love me, you should be happy for me.'

Whatever. The fact Carolyn's behaviour had made it difficult for Sharon to see much of her father in later years was his bad karma. The price *he* paid. Having never stood up to her, did he finally feel trapped at the end? Maybe.

She tried to push the negative thoughts away, and looking at her father now, she just wanted to tell him how many memories she would carry of him. How she would always remember him with love. And to look out for her on the other side.

She started to speak softly to him, when Esme unexpectedly came back into the room.

Remembering their brief time as kids together, Sharon felt a small bond in such a sad situation.

'How long has he been breathing like this?' she asked quietly. Her father would take a deep breath, then stop for what felt like forever, then breathe again. Each breath one wondered if it actually would be for eternity.

'Since lunchtime, for about four and a half hours. I think I'll get my mother to come in again.' No! thought Sharon, experiencing the queasy fear Carolyn's presence always made her feel.

But Esme had left to get her, leaving Sharon in a panic. She had thought they would at least give her twenty minutes when Sharon had first arrived. But, suddenly, that was to be snatched from her. She hadn't said anything near what she wanted; hadn't said she loved him. Hadn't kissed him goodbye. Before she could gather her thoughts, Carolyn flounced in, and draped herself across the bed.

'Please, just give me two minutes to say goodbye,' said Sharon, shocked, so wanting precious seconds alone with her dad for the very last time.

'I'm his wife. I've been his wife for nearly ten years. I deserve to be here.'

Sharon was horrified. This woman had enjoyed many weeks to say her goodbyes. Many sweet days, and hours at the end, when her father was actually capable of responding. But she wanted to steal the little time Sharon had as well. The selfishness was indescribable. Shocking. Despite a three-hour dash through the storm, Sharon was going to be left with no tender farewells, nothing. The cuckoos were once again taking everything they could from her.

'Wife for ten years? I've been his daughter for 21 years!' Sharon counteracted. She believed the odds of him actually going in the next minute or so was about the same as him sitting up for a game of Chess.

She begged and pleaded again, 'I'm only asking for *two* minutes.' At the very least, Sharon knew Carolyn could have easily chosen to stay out of her sightline and wait by the door for a few moments.

But no, she still refused to leave, settling herself even closer to Joe in a pathetic act of possessiveness. Sharon stood back, disgusted.

'You really are an *evil* woman!' she cried in desperate anguish; a feeling retched up from the bottom of her damaged soul. Words long overdue. She stood to leave the room, and away from the hellish woman forever.

Unmoved, Carolyn pursed her lips self-righteously.

Her father didn't actually die until twenty hours later. Sharon was sent the date of the funeral by text.

Chapter Twenty-eight

It was night outside. Sharon lay curled in a ball, eyes staring at the tissue-strewn floor. Weeks had passed. Or was it a day? Maybe it was just an hour? Sharon had lost all track of time. The loneliness and the knowledge she'd never see her father again came sporadically and often. A sudden memory surfacing would create a wave that would crash over her, leaving her sitting in a sea of salty tears. She'd had a few phone calls from Debbie, Jules D. and Simon, but didn't have the energy to reply. What the hell, none of them really cared anyway.

At random intervals she had dragged herself up to the scales and stepped on. It seemed her weight had finally settled at 114lb. At nearly six feet tall, the falling elevator had juddered to a halt leaving her an American size 0. At least she wasn't going to disappear, she surmised miserably. But how had she ever thought this look was stunning? To Sharon, now brainwashed into thinking big was beautiful, her head seemed too large for her body, a little alien in appearance; whilst her sad shoulders jutted sharper than a wire coat hanger. She was so gaunt, she could fit into children's clothes. *Infants'* clothes, at that.

The thought that tortured her equally was her lack of willpower, and what fame and beauty she had lost. Over and over again, she remembered the scene in the cubicle, berating herself again and again for eating the fairy cake. How could she have not lasted *two* pathetic little hours? Regardless of her mixed-up life as a kid, she was now an adult. There was no excuse, she should have had more control. But instead, she had been a deliberate back-seat passenger as she drove along the highway of self-destruct – and it had taken this to see it.

Whatever. One thing was for certain – she had thrown away her big chance; destroyed the one miracle that had truly changed her life.

Well done, Sharon.

On the occasions she could raise herself up, she trawled the Internet in a desperate fervour. Dr. Marvel and his Miracle Weight Clinic were nowhere to be found. But she did find sites totally dedicated to stars' weight – whether up or down, every pound was monitored. The truly obsessed fan could even receive emails announcing if their idol had lost or gained a 1/4lb. It was more sick than her own body, thought Sharon.

She lay there trying to think of one good reason to live. But it was hard. She now had no family. No one to care about her. No one to call on Christmas. Or to call her.

She also had no work. She had been dropped from Glacé Inc. like a melting dollop from an ice cream cone. Splat. Contracts cancelled and money owed back. To add to her woes, she was due to move out of her home and sanctuary for five years in just two days time. Not only had she so far failed to pack a nail file, she was moving to a strange new place with a staggering £600,000 plus mortgage. And since she wasn't working, she'd probably have to use the last of her money to pay it off. What to live off then?

But worst of all were the papers and magazines and their merciless onslaught. She couldn't pass a magazine rack without seeing '*Skinny Shaz*' paparazzi-snapped covers. She felt she was everyone's figure of fun. All she wanted to do was crawl out of sight, like a wounded bear. No, she was flattering herself. That animal was warm, big and cuddly. She was a starved little mouse. A measly little wounded mouse, that had scabby fleas.

If only she could hide somewhere forever. Move away. As she thought about it, the idea grew more and more appealing. Who the hell would miss her? Not Jules D. She just saw her as a client. That was all. Not Debbie. Instead of best friend, now Sharon was just her boss and passport to a glamorous life. A life Debbie was already experiencing with John… Joe… Jack? What's-his-name. A life Sharon was never going to experience again. Then there was Simon. Handsome, funny, witty Simon. He'd never fancy her now. Oh, get real, face it. He never did. Sharon groaned in pain. If only she could stop the hurt. If only…

Then she realised, actually she could go away forever. The drawer in her bathroom contained the answer. A supply of sedatives that would send her to dreamy, sleepy bye-byes, and all her problems would fade away. Just like her. What a great idea! A feast of barbiturates.

She wrapped her old fluffy dressing gown round her almost twice, and made her way slowly to the vanity unit. Her long legs shook with what she knew she wanted to do. She reached inside, and took out two bottles of dainty white pills and carried them back to her messy nest bed.

Swallowing a couple with a third glass of wine, she laid her head back.

She rang Debbie.

'Hi Sharon! Long time no speak! How are you coping?'

'Not great. Not great at all. Oh, Debbie… I feel so alone.'

'Sorry, what did you say? Alone?'

'I feel so… can't you hear me?'

'Not too well. You're re-routing to my mobile. Hey, guess what!? Remember that crappy Saturday job we had at The Cut Above? Well, I'm *there*! They're having a launch party. Can you believe this, as your assistant they want me to open their new salon two doors down. I'm *so* excited! *Me*, a celebrity! They're actually paying me. What a hoot! Have to go over and cut a ribbon – I just heard that cow manageress saying she hopes I can do it better than I cut anyone's hair!'

'Sounds fun. Hope you have a really good time,' said Sharon weakly.

'You okay?'

'Sure. I'm okay, Debbie. I'm fine. Bye. Have fun now. Have a good time for me.'

She started to feel slightly drowsy. She had to make the decision to go for it or not, before she fell asleep. She held up the pills in the bottles and shook them like baby carnival maracas.

'All I wanted was to enjoy life a tiny little bit more. That's all,' she murmured. What to do, what to do? She held a bottle outstretched, in an upturned hand.

'To be, or not to be, that is the question.' She struggled to remember her classroom Shakespeare lessons. 'To be fat, or to be thin? Whether 'tis nobler in the mind to suffer the slings and arrows of outrageous fortune… each has brought with it? Or to take skinny arms against a sea of troubles, to die. To sleep?' she finished dramatically, pleased with her own Sharonspeare version.

However, there was no one to hear her performance. She sobbed with loneliness, slugging back a fourth glass of wine in despair.

Did she really want to do this to herself? Could she do this? No.

She decided to ring Jules D.

'Darling, how are you?'

'Okay,' said Sharon sadly.

'Okay? Not okay, by the sounds of it. Look, I can't talk – I'm with a client right now. I'll call you back, okay?'

'No, no, don't worry. Don't. It doesn't matter. You stay with your client. I'm fine. Really fine. See ya. Must have lunch. Bye…' Sharon hung up, tears making her sore eyes even redder. She felt so let down. So alone.

All she knew was that she didn't want to 'feel' anything anymore. Ever.

Maybe that meant she had to die…? Hopefully heaven was a place where people didn't have bodies, nobody was judged. Maybe everyone's soul just floated around in a swarm of happy atoms?

Her mind was rambling as her eyes felt heavier. She tried to pour another glass, but, hands unsteady, spilt it all over her.

Grabbing the bottle instead, she tossed back a gulp, then took a long, hard look at her body in the full-length mirror at the end of her bed.

The irony was she was exactly as she had dreamed she once wanted to look, all those weeks and weeks ago in life before the Pill.

You did it, Sharon! she sighed in sarcastic disgust. So there she finally was. Size 0. A great big round nothing. An empty hole she'd fallen into. No, make that slipped. An oval mouth that gaped ready to swallow what was still left of her whole.

At only 21, the elasticity of her skin meant it had shrink-wrapped back around her bones, leaving her looking taut and firm. But now that just seemed bland. Boring and bland. Not a pretty wrinkle, dimple or roll to be seen. Tears silently falling, she looked at her back view with a hand mirror. The gap between her stick-thin thighs gave her legs the emaciated look of a famine-struck African infant, her protruding ribcage the carcass of an antelope. It was horrible! She smashed the hand mirror against the wall, shattering its glass across the wooden floor. Wobbling now as the drink and drugs took effect, Sharon sank to her knees in despair, rocking herself back and forward, back and forward. She rocked incessantly, silently, like an orphaned cot baby that would never be picked up. Being slim, being fat… It didn't matter. All she ever wanted was to be normal, to be loved.

The papers now said she was a skinny freak. She picked up what was left of the mirror, and stared at her reflection, distorted in the remaining shards. She hated what she saw – the pain in her eyes frightened her. Forget the pills, they took too long. She could end it there and then. A couple of slices on the flesh… Quick and easy. She picked up a large, vicious shard that had skittered behind her, her green eyes reflected back, a dull, muddy sludge. Then, with her other hand, she reached for the pill bottle.

To be or not to be? Which to use, which to do? The irony was so heavy, she gave a bitter laugh. The mirror had ruled her life. A pill had changed it.

Ah, how about both? she thought, cleverly. A homage to both.

She downed another swig of wine, popped another pill, and held the glass sliver poised.

'Ouch!' It hurt as it sliced her wrist. But apart from a superficial cut, not a lot happened. She was doing this all wrong. Pathetic, pathetic, pathetic. Maybe the Grecians got it right, a nice hot bath… cut the wrists and take the pills. Or maybe, take the pills and cut the wrists? Either, both … or none?

Slowly, she crawled towards the bath like a poisoned slug and turned on the taps. She pulled herself up and over the side, settling into the cold walls as warm, comforting water embraced her body. She was a baby in a wonderful white cot…. It rocked. …It was a cradle. It was a 'coffin'. Her mind drifted along on the tide.

She didn't care. Not long now, then I can just switch off… she thought sleepily. Peaceful, lovely …loooovely sleep.

There was somebody banging at the door.

How irritating thought Sharon, eyes shut heavily, head rocking gently.

'Go away! I'm too tired,' she shouted. But it only came out as a whisper.

Keys jangled, and the voice of Mrs. Lucas, her landlady, could be heard. And a man's.

But by then Sharon had gently slipped into blissful oblivion.

Chapter Twenty-nine

The flat was quiet. Deathly quiet. Outside an approaching siren wailed.

Simon sat on the bed's edge, his head in his hands. He shuddered at the sound of the siren, as if being shaken awake. His head was throbbing, and the siren only made it worse. Then it faded away.

'Why?' he asked aloud. There was no one there to answer.

The landlady was gone now. She had let him in, but that was all she could do. That was all anyone could do now.

He put his head back in his hands, supported on his knees. This was so awful.

'Why did she do it?' he asked himself. If only she'd talked to him more. 'Oh, Sharon, why? Why did you do it?'

He felt a hand on his shoulder, and looked up to see a familiar, but equally distraught, face.

'It's alright,' said Debbie, looking down on him, trying to comfort him with a smile. 'I'm here.'

'I just don't understand,' he said. 'I don't get it.'

'There's nothing to understand,' Debbie sighed, feeling the pain of guilt and sadness. 'Poor Sharon, she was going through so much. We should have seen it coming. I think she just felt she had nothing to live for.'

'But she had us,' he said, eyes welling.

'I know, but I don't think she knew,' said Debbie, sitting down on the bed next to him. 'She was always so insecure. Ever since her mum died. She just never believed she was worth loving.'

'Oh, Sharon… you silly girl. You were always so lovable. I was falling in love with her, you know. I should have told her earlier.'

In love with her?

The voices were floating along, disembodied, like a dream.

I'm dreaming, thought Sharon.

No, not a dream. The last moments were coming back to her.

I'm in Heaven! she thought – relieved she'd actually made it over to the other side. And it sounds like someone is saying they love me. Somebody actually loves me… What a heavenly place this actually is, she sighed, her body bobbing lightly on a soft, fluffy cloud.

The voice sounded deliciously familiar. It was Simon's. What was he doing up here?

Wait, it's coming from far away... Well, of course. Obviously, in Heaven you can hear those on earth who you care about.

Ummm… She loved Heaven. It seemed she'd be able to see as much of Simon as she wanted. Good being a free spirit. But it was surprisingly dark. She couldn't see a thing. Nothing. Where were the bloody lights that were supposed to guide you? She wanted to look for her dad. Shouldn't he be waiting, hands outstretched for her at the end of a tunnel, or something?

Sorry, but it really was too bloody dark. Must find an angel to complain to… She strained to see in the pitch black.

Her eyes flicked open.

'Great,' said Debbie. 'Simon! She's coming round again!'

'Sharon, you're going to be okay. We're here,' said Simon, holding her hand and stroking her forehead tenderly.

Sharon looked into his eyes, and breathed a deep sigh. She was alive.

She realised she was lying in her bed. The wet tendrils of her hair spread over the pillow like a beached mermaid.

She tried to lift her hand to his, but it was leaden and heavy.

She noticed a rough piece of cloth tied around her wrist in a makeshift bandage.

'Do you remember what happened? How many pills have you taken?'

Sharon squeezed her mind hard to try and concentrate.

Not many… two, maybe three.

'Debbie, go down and stand by the door – take the bottles to show them… the paramedics should be here any second.'

'Think, Sharon, what else do you remember…?'

She remembered him dragging her out of the bath. What had happened? It slowly came back to her…

She remembered the banging on the door, and then his voice. 'Sharon, speak to me. It's me… Simon.'

'Oh God, no, …I look like shit.'

He'd sighed, 'Great! You're still with us! What the hell did you think you were doing?'

'I… I don't know. I just want to sleep. Please, I really need to sleep.' She recalled trying to turn into a foetal position, but Simon had lifted her light frame up into his arms and cradled her gently, like a little child.

'Sharon, come on. Wake up,' he'd said as he headed towards her bedroom.

'What are you doing here?' she'd tried to ask him, but her mouth was working strangely, like chewing on balls of wool.

'Debbie rang me from Croydon, Jules too. You hadn't called any of us back for three days, and then you rang all three of us in one go.'

'You rang me before?' Sharon was all confused.

'Many times.'

She had looked at him through her half-closed eyes. She had felt so drunk, so floaty, and she was sure she was going to die. So, like a pissed ladette on a girls' night out, she felt she had nothing to lose. Not a jot.

'Soooo, tell me, Simon, what do you think of me? Really think?' she had slurred, dizzy headed as the room swam around her.

'What do I think? I think…' He weighed up the situation.

'The truth? Okay, why not. Here it comes. You always make me laugh. I love being with you. In fact, I probably love you. There, I've said it. I'm crazy about you. Adore you. Always thought you were cute as hell.'

'What, me? Always? …Fat or thin?'

'Sure. I've told you it's all in the mind, anyway. And, hey, I'm not exactly Adonis!' he had added modestly.

Actually, in her eyes he certainly was. Sharon remembered trying so hard to swallow the facts he'd just fed her. When she had finally digested his words, it was the best meal she'd ever had.

As he dropped her onto the bed, he bent his head and brushed his lips across hers. Then he softly kissed them. Twice, causing a tingling sensation *all over her body. He tasted sooo… sweet, like strawberries and double cream… like chocolate crème brulée… like coconut cookie ice cream… She was finally getting her just desserts. Sharon had managed a groggy smile then closed her eyes, desperate to sleep.*

Then there was a blank in her memory. She looked at Simon standing over her like a concerned medical student, then looked at Debbie. Even though she weas dressed in her finest designer suit, her lipstick and mascara were smudged. And her face looked extraordinarily pale. It's Coco Chanel the Clown, Sharon thought with naughty irreverence. She closed her eyes, and tried to remember what had happened next.

The sound of clattering stilettos on wooden floors and Sharon saw Debbie's chubby legs stalking into the bedroom clad in a high pair of red fake Louboutins.

'I got here as soon as I…Oh, my God!! … I'm too late!'

Through half-closed eyes Sharon had seen Debbie throw her hands to her mouth in dramatic diva hysterics. Simon turned and calmed her.

She was screaming.

'No, no… I know there's a lot of blood, but it's just a superficial cut. I think she's going to be fine,' said Simon, turning back to pull Sharon close, wiping the damp locks off her forehead tenderly with a cold sponge.

'Debbie, you came too?' Sharon had said, struggling to open her eyes properly.

'Of course I did, you silly cow. Missed me big moment too! You had me so worried, Sharon. Really worried. I love you, you know. You're my oldest mate.'

'And now your skinniest!' Sharon recalled, smiling soppily. 'Love you too,' she had managed to say back.

They had bandaged her wrists. And had told her the paramedics were on their way. It had gone dark again.

But it seemed now they had arrived.

'You go downstairs, I'll stay with her,' said Debbie.

'No, you go,' said Simon. 'I don't want to leave her.

'In truth, I don't ever want to leave her...' he uttered quietly – this time looking directly at Sharon's sea-green eyes.

She gave him a subtle, impish smile, and slipped into semi-dreams. What had the gypsy said? 'I see a man involved in "pictures".' It wasn't Brett. Of course it wasn't. Simon touched her cheek and caught a tear on his finger.

...She'd ask her father to walk her down the aisle, she'd throw her bouquet to Jules D. and the waiting crowds... and...

And then the image faded. Her mind blanked.

What type of wedding? She couldn't picture it. But it was nothing to do with the sleeping pills or the wrong man. She didn't want to this time. Sod it.

He deserved more than a stupid fantasy because he was different. This was real. And she would take it one step at a time. Right there and then, she knew the only thing that mattered was he really cared about her, fat or thin.

And they were finally going to get together.

The Epilogue
A Year Later

The studio lights shone in her face, the music blared, and Sharon gave a famous toss of her Scandinavian blonde hair.

'Love it, Sharon. Give it another shake,' said the renowned photographer with a disarming smile.

The team buzzed around her like busy worker bees attending their Royal Queen.

She was so happy, she imagined the swarm were carrying little placards saying 'Sharon Rules Okay!'

Cheekbones sharp, green eyes glinting like a cat, she twisted her long limbs and slender torso to show off her tiny butt in the tight white jeans and cropped T-shirt top.

'God, you look fantastic. I love you, kiddo,' said Simon from behind the camera.

'Love you too,' she trilled, with no fear of rejection.

'Darlings, isn't it time for a break?' said Jules D., coming out of the studio kitchen with a tray bearing large champagne flutes and fresh buttered *pain au chocolat*, with Max at her side, laughing at some private joke.

As Sharon took a mouthful of the delicious, home-baked pastry she gave Jules a giant hug.

'I owe you so much, Jules, thank you.'

'Really, I thought the croissants were a little stale myself?' smiled Jules D.

'You know *exactly* what I'm talking about!' insisted Sharon.

'Ah, you must mean my dinner with Mr. Grey. Marvellous man. Mar-vell-ous. There I was, eating and drinking away with him, whilst you were popping pills and slitting your wrists. Silly girl.'

'Well, had I known at the time you'd set up a meeting with him, I might have given that bit a miss!' said Sharon.

'I told you, you'd had so many knocks, I didn't want to get false hopes up. But then again, maybe I should have. I knew I could pull it off. More champagne?'

'Make that a coffee,' said Debbie protectively, emerging from the dressing room with a big grin.

Armed with a stack of clothes in one hand and a pot of coffee in the other, she clip-clopped over in a short velvet skirt and a pair of thigh-high, brown suede boots that made her chubby legs seem even more curvaceous.

As Sharon poured herself a steaming, aromatic cup, she recalled the moment she found out her life would change again.

It was when Jules had visited her in hospital later that awful night she'd tried to end it all.

'Is she okay?' Jules D. had asked, rushing into the room.

'She's going to be fine,' Simon had replied, sitting at the side of the bed.

Sharon had opened her tired eyes to see Jules, normally so together and controlled, looking shaky and ashen-faced.

'Thank God!' Jules had said.

She saw the shock register on her face as she noticed her bandaged wrist.

'I'm sorry,' Sharon had apologised, lamely. 'So sorry. I just didn't think anyone cared. Gosh, you left a client for me!'

Jules knelt down and hugged her tightly. Sharon had felt a warmth sweep over her, a feeling of protection she hadn't felt since her mother died.

'Of course I did, you sounded so strange. Darling, you're one of the funniest, most lovable women I know, okay.

'Listen to me Sharon, I know you don't think you are, and I also know exactly why you don't think you are.

'But, believe me, you are, okay? I'm going to have to get you a pile of those self-esteem books… and a free consultation with one of my clients, he's a top therapist, okay?'

'Okay' Sharon had answered meekly. 'In fact, it seems my life is always "okay" when you're around,' she whispered.

As Sharon closed her eyes, Jules softly placed her hand against Sharon's cheek and let out an unaccustomed sob.

'We've had such a fright. Why did you try it, Sharon?' asked Jules D., trying to compose herself.

'Tell us why. I know things were bad, but you've got lots to live for.' she added, gently.

Sharon struggled for words, embarrassed. 'It didn't seem that way. … no family… no work. A failure. Nothing lined up.'

'Not true, Shaz. For a start, what are we? You've got us. And as for work, darling, things can always change. As it is, I've got some amazing news to tell you, but I don't think now's the time…'

'Oh, it is, it really is,' said Sharon. 'Please? Go on…'

'Okay, if you're sure. Well, when you rang, I wasn't really with a client, I was having dinner with Michael Grey.'

Sharon was still groggy, and had struggled to remember a face to go with the familiar name.

'You know, the man who wanted you to design for Bessie B.'s?' reminded Jules.

'Why were you with him?' Sharon had asked, unclear what Jules was leading up to. Was she dating him?

'…My poor darling, you were so miserable, so distraught with all the horrible things happening to you, I wanted to see if I could salvage anything for you. And guess what…? He told me he still thinks you have amazing style, fat or thin. He told me that, when he met you, he was completely knocked out by you…

'So, I made a suggestion. And he thought it was brilliant.

'Guess what…? He wants you to be the figurehead for his Minus Miss chain of shops for slim women. How about that!! And he accepts the fact you're famous, so it's going to be the same mega-deal as he offered you for Bessie B.s!'

'Really?!' Unreal, Sharon had thought to herself.
Life had a funny way of reversing when you least expected it.

And here she was. The third shoot, and it was going brilliantly. Sales had increased dramatically, Michael Grey was thrilled, and she was now *really* in charge of the collections.

She looked at her gang, teasing and chatting with each other, and felt a great sense of belonging.

She took another sip of coffee.

As the taste of the liquid tingled on her tongue, a thought began to percolate…

She had a formidable team around her, right under her nose.

With Simon taking the photographs, Maxine designing, Debbie organising, and Jules D. in charge of marketing and PR, she had a feeling they could make *Minus Miss* a really major global brand.

What they needed to do was make the customers feel good about themselves. Not ashamed. To make them believe there was nothing wrong with being slim. They should design the clothes in far brighter colours. And maybe tighter? Why not? It would be great to make these women feel proud about the shape and definition of their bones.

In fact, with the right promotion and media support, maybe there was a way they could actually make it 'in' to be thin?

She smiled secretively.

It would probably take a miracle… but there was always a *slim* chance.

The End

To find out more about the author please visit:

www.russellartist.com